DREAMS OF LOVE

Her eyes pooling with tears, Sass touched Shay's cheek. He was everything she ever imagined in a man and more. Was it any wonder she found herself loving him more desperately each day?

"That was so kind," she whispered, leaning close and kissing his lips. Suddenly Shay's arms were around her, pulling her close.

"Ah, Sass," he whispered when their lips parted and his cheek was next to hers. "I'm not so kind. I think that I need to have you in my bed, beside me, loving me, and that's all I think about."

"Shay," she whispered, feeling the heat rising from him, infecting her until she was lost in the passion of his words. . . .

REBECCA FORSTER

DREAMS

ZEBRA BOOKS
KENSINGTON PUBLISHING CORP.

ZEBRA BOOKS are published by

Kensington Publishing Corp.
850 Third Avenue
New York, NY 10022

First Printing: May, 1995

Printed in the United States of America

To my sister, Elizabeth Barnes,
who makes her dreams come true

One

Sass Brandt lay in bed looking at the ceiling. Her chest rose and fell with the gentle breathing appropriate to the pink-tinged moments before sunrise. Beside her Curt Evans slept, oblivious of the fact that the woman he, and millions of other people in the world, loved, was not a woman content with her life. If he had been a different kind of man, Curt would have seen beyond her beauty, listened to the meaning of her words rather than the sound of her voice and felt her dissatisfaction. Instead, he woke and thought this was nothing more than a passing mood; he imagined beautiful, rich, successful Sass was in the throes of an artistic, or female, temperament.

Eyes still heavy with sleep, Curt thought Sass Brandt, in her filmy cotton nightgown, was more titillating than Julia Roberts lying stark naked on a bed of ice. Breathing deeply he stretched his well-muscled arms above his head before reaching for the goddess beside him. He wrapped his hand about her tiny waist, leaned over and nuzzled her neck. Curt kissed her cheek and made all those warm, wonderful mating noises that usually worked magic on any mood.

"Don't," Sass murmured, moving her head on the pillow, keeping her distance without pulling away. Curt's morning fog disappeared as quickly as his ardor. His smile faltered, then evaporated. He rolled onto his back, his hand sliding away from her waist. Rebuffed once again. Lately, it was happening far too often.

"Sorry."

Sass sighed. "No," she whispered, "I'm sorry, honey. I really am. I just . . ." Sass raised one long fingered hand as if to touch him, but it fell back onto the covers without making contact. "I don't know what's wrong. I guess I'm just tired."

The heaviness of sleep was completely gone, leaving Curt awake and thoughtful and curious. One minute Sass was the woman he adored, so full of life and energy; the next she was acting like Camille, lethargic and petulant. He'd love to know what triggered these episodes. Running a hand through his tousled hair, Curt watched her when he asked, "Of what? What are you tired of?"

"What makes you think I'm tired *of* something?" Sass whispered, hoping perhaps he actually had an answer.

"A wild guess. You've been going to sleep so early you couldn't possible just be sleepy, and you're not inviting me along so you couldn't possibly be lonely." He laughed, but there was a sad edge to his voice. How he feared it might be . . .

"I suppose you're right. I am tired of something. I'm tired of it all," she said, suddenly adamant and ready to talk. "I'm tired of *Crossfire*. That film took a lot out of me. I'm tired of everyone bugging me about doing publicity for that movie.

I'm tired of working out, of watching what I eat, of stepping on that scale every morning. I'm tired of my bedroom painted this color. I'm tired of being Sass Brandt— movie star, and I wish I wasn't for a while."

Curt laughed even as he felt his heart clutch. This was serious.

"Watch what you say, you might get what you wish for. There are a thousand blondes in Hollywood waiting to be the next star of the century. Besides, if you weren't who you were, then I wouldn't be lying here with you. I wouldn't be loving every inch of you, and I wouldn't be trying to figure out just what it is I can do to make it all better."

Mischievously, Curt let his hand drift under the covers but the edge was back in his playfulness. He'd never heard Sass talk like this. Tired of her life? Impossible! Sass Brandt had been a movie star since she was a kid. Sass Brandt was rich, powerful, talented, and damned sexy. He wanted her to stay that way. He wanted everything to stay the way it was.

He drew one finger over the curve of her knee, stopping only when finger met fabric and the normal trembling response to his caress wasn't forthcoming. He counted his blessings. At least she didn't tighten the way she had the past few weeks. Deciding not to press his luck, Curt patted the cotton of her gown and rolled over again. This time he tucked his arm under his head and watched her with as much selflessness as he could muster.

"You really are gorgeous, you know that?"

"It's not enough, Curt," she said gently and

even he heard the catch in her throat. "I don't feel gorgeous. I look in the mirror and see the same old me. I look tired and bored and I don't understand why." Sass plucked at the English cotton sheets, twirled her finger around the intricate embroidery that edged them. She looked near tears, and Curt marveled at the depth of her frustration. He never felt anything so passionately except love for Sass.

"Maybe it's not you, Sass." Curt ventured.

She turned her head, her long hair creating a bed of shining gold on which she lay her cheek. Now her fingers were quiet, wound tight in the exquisite sheet she had pulled close to her throat. She looked as if she were protecting herself.

"What do you mean?"

"I mean, maybe it's me you're tired of," Curt said solemnly, his voice a mere octave above a tortured whisper. Much as he didn't want to think it, perhaps he was making her unhappy. If he was he would leave. He loved her that much and the thought surprised him. "Maybe you should get rid of me."

"Curt, I would never do that," Sass murmured, disappointed that he, who knew her so well, couldn't perceive how deeply personal this discontent was. Disappointed that once again, Curt thought first of himself. "I can't believe you would even think that."

"Then you still love me?"

"Of course I do," she said and he smiled without seeing that small vacant place in her eye where despondency lay. Instead, he attended to what she did and said, not how she said it. He closed his eyes, reveling in the feel of her hand as it cupped his cheek and framed his face.

Sass looked closely at him and realized that Curt could have almost been a caricature of beauty, instead of beauty itself. She smiled sweetly, an expression that came easily with trust. Curt was right as always. She was a damned lucky lady. He had walked into her life during the production of *Peter's Wife* three years earlier and never left it. She adored him for his easygoing manner, his wit and charm and his need to succeed on his own rather than ride her coattails. She loved his honesty. Yes there it was. She loved how he was really trying to understand what ailed her. Unfortunately, he couldn't help. She didn't even know herself. This feeling of restlessness just wouldn't go away no matter how many times they made love or how hard she worked.

"What are you thinking?" he asked.

"About you," she answered truthfully.

"What about me?"

"About how I love you dearly, how special you make me feel. I'm thinking that you are an unusual man." Sass raised her shoulders in an attempt to show how difficult all this was to explain. Voicing real-life emotion sometimes sounded so insincere. How she wished she had a script.

"But, Sass, you are special. To me and about ten billion other people in the world." Curt laughed dryly, uncomfortable with the direction this discussion was taking.

"No." Sass held her fingers to his lips as she objected. "I said the way *you* make me feel special. I can't thank you enough for that. My mother was the only one who ever made me feel that way until you came along. I honestly believe it's me you love, not the image of me. For that I thank you from the bottom of my heart."

Curt pushed himself onto his elbows and looked at her. His handsome brow furrowed, his eyes half hidden by his long lashes. There were times her odd näivetē amazed him. Sophisticated to a fault on one hand, her need to be loved for herself was close to obsessive at times. And it was at times like this he felt guilty. How could he explain that, to him, she was as much her image as herself, as much the picture on a marquee as the flesh-and-blood woman lying beside him. He didn't have the words, or the ability to communicate these deep and conflicting thoughts, so Curt Evans did the only thing he knew how to do. He began to love her.

He plucked the buttons of her nightgown open, whispering something about how much he needed her. He kissed her with the softest lips, leaving behind a trail of breath high on her cheeks as those kisses trailed to her neck. He lay his lips on the rise of her breasts, and was just about to ease the Swiss cotton gown over her shoulders, when three unapologetic knocks sounded on the bedroom door. The housekeeper's signal. Curt collapsed on Sass with a frustrated groan. In dismay he rolled over to his side of the bed and slipped back under the covers.

"Oh, Curt," Sass breathed in an expression of sympathy. Actress that she was, she made it sound as if her disappointment was as great as his. Yet silently she thanked her housekeeper for the interruption. Pulling her gown over her shoulders, she called, "Yes, Winifred?"

On cue the door opened. Winifred, fifty and a bit, stood framed by the jamb. Her hands were folded in front of her as she looked, without interest, at the two in the bed. She liked Sass and Curt well enough, she just wasn't all that attached the way she had been to the Carson family. All those dear, sweet little ones. Winifred much preferred the clamor of children to the overly expressive sounds of lovemaking. With these two, one accidentally stumbled upon the strangest things.

Not that Miss Sass wasn't discreet, but Mr. Curt had a habit of initiating the unthinkable in the oddest places, at the most unsuitable times. At least he used to. Lately the household hadn't quite been so happy-go-lucky. Winifred cleared her throat and her mind. She wouldn't leave even if they decided to indulge their carnal senses atop the dining-room table. No one else paid like Sass Brandt and no one else demanded so little.

"It's Mr. Maden, Miss Sass."

"I didn't hear the phone ring," Sass said, looking at Curt for corroboration. He shook his head and made a face. She laughed, knowing he would have preferred a phone he could unhook to Winifred who was impossible to ignore.

"No, ma'am. Mr. Maden is in the sunroom. He said you had an appointment," Winifred answered patiently.

"Oh my God!" Sass leaned over the bedside table and checked the calendar Lisabet faithfully updated every evening. She fell back against the pillow, starting to pull herself together. This problem—whatever it was—was getting the best of her. She was losing her mind. "You're absolutely right. I completely forgot. Lord, Lisabet told me about it just last night. Is she with Mr. Maden?"

"Yes, ma'am. They seem to have quite a bit to talk about."

"I'll just bet they do." Sass chuckled. "Those two will keep me hopping until I'm a hundred and ten if they can. Go down and ask Mr. Maden if he'd like breakfast. I'll just have juice, melon, and a slice of toast. No butter today."

"Miss Lisabet already told me, ma'am," Winifred sniffed. Sass's assistant was uncanny. Lisabet could tell what Ms. Brandt wanted before it was thought of. Winifred so admired that talent and actually found it comforting. The house ran better for it.

"Lisabet is a wonder." Sass sighed and threw back the covers. "I swear I must be the most predictable person on earth, or she's psychic."

"Yeah," Curt muttered. Shifting in the bed, he tried to catch her hand and draw her back.

Sass shot him a glance and eased herself away. His dislike of Lisabet pained her. The woman was not only Sass's assistant, she was Sass's best friend. Living together as they all did in this sprawling Malibu compound, it was difficult when there was friction. One of these days Lisabet and Curt would have to straighten things out. But this wasn't the morning, and Winifred wasn't finished.

"Mr. Curt?" The maid cocked her head and looked toward the bed without really seeing him. Women worldwide would have given anything to be in her shoes, but the sight of Curt Evans naked under the sheets didn't even give Winifred a shiver.

"Nothing for me, thanks, but I'd love one of Amy's Chinese chicken salads for lunch. Would you mind passing that along?" Curt's request was as far from arrogant as it was from apologetic. He was awfully comfortable with servants. "How about you, Sass?"

"Yes, that's fine. Winifred, please tell Mr. Maden I'll be down in half an hour. And tell them not to make any plans for me. I hate it when they do that when I'm not there," Sass warned, knowing neither Richard nor Lisabet would pay one bit of attention to Winifred.

"Yes, ma'am."

Winifred disappeared. Sass sighed, and shed her nightgown as she headed for the glass-enclosed bathroom, her naked derrière looking as pleasant as anything Curt could imagine.

"That's it," he muttered. There was, after all, only so much a man could take.

Surprised, Sass looked over her shoulder, her light eyes wide as she saw Curt toss aside the covers. Then she grinned. That was all the encouragement he needed.

With a single leap he bounded out of bed and was after her. Sass squealed as she raced into the bathroom, almost skidding on the white tile that covered the floor and walls and ceiling. Curt caught up with her easily. Grabbing her around the waist he pulled her toward him, their exquisite bodies melting into each other. On one side of them was a wall of glass through which the sun streamed in white gold rays. A man-made forest surrounded the glass and kept them from prying eyes. It was there Curt and Sass finished what they had begun in bed. This time Curt convinced Sass in no uncertain terms that this was the one and only cure for her fretfulness.

It was a contrite, but glowing Sass, who joined Richard and Lisabet an hour later. Enjoyment out of the way, discontent banished, if only for a moment, Sass was ready to get down to business.

"More coffee, Richard?"

Lisabet Sheridan stood by the Regency table, her fingers laying atop the silver urn. Hers was one of those spare, yet eloquent, gestures most people choose to interpret as arrogant. Richard was no exception, and it was no secret he thought Lisabet overstepped her bounds as an employee. This animosity had become such an accepted standard that Sass was no longer upset by it. Instead, she watched Lisabet without really being aware of it, and considered the odd competition that raged between her manager and her assistant.

Lisabet's skin was so pale that Sass, even from where she sat, could trace the map of blue veins that ran across the back of her hand. She had instinctively turned her head at the sound of Lisabet's low, melodic voice and, as usual, found Lisabet's huge plain eyes fixed on her, not Richard. Sass smiled, ignoring the odd uneasiness that often accompanied the other woman's attention. It was a pity Lisabet couldn't be happy outside her work.

Orphaned like Sass, Lisabet's need to be loved translated into an almost unhealthy devotion to those she loved. And Sass was the friend Lisabet loved. Sass, understanding Lisabet's need to be needed, had tried to help her along in the outside world. Sass had offered her hair dresser, her makeup man; she had introduced Lisabet to nice, eligible men, paid for elaborate vacations, taken Lisabet shopping. Nothing worked. Lisabet seemed content in her low heels, long skirts, and perpetually proper cardigans. The day Sass figured out what made Lisabet truly happy she would buy her a lifetime supply. It was the least she could do for the years of faithful— how could she think obsessive?— service.

"No thanks," Richard said. "I've had enough coffee."

Sass flinched. She'd half forgotten they weren't alone so mesmerizing was Lisabet's flat, yet strangely intense, gray gaze. Lisabet let her fingers slide away from the urn, retrieved her dictation pad and took a seat to the right of Richard so that she faced Sass. Richard shifted on the couch, anxious for her to settle so he could get on with business. "Okay, are you listening, Sass? I feel like you're floating again."

"Richard, when have you known me not to pay attention to what you say? You've been arranging my life brilliantly for years." Sass smiled, but her eyes were fixed on the far horizon. It was the only thing she seemed able to focus on that morning.

"You make me sound like a drill sergeant," Richard complained, though his voice softened as it always did when Sass called him to task. "Always had your best interest at heart, you know. Haven't steered you wrong yet, have I, kiddo?"

Sass shrugged and smoothed the pewter-colored tassel on the crewel work pillow she was holding. Now his feelings were hurt. She hadn't meant to do that. She only wished he was a bit more sensitive about hers. Lately all this arranging and planning was enough to make her scream. If it wasn't Richard, it was Lisabet. If it wasn't Lisabet it was Curt wanting to go here and there, to see and be seen.

"I suppose you haven't," Sass said with less conviction than she should. She tucked her bare feet underneath her.

She was wearing her favorite jeans, the ones that were at least ten years old and had the patches to prove it. She'd thrown on an old cotton sweater and pulled her red-gold hair into a ponytail. To say Sass looked stunning was the understatement of the year; to say she looked ready to jump out of her skin was not.

"Sass," Richard cajoled, bravely trying to get her interested in what he was saying. "Don't do this. You sound as if your heart is breaking, and this isn't about heart at all. How many times have I told you, business is business. Wanting to do something that isn't good for the Sass Brandt business just doesn't make sense." Richard leaned forward a bit trying to catch her eye, but she was firmly fixed on that horizon again. It amazed him that, after all these years, Sass was suddenly temperamental. He would have expected it in her teens, maybe even her early twenties, but not now when she was a professional on the other side of twenty-five.

Still, he should be counting his blessings, fits of pique or not. Sass could have been one of those flash-in-the-pan starlets who bare their body and souls and disappear. But Sass had endured, growing with her craft and in her stature. With her there was longevity and that meant security in Hollywood. A bout of annoyance now and again didn't really bother him. Not really. He smiled, a rather fatherly smile.

"Sass, I don't like to argue, you know that. I love you, kid. I admire you. I wouldn't have represented you exclusively all these years if I didn't. But liking you and good business are two different things— understand?"

Sass nodded and rested her elbow on the back of the sofa. She clicked her nails as she looked out the window toward the ocean, down at the couch, up at the wall, anywhere but at Richard. It was her I-hear-you-but-don't-like-what-you're-saying look. Richard tossed his pen on the table.

"Aw, come on, Sass. I don't want you to do something that would put a kink in your image. That's all."

"Richard, this has nothing to do with that Wilder comedy. I know you don't want me to do that," Sass said softly, trying not to criticize. Finally she looked his way, her expression one of such sadness that it broke his heart. "I don't think we have to be that careful anymore. It isn't as though I'm at a critical point in my career, you know. I should be allowed to have a little fling, some creative leeway, instead of you picking and choosing every project I'm involved with. I deserve that, don't I?" Her arm was down, those long legs unfurled and she was leaning her weight on her knees. Those damned clear eyes of hers were cutting through

Richard like a knife through butter, and he had a feeling something not so good was coming.

Richard sat back appearing to consider what Sass was saying. In reality he was formulating a diplomatic answer. Finally, in his most appropriate voice, he said, "A little fling could set you back years. And you've worked too hard to get where you are."

"Don't be silly," Sass scoffed, waving her hand as if she could brush away his objections like offending smoke. "I've been doing the same kind of movies for twenty years. I've got more than fifteen serious films to my credit. You honestly think my fans will turn up their noses if I decide to do a little slapstick?"

"I do."

It was Richard's mouth that opened, but Curt's voice they all heard. He ambled into the room and headed straight to the coffee urn, his hair slicked back and wet from his shower, his cheeks red from the heat of the water. His grin shined on them all.

"Hi, folks."

"Curt." Richard acknowledged the younger man with a nod of the head. Curt wasn't his client so there was no need to be effusive.

"Good morning, Curt." Lisabet greeted him out of habit, not expecting him to acknowledge her. They had settled on a noncombative coexistence long ago. Poor Lisabet. Definitely not a man's woman.

"So you're ganging up on me, are you?" Sass laughed uneasily, uncomfortable that this was turning into an all-inclusive meeting.

"We are not," Curt objected, taking a place beside her on the deep blue sofa. "I haven't seen

Richard in ages so we couldn't be in cahoots. He refuses to handle me despite the very special relationship I have with his exclusive client."

Curt kissed Sass's cheek, grinning at Richard all the while.

"Can't blame me for wanting to keep Sass to myself as much as possible," Richard quipped.

"Nobody can be blamed for wanting that," Curt said, his good nature coming to the fore. Even Sass had to smile when he did. There was a truly enchanting quality about his grin. So unlike the one he flashed in public. Sass swore the people in her home were the only ones to see how lovable, not just desirable, Curt Evans was. She smiled back at him while he talked. "But aside from that particular failing, you're a pretty good guy. And I think you're right about this Wilder thing. I read the script . . ."

"You did what?" Sass interrupted, her smile gone. Her first feeling was one of betrayal, her first reaction one of anger. That was her script! Until this moment Sass assumed they paid each other a certain professional courtesy. Though they lived under the same roof, Sass believed her projects were private unless she asked Curt's opinion.

"I did," he admitted with a boyish shrug, dismissing, or ignoring, her distress. "Sorry. I was curious and it was on the coffee table." Curt didn't sound as sorry as she would have liked, but Sass took a deep breath and let it ride. This was a small thing after all, wasn't it?

"It's my fault, Sass," Lisabet broke in, ready to take the blame. To her, Sass's displeasure was as welcome as her smile— both gave Lisabet the attention she craved. "I must have left it out instead of locking it in the file with your current projects. I apologize. It will never happen again."

"Oh for goodness sake," Sass snapped, all her restlessness falling in on her again. Lisabet was acting like a wayward child anxious to have her hands slapped. "It isn't anyone's fault. It isn't a thing to have a fault about. I was merely surprised that Curt read my script. Can we move on to Curt's opinion of the Wilder project since he seems intimately familiar with it."

Richard cleared his throat; Lisabet hung her head. Neither knew how to handle these strange outbursts. Only Curt seemed unaffected, responding to Sass's mysterious displeasure much better than the rest. He sipped his coffee, ignoring the thin thread of tension in the air.

"As I was saying, I don't think Sass should even consider comedy of this sort. Wilder already has a well-established niche in physical comedy. If you want to move away from what you've been doing then find a comedic script that's closer to the stuff Hepburn used to do."

"Which one?" Lisabet asked sarcastically. She didn't have a great deal of respect for Curt's spy thriller career and even less for his opinion about classic films.

"Either one, my dear Lisabet," he replied easily. "Although Sass might be a little old for the ingenue-ish stuff Audrey used to do with Cary Grant."

"I beg your pardon." Sass's spirits rose. She took the last piece of toast, sat back and munched.

"Just joking," Curt said smoothly. "But I think

you'd really shine in that kind of thinking-woman's comedy. Sass isn't Lucille Ball, so if she wants to do comedy she should keep it within the limits of her reputation."

Richard shrugged, "Hate to say this, Lisabet, but I think he's got us. Sass could pull something like that off beautifully."

Richard's comment remained rhetorical as Lisabet pretended to be scribbling a note to herself to hide her annoyance. She should have thought of that long ago rather than immediately dismissing the genre. Now Curt had endeared himself to Sass even further. At least there was some consolation in the fact that Richard hadn't been terribly bright about this either.

"That sounds reasonable," Sass said, "if we can find a script. Good ones have been few and far between lately. Richard, would you take a look at what's out there? I'm going to be at odds and ends now that *Crossfire* is wrapped up." Richard laughed outright. Curt joined in. Lisabet rolled her eyes. Sass looked from one to the other, an incredulous half smile on her lips, an insistent edge to her voice. "Well, I am."

"Sass," Lisabet said, "just because *Crossfire* had the biggest box office ever for an opening weekend doesn't mean you can just forget about it. You know that. You have a string of personal appearances across the country to promote the film. We have to devise a strategy for the Oscars, we have to . . ."

"Lisabet, stop! I already have an Oscar. I don't want to devise a strategy for number two." Sass felt it now. That impotent impatience that took her to the edge and let her teeter there, unsure whether she should scream at her friends and confidants, or plead with them to help her figure out what was wrong with her. Crazily, lately, she had begun to feel that they cared more about her career than she did. How untrue that was.

Sass did care, but in a different way. She needed more than fame, more than money. She needed— what? Satisfaction? Could it be as simple as that? She turned to Richard, imploring, "I don't want to have to sell myself to the academy, Richard. Please. Let's not do that this year. It's degrading to take out ads about myself in the trades. If *Crossfire* is as good as everyone says, it will do fine when Oscar time comes around. Leave it alone, and let me move on to something different. Just bring me the right script, find a property that will make me want to act like I've never acted before in my life. I know it's out there somewhere. A story I can really sink my teeth into. Please, Richard."

"Sass, you're being unrealistic. This business won't allow you to let *Crossfire* float on its own. You've got to get out there and promote the hell out of it . . ."

Richard couldn't finish his sentence because there was no room for words in the heavy air that surrounded them. The room was dominated by Sass, and she had made it inhospitable with her sudden, controlled and tense silence. When she spoke it was with a cheerless determination.

"You know, Richard," she said flatly, "that is so frightening. You just said the *business* won't *let* me do things. I had no idea that a business could allow me anything at all. At least when Mother was managing my career— or with you in the beginning— it was a human being who objected to what I might want. Now you've reduced me to dancing to the tune of 'the business.' You're not even talking about me, the person, anymore, Richard. You're talking about me, 'the commodity.' "

Sass held up the fingers on one hand and wiggled imaginary quotation marks into the air. She looped her thumbs over the pockets of her jeans, disgusted as she stood up and talked to all of them but mostly to herself.

"That's scary. Damned scary, and I won't stand for you talking that way or thinking that way. I won't take it from any of you. This business will not tell me how to act or what to act in. That's like saying the clock can tell me when to breathe. If everything went away tomorrow— no scripts, no movies, no money— I would survive. If I had to work as a grocery checker, I could do it without blinking an eye. But what I won't do is kowtow to something that doesn't exist. The 'business' doesn't exist. We make it what it is. You with your wheeling and dealing, Richard. You with your schedules and promotions, Lisabet. Curt with his image and good looks; me with my personality. That's all this business is. It's people. Remember that. Remember . . ."

Sass wasn't quite finished but she couldn't find the right words to express the pain she was feeling, the disappointment, the aloneness. She needed to leave the room fast and get away from the expressions of shock and amazement. If looks could kill she'd be tied to a stake and burned as a witch for this heresy. If Sass could have, she would have climbed out of her skin and left it there for them to haggle over. Since she couldn't do that, she did what was possible. She called an end to the meeting.

"Now, if you will excuse me, I'm going to go to my room, change my clothes, grab the pile of books Lisabet brought me and settle down by the pool. I'm going to forget that all three of you seem to have forgotten about me. The next time I see any of you I expect to first be your friend, then I'll be whatever else I must." Sass straightened her shoulders and headed to the stairs. "Goodbye, Richard. Call when you have something wonderful, something that will make me laugh or cry or whatever regardless of box office predictions."

Lisabet began to follow Sass. "I'll bring out your appointment book, Sass."

Sass held up her hand, without looking back. "Not now. I'd just like to have a little private time, and try to forget that my life has been reduced to nothing more than one publicity stop after another."

"Come on, Sass. No one meant to imply that you had to be led around by the nose." Curt reached for her as she passed. She hesitated as he touched her arm.

"I know you didn't. Maybe it's me. Maybe I'm overreacting. But I sure as hell don't like being told in absolute terms what I can and cannot do. Especially by 'the business.' "

Then she laughed a little at the ridiculousness of it all. Sass knew exactly what Richard had meant, yet she chose to make an issue of it. Maybe she was coming down with something. Or maybe, just maybe, she was simply uninspired. Whatever was bothering her, Sass sure hoped she could get in touch with it fast before she talked herself out of one helluva career and her few dear friends.

"Sorry, folks, but that's it for today. Sass Brandt is going to be a housefrau. I'll talk to you after I've had a good dose of sunshine, a wonderful lunch, and read myself to sleep."

Sass swept out of the room, leaving three stunned people in her wake.

Sass stood in front of her mirrored wardrobe ostensibly looking for something to wear. She wasn't making much headway. Her hands lay in the drawer that held twenty bathing suits, yet her fingers weren't rifling through the little bits of fabric looking for the one that suited her mood. Instead she was trying to remember when the last time was that Sass Brandt, superstar, had made a real, honest-to-goodness decision about her life without Richard or Lisabet, Curt or her mother, bless her soul, getting in the way.

Unfortunately the answer wasn't one she wanted to acknowledge. The last decision she had made was to decline an invitation to join the Girl Scouts, opting instead to audition for a local commercial. She had been seven years old. Nineteen years ago. Too long to go without exercising your God-given right to self-determination.

Intrigued by this thought, Sass reached into the drawer and pulled out the first suit she found. She was out of her jeans and into the gold Brazilian thong a minute later. Still engrossed in her thoughts, she took the books Lisabet had put by her bedside and headed for the pool. Something had to give here, and it damn sure wasn't going to be her anymore.

Two

Winifred paused as she passed the study. Under normal circumstances there wasn't a sound in the world that would have broken her concentration or kept her from her appointed rounds. She was, after all, paid to keep the house, not the people in it. But when she heard raised voices, angry voices, frustrated voices, well, one just had to stop a moment and reflect on what that might mean to the household in general.

Winifred's initial thought was that this was the beginning of the end for Mr. Curt Evans. Perhaps he'd be out on his ear soon, and that would suit her just fine. Him and his fancy ways and love-making every hour of the day didn't set quite right. Yet, upon analysis, she decided that was not the case. It seemed it was Mr. Richard's voice raised to new heights with Miss Sass joining right in. This was more than a bit unusual. Surprisingly when Mr. Curt's voice was heard, it seemed to be that of the peacekeeper of all things. And Miss Lisabet, where was she? Winifred leaned closer, her ear almost on the door. Where, indeed, was Miss Lis . . .

"Can you hear well enough, Winifred?"

Lisabet walked purposefully past the house-keeper, hesitating as she opened the closed door long enough to give the older woman a withering look. Winifred managed a huff and hugged the linen she was carrying to her substantial chest.

"I was only concerned, Miss Lisabet. Just a bit concerned, that was all."

"No need to be," Lisabet muttered, dismissing Winifred as she slipped past her into the room, notebook in hand. The door closed in Winifred's face and Lisabet was back where she belonged at Sass's side: silent, watchful, and ready to do her bidding no matter what it was she desired. But no one, least of all Sass, noticed she'd returned. The debate was too heated, the anger more pronounced than when she'd left.

"I don't believe you, Richard," Sass cried, her cheeks stained with the color of righteous fury. "Not for one minute do I believe that you did as I asked."

"Don't be absurd, Sass. Why shouldn't I do it? I've given you the proof that I did just exactly what you wanted. It's right there."

Richard slammed his open palm onto the memo in front of him, surprisingly angry that Sass should question him, accusing him of doing less for her than he had done all these years. Lisabet jumped. Sass rolled her eyes, undeterred, every inch the star in command of her universe.

Curt watched, enjoying the contest of wills. This was a new Sass. The ultimate professional, she'd always listened to Richard, and her mother before that, when it came to career decisions. She respected directors and producers. She gave her input and she was never, ever, unreasonable. Now, though, there was a bee in her bonnet. It was buzzing like a son of a bitch and he didn't want to get stung so he didn't get involved. There was merit in both sides of this argument, and Curt knew his vote one way or the other wasn't going to make much of a difference.

He sat back, mentally taking bets on the outcome. Sheer stamina dictated Sass as the winner; Richard was getting tired, his hands were over his face and he pulled them down to reveal an expression of frustration and bewilderment.

"Sass," he pleaded, "look at that memo again. If you're having trouble understanding it, then let me verbalize the specifics— again." Dramatically he picked it up and shook it out. "Ready now?"

"There's no need to be condescending, Richard," Sass drawled, but Richard ignored her and forged ahead. His tone was clipped as he tried to defend his integrity.

"Per my memo of the third, the book entitled *The Woman At the End of the Lane* was written by Tyler McDonald. He is dead. He died two years ago at the age of seventy-seven. The man who controls Tyler McDonald's estate, including the film rights to *The Woman At the End of the Lane,* is Shay Collier. He lives in Alaska. I have written to Mr. Collier, and he has replied that he has no desire to discuss the possible sale of the rights to this work for film or any other purposes." Richard sighed and looked up, his expression strained. "Now, I have shown you the handwritten note he sent attesting to that. The question is moot. You cannot produce, direct, or star in *The Woman At the*

End of the Lane because you don't have any right to do so and you never will. Period."

Richard threw the memo on the table and himself back onto the sofa. His face was flushed, his eyes were red. He was looking angry and stymied and Curt wasn't sure Richard would last another round. Richard dropped his head back for an instant, took a deep, cleansing breath, then quietly, as calmly as possible, addressed Sass.

"Sweetheart, this kind of thing is the kiss of death at the box office anyway. It's a stupid project, Sass. I don't even know how something this old got into your reading pile."

"Lisabet picked it up during one of her turns at an estate sale. But how is immaterial. What's important is why. And why this book found its way to me is because it is a story that needs to be told on the screen."

"For God sake, that is the most ridiculous thing I've ever heard. Let it go."

"I won't, Richard," she said quietly, her arms crossed over her gorgeous chest, her golden eyes trained on him with an intensity none of them had ever witnessed at home. *"The Woman At the End of the Lane* is a stunning book. My God, the characters are incredible. They're urgent and desperate to be brought to life. You did read the book, didn't you?"

Richard nodded, "Yes, I read the book and it put me to sleep quite nicely, thank you."

"That's because you didn't want to like it. You want me to go with that thing that Spielberg is doing, but I will not share center stage with his latest special effects. My God, Richard. Think about it.

Close your eyes and envision me as Eileen." Sass's voice became rich with drama and determination. "That woman is so tragic. To be torn by her love for her husband and her desire for another man— a man old enough to be her father. To be alone in that Irish village where women, once married, were no longer anything but their husband's wife. Lord, the dialogue alone is enough to make me dream about playing this woman. I can see the scenes in my mind. It's like a vision, Richard. A vision that I want to make a reality. I already have Jay Williams working on the first draft of the screenplay because I thought you were going to work your magic with these negotiations. . . ."

"What a waste of money, Sass," Richard scoffed. "That was stupid. What kind of contract did you draw up with Jay without my knowledge?"

"We don't have a contract, Richard. I'd never do that without bringing you in on the deal." Sass waved away his complaint. "Jay is my friend, for goodness sake. Curt and I have known him for years and so have you. I would never screw him on the deal and he knows that. Besides, he's the only one I know who can do this book justice."

"A book you don't own, Sass," Richard railed. "I would suggest you get Jay on the horn and ask him how much time he's got into this thing. Then pay him off and forget it."

"I can't . . ."

"You will! Come on, the time for this kind of character-driven film is gone. It's the stuff small budgets and smaller distribution deals are made of. There might be a couple of awards in it for you if you ever did get it made. But what of it?

The big box office isn't going to be there. *Howard's End* and *Enchanted April* swept this genre a couple of years ago, and the public just isn't going to want to see it again for another century. We're moving on and you've always been on the cutting edge. Sass, you're not the kind of star who does a project that was yesterday's news. Sass . . ."

Richard opened his hands, begging her to drop the subject. But her beautiful jaw was set against any reason, so Richard gave up on her. He appealed to the troops for help.

"Curt, come on. You've got to agree with me. You're no dummy when it comes to reading the trends. Tell her . . ."

Curt chuckled, "No can do, Richard. I've already thrown in with Sass. I get to play the wronged husband." Curt threw a wink Sass's way. She didn't notice. He got serious. "I think it's a damn good role."

"You would," Richard groused. "You've been trying to shed that double-o-seven image of yours for years. Even if the thing bombs, you could give a good performance and come out smelling like a rose while Sass twists in the wind."

"Right." Curt looked at Richard who looked right back. That wasn't the admission Richard expected at all. He thought Curt was smarter than that.

"Sass, did you hear him?"

"Absolutely. And I think he's right. You know Curt actually does have a mind, Richard. That's why I love him. I also love him because he knows this is an exciting project and you continue to ignore that fact. He wants to do it because it's something different. Different, for God's sake! And I want to do it."

"Think about it, Richard," Curt interrupted. "If I do this project and it gets legs, then I'm a star and more worthy of Sass. If it bombs, at least I've had a chance to see what I can do. Sass would never cast me if she didn't think I could do the job. I know it and you know it, so it's not like anything weird is going on."

"And if it bombs, what about Sass?"

"I'll answer that." Sass moved to Richard. "If the movie bombs I have enough equity in the business to come out on top. It will just be a fling for me. We'll laugh it off. I've never had a fling before, Richard. Nobody's going to deep six me because of it. If this project is a success, then I'll have proved to myself that I actually have good instincts. Good enough to choose my own properties." She squeezed his hands instinctively, pleading with him, talking through him to all the people who had made decisions for her in her life. "Richard, if it works then I have something I've always wanted."

"What, Sass? What is it you don't have that you think you can get by doing this?"

"Self-respect, Richard."

"Oh, for God sake!" Richard shot up so fast Sass almost fell backward. He scoffed. He glared at her. He looked from lounging Curt to wary Lisabet. He was alone in a den of lions. They were all on her side. "This is ridiculous. Self-respect, my ass. If you don't have self-respect by this time, then I have definitely been doing something wrong. And so did your mother. . . ."

"That's uncalled for, Richard . . ." Sass countered. Curt swung his feet off the sofa, ready to go to his lover's defense if Richard was going to hit below the belt. He could have saved himself the trouble.

"Sorry. Sorry." Richard's head hung in shame. "Your mom was a great woman. She did incredible things for your career. But more than that, she raised you to be an amazing woman. How many people do you think could survive the stardom like you have? None. You're one of a kind, Sass. You've got money, talent, fame and you've never, ever spent one thin dime on therapy. If you don't have self-respect now, you'll never have it."

"Okay, maybe that was the wrong word." Sass stood up and put her hand on his shoulder. He didn't turn around. "I just want to find out if I can make my own decisions for a while. I appreciate everything you've done for me. I'll listen to your advice, but I think now is the time for me to stop doing what I'm told just because it's good for business. I want to do something for my . . ." Sass hesitated. She blushed and chuckled lightly, knowing how strange this would sound to her three friends. ". . . I want to do something for my soul. It might sound silly to you, but it isn't to me."

Sass turned him to her and studied the face she had come to trust over the last sixteen years. Richard had become more handsome over time. Gray hair suited him as did the pleated trousers and paisley suspenders. He wore the uniform of a powerful man with ease. But he had lived for power, understood only the specifics of contracts and not the need for emotion and expression and self-determination. How could he? His job was to keep his client, Sass, on the straight and narrow so that she would gain money, fame, and notoriety. He didn't understand that these were not the only things from which happiness was derived. These were not the only ends to her means. Sass let her hands drop. They weren't close at this moment; they shouldn't show affection when they were at such odds.

"Richard, I'm sorry. I honestly don't believe you tried your hardest on this one. I want this property. I want— no, I need— to make a film out of that book. I will be Eileen. I will be *The Woman At the End of the Lane,* and I will have Curt star opposite me no matter what you say. I can buy anyone, including this Shay Collier. If I can't do that, I'll charm him. If I can't do that . . ." Sass shrugged, apologizing for Richard's discomfort. "I've never had to find out what I would do if someone said no to me, but I guess the time has come. I'm not going to give up." Sass was done with cajoling, it was time for action. She turned to Lisabet. "Lisabet, have you got it?"

Lisabet was ready on cue. She was at the telephone dialing while Curt laughed, suddenly realizing what Sass was up to.

"Sass, you vixen," he said.

Richard looked left and right. Sass was already beside Lisabet, waiting. Then Lisabet was speaking and Richard was throwing up his hands.

"Mr. Collier? My name is Lisabet Sheridan, assistant to Sass Brandt. If you'd hold for Miss Brandt please. . . ."

The phone was passed from Lisabet to Sass who

gave her a triumphant wink. Shaking her hair back, flipping off her earring, she put the phone to her ear and a smile on her face.

"Mr. Collier . . ." she purred, her voice dripping with milk and honey. Irresistible. "This is Sass Brandt. Thank you so much for taking my call. . . ."

Sass went no further. Instead she pulled the phone from her ear, looked at it, then incredulously at Lisabet.

"He's not there."

"He was. I spoke to him myself," Lisabet insisted, looking puzzled as she reached for the phone. Sass pulled it back.

"No, give me the number. I'll dial. Maybe he just didn't understand he was supposed to wait . . ." Sass dialed as fast as Lisabet spoke. She shook back her head again and unclipped her other earring. Sass stood up straighter when the ringing stopped.

"Mr. Collier. Sass Brandt. I think we were cut off. I'm calling about acquiring the rights to Mr. McDonald's novel, *The Woman At the* . . ."

Slowly, Sass lowered the phone and looked around the room. She held the receiver out toward them as though they could see what she had just heard. But all looked at her silently, waiting for her to fill them in. When she did, it was with complete and utter astonishment.

"He hung up on me."

He looked out on the darkness that had surrounded him for months. Morning and night were one in the same in this place, and it was just as

well. The darkness was one of the reasons he lived
in this godforsaken place of ice and snow, forests
and mountains. The darkness was why he was away
from the hills of home, where light was not just
illumination but a state of mind, a way to live. Yes,
he was here because his soul was as black as the
night; cold was why he was here, for the flame in
his heart no longer flickered to warmth.

But now someone had called.

Someone was trying to let the light back in.

A woman with a voice as deep as a lough, as
inviting as a bed of heather. She said the words
and stirred the ashes that once burned inside him,
scorching the very essence of his being until he
thought he might die from the agony of it. But it
was all so long ago. He was wiser now. Harder. He
had healed from the wounds and his hide was as
tough as a grizzly bear, as impenetrable as the face
of a glacier.

So he sat in the blackness not knowing what time
it was in his northern prison. He put his head back
on the old green leather upholstery, his long,
strong body curved into the great chair that had
been carved for a man as tall as he but bigger,
maybe even harder, even than he.

With a great start Shay Collier moved from the
chair, arms reaching out into the darkness to hit
at whatever could hurt him. He wanted to be reminded that pain came from other places, not just
the heart. With a mighty swipe his arm was thrown
across the table beside him. Phone and candle,
book and picture clattered to the floor. A bell, the
crack of glass, the single beat of the book crashing
to the ground broke the silence and gave solidity

to his fury and his suffering. Oh God, he felt it coming again. Just now, when he thought it was gone forever, when he was sure it had been buried in the deepest part of him and forgotten, grief came furiously at him once more.

Shay was up and his boots sounded hollow on the floor, as hollow as the man who wore them. He looked at the stove, the fiery glow was low and the place was chilling. He didn't care. He welcomed it.

The fear was coming, too, and it was great. Fear that he might feel again, and want again, and ask questions that could never be answered. He wanted no part of the woman with the honey voice, nor the questions she was asking. He wanted no part of living though he had no choice but to follow till the end of his days. For to do less, to put the gun to his head, would be against all the laws of God and nature. But nobody— nobody— could make him live again.

With a mighty hand he tore his fur jacket from the hook where it was kept, striding into the frigid darkness with it still in hand. He had gone far, was breathing hard, before he remembered to put it on. It was just as well. Frozen as he was, he had forgotten his pain. Numb now, far from his cabin, Shay Collier was safe again. Sweet words, and visions of the woman who spoke them so long ago, were suspended, sleeping in the ice of his heart once more. All was as it had been. He would sleep and fend for himself and put one day of life in front of the other until he was at the end of all his days. Only then would he truly be at peace. Only then, when his body joined his soul in death, would he find what he was looking for.

"I don't think you had a very good time."

Curt hung his tie on the rack, meticulous as always. Sass sat behind him, removing her makeup. His eyes flitted her way. "The way you're going at that makeup you're going to dredge a few canals around your eyes, and then where will you be?"

"What?"

Sass's eyes flashed, catching Curt's gaze in the huge mirror of her deco dressing table before she wiped away the last of the mascara and eye shadow. He was right. She was rubbing herself raw. That's all she'd need. Red eyes in the morning and some tabloid would have Curt beating her. She tossed the cotton ball into the white wicker wastebasket at her feet. She sighed and smiled.

"I must be nuts. I want that book so bad and I can't explain why. It's as if I was meant to be a part of it. You know, I could feel that woman's heart tearing in two as she tried to choose between those two men. No . . . no . . ."

Sass held up a hand as if to stop Curt from interrupting, which he had no intention of doing. The sight of her half naked, reflected back to herself, red gold hair laying over her shoulders like a silk shawl, her face pale without the makeup but still naturally beautiful, was too much for him. To interrupt would have changed her, the picture ruined, the dreamer awakened, the masterpiece marred. So he listened and felt along with her. Not as deeply, but with respect and appreciation.

"Eileen, the woman at the end of the lane! That's not what that character was doing at all. She was choosing between them and herself. It was a triangle, Curt. Because there was something she could give one of them by refusing the other and there was something she could gain by rejecting them both. Do you understand that?" She gave him a cursory look, not wanting his input as she fell under the spell of the memory of the written word. "That woman couldn't choose between the men because she had never come to understand who she was or what she wanted. Yes . . ." Sass leaned back in her chair with satisfaction, a private smile on her lips, eyes downcast as though the problem had fallen into her lap for her consideration. "That's what intrigues me. I would be able to make that choice for her on the screen. I would be able to bring her to life so that she could make the right decision, or fight back if it was the wrong one."

"But she died, Sass. In the end, she killed herself. How could she fight back?"

Confidently she raised her eyes and they looked at each other through the mirror once again. "She would die with honor, Curt. She wouldn't go to her death a broken woman, but a woman making amends. That's what I mean by finding herself. I know I could make that story explode on the screen. I feel Eileen. I feel her here." Sass touched the place above her heart gently, as if it were a most precious place on her body, as if her flesh protected secrets she had never shared with Curt.

He opened his mouth, a pithy comment on the tip of his tongue, but he couldn't bring himself to make light of this. He had never seen Sass so involved even though this project was out of her reach. He shook his head slightly, realizing his mistake. Sass wasn't just involved, she was on a mission. This book was her vision. There was a prescience to her preoccupation that hushed Curt and made him wish he could peer into the night and see what she saw.

"And what of the men, Sass. Do you feel them?" he asked quietly.

She nodded.

"I feel him," she whispered.

"Which one?" Curt asked, feeling himself drawn into the fantasy. "The husband? The part I'd play?"

Sass turned slightly in her chair and considered Curt, her expression one of confusion, her lips parted as though he had lifted her from a sleep so deep she'd awakened frightened.

"I feel him," she said again, then shook her head when she realized that had not been the question. "I mean, of course I see you as the husband, the younger one. Who else would you be?"

Suddenly she was all motion. Pots of pretty colors were put in place, brushes whisked away. She was up and at the closet, pulling out a wisp of a thing that was less clothing than colored air. When she turned back to him her smile was too bright, her cheeks too pink. Curt neither noticed nor would he have cared. She was back with him, not wandering around with a character from a novel. Whatever was in her head was gone now, banished and that's all that mattered. Tonight was just another night. They were together, their life was good. If she wanted the damn book she'd have it, he had no doubt. But it was only a book, the characters only acting out at the discretion of a real person who knew how to type. More than likely it was Mr. Collier's bad manners, his refusal to dance to her tune, that fed Sass's obsession.

"I like it," he said, having no more use for Mr. Collier or discussions about the book. His interests, and his needs, were more immediate. Pushing himself off the bed he walked to Sass and took the filmy nightgown from her fingers. He tossed it aside. "I think we'll work from the inside out tonight."

Sass watched as his head bent to her shoulder and his lips met her skin. She smiled softly, knowing the stirrings inside herself would match his and her problems would be banished in moments— perhaps only for moments— but it was enough. Instinctively her hands cradled his head, her fingers winding themselves through his soft light hair. There was no need for guidance. They had loved too long for that.

Yet as the lingerie was discarded, as her head came forward, encasing her lover in a curtain of satiny hair, Sass felt a jolt so deep inside even Curt could not have created it. Sass Brandt had been touched by another, by a soul or a mind or a spirit somewhere far away. She shuddered. Encouraged, inflamed, Curt's hands roamed farther. Sass breathed in the scent of her lover, she buried her lips in his hair and suddenly, sadly, wished she was alone.

* * *

In the garden, under the balcony that graced the French doors of Sass's room, Lisabet sat and smoked. Even Sass didn't know about the cigarettes. Certainly this was nothing to be proud of, nothing she would want to broadcast. It was a filthy habit that someone as disciplined as herself should quite easily be able to discard. Actually, she had all but quit— except at times like this.

Sass had looked gorgeous when she left for the party, fabulous in the new Givenchy sheath. All golden lace, the color of her eyes, threads the color of her hair woven into the floral pattern. Lisabet had never seen her employer, her friend, her . . .

Her nothing. Angrily Lisabet pulled the smoke through the tobacco and drew it into her lungs. Sass was no more to her than employer and, if she was lucky, friend. That was all she would ever be even though she, Lisabet, understood Sass Brandt better than anyone on this earth. Certainly better than that man who shared her bed. That man couldn't possibly understand the depth of the woman in his arms. There wasn't a man in Sass's life who understood what she needed. Sass Brandt was a one-woman industry. She was money in the bank and that's all those men cared about. It was no wonder she was focused on that book.

Sass was calling out and no one was listening. All she wanted was for them to accept her idea. To respect her creative decision, to fight for this one thing she wanted. Sass would be so grateful to the person who did that, and Lisabet was going to be the person to oblige. Lisabet was going to show Sass just how understanding another human being could be. She wouldn't deny Sass nor demean her. She would raise her friend up and let her be whatever she wanted to be. She, Lisabet, would be responsible for the final stroke that perfected Sass Brandt.

Suddenly Lisabet jumped and threw her cigarette away. It had burnt down and singed her fingers. She blinked and brought herself back to the here and now. So engrossed had she been in her dreams she hadn't realized she was staring at Sass and Curt. They were at it again. Two bodies as one, silhouetted in a window Sass thought no one could see. But Lisabet could. Lisabet knew all the secrets of the house, and the house couldn't run without her. So in a way Sass was right. No one could see except someone privileged to roam this marvelous compound. Someone like Lisabet. . . .

Slowly Lisabet lit another cigarette, smoked it down and dropped it on the graveled path. The butt glowed red in the night. Automatically Lisabet stepped on it, watching the shadows, watching the love play, thinking something was different that night. Sass might be tiring of him for their movement was languid and halfhearted. The toe of her shoe ground harder and harder until there was nothing left but bits of paper and dry tobacco to be taken by the wind.

Lisabet turned her head, believing she hadn't meant to watch, convincing herself her audience had been an accident. And assure herself she did, as so often happened, in the depths of the night. The silhouette had disappeared, collapsing to a bed or the floor, retreating to the shower, to some place Lisabet could no longer see. There was no sense watching any longer. Sass was in her home, safe. There would be no more need for Lisabet.

None at all. . . .

Three

"I don't think we're in Kansas anymore, Toto."

"Beg your pardon?" Lisabet said, hurrying to catch up with Sass, fumbling with her gloves as she did so. She hadn't expected the place to be so cold or so barren. What were they doing in Alaska? And the darkness! My Lord, there was something about darkness at three in the afternoon. It left Lisabet feeling bewildered and alone, despite the fact that people went about their business as if the sun was shining. Up and down the streets they moved, just like it was any other small town in the United States.

None of this seemed to bother Sass though, not even this odd, hushed life lived under snow flurries and a blanket of blackness. She just forged ahead, bundled up in her sheepskin coat, her brimmed hat pulled low over her eyes, her chin tucked into her high collar and double-wound muffler. Lisabet looked dowdy in her stretch pants and rubber boots, clumsy as she tried to reach Sass. When she finally did, Sass was shrugging off whatever it was she had thought important enough to talk about a moment before.

"Nothing, Lisabet. Forget it."

Sass's foot hit the raised wooden walk and her cowboy boots thudded as she hurried on. Lisabet puffed by her side, giving Sass a wide berth. Her boss was wound tighter than a spring, her eyes darting about. Only she knew what she was looking for. When she found it, Sass steered Lisabet back into the street. They waited for a truck to rumble by, its huge snow tires pulverizing the thin layer of ice into a thousand tiny pieces, before they crossed. They were back up on a raised wooden sidewalk again.

"This is what I want. Petersburg Police Department."

Sass hitched her purse and opened the door. Lisabet followed, thankful for the warmth. Petersburg, Alaska, was not where she would have chosen to spend Thanksgiving. Instead of throwing herself at Sass's feet and begging to go home, though, Lisabet rubbed her hands and stood back as Sass leaned over the counter and caught a deputy's attention.

"Excuse me. I'm sorry to bother you . . ." Sass said in her sweetest voice. The man was out of his chair in no time.

Lisabet smiled ruefully. It was the same everywhere. Men reacted to Sass as if they'd never seen a woman before. This fellow was no different. He pushed his chest out, pulled his stomach in, and instantly became more attentive than if Lisabet had come in on her own. Thankfully he didn't seem to recognize Sass, and that was good. At least they wouldn't be hanging around the police station for an hour or two while the staff called their mothers and brothers and best friends to come see the movie star.

Lisabet wanted to be back in Los Angeles where she knew what was happening to their lives, where there were schedules to refer to and people to talk to who understood and adored Sass Brandt. But Sass wanted information, so Lisabet tuned into the conversation going on over the scarred wooden counter. The deputy was shaking his head. Sass wasn't getting very far. Even here, Lisabet imagined, giving out someone's address wasn't considered good form. But Sass was determined.

". . . and we came all the way from L.A. to see him, but we don't have an address. I have his post office box because I've written to him. But I need to find his home. I looked in the phone book and he isn't listed. I called directory assistance. They say they can't give out his address. It's awfully important that I see him. It could mean a great deal to him. He's the executor of a will and . . ."

"Hey, wow, an inheritance!" Now she had the deputy's attention. Money had a way of doing that. "Well, you should have said that right up front, ma'am. I can understand that. Sure, I hear about that kind of stuff all the time. So I guess he's coming into some money, right?"

"Well, not really . . ." Sass began, but Lisabet interrupted. Sass was far too honest to handle this.

". . . Not really a fortune, but a substantial amount. We've been looking for Mr. Collier to discuss with him the ramifications of a legacy that could mean quite a bit to him, indeed. Of course we could take out an ad in the newspaper, but since we've traced Mr. Collier this far we'd like to see him. We'd be ever so grateful . . ."

Reluctantly the deputy looked away from Sass

and listened to Lisabet. A rocket scientist he wasn't; impressed he was. First by Sass and her beauty, then by Lisabet and her obviously official bearing.

"Gee, I'd like to help you, ma'am, but I don't know Shay Collier. Name just doesn't ring a bell, and I know most people 'round these parts . . ." The deputy pulled his brows together, his chest was falling, his stomach pouching again. He half turned from them. Sass gave Lisabet a hard look. Lying was not something she cared for, but Lisabet reciprocated with a cool glance. Her job was to get the things done that Sass wanted done. Lord knew Sass wanted this thing done.

". . . Hey, Frank. You know anybody named Collier? Shay Collier?"

The man behind the glass looked up. He gave Sass and Lisabet a passing glance, then let his gaze linger a bit longer on Sass. He yelled something, but the words were muffled by the glass. The deputy at the desk ambled toward the back office and stuck his head around the corner. He was back a second later.

"Frank knows the guy. Lives out on the highway a bit. Then you've got to turn off, right when you see the first fork. 'Bout ten miles in and up. Roads are good, but I don't know if you want to try this on your own if you ain't familiar with our terrain. . . ."

"We'll be fine," Sass assured him. Trying to control her excitement, she pulled a map from the deep pocket of her jacket and spread the piece of paper in front of the deputy. "If you wouldn't mind just showing us the way, we'll do the rest. Believe me, Mr. Collier's going to thank you, and every one of his lucky stars, once we get in touch with him."

"Well, if you say." The deputy picked up the pen, then traced the route through the mountains. When he was done a big **X** marked the spot where Sass Brandt would finally meet Shay Collier, the man who owned the book she wanted to film.

"Christ! Lord! Can you believe someone lives in a place like this. Jesus! This is absurd-d-d-d. . . ."

Sass's complaints sounded like a poor imitation of Elmer Fudd as the four-wheel drive hit another rut and bounced over God knew what kind of rock, fallen branch or other item Mother Nature had tossed in their path. She was almost afraid to stop the car and get out to look. With her luck Bambi would be under the wheels.

"Sass," Lisabet begged, "let's just turn around. We'll start again tomorrow. It's already five o'clock, and every mile in this wilderness is like twenty at home."

"No way. Not when we've made it this far," Sass insisted, ignoring the concern in Lisabet's voice. Poor thing, how she hated to take risks. But Sass had the situation well in hand. Nothing was going to happen to them. Success was at hand and Sass reassured Lisabet with a touch on the shoulder before she had to grip the wheel with both hands again. "Don't worry, Lisabet. I'm not going to let anything happen. If I really thought we weren't headed in the right direction . . ." Another thump of the right rear wheel. Sass gritted her teeth. "If

I wasn't sure about this we'd be headed back right this minute. I promise. Oh, look. Look, Lisabet. There it is . . ."

Lisabet took her eyes off Sass reluctantly and peered through the darkness. She closed her eyes and offered a little prayer of thanks. A cabin, lit and welcoming could be seen ahead. Of course it might not be Shay Collier's, but right now she was happy to see any sign of life. The Alaskan mountains were no place for women like them, much as Sass would like to think she could manage any situation in heaven or on earth. This was actually no place for any kind of woman and that brought up another question. What if Mr. Collier were not only rude, but a dangerous sort of man? Then what would they do?

Lisabet was just about to pose this question, when all thoughts were wiped from her mind. She flew forward, instinctively putting out her hands to break her movement before being pulled sharply back by her seat belt. Sass was throwing the gear into park and pulling on the emergency brake, ignorant of Lisabet's discomfort as her excitement rose.

"That's it. This is as far as this baby will go."

Sass was grinning, chattering as if they were headed to The Bistro for lunch, full of life and breezy expectation. It was as if she had forgotten this was Alaska and they were chasing after a man who not only had no idea they were coming, he'd made it clear he didn't want anything to do with them. From the looks of his cabin, he didn't want to see many people. There was no clearing for cars to park nor even a path to welcome his visitors.

"Sass, the more I think about it, the more I think we ought to go back to town and call. You know, this man lives away from other people for a reason. In a place like this . . ." She waved a hand as if that could dismiss the wilderness about them.

"Lisabet, this is the man's home," Sass said. Though she laughed, there was an underlying frustration in her voice that Lisabet recognized. Sass thought Lisabet was being too protective. "There's no need to act like we've just stumbled on the wicked witch's house."

Lisabet sniffed, chastened and embarrassed by Sass's good-natured scolding.

"I wasn't saying that at all. I was only being cautious. You must remember how very precious you are, Sass." Lisabet swiveled in her seat, unsnapping her belt as she did so. Her clear gray eyes looked deep into Sass's golden ones and Sass's authority faltered under their scrutiny.

There were times, like now, that Lisabet seemed the powerful one, unfairly influential on a life that shouldn't be easily controlled. Her comments seemed so personal they made Sass want to leave the car, walk on by herself, seek refuge with a stranger in his cabin rather than stay with a woman who indefinably wanted so much.

Lisabet, sensing Sass's withdrawal, spoke again, qualifying her concern so that Sass wondered if she hadn't been imagining the intimacy. "Professionally, that is, Sass. You're valuable and recognizable. We haven't a clue what we're getting into. This man hung up on you. He told Richard to go to hell, and he lives like a recluse."

"And I want something he has," Sass insisted

petulantly, tired of delay. "I don't know what it is he wants, Lisabet, but I'll find out. If he's impressed by the stardom I'll use that. If it's money he wants, no problem. But he's not going to get away from me. We've come too far. I want the rights to that book."

"Why is it so important, Sass?" Lisabet asked, unable to fathom this obsession. Certainly a person could ignite that kind of desire, Lisabet knew that all too well, but this was a book. Only a story.

"Because I feel as if this is the role I've been waiting for all my life. I can hardly wait to become that woman, speak to those men in those words. I know they were written by Tyler McDonald, but somehow they seem to be mine. Please, Lisabet, help me get the rights. I need this like I've never needed anything in my life. If I pull this off, it will prove that I am more than what someone else molds me into."

"You've never been that," Lisabet assured her and there was anger in her voice. Sass ignored it. Lisabet was always angry when Sass stepped out of the predictable schedule of her life.

"I have been. I've been moved about like a chess piece. I'm smart enough to know that. And I was smart enough to listen to those people. I wouldn't be where I am except for my mother and Richard, and you, of course. Don't you think I'm grateful that you all helped point me in the right direction? But I was educated so I could think for myself. That's what makes me smart enough now to know that if I don't try to do this thing— no, if I don't accomplish what I set out to do— I'll never be exactly the same again. Now, are you with me?"

Lisabet reached out, her gloved hand catching Sass's and for a moment the women were linked with one mind. Sass grinned, her energy back in full force, her hand slipping out of Lisabet's as she opened the door.

She was out, stamping in the cold, ready to charge the house and take prisoners to get what she wanted. Reluctantly, feeling fate closing in on her, Lisabet followed. They hiked the last few hundred yards over inhospitable ground, slipping on the ice, crunching over frozen snow until they stood on the small porch. With a thumbs up, Sass knocked. It was Sass who couldn't contain herself and called excitedly.

"Mr. Collier. Shay Collier, are you there?"

Tight-fisted, she knocked again, calling as if the sound of her voice would make her more welcome. When she tired of calling and knocking, Sass stepped back and looked over her shoulder at Lisabet, fright in her burnished eyes.

The lights still shone inside, the cabin looked inviting but the door remained closed to them. There was no welcome. Perhaps there was no man named Shay Collier inside to listen to them. Squaring her shoulders she raised her hand again, filled her lungs to call once more and, before she could do any of it, jumped back, almost into Lisabet's arms as the door was flung wide, the doorway filled by a tall man.

They stood in the dark, he in the light of the fire so that they saw nothing except a halo of light around tousled black curls, the outline of his body, powerful and broad shouldered. In the blackness, in the wake of surprise, the man who confronted them seemed brutish and threatening. But Sass saw beyond the height and the breadth of him to the poetry in his power, the symmetry in his body. Slim hips, long, almost delicate fingers on the big hands that grasped the doorframe. His hair wasn't wild and unkempt, but thick and naturally unruly, curling and framing his broad brow, tipping at the collar of his plaid shirt. But his face was still hidden, shadowed by the dark in front and the firelight in back.

If Lisabet hadn't been holding her, Sass would have picked herself up and gone to him, turning him to the light the way a director might move her until she was perfectly exposed. Yet, before she could do anything, the faceless man spoke, his voice cutting through the frigid night, warming Sass to the core of her being. In that voice was pain and the lyrics of loneliness. She perceived this without understanding how he came to be so separate. He spoke with an Irish lilt, the words precisely uttered with the cadence of valiant poetry.

"What is it you want, ladies, for I'm short of time and even shorter of temper."

"Shay Collier?"

Sass roused herself first, shaking off Lisabet who would have held her back in timidity. Strangely Sass felt no fear, only curiosity and need. But the need seemed less professional now, the desire almost personal. She took three steps, close enough to see more of him. A long straight nose, a face carved by high cheekbones and a broad brow. His eyes were shadowed, perhaps sunken, and dark. This was the face of a tortured man. He wore a beard and mustache, a mountain man, a bard, a man without guile for he wore his torment for all to see, even in the shadows. And in those shadows Sass could see he was unaware of any of this. From him she felt anger. To anyone else his fury would seem directed at the people who harassed him on this winter night. Sass knew the outrage was deeper and long held. It was a festering wound that he licked alone in this den of his. She held out her gloved hand, tentatively.

"I'm Sass Brandt, Mr. Collier."

It was clear her name meant nothing to him. He didn't flinch, his eyes never left hers, not even to look at the hand she proffered, not even to change in depth as he registered her beauty the closer she came. Sass let her hand fall, but not her bravado.

"I called you from Los Angeles as did my manager Richard Maden. We've been trying to contact you because you have something that is very important . . ."

"I know who you are. Sure, and don't I recall making myself clear to the gentleman and to you about what it 'tis you want. So I suppose that leaves us with one question, Ms. Brandt. Are you daft or simply rude?"

So quiet. He had spoken with hardly an effort and raised his voice no higher than the drift of the wind, yet Sass was ablaze as if he had assailed her with an oratory of fire and brimstone. Interesting man. Charismatic man. She leaned closer still, moving until she stood almost in the doorway, under his outstretched arm that still barred the entry to his home. The closeness of him made her

tremble, or was it only that she could see his eyes
and they weren't sunk in shame or in pain. They
were simply black as the night into which he
looked.

"I'm neither, sir. But I am cold and my car is
at the edge of your property. I'm so low on gas,
I'm afraid we won't be able to leave here unless I
can call for assistance. My friend and I would appreciate the chance to warm ourselves and use
your phone. Even you wouldn't deny us that,
would you?"

Sass had his attention now. He had noticed her
though it was hard to tell from his stony expression. Yet in his eyes she saw a flicker and knew
she had made an impression when he sized her
up with one swift look. The man seemed neither
pleased, nor attracted, nor surprised. He had only
made note of her and was now searching for his
long, unused sense of courtesy. Sass waited, wondering if Shay Collier would prove himself the
brute he first appeared, or the poet she saw beneath the angry stance.

They faced off: Sass with her breath held, Lisabet rigid with apprehension, Shay Collier domi-
nant by both his presence and his silence. The
women, independent and proud, found themselves in a curious situation of waiting on his
pleasure.

"No need for anyone to be called. Come in. Sit
by the fire. I've fuel you can have."

He stood aside but just barely. Sass slipped by
him, aware suddenly of how small she was, how
delicate she was when compared to a man like this.
He turned to follow her as if he'd done so all his

life, but stepped back, remembering Lisabet on the porch. With a spare gesture of welcome he held out his hand allowing her to follow Sass before closing the door behind them.

Shay Collier left the room without a word or a nod. The women watched him go, and it was Lisabet who skittered to Sass's side, whispering.

"Let's go, Sass. I don't think this was a good idea. It'll be late soon. We're not going to find any help on the road if we wait too much longer."

"Don't be silly, Lisabet."

Sass's voice was gentle, a laugh of amazement hiding somewhere in its silky depths. She unwound her scarf slowly, watching the doorway through which Shay Collier had walked. She slipped her hat from her head and shook out her long coppery hair. Lisabet was about to speak again, but Sass held up her hand. She wanted silence, she wanted to appreciate the scene.

From the next room she heard sounds: metal upon metal, drawers opening, the man moving about with gestures that were practiced. He was in the kitchen and that was a good sign. Content that she had a handle on his movements, Sass turned her attention to Lisabet.

"Don't be ridiculous. We wouldn't get more than two miles on the amount of gas left in that tank." Smiling reassurance she realized that Lisabet, far from being intrigued as she was, was actually frightened. "Lisabet, there's nothing to worry about. He's gruff, but he's not dangerous. Do you think he'd do us in with the fireplace poker, then bury us in the forest just because we knocked on his door?"

"No, of course not," Lisabet answered, hurt that Sass would think her so childish. She was embarrassed to realize, though, there was some merit to her observation.

There was danger here. Lisabet could feel it, and it was as lethal as if the Irishman came at them wielding an ax. She'd seen the man's eyes, she'd seen Sass standing next to him, her entire body vibrating with the chemistry that imploded between them. Yes, there was danger here, and Lisabet wanted to run from it as fast as she could, dragging Sass with her. This was more frightening than the dark, more frightening than the cold and the strange godforsaken country in which they found themselves. Somehow she had to take Sass away. But Sass was settling in, unaware of what was happening here.

"Lisabet, come on, loosen up. We're in and that's half the battle." Sass unbuttoned her heavy jacket and slipped out of it just as Shay Collier reappeared.

He looked at her and she at him and there, Lisabet thought, was the peril. It was as clear to her as Sass's eyes. But Sass and the Irishman didn't notice because he moved too quickly, not without grace, but with no hospitality.

"Coffee. It's hot." Leaning down he put a wooden tray on the raised stone hearth and backed away. Sass hid a smile. Even this unfriendly man was bound by social graces. Obviously some mother or wife had bred politeness to the point where it was second nature. On the tray were not only mugs of coffee, but English biscuits and napkins, a small pot of cream, and a bit of sugar.

"Thank you," Sass said, hoping for an opening to chat. She wasn't to have it. Shay Collier was already shrugging into his jacket by the door. He stooped and picked up a huge flashlight.

"I'll be ten minutes. You should be warm and ready to be on your way then."

With barely a glance he took his leave and something vital seemed to follow him out the door. Sass sighed and Lisabet listened to it for barely a moment before handing her a mug.

"Here, drink this. He won't be gone that long. You might as well get your jacket on, too, so we can be ready . . ."

"Lisabet!" Sass scolded her with an incredulous laugh. "I can't believe what I'm hearing. You want to go? We just beat down the door. We entered the bastion. We took the keep. Come on," Sass flopped herself onto the sofa, made a face when she realized it wasn't as soft as it looked, and patted the seat beside her. "We're halfway home. We're going to sit here until Mr. Collier either hears what we have to say or throws us out bodily."

Ignoring the invitation to sit, Lisabet wandered to the window. "I'd imagine the latter is going to be our situation. He looks like he'd have fun doing that."

"You must be blind, Lisabet."

"This isn't a movie, Sass," came the retort. Lisabet closed her eyes, immediately sorry she'd snapped. Slowly she turned toward Sass, knowing she had to make up, fearing if she didn't Sass might send her home alone. "All I'm saying is this isn't a predictable situation. We don't know this person. We're alone and the policemen who gave us directions weren't the brightest. We're not from here, and I doubt they'd come looking for us if they don't see us at the hotel tomorrow. You didn't tell anyone in Los Angeles that we were coming here. Curt is away on location. Richard has taken a few days off. This is a reckless situation. One we shouldn't have gotten ourselves into. I think it would be wise to leave this man's house, go back to town and either go back home or figure out a better way to approach Mr. Collier."

"Lisabet." Sass sighed. "You're a wonderful secretary, a marvelous assistant, a dear friend, but you are incredibly unadventurous."

"This has nothing to do with adventure, this has to do with that man's right to privacy and our own safety."

"Okay. Okay." Sass leaned forward, her hands wrapped around the warm mug, realizing just how nervous Lisabet was. "I'm sorry. I know I sound flippant but it's the excitement talking. I honestly wasn't sure we'd get this far and look, here we are. We're sitting in the lion's den. Lisabet, you know me. I don't do stupid things. I'm very cautious. But I'm also determined to do everything I can to secure the rights to that book. Believe me, if I really thought something was amiss, I'd be out of here in two seconds."

"But, Sass, this is getting ridiculous. We're like two kids breaking into the local haunted house to prove we can. You're obsessed with this book. I can name ten others that are better properties than *The Woman At the End of the Lane*. And they'd be available. The authors would beg you to produce their work. Why are we going after someone who lives in the middle of nowhere, and obviously can't be bought? Why, Sass?"

Slowly Sass pushed herself off the couch. Carefully she put her mug back on the tray and stood there for a moment as though trying to decide whether or not to indulge in a biscuit. Lisabet knew better. Sass couldn't be tempted by anything so mundane. Her temptations were of the spirit, creative bait like this book that could snare her with its images and thoughts and words. It was that she was thinking of now and that of which she spoke.

"When I read that book, Lisabet, I was transported. I went beyond my home, beyond my body to a place in my mind that I'd never been before. It was there I realized that something about this book was wrapped up with my fate. I don't know if it's meant to be the best project I've ever worked on. I don't know if it's meant to be the vehicle of my comeuppance. I only know that, deep inside me, I will never find contentment, much less happiness, if I don't try to figure out what this is supposed to mean in my life."

Sass turned toward Lisabet, her beautiful face set in an expression of the utmost seriousness. Seldom, if ever, had Lisabet been privy to the most secret parts of Sass Brandt.

"Lisabet, I live a very odd life. People who don't know me adore me. People who have never met me, hate me. Curt and Richard, yes, even you, who know me best of all aren't sure whether your affection is for me or for what I do. . . ."

"Sass, not me . . ."

"Shh, Lisabet. Of course your feelings are all tied up with my career. They must be, because mine are, too. How I feel about myself is often colored by what I'm doing at the moment. But reading this book, thinking of myself as Eileen, I felt that I was being offered a chance to bare myself in a way I'd never done before." Sass waved her hand as if brushing away a thought that was particularly bothersome. She walked to the old leather chair and ran her hand across the back of it. Her expression softened as if she had somehow connected with the owner just by touching the cracked leather. She laughed gently.

"I know that sounds ridiculous. You can argue it's simply another part, another chance to test myself as an actress. But I think it's more. I had a vision, Lisabet. I saw myself, and yet I didn't. I suppose I felt something— that through this work I would understand what heroism felt like, what true suffering felt like, what true achievement was and honest risk. I've never felt any of those things really. God, my life has been so easy. Lisabet, you must understand. I read that book and I saw . . . a vision . . ."

The door opened and a cold wind blew through before Sass could finish. Her hair caught it and rose in tendrils, blowing across her cheeks, her lips, the frigid air knifing through her heavy sweater. But she didn't move. Instead Sass, straight and tall, looked at Shay Collier. Standing by the door now he looked so different from their first encounter. Now she could see him clearly, every inch of him, and she was impressed to no end.

The sight of Shay Collier kept her rooted to the spot on which she stood. Carefully, she pulled her long hair away from her lips. They were full and red, tinted first with the cold, then the warmth of the coffee. Her color was high on her cheeks, and she spoke as if in a dream, continuing the thought she was trying to impart to Lisabet, finding herself suddenly sharing it with Shay Collier.

"I had a vision . . ." she whispered. Remembering herself and this very real moment, she shook herself free of the memory of Eileen and Tyler McDonald's book. It was time to make a frontal assault. "Mr. Collier, I did have a vision, and it was because of the book you hold the rights to. I'm here to talk to you about *The Woman At the End of the Lane*. So let's talk. Forget this tantrum of yours, and let's get down to business."

Sass grinned at him, but her smile failed her now. Shay Collier removed his coat and hung it on the peg beside the door as if he hadn't heard a word she said. Undaunted, Sass headed for the hearth and the tray while Lisabet tried to make herself small. She wandered about the cabin sipping at her coffee, knowing there was nothing to stop Sass now.

"Here," Sass said, bustling about as if she owned the place, "You must be freezing. Come near the fire. Would you like me to fetch another cup for coffee?"

"I know my way around my own kitchen."

"Sorry." Sass's hands were up in the universal sign of peace. "Just trying to be helpful. I appreciate your filling up our car."

" 'Tisn't filled, but it should get you where you're going," he grumbled, still unable to settle himself with these women in his house. "I suspect it might be a proper time for you to be going."

"Mr. Collier, be reasonable. What good is it for you to hold onto the rights to that book when it could do so much good if you sold them?"

"And for whom would it do the most good, Miss Brandt? For you? To make you richer? To make you even more famous so the man in the moon might know your face as well as we poor louts in the back country here?"

"Okay . . ." Sass lowered her hands and wiped the gratuitous smile from her face. She sat opposite him on the horrid lumpy couch. "Okay. You're right. Let's talk. I have put you out horribly. I have disturbed the silence of your life. Obviously you enjoy your solitude, and you have a right to it. But we wouldn't be here bothering you if you'd lived up to your responsibility as executor of Tyler McDonald's estate. By accepting that charge, you have an obligation to the business of that estate."

"I have no such obligation, Miss Brandt. Tyler McDonald is dead. I have been left to make decisions regarding his estate. I choose to take no action. That in itself is a decision."

Shay spoke and Sass was mesmerized. Beneath the dark beard, partially hidden by his mustache, she saw that his lips were beautifully sculpted. They opened slightly, almost in amusement, while he waited for her to respond. He had no intention of listening to reason or changing his mind. She knew that now, yet still she couldn't stop herself and forged on, as afraid to stop fighting for this project as she was to leave this little house in the wilds of Alaska.

"Then Mr. McDonald made a poor choice of guardian for his work of . . ."

"S.J. Collier."

Lisabet's voice startled Sass. She had almost forgotten the other woman was there, silently roaming around the living room. Her eyes snapped toward Lisabet, then quickly back to the man in the leather chair. His lips were pulled together. The amusement she'd sensed a moment ago had been replaced with a cold wariness. Once again he was the brute in the dark, unknown and frightening. His handsome face, his coal black eyes, were as closed to her as if he had put a steel door between them. He didn't move. Instead, Lisabet came forward, forgetting her apprehension, holding out a wooden plaque.

"You're S.J. Collier, the Irish novelist who refused the Nobel prize for literature. No," Lisabet shook her head, remembering, "you didn't refuse it. You disappeared and never claimed it. You're . . ."

Four

"You're Tyler McDonald's son."

Sass and Lisabet exchanged a glance, putting the pieces together at the same time. Their research had been minimal, but it was enough to know that the man in front of them was no mere executor of a will. The keeper of Tyler McDonald's literary legend had been well on his way to creating his own when he dropped out of sight.

"How can you possibly sit here and refuse me? How can I possibly understand that?" Sass asked, quietly indignant, her body regally held, tight and hurt that this man should refuse her when he was a creator himself. "It's one thing to end your own career, but how dare you stand in the way of your father's creation living on? Or my creativity expressing itself? You must be a horrible coward, Mr. Collier. You ran from your own success, and you're jealous that your father might enjoy more of it even in death. My God. This is unbelievable."

Shay Collier pushed himself out of his chair to tower over Sass. She looked up at him, unafraid, disgusted that he should be so petty. Lisabet moved to Sass's side, but kept silent. Slowly Shay reached toward her and slipped the plaque from her hands. In the silence of the cabin they heard only two things: the fire crackling and spitting and the sound of Shay Collier walking across the bare wooden floor to the desk in the far corner. There he replaced the plaque exactly as Lisabet had found it. His fingers lingered on the polished brass surface, wound their way slowly over the dark wooden frame. Sass thought she saw a tremor tear at his body, perhaps she heard a sigh. But the dry wood hissed as the fire consumed it and she couldn't be positive she'd heard anything except that. Sass didn't move. She dared not look at Lisabet. Now even Sass was afraid.

In the silence, Shay Collier's back to her was more menacing than his appearance on the doorstep. She could feel something emanating from him, an anger so deep and silent that it might border on madness. Lisabet didn't feel it, but Sass did and she wanted to feel more. The intensity of his emotions intrigued her as much as the realization that there would be no emotional outburst. Nor was she privileged to see his face again.

"My life is my life, Ms. Brandt. I live it as I choose, and I choose not to be reminded of my heritage or of my father. Now, I believe it is time to be on your way."

Shay's voice was controlled and masterful, leaving no question that they should do as he said.

Sass hesitated for only a split second, then slid her coat off the back of the couch and put it on. She didn't bother to button it. Her muffler was draped over her neck, her hair stuffed back under her hat. She paused and looked at Shay Collier. He hadn't moved, he barely seemed to breathe.

Sass swayed forward, her lips parting to speak though she hadn't a clue what she could say to make him look her way again. Lisabet put a restraining hand on her arm and Sass realized she was right. Now wasn't the time, perhaps there never would be a time, to approach Shay Collier. Surprisingly Sass didn't feel defeated. Instead she felt an overwhelming sadness, a great loss.

Knowing it was time to cut her losses, Sass slipped on her gloves and out of the house with Lisabet close behind. On the porch Sass pulled her coat shut and buttoned it quickly. She hadn't realized the cabin had been so warm and welcoming until she was banished from it. Though it was late afternoon, outdoors felt more like the dead of night, even though they stood in a pool of light that filtered through the curtains of the cabin. Beyond that there was nothing but blackness.

"Jesus, it's dark," Sass muttered.

Lisabet looked about. "I see a lantern over there." She was on it and back before Sass even turned. "Do you have any matches?"

Sass shook her head and laughed nervously. "Not a one. I should have taken up smoking in anticipation of a night like this."

Lisabet, never one to indulge her own sense of humor, grimaced and shook the thing. There was fuel, but she was matchless, too.

"Well, we're not going to be thrown out into the cold like this. The least he can do is light the way back to the car."

"No!" Sass caught Lisabet before she knocked

on the door, her eyes flickering to the window. He wasn't watching them, she would have felt it if he was. But he was in there, feeling things she couldn't even imagine. "No," she said more gently, "we can go on our own."

"Sass, if you recall that was a bit of a hike coming up and, hard to believe, the snow was lighter than it is now. What if you fall?"

"Then I'll twist my ankle. I'll scrape my knee. For goodness sake, Lisabet, I'll heal." Sass laughed but her frustration with Lisabet's overnurturing was evident. "The man didn't ask us here, but we came anyway and he let us in. Now he's asked us to leave, I think it would be best if we did just that."

"All right. But hold my hand. We'll go slowly."

"That's the spirit, Lisabet. We'll have you wanting to hang glide soon."

Linked as they were, the two women stepped off the porch and into the night, picking their way silently over the ruts and branches and rocks of the wilderness that was Shay Collier's domain.

They made it to the Land Rover without the dire consequences Lisabet feared. Sass slid behind the wheel, gunned the engine and, with great care, turned the car around and headed down the mountain. She grinned the minute she maneuvered the car onto the four-lane highway. At least there was one triumph this day.

"There. Feel better?" she asked.

"Much," Lisabet said. She shifted in her seat, peering ahead, anxious to be back in town. She wouldn't fully rest until she was settled in a hot bath and Sass was doing the same in her room. But she was feeling better by the minute. In fact, she was feeling quite well, almost happy. "I can't tell you how glad I am that that's over, Sass."

"Oh, it wasn't so awful. It wasn't as if he was going to chop our heads off, you know. He's quite a charming man, I'll wager, once you get past whatever chip he's got on his shoulder."

"I wasn't referring to our visit with Mr. Collier, Sass. I'm glad the whole thing is over. Now maybe we can get back to doing some real work," Lisabet said.

To her surprise, Sass laughed. She laughed so hard the Land Rover swerved over the center line causing Lisabet to yelp in surprise. As Sass righted the huge vehicle she sucked in her breath, desperately trying to control her giggles.

"My God, Sass, what's the matter with you?" Lisabet snapped.

"Nothing's wrong with me, Lisabet." Sass chuckled. "I just can't believe you said that."

"Said what? I don't know what I said."

"That you're happy this is over."

Lisabet gave Sass a puzzled look. "I don't understand why you find that funny."

"Because, Lisabet, it's not over. Not by a long shot."

Alaska was gorgeous on a winter morning. Three hours of light, that's what they had promised when she filled up at the gas station at six. Three hours in which she could drive to Shay Collier's cabin, talk to him in terms he would understand and hopefully walk away with the rights to *The Woman At the End of the Lane*. Lisabet had been left sleeping, a note dutifully left at the front desk. Lisabet was a drag on Sass's concentration and that's all there was to it.

Though Mr. Collier had been quite circumspect, Sass hadn't missed the initial message. He'd found her attractive, even interesting. Perhaps he'd been in the woods a long time, but not long enough to have lost his mind. She would use that to her advantage now that Lisabet wasn't there to edit the encounter.

And, if the truth be known, it was an absolute delight to be alone. There was an incredible sense of freedom that all Sass's money couldn't buy. She felt downright girlish again, though the notion of her lost youth would make anyone laugh. If there was a person on this earth who epitomized the beauty, the adventurous spirit, the verve of youth it was Sass Brandt. Yet much of that appearance was a facade, as well acted as any of her roles.

Her youth had been given to her mother, Francesca, no more than a girl herself. Pregnant and alone when she gave birth to Sass, Francesca Brandt savagely protected her daughter, guarding her talent, only using it to create a world so much better than the one she had grown up in. No trailer parks for her baby, no poverty, no hunger. She was father and mother and, when cancer proved her undoing, she transferred her protective spirit to Richard and Lisabet until Sass hardly remembered the mother love. It had been replaced by the ever more cloying devotion of people who depended upon her wealth and talent for their own peace of mind. Unintentional though the gilded cage had been, that's what Sass's life had been when growing up a normal little girl would have served so well. But Sass had loved her mother and done what was expected with an open heart. Still, at times, she wished it could have been different.

Going to auditions she watched the children in parks and dreamed of stopping to play. Sass longed to ride a bike rather than be chauffeured in limousines. She wished for a best friend for Christmas and got a trip to Cannes. Never complaining, Sass wistfully loved her mother and Richard and Lisabet through it all. Now, in her late twenties, Sass was ready for freedom. This was her time, and damn it, Shay Collier wasn't going to stand in her way any more than the rest of them. She was strong and she was right about this project. One way or another that book would be hers.

Her memory, honed by years of learning scripts on a moment's notice, Sass made the turn off the highway and up the mountain without hesitation. She marveled at the beauty around her. In the hazy light of morning Sass realized that Shay Collier might have good reason for wanting to hide away in this fabulous country. Perhaps he wasn't driven by the things normal people desired: money, success, companionship. Maybe Mr. Collier was of a more spiritual bent.

Sass slapped the steering wheel thoughtlessly, feeling lighthearted and sure of herself in the light of day. Funny how setting the scene could change an attitude. Last night she was almost ready to catch Lisabet's fright and resignation. Now, Sass was ready to meet her match and Lord what a match he was.

At that thought Sass chuckled, wondering what Curt would say about the little gnats of enchantment that buzzed about in her brain for the elusive Mr. Collier. What an interesting man! Gorgeous, to say the least, but it wasn't his physical being that so intrigued her. No, it was much more than that. She would have found him irresistible if . . .

She shook her head. Forget the "if," think about what is, she demanded of herself. She had so much new information on him there must be something that would stack the deck in her favor. This man had walked away from a Nobel prize in literature. He wasn't much older than she. Could he be so altruistic as to think that a commendation such as the Nobel prize was even too commercial to acknowledge? Could it be that here was a man her money, her power, or her celebrity couldn't tempt? What an exciting thought— if it were true. It would be the immaterial benefits she would stress when talking about *The Woman At the End of the Lane*. She could hardly wait to meet Mr. Collier face-to-face again and from the looks of it, she wouldn't have to wait too much longer. The cabin was ahead. The stretch between the road and the front door seemed almost welcoming at this early hour.

Sass pulled off the road, tugged on the emergency brake, and then sat back. This time she was going in prepared. Every instinct was on alert, every ounce of intelligence and all her powers of observations were called into play.

In the soft, hazy light that passed for sunshine in these parts, Sass saw that the house truly was a cabin. Made of real logs not plaster and a facade.

She guessed its size: living room, which she remembered well, the kitchen, possibly two bedrooms, and a small room jutting out to the side near a shed on the left. Just enough room for two and plenty for one. Lazily she wondered if Shay Collier entertained overnight guests of the female persuasion, then realized that was the least of her worries. Though a lady friend might actually help this situation, Sass doubted she'd find one stashed away. There hadn't been a feminine touch about the place.

There was no sign of a car or truck. Could it be that S.J. Collier walked everywhere? A true mountain man, throwing a bear skin over his jacket, slinging a rifle across his shoulder as he hunted and scavenged for his daily bread? Sass laughed. The scenario sounded just like that movie, *Jeremiah Jones.* But Shay Collier was no Robert Redford. He was much more attractive.

Sass blinked, then grinned. Her concentration had been so deep, she failed to notice the snow. Little pieces of lace fell from the sky like pixies coming down from heaven to play. How delightful. How wonderful. It was like a fairyland and Sass was filled with an overwhelming sense of confidence.

"Deny me now, Mr. Collier," she said to the cold.

She was invincible and she was ready. Opening the car door Sass stepped out, playfully raising her face to the sky, opening her mouth and letting the snowflakes melt on the tip of her tongue.

"Watch out, Shay Collier, Sass Brandt is headed

your way," she muttered and headed straight toward the front door.

She was breathing hard by the time she hit the front porch. Her L.A. lungs might be used to the smog, but this altitude was another matter. Smiling, Sass turned around to look at the snow. It was falling harder now, a beautiful veil of Chantilly lace covering the bride from head to toe on her opulent wedding day. Beautiful images of an incredible natural phenomena. Strange how the snowfall could quadruple in the five minutes it took her to reach the door. Well, if last night was any measure of what was to be, she'd soon be sitting in front of a roaring fire with a tin of biscuits at hand. Hopefully he wouldn't turn her away before she had a chance to sample his hospitality once again. She'd like the chance to sit across from him, his black eyes on her, as she tried to figure out what exactly it was that he wanted.

Raising her gloved fist Sass knocked and the hollow call was greeted with an even more empty silence. She tried again, and a third time. Walking the length of the porch she saw the lantern they had abandoned the night before had been carefully put back in place. A very proper man, this. Nothing out of place. Yet something was out of place with him. Hadn't Sass felt it last night?

Poking her head around the cabin she saw the woodpile, carefully covered, an ax embedded in a half-split log. No Mr. Collier there. Stepping off the raised porch she looked toward the chimney, squinting against the sting of the snow. No smoke. Damn. He wasn't there. Well, there was nothing to do but find him. How far could he go in this—blizzard?

Though she hadn't meant it quite so literally, Sass was beginning to wonder if that's exactly what this was. Skiing at Aspen had always been such a pleasant experience, but this much snow in the wilderness was downright annoying. Cupping her hands around her lips, Sass called.

"Mr. Collier! Shay Collier! It's me, Sass Brandt."

With the first word Sass was satisfied that her stage yell would hold her in good stead. But by the time she called her name, the wind had picked up the sound of her voice and whisked it away, only to be completely muffled by the heavy blanket of snow. Sass had gone no more than a hundred yards when she turned back. Even she, a city girl, knew this wasn't good. When she turned and couldn't see the cabin she understood how very bad the situation was indeed. Though she'd heard about whiteouts, Sass had never seen one. Aspen and Tahoe didn't allow for that specifically horrible freak of nature when up becomes down and sideways is nothing but a circle. Alaska had no such rules against nature's pranks and Sass Brandt was now caught in the most unbelievable mess.

The world was completely white. Now and again, in a tiny tear in this phenomena, Sass could see a tree here, a rock there, but nothing more substantial than a glimpse of either. There was no full picture to ground her or guide her. In the very center of her being, fear began to grow.

Forgetting about Shay Collier, Sass stumbled in a direction she prayed would take her to safety, not farther from it. She remembered the car, half pulled off the road. She had walked right to the cabin door to the left in a straight line so the Land Rover was another straight line to her left. A perfect triangle. Yes, that's exactly where she needed to go. But this white world wasn't precise nor did it seem linear. She was inside the beautiful seamless dome of an egg, no in or out, up or down, no point of connection. Still, Sass knew she had to try to get through it. The cold was numbing and concern hovered on the edge of panic.

Gritting her teeth she took one tentative step. She would go to the car. A simple enough goal. After that she need go no farther. *Don't be afraid,* she repeated over and over again in her mind until it became a prayer for salvation. Again she called and again her voice was engulfed by the furiously falling snow. She fell, too, faltering more often than not, her knees sinking deeper into the drifts each time. And each time hysteria hit her in the pit of her stomach, harder and harder until it seemed like it would pummel her into the ground. Yet each time Sass fought off terror. She lifted her head and flailed her arms and screamed useless screams as if this were a real enemy that could be pushed away. Her hat flew off, loosening her hair, exposing her face to the freezing elements. Desperately she snapped up the fur collar on her coat, knowing even that wouldn't be enough to keep her from frostbite if she didn't find shelter soon.

Recklessly Sass used what she could to save herself: her voice to call though she knew no one could hear her, her legs to wade through the heavy snow, her arms to push away the branches she felt, but did not see, in this white, white world. She pricked her ears but there was no noise except the roar of her heart beating away her life. No sight. No sound. Lord!

Sass thought of Lisabet, still sleeping so warm in her bed, unaware of what was happening on this mountain.

And there were tears. They were pushing out the side of her eyes, freezing on her lashes before they could fall. Her hair was wet from the snow and still that damned stuff came, heavier and heavier, pearly and frosty until Sass was beyond fear. What if she never found the car, or the cabin? What if . . . she died?

Then, with a gasp of despair that turned to a cry of relief Sass's hand touched metal. The car. She had found the car. Hand over hand Sass used it as her guide, caressing it, trying not to sob with gratitude, wasting what little energy she had left. Finally her fingers wrapped around the handle. Unlocked, it was a simple thing to slip inside. Her head fell back on the seat, her eyes were closed. She was safe.

Sass took three deep breaths. Meant to quell her dread, they sounded only frantic and fearful. It would be a long, long while before she was calm but warmth must come immediately. Fingers trembling, Sass forced her head up. She couldn't feel her nose, her lips were frozen. She was so cold she couldn't shiver, so tired she could hardly move.

How long had she been out there? Ten, fifteen, twenty minutes? Time had been lost along with a sense of direction. Such a short distance, yet every ounce of her energy was used traversing it. Unsteadily, Sass grasped the key and concentrated on inserting it into the ignition, afraid to look through the window and into the white for fear she would lose all sensibility. It took so long Sass almost cried, but finally she managed to turn the key and the car rumbled to life. Frantically she adjusted the heat settings, desperate for the life-giving warmth since the temperature was now deadly cold.

Sass swiped at her face, her hair, ran her hand around the collar of her coat trying to rid herself of the now melting snow that all but covered her. She collapsed back on the seat, exhausted, unable to do anything but breathe until she felt the air pumping through the vents become warm and finally, blessedly hot. She sobbed, hiccuping through her tears, and thanked her lucky stars for modern technology.

Closing her eyes, Sass was immune to the needle-like pain that tortured her now thawing flesh. Half-heartedly she attempted to remove her gloves, but they were too wet, plastered to her hands. The effort proved too much for her.

"This is a fine mess you've gotten yourself into," she whispered. Outside the windshield the world was still as white and smooth as the inside of an eggshell. No sky, no ground, no depth. White, white, white and full of fright. Afraid to open her eyes and look again, Sass rested as the engine purred and the warm air slowly seeped through her wet clothing. She was fine now. As long as she was safe in the car there was time to think.

First, Shay Collier was not in the cabin. That much she knew.

Next, Shay Collier might not be about at all.

If that was true, Sass was on her own and would have to do whatever it took to get herself out of this mess.

Finally . . . finally . . . finally . . .

There was no final thought because, with the heat and fatigue, her thoughts spiraled out of control and her fear was sucked into the vortex until sleep claimed her.

She woke with a start. Disoriented Sass was heavy with slumber and something else. Something very inviting. It was a heavy weight that felt marvelously comfortable. She felt herself smile, knew she was thinking about this interesting sensation, yet she also knew she was powerless to explore it. Her eyes closed again, shutting despite her desire to orient herself. Tired. That's all she was. There was no harm in dozing a while longer. But something nagged at her, some horrid idea that lurked in the back of her mind. She fought desperately to wake up and face the problem head-on, Sass Brandt's way. She would have laughed at that had she had the energy. She couldn't face anything if opening her eyes was such a problem.

"Please open."

Sass was sure she had spoken, begging her own body to do her bidding, but then again she wasn't sure. Perhaps her voice had only been bouncing around in her mind instead of the still interior of the Land Rover. The still interior . . . the silent interior . . . the quiet . . .

Oh Lord! The quiet. That was what was wrong. She was dying. She was freezing to death. The whoosh of the heater had stopped. The hum of the motor no longer rocked her to sleep. It was the grim reaper's icy fingers that lulled her into unconsciousness; it was the cold that was shutting her down as easily as the old battery had turned off the life-giving warmth.

Damn. She was dying. Her mind knew it, and her body didn't seem to care. Sass struggled now, using the only tool she had at her disposal— her will. Her brain was working. All she had to do was get it to access that marvelous little place where her will was hiding. That was all she needed, a little bit of drive, a pinch of chutzpa. She was Sass Brandt and she wasn't about to freeze to death a hundred yards from a warm cabin where there was food and shelter.

Her eyes were open. Even though she was groggy and terrified, Sass knew each little step was one in the right direction and open eyes was the first one of many. Now came the real magic. Her body had to move. First her hands. Afraid to close her eyes in concentration, Sass stared at those hands, willfully insisting that her fingers wiggle. It was so hard in her leather gloves. Soaked by the snow, they dried in the intense heat before the battery went dead and were now like a second skin, the cowhide shrunk and stiff until it felt as if her hands were encased in cement. But move they did. Another triumph and this one pushed her on to bigger things, better things, things that would make her responsible for her own destiny no matter what that destiny might be.

Sass shifted, her body responding sluggishly and painfully. Her legs uncurled and her arms unfolded until she was sitting upright. Dismissing the cold, Sass refused to imagine what her feet looked like beneath her boots and socks. They were feet Sass couldn't feel. L.A. bred though she was, she knew this wasn't a good sign. But those feet were still attached to her legs and those feet would move, by God.

Shaking her head, Sass pushed her hair out of her eyes and peered out the window. Thankfully she could see the cabin dimly in the distance. The snow still fell heavily, much harder than she'd ever seen snow fall, but it was no longer a whiteout condition. She could manage this. Certainly she could.

Thinking that, letting the mantra tumble about in her mind, Sass opened the door, abandoning the useless vehicle and the keys. Damn the old piece of junk. When she got out of this she would sue the pants off the rental agency that dared give her a car with an old battery. That would be a pleasure.

No, it wouldn't.

Pleasure would be sitting down to a warm dinner. Cuddling under a heavy comforter. Curt holding her. Seeing Lisabet.

Stumbling on, she recited her pleasures to keep one foot moving in front of the other as she squinted against biting, driving snow. Making love to Curt . . . Sass tripped and fell to her knees but pushed herself up and continued her recital. Making love to Shay . . . No . . . She shook her head and laughed. She was out of her mind. Surely dementia was setting in. Beginning again, her narrative more guarded now, Sass moved on. It was so cold. So damnably cold.

"Try again, Sass," she told herself through gritted teeth. "Say it out loud."

There was a lump in her throat and a big rock up ahead. Calling up all her concentration she focused on the rock and began to talk, the lump in her throat making her words sound like sobs.

"Making love to Curt. Making a movie. French Onion soup with cheese bubbling . . ."

She was at the rock, falling toward it, then holding on for dear life. The rock was solid and it was real and it wasn't snow white. Sass was so grateful for that rock. But she was cold and she didn't seem to be getting warmer or stronger no matter how much she moved. Sass needed more of everything: strength and savvy and the sound of her voice.

"Pleasure," she breathed, reminding herself to remain sane and focused. "Things that would be a pleasure."

Sass pushed off the rock. The cabin was so close. She could see the woodpile. Twenty more yards. "Pleasure. A warm puppy. A blanket. Pleasure would be . . ." She huffed, the breath suddenly gone out of her. Ten more yards. "Pleasure . . . arms around me . . . pleasure . . ." Five more yards. ". . . strong arms . . ."

She was there. Her hand touched a log, rough hewn, split by the man who owned the cabin. Strong arms, that's what she thought of, that was the vision in her mind even as she gave herself up, not to a man's loving embrace, but to nature's deadly one.

"You don't understand. There ain't nothing I can do about it right now."

"No, you don't understand," Lisabet railed. "That is Sass Brandt, the movie star, out there. She's gone driving off in this blizzard to Mr. Shay Collier's cabin, and I want you to go find her."

"I don't care who she is we ain't goin' out till it lets up. I got two deputies in this town. One is out with a lady givin' birth, and the other one is trying his best to get the roads cleared on our one and only plow. Now if your movie star is out there and havin' trouble, she's just goin' to have to wait like us mortal folks for help. 'Sides, you don't even know if she's in trouble, do you?"

"I can feel it," Lisabet insisted, realizing the minute the words were out of her mouth how ridiculous that sounded. But what would these backwoods people know about her bond with a woman like Sass Brandt? They were too practical, too concerned with the corporeal rather than the spiritual. Lisabet threw up her hands, the proper words, the convincing words eluding her. "Oh for goodness sake. She's from Los Angeles, she doesn't know her way around this place. The man she's gone to see doesn't want her on his property, and she's pushing him to the limit. What else do you need?"

"A break in the weather, ma'am. You get me that and I swear, I'll get a car up to Collier's place. Till you can do that I'd suggest you stay inside out of the cold. 'Cause if you don't, we may be lookin' for you along with your friend when this is over. Now, if you don't mind, ma'am . . .''

The man behind the desk grimaced as if to say he had better things to do than talk to her and he was damned sorry about it. Lisabet began to object, thought better of it and cut her losses. Obviously there wasn't help to be had here so she'd have to take matters into her own hands. Abandoned, she went to the door and stared through the window before opening it. Yes, she'd have to take care of things as she always did. She'd have to . . . What?

What on earth could she do? Walk ten miles to Shay Collier's cabin and hope she found Sass along the way? She'd call, but the lines were down as she found out when she tried to reach Richard. He was too far away to do any good anyway, and Sass didn't want him to know what she was about. Curt. Well, Lisabet would have preferred to deal with him, but he was on location somewhere in the sunny Caribbean. There was nothing to do, nothing Lisabet could change. Not the snow or Sass's departure or her own ineffectualness. She was useless. But one of these days, well, one of these days she'd prove to everyone, especially Sass, that it was she, Lisabet, who was invaluable.

Throwing open the door, Lisabet braved the elements long enough to get back to the hotel. There was nothing to do but wait.

The snow fell softer and the wind was down. It didn't moan through the pine trees that towered as tall as twenty men, it didn't blow the snow horizontally so that each flake felt like the sting of a dart against the skin. Everything was beautiful now, quiet and manageable. He could leave. Not that he really wanted to. He'd handled things quite nicely out in this wilderness for a lad from the green isle.

When the whiteout hit Shay was ready. He dug into a snowbank and covered himself with the insulated blanket he carried in his pack, then waited it out. It had been cold but from the inside out Shay was dressed for an event like this. He laughed, thinking of the tourists who came dressed in their fancy coats and high-heeled boots, ridiculously decked out for the cold. Just like that woman. Sass Brandt. Dressed like a movie star she was, that sheep coat, the sweater and jeans that fit her like a glove outlining every nip and curve of her body. Damn stupid woman, he thought, uncurling himself under the blanket. Anyone with sense knew that clothing had to be loose enough to cover a bit of long underwear that a woman like her wouldn't be caught dead in if he had a bet about it. But he didn't. She wasn't worth a thought one way or another. Still, she'd been nice to look at, nice to sit with for a wee bit— when she was silent, not talking about that damnable book.

With a grunt he pushed himself up and shook off the snow. Expertly he folded the silver survival blanket and hoisted his pack, sorry that he wasn't returning home with a rabbit or two for supper. Not that he was at all sure hunting had been on his mind when he left early that morning. He'd simply needed to get out of the place, away from that lingering scent of perfume that had no place in any

home of his. Female things. Never again. Well, now
his head was clear, of that he was sure. Home he
would go to do the things he did every day: to ignore
the typewriter and the words that flew through his
head, to scorn the work that called to him with more
strength each day. He would chop some wood and
fix the pump. He would . . .

Funny, wasn't it. He was running out of things
he would do. God save him from time and himself.

Adjusting his pack Shay began to walk. He left
behind his thoughts, or lost them along the way,
as he pushed through the forest in the cold and
snow. Either way, he didn't care where they went
so long as they didn't go with him. Twenty minutes
later he was home, throwing his pack in the house
before heading to the woodpile. Damn the repairs.
A roarin' fire was just what he needed. That and
a cup of ale and . . .

"Jesus, Mary and Joseph . . ."

There, behind the wood, curled tightly into herself, her copper-colored hair covering her face, her
body half covered by snow, lay Sass Brandt. In the
blink of an eye he had her in his arms. Her hair
fell away from her face and he saw it was pale as
the snow that fell upon it, except for her lips.
Those were tinged the color of azure, the clear
and precise tint on death's calling card. Shay Collier hesitated no longer than it would take a lep-
rechaun to twinkle out of sight when stumbled
upon. He was upon her, arms scooping her up
roughly in his amazement and terror.

Clutching her to him he carried Sass to the
porch, he kicked open the door, spinning through
it into the cabin before it slammed shut behind.

Without a thought he did what he had to. Sass was laid on the couch, a blanket tucked around her haphazardly while he worked. The fire was stoked and piled with dry wood until it flamed enough to warm the room. Out Shay went again into the snow to bring in more wood, not giving Sass a thought until the fire was blazing. When it was done he turned to her and pulled off the blanket. Sass moaned, half turned but he kept her still, putting his hands on her shoulders. The fire blazed, illuminating her chalk-white face so eerily it frightened him to gaze upon it.

Without care he stripped off her clothes: the wet coat, the sweater and jeans, her boots and socks until she was almost naked. Quickly Shay looked at her, seeing only what he needed to see. Her feet were bad but not beyond hope, her fingers had fared a bit better. Frostbite had not claimed her extremities, but she must be treated properly lest he do more harm than good.

Kneeling at her feet Shay lay the blanket back over her and took each foot in his hands, massaging and kneading them slowly so that her blood flow would come back naturally, gently to warm her. He was thankful she wasn't awake, for certainly this would be painful, and Shay knew he couldn't stand to see anguish in those eyes of hers.

He worked Sass's fingers in the same way. She cried out and tried to jerk her damaged hands away, unaware he was trying to help her, lost as she was in the deep sleep of hypothermia. Surprised, Shay pulled back gently, looking up from his work, his eyes lingering self-indulgently on her face. Mother Mary she was beautiful. Too beauti-

ful. Even more so than she whom he had loved . . .
once . . . so long ago. . . .

Unable to help himself Shay abandoned his
work. Her fingers were warming, the color coming
back slowly as her blood began to flow once more.
Tears in his eyes, memories overflowing the tight
boundaries he had built for them, Shay tucked the
blanket under her chin, unable to look at such
beauty, unable to be reminded of death for fear
he would seek it himself.

Covered, sleeping quietly now, actually resting,
Shay turned away from Sass knowing there was
nothing more he could do. Yet something called
him back to her, some need to convince himself
that all was right and she was safe. Once again he
sank to his knees and this time his long, strong
hands cupped the sides of her chilled face. Her
lips were ashen, no longer blue. God, to waste such
beauty as this, to waste such spirit. If she only
knew how foolish that would be. It hurt his heart
to even imagine it.

Knowing he could watch no longer without losing his heart to despair, Shay Collier lowered his
face and lay his cheek ever so softly against hers,
willing his warmth and his life to her. When he
was sure the gift had been accepted, when the first
tear fell from his eyes to her flesh, he rose and
left her.

Five

Sass had Shay's attention the moment she moved. She came slowly to consciousness. He watched carefully, noting every change in her.

There was the color of sunrise in her cheeks. Her lips were still near white and he crazily thought to kiss them to tint. Someone watching would never know he was even concerned about the woman on the couch. His expression was stony and the only motion about him was the occasional blink of his eyes. She had thrown the covers off so that one graceful arm and shoulder were bared. Shay, who had been watching for so long, realized now that he actually knew her quite well though they had not spoken a word.

Sass Brandt was simpler than he had first imagined. No polish on her nails, they were short and well cared for, but not a source of obsessive pride. Yet her skin was pampered, oiled everyday, he was sure, steamed and caressed by people who were paid to care for it. They'd done their job well. Her flesh was the most exquisite he had ever seen and, even before the other one, the one he loved, there had been many beautiful women for him to compare her to.

Her hair was tangled now, yet, as it dried, lost none of its luster. There was no dye, no streaks that weren't naturally red and gold and he liked that. The night wore on now with only the candle-light and the fire to illuminate the cabin, yet still her hair glimmered like a fiery halo about her face.

Her ears were pierced, but no diamonds for her. Small gold hoops were the only bright spot against her pale skin. She would wake soon. She would be looking at him with those eyes. What color were they? He couldn't remember. He knew they had looked almost through him. They had shone like a star. Nursemaid he'd been for the last hours, now he would be caretaker and then she would be gone. Pushing out of his chair he stood, took one last look and turned on his heel. But he hadn't gone far before he was stopped.

"Where are you going?"

Her voice was weak, yet as lovely as if it had the strength of the day before, more beautiful perhaps because he could imagine it speaking other words to him, asking him to stay for other reasons than fear and confusion. More pleasurable reasons. He remained still, letting the question hover at his back. Put out he might be, rude he was not. He turned to face her.

"I'm going to the kitchen. You'll be needin' something warm to eat, somethin' simple. I've had the kettle on the stove heating for the moment you woke. Tea and some soup."

"Thank you." She tried to smile. It was diffi-cult. Shay didn't encourage her but remained stoic, looking at her from hooded eyes. She was dangerous to him, that much Shay knew. Though he would help her, he wouldn't make the lioness too comfortable in this den. Now that she was here out of necessity he couldn't afford to befriend her.

" 'Twasn't a matter of hospitality, woman. You were near dyin' when I found you. I should thank you to do that on someone else's property. Now that you're on mine, I'll patch you up."

Now Sass did manage a smile, feeble but beautiful nonetheless. Bravely, clutching the blanket, she tried to push herself up to sitting, but Shay was upon her.

"What are you doing? You're daft as the day is long," he said, more gently than he intended.

His hands were on her bare shoulders, warm and strong and insistent. His fingers dug into her skin without pain, the pressure pleasurable even as she realized she had no strength to fight him.

"I'll leave. I know when I'm not wanted."

"Don't be a fool. You can't leave. Look!" He shoved his head toward the window. Still the snow fell and, even in the darkness, Sass could see high drifts where once there had only been rocks and patches of ice. "Sure, since you were foolish enough to almost freeze yourself to death, use whatever brain you've left to save yourself from doing it all over again. I'll get you something warm. Then we'll see how you're feeling and worry about things like sittin' up."

Sass nodded, knowing he was right. Her head was spinning and her body was weak. He was gone before she could utter another word. When he came back he had the same tray on which he'd

served her the day before. This time there was soup
and some wonderful concoction that smelled of hot
apples and cinnamon.

Without a word he laid a cloth over her chest
and propped her head higher on an extra pillow.
Intent upon his task, Shay sat on the sofa beside
her and spooned some of the steaming liquid between her lips. Sass pulled back.

"Hot," she whispered and he blew away the of-
fense until it was warm enough for her to eat properly. They sat this way for ten minutes, he
spooning, she concentrating on eating. No sound
in the cabin other than the clink of the spoon
against the white bowl, his murmur as he urged
her to one more sip of spirits, one more taste of
the soup. And with each spoonful, each sip, Sass
felt herself coming back. At one point she shuddered and said, "I almost died."

Shay nodded. The observation needed no corroboration. She would need to talk about it sometime. Now was not that time, and he had no desire
to be her confessor. The less he knew of her the
better, for surely she could become too easily cared
for and that was the last thing he needed. So Shay
Collier resumed his ministrations and they spoke
not another word until Sass turned her head, unable to eat more.

"Better?" he asked, keeping his eyes downcast
as if the bowl of soup needed a great deal of attention. He had seen the color of her eyes now,
golden like the first spring wildflowers on the
mountain. Disconcerting, that's what they were.
Too clear. Too bright. The eyes of someone who
never suffered. Suffering had turned his coal

black, and he couldn't endure to look at himself in the mirror for fear of being reminded of his anguish every day.

He looked up only long enough to see her nod, see her try to smile, but the exhaustion was deep in her body and she was already drifting off to sleep again. Though he wished her gone, Shay found himself standing as quietly as if she were a babe in a cradle. He moved softly for a tall man, gracefully over the floor to the kitchen where he washed the dishes and tried to banish these feelings that rushed in on him. The avalanche of emotions that dared try to bury his indifference, his hatred of the world, was frightening. She was nothing, yet he watched as if she were the only thing in the world worth tending.

He had thrown her into the dark the day before, and now protectiveness reared its tender head to prod his heart. Finally, controlling the part of him that would open up and care for Sass, Shay left the kitchen, turning off the lights behind him. In the living room, as he expected, Sass slept. She had turned and he could no longer see her face, buried as it was in the white down pillow. But ah, the sight before him was one to behold even without the gorgeous planes of her countenance. Her hair flowed over her bare shoulders and down her naked back. In her restlessness the blanket had been drawn close to her chest, gathered up in her fist like a child so that now it lay draped over her hips, baring her exquisite skin. Had he been one of the great masters he would have been moved to paint, had he been a poet he would have been moved to verse, but he was only a man and the sight of her moved him to thoughts and desires he hadn't allowed himself for what seemed an eternity.

Since he dare not go close, for fear the touch of her, the mere act of covering her, might bring him to the brink, Shay Collier walked around the couch and drew his fine old chair close to the fire. Then he pulled on a worn quilt and spread his legs in front of him, staring into the flame so he might not think of the woman who lay deep in sleep behind him. Soon he had his wish. All was dark.

Shay Collier slept dreamlessly for the first time in years.

He woke with a start, reaching for something—what he didn't know. But there was danger in the room and he needed to defend himself. From this danger, though, there was no shield and he realized it the moment the sleep left his eyes, and the dreaminess withdrew from his mind.

It was only her, looking like a vision, dressed in his old robe, the one he never wore. It engulfed her from chin to toe, the collar turned up against the chill in the room now that the fire was burning low.

She looked at him. Her hand was raised to her head, a comb hovering near her hair. That hair seemed darker now. Then he realized why that was. It was wet, her face was shining. Shay pushed himself up in his chair, taking a deep breath to clear his mind only to find it muddled by the scent of soap and Sass.

"I'm sorry," she whispered. "I didn't mean to wake you. I wanted to dry my hair. It was so cold after . . ." Sass laughed gently, clearly embarrassed. "I hope you don't mind. I took a shower. Just made myself at home." She shrugged and pulled the comb through her long hair before throwing it back over her shoulders, pulling her knees up and hugging them. She looked at him, straight at him, with no apology and truly little shame. An odd woman this. Very American yet softer, kinder perhaps than the ones he had run into. They seemed hard and practical, unlike the women he was used to at home . . . the place he used to call home, he reminded himself.

Shay tossed off his quilt.

"No, I don't mind. 'Tis probably best."

Sass listened. There it was again, that marvelous lilt in his voice, the calling of a land far away, a land of mists and loughs. Ireland. She never thought the sound of a voice could conjure up such visions. Then again, perhaps it wasn't his voice. Perhaps it was him: tall, dark-haired and bearded, pale skin, black, black eyes. He'd look wonderful in a kilt. But then, wasn't that the Scots who wore such things? Sass smiled up at him as he stood. He was so tall, so graceful in his stance, as if he had been born strong and confident, not grown that way learning his lessons from life.

How curious she was about that life of his. The little she knew of it was so contradictory. Impassioned novelist, award-winning talent, a man who disappeared and now lived like a hermit away from the world he wrote about. Strange. So odd. She tipped her head, wanting to speak of these things, but he was moving now as if away from her was the only place he wanted to be.

He folded his quilt and draped it over the back of his chair. He did the same with the blanket she'd lain under. He moved her clothes, gingerly as if they might burn him. He blushed when the skimp of silk she called a bra fell at his feet and had to be retrieved. He was headed to the phone when Sass decided she'd better start the conversation before he had a heart attack trying to figure out ways not to talk to her.

"It doesn't work. I tried. I knew you'd want me to leave as soon as possible but I couldn't even get a dial tone. I'm sorry."

"No bother. We can wait. Plenty of food," he mumbled.

"And wood and everything else I'm sure." Sass laughed, her voice gaining strength as the sleep left both of them. "You seem to have thought of everything."

"What in the hell were you doing out there near dying on my doorstep!" Shay's eruption was so sudden, so intense, Sass tightened her hold on her knees and dipped her head as if to protect herself from his anger. He twirled back on her and from across the room she could see a blaze deep in his eyes, feel the tautness of his body and she knew instinctively this was not a reaction of fury but of fear. "Sure I cannot believe you could have been so stupid as to come here, and not leave when you saw what was happenin'!"

"But it was so fast," Sass countered, raising her head, refusing to be cowed. Heaven knew she'd been scared, too. He didn't have a monopoly on that particular emotion. "It was snowing so prettily one minute, the next I couldn't see a damn thing. I assure you, Mr. Collier, had I known what would happen I wouldn't have ventured within ten miles of this place. I assumed, when I drove up here, it was only my dignity that was in danger, not my life!"

"I doubt your dignity would have been much in danger, madam. By the saints, you seem to have none. Your sense of decorum is badly defined. You invite yourself to places you are not welcome, you continue to request things that have been denied you, and in general make quite a nuisance of yourself." Sass's lips tipped in the beginnings of a smile. He raved beautifully. But it made Shay Collier crazy to see her so. Though words had never failed him, they did now. "By the saints, you don't even have the decency to be shamed, miss. Not even that decency . . ."

He was at the door, ripping his coat off the rack, his hand on the knob when Sass called.

"I already looked. Even a mountain man like you couldn't get outside right now. The drifts are up to the sills, Mr. Collier. We haven't a phone and it's the middle of the night though I realize it's difficult to tell around here exactly what time of day or night it is. Anyway, what I'm trying to say is I'm afraid you're stuck with me . . . and my misguided sense of decorum."

The door remained closed. Shay listened, his head hanging lower with each word she spoke. Sass tried not to laugh. How awful it must be for him to have her naked under his robe in front of his fire, her hair freshly washed, her skin smelling of

soap. She was no fool. Even those eyes of his
couldn't hide his appreciation of her as a woman.
Granted she did feel badly that he had no choice
in the matter, but Sass also knew this was not the
hardship he made it out to be.

"Please, Mr. Collier, sit down with me. We'll
talk. This has been the most frightening, in some
ways most wonderful, day of my life. Could we talk
until morning? Someone will come then. They'll
clear the roads and I'll be gone. Until then, please.
Please, couldn't we just talk? I was so afraid."

Looking over his shoulder Shay saw an angel sitting on his hearth, her legs tucked up to her
breasts, his old plaid robe looking nothing more
than the garment of Venus. One hand still
wrapped about her knees, the other was held out
to him in a gesture of peace, not seduction. Try
as he might he couldn't help himself. He smiled.
He smiled and sighed and tossed his coat back on
the hook.

" 'Tis certain you're a convincing woman, Miss
Brandt. I'll see what the larder has left. Perhaps,
even after all this time, I have the proper things
on hand with which to entertain a lady."

He began to talk about the book when the clock
struck four A.M. Sass knew it was not the wine they
had drunk or the lulling of the embers that
brought him to this point. It was the things they
had said to each other or rather, the things she
had said. How easy it was to talk to him. This dark-
haired, dark-bearded man listened to her with his
heart and soul. His mind didn't spin off in a mil-

lion directions, translating her conversation into dollars and cents, promotion and production. He simply listened. And, with every quiet bit of sharing Sass did, Shay Collier's respect and interest grew until he, too, was ready to speak. It was he who opened the door by mentioning the book. Sass walked through it, not knowing what the hell she would find on the other side.

"I'm sorry, Sass," Shay said, twirling the tumbler he used as a wineglass between his long-fingered hands. He was sprawled in front of the hearth, one long leg bent, the other straight. He leaned against the couch and stared at the fire while he spoke. "I'm sorry I can't give you the rights to that book. Sure, you're a fine woman and I'm sure I would admire the work you'd be doin' with it . . ."

"But?" Sass urged gently.

"But you may have any other book you wish, not *The Woman At the End of the Lane*. That I cannot give you, lass. That you cannot ask for."

"But, Shay, I do ask it," Sass insisted, sensing that this was the moment to press her advantage. "And I will not stop asking until you throw me out of here. It's so important. I feel it in my bones that this project, that book, will somehow change my life. It might even change yours, Shay, if you let it. You won't admit you need a change, of course, but you do. You're not meant to be locked away like this. Not a marvelously talented man like you."

Sass laid her fingers on the back of his hand. She felt the softness of the dark curling hair at his wrist, the spareness of his hand, all muscle and flesh. She would have taken it in hers had she not felt him stiffen—perhaps in fear—at her touch. What hurt he must harbor if she could make him afraid. So she let her fingers lie as she continued to speak, low and insistent, hopefully convincing.

"Shay, I promise you, I won't do anything to undermine the spirit of that book. I will be as true to the words, and the spirit, as I can be. There will be no gratuitous commercialization. I promise you that with all my heart, and you know I can deliver on that promise. I'm not a producer out to make my fortune off your father's work. I have fortune. I have fame. I don't need to bastardize this property. In fact, there are people who think I'm crazy for wanting to make this movie. But I know I'm not. The story is too powerful, the people too real. Please, Shay. Please believe me. I can make it come to life on the screen."

The promise slid from her lips into the air and away from them. Shay was not moved by her plea. Perhaps he'd heard too many promises before and wouldn't bother with this one. He sat quite still, looking at her fingers resting on his hand. For a moment she thought he would take hers in his own, hold it so that they would be linked together while he spoke of his private reservations.

Instead he gently laid it aside. She no longer touched him, yet her hand was close enough should he need to feel her again. With his other hand he put aside his glass. The wine was almost gone. It wouldn't help him in this anyway. There was no strength in the bottle, didn't he know, only foolhardiness. It hadn't helped him in those many days past when putting it aside hadn't been so easy. Then he'd run a continent away to leave the damnable brew, and the pain, behind.

Now this woman insisted he speak of it all, everything that had happened and brought him to this place, this time. She would lance the boil that had tortured his heart, and he was terrified of so painful an operation. Strange that he would allow this; strange that he seemed to know it was needed. So as he set aside the wine, Shay Collier took courage in a moment of silence.

With a deep breath Shay let his chin fall to his chest. His eyes closed as if in prayer. In the firelight his hair shimmered blue-black, waving exquisitely away from his broad brow, curling over his head and down the nape of his neck. She wanted to take his head in her hands and draw him to her. But whatever it was that tore at his heart, seemed too deep a wound for her to heal. When he raised his face he looked, not at her, but at the charred logs, the desperate red glow of the dying fire. The story he had to tell her was unlike any she'd heard, and excruciating in the telling because it was, in reality, his own.

"My father," he said simply, "was a genius. I shared a bit of that with him, you know. From the time I was a wee lad, and should have been rushing about the village with the boys, I was waiting on Tyler McDonald, knowing that my talents and my life were tied up with his. I waited for him to notice me, not caring, mind you, how he did it. A kick, a slap, a hug. To an Irishman like him, with a soul tortured beyond my young knowing, they were all the same. My mum had long since ceased to care about that man. She wanted him only to write his stories and bring us some money to pay the taxes or buy a few new clothes. She cared for nothing other than that. But I cared. God, how I cared . . ."

Shay shook his head slightly, his lips trembled. But he was a courageous man, had been a courageous boy, and Sass knew he didn't need her help, only her ear.

"So Tyler McDonald was in and out of my young life, and the village tongues waggled. Oh, how they loved to talk about him. But there wasn't a bit of gossip I concerned myself with, for he was mine, my da, and I knew he was a brilliant man. Even as a boy, though, I knew he was tormented. When I became a man and tried to do him proud by emulating him, I realized it was I who tortured him, I who persecuted him. Mother Mary, it was me . . ."

"Shay, no. Don't go on . . ."

Sass's plea had the edge of horror to it as she realized what she was hearing. She watched his face lengthen and harden, becoming taut with misery. His eyes snapped her way briefly, quieting her. He was angry that she should try to stop him now that he was doing exactly what she wanted. If she hadn't the courage to face what she had stirred up, then Sass Brandt should never have sought him out.

"Don't be silly, woman. You want something I have. If I won't give it to you, don't you at least want an explanation? Now sit and listen, lass. I'm sure the story will thrill you, a woman of your creative bent. Perhaps you can use this story—a bastard of *The Woman At the End of the Lane*—but something for your beloved films, nonetheless. I'm giving you part of what you've come for, woman. Be grateful."

"Forgive me," Sass muttered, her hand slipping away from his, her body willing itself to nothingness so that he could feel safe with his words.

Shay stood up. In front of the hearth, his legs splayed, his thumbs looped at the waist of his jeans, he considered the fire a moment longer, then laid another log on. The spent wood crackled and moaned and threw its last embers up in protestation while the dry new log caught quickly; the flames lighting Shay's face eerily. He turned from the heat and the illumination and walked to a cold, uninviting corner of the room. From there, he continued.

"I began to write when I was only twenty. My first efforts met with great literary success. Sterling reviews, a great deal of acclaim. I was so young, and I was so proud. Lord in heaven, I was proud and it was pride that was my downfall."

Shay walked about, quieting finally when he leaned against the rough-hewn wall close to the small desk where Lisabet had discovered his identity. He fingered a pen, ran his hand along the curve of the wood as if it would help him think back to those times he found painful. With a sigh he went on, talking softly, speaking more for his benefit than Sass's.

"In my pride I thought, now, finally, Tyler McDonald will embrace me, his only son. I shared so much with him— not my looks for he wasn't a comely man— but my ability to use words, to write them down and create worlds of my own that matched his. How could I have made such a mistake? Those words did not match his, Sass, they rivaled them. The great Tyler McDonald had met his match and 'twas his son who threatened him, poor man. Poor, poor man who didn't understand that never did I want to do that. I wanted nothing that was his, for I adored him and worshiped him. It was gratitude I felt to be sharing his profession. It never occurred to me he wouldn't want that. I only wanted to understand what brought his fists up to beat me or his arms around to hold me. I thought if I wrote, I would find . . . something, come to an understanding."

Shay paced as his hands came up toward his face, his arms bent as though he would embrace himself to keep his soul from flying out of his body. Sass thought her heart would break listening to him admit his sadness. Instead, she sat silently, trying only to listen and not judge.

"I would never understand why such a great man would want to hurt my ma, or me, or anyone else. You see, Sass, I hadn't that much of him in me. Not the meanness. I couldn't feel the fury, only the love. I couldn't feel the fear of life, only the exhilaration of writing about it. We shared half our heart and soul. No more. Try as I might, I couldn't fathom the dark half of his."

Shay hesitated. He raised the fingers on his hand like a priest offering a blessing.

"No. No. 'Tisn't true, that. I understood it later. Much later. But I didn't appreciate how he could act upon his hatred, these frustrations, these worries of his. As though beating me would make everything go away, perhaps even make him happy."

Shay shook his head sadly. "What ailed Tyler McDonald could never be made better. It was the way of the world that troubled him, the nature of the beast of man. I was simply the personification of the inevitable."

Shay laughed a bit, and cocked his head toward her in a charming manner. But his eyes glittered darkly and Sass knew this was not to be a playful exchange. "Ah, and wouldn't that make a fine title for the definitive work on the aging of a man? 'Twould explore the beast's last throes of strength as it tries to dominate the life it's leaving, Sass. Personification of the Inevitable. Shouldn't I then be thought quite the literary genius with a work like that? Shouldn't all those sage men nod their heads, all those grand men who know best about such things, and say "he is his father's son"?

"But I wasn't my father's son. I was my father's tormentor. To Tyler McDonald I was the devil himself, shown up on his doorstep. Such a sad story, my darlin', that I'm going to tell you."

Shay let his head hang, there was a wryness in his voice shaded by borders of bitterness. Sass didn't move. The fire popped behind her, but Shay didn't notice. He was lost in his litany, a story now started that had to be finished.

"My father hated me because I had what he so desperately wanted. Not the talent, of course. He'd had that well before me, and more of it to boot. What I had was happiness, Miss Sass Brandt, and Tyler McDonald couldn't stand it. My contentment ate at his soul, it made his heart black until all his genius, all his creativity was called to bear and unleashed against me, the boy, the man, who loved him. Yes, I was a man. He could no longer pummel me, but he found another way to do the deed and it was far more dreadful than the fall of his fist."

"Shay . . ." Sass whispered, not wanting him to go on, sensing that what was to come was so painful Shay might not be able to live with it once she was gone. But he didn't hear her. She was no longer in the room that he roamed like a caged animal, touching things, picking them up, putting them down as he battled his anguish and fury.

"I was married, Sass, to a beautiful woman. Moira was eighteen when we took our vows and a more beautiful girl the world has never seen. Her hair was red gold." He paused and looked contemplatively at Sass. "Much like yours, but shorter with softer curl." His hands mimed the bob of the woman's hair, then rose in the air as if he could touch her. "Her face was that of an angel and a siren. Her body was full, the way an Irish lass's should be, and she carried herself properly as if she delighted in every breath she took. I loved that woman beyond anything in this world. I bedded her with delight, with love, with passion, and above all with tenderness. I thought of her and me and us as some men are unable to do. Because of her I could feel every ounce of life in me. It was a marriage of exquisite proportions, a life of such adoration that it seemed sad to play it out in our little village. We should have made the world watch us and learn how love was done."

A short harsh sound burst from his lips, but Shay fought it back before Sass could define it as a sob or cry of anguish.

"God, how I loved that woman. And how I rejoiced when my father danced at my wedding, and slapped my back, and kissed my bride even while his own, third marriage disintegrated. He was old now and had been cantankerous for some time. Yet, when I married, when I brought Moira to my family, my father, Tyler McDonald, came to life again. He began to work, which he hadn't done for years. In my arrogance I thought I had brought him this contentment. No doubt I had brought him something, but it wasn't pleasure or peace of mind. What I had given him was much more valuable. Something . . ."

Shay shook his head and waved his hand perfunctorily in front of him. He shot her a dark look, his black eyes hidden by the shadows the fire was throwing. He was agitated, but Sass wasn't afraid. She was enthralled.

"I'm getting away from the drift of the story. What good is a story if the plot doesn't unfold properly? So I'll do my editing now. I'll go back, Sass, to where I should have been.

"So. After my wedding he sat himself down and he began to work. I would go off to work in the mornings, still not making enough for a family from writing my tales, and I would come back to hear Moira laughing and my father laughing. I would come to my cottage and join in, delighted to see the old man working and enjoying life as he'd never seemed to fancy it before."

Suddenly Shay sat down on a wooden chair near a desk. The chair seemed small with him in it. He propped his head on an upturned hand and held a picture frame with the other. He spoke slower now, sadly, all trace of turmoil gone, given way to his melancholy.

"I was a boy, Sass, not the man I thought. I didn't recognize what was in his laughter. Triumph was there in that sound. It was the noise of a victor and it took the vanquished a very long while to understand that. And in Moira's laugh there was something misplaced, too. But I didn't hear it. I didn't see the things I should have seen in her face, feel the things I should have felt in her touch. I didn't know until he finished the book, what Tyler McDonald had been about." Shay's voice caught. Sass thought it might have been a muffled sob that made him stumble, but it was a wail of grief caught before it burst loose. Then he muttered, "That damnable book."

When he continued, his voice a bit louder but oddly monotonal as if he'd lost his stamina. Sass knew the story was coming to an end. She didn't want to hear anymore. This wasn't happy, this wasn't what she had expected. But she had no choice. She had to listen. Any movement on her part might shatter Shay's concentration. That would be worse than listening.

"I was home the day his copies of this new book came. *The Woman At the End of the Lane*, it was titled. A nice title, I thought. I was home working on a book of my own. My first three had been published. I was starting to make money from my writing, and one novel had been nominated for the Nobel prize. I was beside myself with joy. My father was working, I was gaining stature as an author, Moira, who had lost none of her blazing sensuousness, was my wife. And on this glorious day, a day when Ireland was awash in a mist that made the entire island sparkle, on this day when I could smell the heather wafting through the window by which I sat, I saw my father comin' down the lane. I saw him comin' and had the strangest feelin'. For that moment, I felt as if I was dead and buried and someone was dancin' on my grave."

Shay let the picture frame fall onto the desk. He buried his head in his hands and Sass had to strain to hear him.

"Tyler McDonald walked into my home, pretty as you please. He grinned at me. That ugly, old man's grin. His chest was all puffed out as if he were young and strong again. Cock of the walk. I smiled at him, welcomed him to my home as was my way these happy days. He was laughing, always laughing.

" 'Lad,' he said, 'I'm delighted to be seeing you on this fine day.'

"But he didn't come near to touch me, and the smile he gave me was curled and twisted." His hands lay now on the desk and his voice softened. " 'Twas a look not unlike the one he gave me as a child, just before his fist found my jaw. Yet I chose not to notice. I smiled at him. Good God, I grinned at him even as he called to my wife, 'Moira, my lovely, come show yourself.'

"And out she came. Yes, she came, and in my mind I can still see her. Beaming at my dad like she never smiled at me. But did I understand that? Did I?" Shay's head snapped up, falling back as though he could gulp the air that would help him continue. This time Sass knew the tears were falling. She remained mute, having no strong voice with which to answer him when he asked again: "Did I see that, Sass, the look she gave him? No, I saw her all lit up from the morning sun that cut through the mist and blazed into our little home. I saw her dress, green like the spring grass just poking through the ground. In Ireland there are so many greens, but her dress that day was the spring green I favored. She had worn a dress I favored. I wonder what she would have worn had I not been home that day?"

Now his back was straight, his head forward, his eyes unblinking.

"Those were the things I saw, and my heart was fairly full to burstin' with the love of all this: those people, the place, my home, my work. I felt my youth and my manhood. I didn't know it was exactly these things that made Tyler McDonald hate me as he hated no one else in this world. It was that moment my da decided to do what he did. He began just then, standing between me and Moira, as he spoke.

" 'I've come to bring you the first copy of me new book, lad. I want you to read it. 'Tis a short one. The story seemed to just flow from me, don't you know.'

"And I thanked him, my chest swelling with pride that I should be the first to have a copy. The cover was beautiful, the pages edged in gold. It was a fine book and he made me sit by my own fire, in my own house, and read it. Read it I did, in my innocence and in my vanity and what I read sickened me. The story was so simple. A young woman married to the man she loved yet giving herself to an older, more worldly man, and loving every minute of their carnal relationship. A suddenly shameless woman, a sad woman, a woman torn between the exotic thing she knew as wrong, and the safe thing that felt so right. Here was a woman I knew and a man I knew. I read to the end.

"When I looked at my father I saw him smile and realized he had dealt me the fatal blow.

"I looked at Moira, a smile faltering on her lips for she knew something was wrong.

"I heard my da say to her 'you're immortal now, my beauty' and then I knew it was the truth. My wife was *The Woman At the End of the Lane;* the man who bedded her my own father. My life was over. He hated me for the things I had, the things learned out of the goodness of my heart. And since his heart was so empty, the only way to fill it up, at least for a time, was to stuff it with everything I was, everything I had. He wanted to make me like him, Sass. He wanted my life; he took it by bedding the woman I loved and still he wasn't satisfied. He had to make his cruelty public. For all the world to see, he destroyed my wife, my Moira, the woman he called Eileen, in that damnable book."

Shay turned his head. He looked at Sass through the ever lightening darkness. She hoped he couldn't see the tears that coursed down her cheeks. She hoped he wouldn't feel her pity, only her empathy. Shay seemed as fragile as aged paper. How hard it was for him to finish his tale; how she wished he didn't have to.

"He died a year later. Moira was dead before that, by her own hand. She was only a village girl, so devastated by the shame she'd brought on herself, on me. She could no more fathom how she would hold her head up walkin' through the village than she could dream of goin' to the moon. Death was preferable to being ostracized in a village like ours. Our children would be laughed at, whispered about. And to leave the village was the death of her soul. My darlin' had no choice, I suppose. She cast her soul free and now it roams about the village, some say that she haunts it. They wouldn't bury her in the cemetery, you see. Holy Mother Church is adamant about takin' one's own life. I suppose they would put me in a right and proper plot, though. Hatred can be sanctioned for sure I've enough of it to test Holy Mother Church. But despair such as Moira's kept her from the words of Christ. The torture of her eternal soul will never be eased. Sure it will wander the earth forever, always longin' for the heavens."

Shay blazed, the tears in his eyes poised to burn their way down his cheeks.

"Sure as the angels above, I didn't take my own life. It was taken from me quickly and brutally on a sunny morning in Ireland. So many times I wish I'd not lived one day longer, how I wished I had died just at that moment. Now that I've been dead so long in the world, I wish it all the more. Sure don't I wish that, Sass . . . Sure I do."

With that Shay Collier ended his story and Sass Brandt her quest.

Quietly she pushed herself off the floor and went to him. Her hands held his face, her eyes saw the depth of his anguish, the endless tears waiting to be shed. Crouching, Sass gathered Shay Collier in her arms and held him until the light had come and gone again.

It was over.

Six

In many ways Sass's home was not what one would expect, in others it exactly matched Sass's status as a megastar. Built on sixty acres of prime land, its extremities were bounded by the ocean on the west. There was a private beach accessible only by rickety, yet serviceable, stairs that wound down a steep hill peppered with Southern California scrub. To the north and south Sass's property abutted her neighbors' equally impressive estates, a producer to the north, an insurance czar to the south. To the east was the Pacific Coast Highway, a busy thoroughfare that ran the length of the state in one form or another, but it hardly mattered to anyone in the house. The entrance to Sass's place was a long and winding road. The moment one turned off PCH, the traffic was forgotten and only Sass's tranquil world remained.

The house itself was an *Architectural Digest* editor's dream. A tribute to California design, it was also a structure of exquisite taste. The sprawling mansion was white, as white as pearl, with a step-stone design that brought to mind the hills of Monaco peppered with stuccoed *pied-à-terre*. The front of the house was starkly beautiful. Two lovely windows flanking a door of rough-hewn wood that curved to a conclusion ten feet above the caller. It was studded with nails the size of a fist. Sass had found the door in Morocco during a lull in shooting and it was her pride and joy, a piece of art that functioned. She thought it wonderful, she felt privileged to own it. Seeing that door made Sass feel content no matter what transpired during the day.

As simplistic and elegant as the facade, it was the back of the house that was truly marvelous, for it was hardly more than colossal sheets of glass rising two stories from the ground. Those on the ground floor looked out onto Sass's stunning garden, her diamond-shaped pool, the cabana and the guest quarters, a miniature of the main house. From the second floor one could watch the sky and the sea beyond, at night it was blackness and stars. To be ensconced on the second floor was a truly uplifting, close to spiritual, experience. It was the second floor that Sass most often chose when she wanted to be alone to read a script, consider a character, think about her life and the future. Even Curt was not often asked to join her in this sky room. She loved looking out onto the clouds and into the heavens. The only thing that marred the view, as far as Sass was concerned, was the wall.

Exquisite though it was with its inset imported tiles, Sass hated it because it reminded her that her life was not her own. She had objected when the house was being built: a wall was unnecessary since no one could access the property without going across the bordering estates and those were heavily fortified by their own walls. But Richard insisted and Sass acquiesced.

The estates on either side, Richard said, were too big to police properly no matter how many security guards she hired, and men roaming about her home were far more objectionable than any structure could be. Still, when the wall was built she wondered if perhaps she'd been wrong. At least she could get to know the security guards. People were manageable, interesting, and welcomed. The wall, that was another matter. It was simply there, tall and topped with, of all things, barbed wire. Her wall had been crowned with thorns. Certainly no one could get in, but equally as certain, Sass felt like a prisoner in her exquisite stockade.

So when she sat behind the huge windows, curled up on one of the pale blue sofas that had been custom made to sweep through the center of the room like a wave, Sass tried to ignore the wall. Hopefully, nature would soon cover it with flowers and vines so Sass could pretend she was in the Garden of Eden.

The house was beautiful by day, but nothing short of fantastic at night. That was when carefully placed landscape lights shone on the white walls, cast shadows over the beautiful gardens, created pools of liquid illumination in the pool and down the paths that wound through her land. Add to that, movement and the sound of entertainment, and Sass Brandt's place became a fairyland. That's what Sass's house was like tonight.

"Bring the endive with shrimp," Lisabet directed and three caterer's assistants jumped to grab the trays. "I wasn't happy with the ice sculpture. It was small," she said and the caterer murmured an equal number of excuses and apologies not knowing which would have more effect on this woman. This was his first job in Sass Brandt's house and he wanted to make a good impression. What he didn't want was this *person* to think he was a pushover. The way she walked around the kitchen you'd think she was Sass Brandt herself. "And I don't want to see any more of those . . ."

He was about to stand up for himself when the lady was hailed from the doorway and the caterer was off the hook.

"Lisabet?"

Curt stuck his head into the enormous kitchen, smiling at an exceptionally beautiful girl heading the opposite way with a tray of endive. He held the door wider. She eased past, her rear end conveniently brushing against Curt's crotch. He moved back a bit more, smiled a bit broader, then noticed Lisabet watching him, her expression a scowl of disapproval.

He slipped into the kitchen as the waitresses filed past, each casting a smile his way in hopes of being noticed. Actresses all, he imagined, waiting to be discovered. Too often their talents were tested in bedrooms rather than sound stages and he thought that a pity. It was only after the last young lady had left that Curt remembered what he wanted.

"Lisabet, I'm not sure the wine's going to hold up. We need at least another couple of cases of the Savignon Blanc and the red needs to be pumped up a bit, too. Can you call and have some more delivered right away?"

"No need. I had them bring extra. The cases are in the wine cellar."

"You're a wonder." Curt smiled, the compliment genuine, yet he was more amused when Lisabet's roll of the eye told him she didn't appreciate his facetiousness. He laughed, defending himself. "I mean it. This is an incredible party, and it was put together on a moment's notice. It couldn't have been done without you. All that calling around, inviting people, food, wine, music. I really think Sass is having a great time." Curt turned toward the door as if he could look through it, anxious, like a little boy wondering if his mom liked the birthday present he gave her. He gave up his impossible task and looked back to Lisabet. "Don't you think she's having a good time?"

Lisabet shrugged. She picked up a towel and dabbed at a pool of water near the sink on the wooden island.

"Come on. Don't be coy. I really want to know what you think, Lisabet. Sass just hasn't been the same since you guys got back from your little adventure."

Lisabet slid her eyes toward Sass's lover. Curt was looking particularly fine that evening. Sun and swimming in the Caribbean, the exertion of those stunts he refused a double for, had left him tan and fit. He was, indeed, a handsome man. That was Sass's one failing. She loved handsome men. Lisabet didn't believe for one instant there was anything deeper than that to this relationship.

Curt's laugh interrupted Lisabet's thoughts. Her eyes snapped his way. He was running his hand through his thick hair, his eyes downcast. He was actually kicking at the tiled floor, laughing, before he planted his tight rear end against the island.

"I still can't believe you two did that. Leave it to Sass to simply *do*. Didn't even tell Richard. Not a word to me. If I didn't know better, I'd say Sass was trying to cut the apron strings to us all."

"Not all of us, Curt," Lisabet reminded him. "She took me with her."

When he looked at her he was still smiling, but his grin had lost some of its charm.

"So she did. Lisabet the confidante, the one with the lists. I suppose that does take precedent over Curt the lover or Richard the adviser. Maybe I should start making lists, too, then she'll take me with her and leave you in the dust."

"I didn't mean anything by that, Curt," Lisabet said dryly. "I'm sorry if I offended you. I just meant that nothing has changed. Sass isn't trying to get rid of anyone. She simply felt going to Alaska was something she had to do. It's over now."

Lisabet lifted a tray of glasses and held them to the light. Finding them acceptable she set them aside and made busy work, preferring that to carrying on a conversation with Curt. He wasn't easily put off.

"Is it?" he said, his voice softening, concern overriding his passiveness toward Lisabet. He shook his head, thinking hard, getting in touch with his feelings. "I don't think so. She's been distant since she came back. Oh, she tries not to show it, but when her guard is down I can see it." Curt reached for an olive and popped it in his mouth. "Do you know she gets up in the middle of the night and sits on the second floor staring out the window? Did. you know that? Insomnia. She's never had insomnia before."

Lisabet nodded. Her radar was sensitive, and Lisabet knew when all was not as it should be in the Brandt household. Many a night she watched Sass sit and stare into the darkness only to fall asleep or wander back to the suite she shared with Curt. Often, Lisabet believed, she could feel something in Sass, a hole where she had once been filled with life or energy or something that was gone now.

It was then Lisabet wanted to glide through the darkness and sit by Sass, take her hands, or hold her in her arms like a mother, and ask her what had truly happened in that cabin with that Shay Collier. Lisabet knew·he had taken a part of Sass and kept it; he was the one who dug the hole in Sass's heart and left it open. Lisabet wasn't even sure Sass realized what had happened and Curt would never understand it, just as he didn't understand Sass's midnight meanderings. So Lisabet said, "Yes, I know."

"Well?" Curt pressed her. "Don't you think that's a bit odd? This sleeping thing?"

"She's just frustrated." Lisabet began stacking dishes but the caterer took them from her, his sidelong glance telling her she wasn't welcome in the kitchen. Why was it so hard to find a place where she was welcome? Reluctantly Lisabet moved aside and let him do his job, sure she could do it better herself. Still, service was what Sass's money was paying for. No, Curt's money. This time it was his dime and that, in and of itself, amazed Lisabet. He must be worried to spend this kind of money just to cheer her up.

"I don't know why she's frustrated. She's had disappointments before. Remember when they didn't cast her for *Wind Song*? She wanted that part so bad she could taste it. But when she didn't get it she didn't mope— no, not the right word. That's not what she's doing." Curt lifted his hands in front of him as Lisabet came alongside. "She didn't retreat or withdraw. She just went on with the next thing on the agenda."

"That's the problem. That ridiculous book was her agenda. It was the first one she'd ever had and she failed to make it a reality. I know it's hard to understand, Curt, but some people find it challenging to be in control of their own lives," Lisabet drawled.

Curt raised a lazy brow. He wasn't dumb, and he wouldn't let Lisabet get away with this.

"Most of us control our own lives. It's only people like you who seem to revel in waiting hand and foot on another human being to the sublimation of self."

"Very good, Curt. That was a two-dollar word."

Lisabet pushed on one of the double doors. It was time to roam the party, poking her nose unobtrusively as possible into everyone's business. Did they have enough to eat? Enough to drink? Were they talking about Sass— to her detriment or not— so that Lisabet could report in the morning? Of course she would make the information sound like gossip, like a snippet of information she found laughable. Sass should know these things. Sass should know who her true friends were.

Curt put his hand across the open doorway and stuck his foot in front of the door so it wouldn't swing back. He glared at Lisabet and whispered.

"You're a piece of work, Lisabet. Most times, I find you amusing and tolerable. You don't bother me in the least on a daily basis. But when you get this high-and-mighty attitude you burn my butt, lady. You think you're the only one who cares about Sass? You think you're the only one who knows what's best for her? Well, I've got news for you. You don't know as much as you think. I sleep with the woman, I talk to her in the dead of night. I know what's going on inside her head and when I don't, I worry."

"That's very noble of you, Curt. I'm sure Sass appreciates it. I've tried to convince you that I have the exact same concerns, but you don't seem to want to hear it. You asked me a question, I gave you an answer. You choose to ignore it and argue with me. I don't see why I should smile and try to convince you that my opinion has merit. It's a waste of time. You have all the answers, there's no need for me to be here. So, if you'll excuse me, I'll do my job. I'll make sure this party is a success. Not for you, but for Sass. The only thing we agree on is that we'd like to see her smile again."

Lisabet walked through Curt's barrier, pushing his arm aside as if it were distasteful, leaving him shaking his head as he looked after her. Lisabet was the most arrogant woman he'd ever met. He'd met women who were beautiful and supercilious, and that he could forgive. Those women actually had something to stick their nose in the air about. But Lisabet?

Still, Sass liked her and she was efficient, slipping easily into the glittering crowd of people who milled around Sass's house. For all intents and purposes, Lisabet had disappeared. Curt supposed there was some merit to being less than gorgeous. After all, without Lisabet who would do the work?

"I've told her ten times that this is the project for her," Richard crowed, beaming at Sass even as he addressed Mark Everette, CEO of Sony Studios. "But Sass is still in the throes of burnout. You know how intense *Crossfire* was. I think she just needs some time to herself. Then we'll be ready to talk about what you've got. Right, Sass?"

Sass blinked. She raised her head, suddenly aware she'd been staring at the studs on Mark Everette's shirt. This wasn't a black-tie affair but he'd come from another party. Sass loved a man in a tux, but there was something about a man in a flannel shirt that was casual, earthy. A man tucked away in the mountains of . . .

"I'm sorry, Richard, I'm afraid I didn't hear."

Mark laughed and Sass looked away from Richard who was watching her with a mixture of barely hidden frustration and concern.

"Sass, there's nothing wrong with you, and don't let this old goat convince you there is," Mark said. "If I could manage to kick back for a couple of months after each production, by God, I'd do it, too. Don't you worry. If you're seriously considering working with us on *The Island,* then give us the high sign. We'll hang on awhile and cast around you. Curt's already looking good for the second lead."

"Oh, Mark, that's wonderful." Sass perked up. This was good news indeed. "I hope he gets the part. Curt is a talented actor. Much more so than anyone has given him credit for. I was hoping to use him in . . ."

"I'm sure Curt will be great." Richard had had enough. He broke into the conversation so rudely Sass took a step back but his warning glance kept her silent. Richard didn't want to hear another word about Alaska, Ireland, or that book. "I don't think Mark wants to hear about what almost was, Sass. I really think we ought to forget business for a while. Let's hit the buffet. It looks marvelous."

Richard cupped his hand under Sass's elbow and Mark's, turning them toward the sumptuous table by the pool. They hadn't gone two steps when Mark was waylaid by an attorney whose name escaped Sass. She moved on with Richard, politely slipping by the people who reached out to her or tried to catch her eye but she was too angry to stop and talk.

"What was that all about, Richard?" Sass demanded, still smiling at him, her voice venomous.

"You don't have to tell your little story to everyone in the business, Sass. You're beginning to sound just a little odd, if you know what I mean. You haven't seen the way people look at you. Nobody has ever heard of that stupid book, and nobody cares that you went all the way to Alaska to buy the rights. Why don't you try to chat about something that will interest your guests instead of making yourself sound like a kid wishing for a pony when you live in a condo in the middle of New York. Nobody cares, Sass."

"Excuse me, Richard, but I don't believe that there are rules for cocktail conversation. I didn't ask for this party, but since all these people are here why not talk about something other than publicity or sets or costumes? Why can't I talk about a book that I think is stupendous?"

"Because you can't ever make it into a movie."

"And that makes it off limits? My God, Richard, have you become so narrow that you think there is no merit in any other kind of entertainment? I think it would do this crowd a hell of a lot of good to read something other than a twenty-page treatment."

Annoyed, Sass walked toward the edge of the patio, away from the flood of lights and out of range of ears that strained to hear what it was that made Sass Brandt angry. Richard scuttled after her, well aware eyes followed them. He tried to smile, reassuring everyone that this was nothing, just a delicate conversation between old friends and business associates. The smile disappeared the moment he caught up with her.

"Sass, what is wrong with you? I don't think you quite understand how horrible you've been acting. It just isn't like you. You slapped me in the face when you ran off to Alaska even though I told you I'd done everything I could to secure those rights. You scared poor Lisabet half to death when you ran off without her."

Sass threw her hair over her shoulder and rolled her eyes. "Please."

"No, you please," Richard retorted and was immediately sorry. He lowered his voice; he put his hand on her shoulder. "Look, you've never been rude. You've never disregarded other people's feelings. But with this thing, well, you've just become so brittle. You're acting like a spoiled brat, and you didn't even act like that when you were a kid. Come on, Sass, it's more than just not securing the rights to *The Woman At the End of the Lane*. There's more to it than that. Tell me. What happened up there?"

Sass slid her eyes his way, then looked out toward the sea. The sight didn't comfort her this night. She saw the wall and that always made her feel sad. Sass sighed.

"Richard, it's hard to explain. That book meant so much to me even before I went up there. But once I met Sha . . ."

"Hello, everybody!"

Everyone in the place turned toward the sound of the greeting and smiled. Kelly Karter was making an appearance. The party was made. Reporter though she was, pain in the ass though she could be, Kelly was fair and Kelly was honest-to-God nice and Kelly was welcome in Sass's home every minute of the day. Even Sass, standing in the shadows, smiled, though she couldn't see the entry where Kelly probably stood like a queen accepting the homage of her very slick, very gorgeous subjects. Only Kelly could feel at home, and very special, in a crowd of incredibly beautiful people.

As she watched, Sass saw the crowd begin to undulate, moving this way and that as Kelly worked them like a politician. But she was taking so long to find Sass. Usually Kelly was like a bullet, shooting through the preliminaries, getting on to the hostess as soon as possible. Sass wished she would hurry. Then Richard might be charmed out of his bad mood and Sass might find herself actually having fun.

"Kelly's really milking her late entrance," Richard muttered.

"Let her. She deserves it. She's probably one of the few people everybody genuinely likes to see."

"That's a charming thought," Richard said, laughing. "If I didn't know better I'd say you're becoming a cynic, Sass."

"I hope so. It would be a whole lot easier getting along. It'd certainly make your life a whole lot easier."

"True," Richard agreed, smiling at her. There was still a lot of the little girl about Sass. Sometimes when he looked at her, he saw the twelve-year-old girl that she used to be. Sometimes he missed her childhood, more than she. He had never had children and Sass was as close as he'd ever come to being a father. Recently he realized that might be a chore he wasn't up to any longer. It was tough watching your little girl grow up and try her wings when you didn't even know they'd sprouted.

"Sass," Kelly called. "Sass Brandt. Come see what I've got. This guy swears you want to see him, and I told him it was my butt if he was lying. Sass, come on out and take a look at this fella."

Kelly was laughing, hardly able to get the words out. She had the loudest voice in the world so Sass couldn't help respond. Sass walked through the shadows just as the crowd parted, drifting away toward the bar, the food or another, equally beautiful body across the room. And in the space that was left Kelly Karter stood in all her glory: her silicone breasts ready to pop out of her beaded top, her thin legs looking insufficient to hold up her heavy body, her tiny fat feet stuffed into a pair of elegant heels. She was painted and primped to perfection and her red, red lips were open. She was already calling, "Sass," when the lady herself stepped into the light and Kelly reached behind her. The last of the hangers-on parted and Kelly drew her friend close.

Sass stepped forward. She smiled. There was warmth and an excessive welcome in her expression. Richard took note because he saw something very telling. Sass Brandt didn't even know that Kelly Karter existed. It was Kelly's friend who was honored with Sass's undue hospitality.

"Shay," Sass breathed, and abandoned Richard in the shadows of the garden.

"I can't believe you're here."

Shay's hands were held lightly in hers, a gesture of a hostess welcoming a new guest. Yet Sass's eyes were bright, her smile luminous and Shay looked down into that face and felt alive again. He almost laughed with relief— he had been so afraid she might be changed. But he didn't even smile. It was hard for him with so many people around, so many eyes upon him, to feel himself.

"Neither can I, Sass. This is a far cry from Irish society and even farther from frozen Petersburg. I doubt the entire state of Alaska could find so

many beautiful people as you've managed to stuff
into this grand castle of yours."

Sass laughed. "Hardly a castle. My home. Big,
yes, but my home, nonetheless, and you are most
welcome in it."

Shay dipped his head and Sass wasn't at all
sure the invitation was welcome. Certainly he did
seem uncomfortable. But then who wouldn't be
walking into a place in jeans and boots when
everyone was decked out in their formal best.
Funny, but it was he who stood out, the rest of
them looking like cookie-cutter people. Sass hid
a smile. She was used to being looked at, he obviously wasn't.

"So, Sass, I didn't know you'd be havin' a fes-
tival. Should I be coming back, do you think?"
Shay looked about, and more than one woman
let him know that he was a most welcome addition to the guest list. "Sass, is it your birthday
or somethin'?"

"No, not at all," she replied gently, leaning
close and smelling the scent of pine and snow.
"It's a cheer-Sass-up party. I'm afraid I came
back to California not in the best of moods and
my . . ." Sass hesitated. Strangely she didn't
want to talk about Curt. Not just yet. "My friends
thought I needed something fun to get me out
of my blue funk. But you're not to worry about
a thing. In fact, I'd much rather have a long chat
with you than play hostess. Your choice: the garden, the beach, the library? Where shall we duck
out to?"

"The garden is best, Sass. A little air, such as it
is here, would be lovely. I'm afraid it's been a bit

too long since I've stood with so many people around. How do you breathe?"

"Very carefully, Shay Collier. Around here, I never do take a private one. Come on. Let's go to the garden."

They had managed to lift two glasses of wine and a plate of food from the buffet without anyone stopping them. Behind them they left a very nosy group. Certainly Shay's arrival was one of the more interesting things to have happened all day, perhaps all year, in Hollywood. He was a stunning curiosity. He didn't bow his head to them as if they were gods and goddesses, he wasn't looking for a part or a deal. He locked eyes with Sass, went to her and left with her. It was simple and it confused almost everyone at the party, much to Sass's delight.

"Your timing couldn't have been better."

Sass walked slowly beside Shay who seemed overly interested in the mechanics of one foot going in front of another. He sipped at his wine, seemed pleased with it; but didn't comment. Sass offered the plate. He chose a huge shrimp and ate in silence, crumpled the small napkin he held, then looked about.

" 'Tis a lovely sight, your garden. I'd forgotten how beautiful a place like this could be. I had one once, you know. A garden and a house. I thought there would be children in it one day. . . ." He strode ahead, visions of Moira and the babes they would never have pounding hard in his head until he wished he could take them out with his hands and toss them away. He stopped abruptly, turned quickly. "Why are there no babes in your garden, Sass?"

Stopping alongside a stone bench, Sass sat down, her long skirt billowing around her feet. Her sweater, so finely knit with threads of sky blue and silver, sparkled under the December moon.

"You have a marvelous way with cocktail chatter." She chuckled, inviting a response. But Shay wasn't one to banter, she remembered. Words were not used lightly with him so she looked at him boldly and answered him seriously. "Because babes need a father, Shay. I didn't have one, I think my children should."

"You'll be old soon, for wee ones."

"My God, Shay, I'm only twenty-eight."

"Mothers should be young. Young enough to chase after them. My mother was eighteen when she had me."

"Is she still alive?"

Shay shook his head. This time when he raised his glass he finished the wine in one long swallow. When he was done he considered the fine crystal, held it up to the stars as if it were a sacrifice and, for one moment, Sass's breath held. Crazily she thought he would throw it far, against the wall she disliked so much. Instead, he held it between his fingers, let it dangle by his side. Looking sideways at Sass, he shook his head.

"No. She's dead. Killed as well by my father. Not by his hand, of course. Only by the sorrow he heaped upon her."

Sass thought to point out that free will is a God-given right and his mother had to choose to leave his father, but refrained from doing so. Considering Moira's disgrace, perhaps Tyler McDonald did have a hand in sending Shay's mother to her grave. She shook her head, having no desire to think of the sadness in Shay's life when seeing him here was bringing her such surprising happiness. Her voice as bright as the stars above them, she changed the subject.

"So how did you find Kelly? She had a hard time letting go of you."

"I didn't find her. She rescued me from the storm troopers you have guarding that high gate of yours, Sass. I told them that I was acquainted with you, but they wouldn't let me come in. What kind of home do you have that friends can't come and go?"

"They aren't here all the time, Shay, and, much as I hate to be guarded, sometimes it's a necessity. But I'm afraid there are bells and whistles. No one can just come and go around here. You're back in the real world where there's more to worry about than freak snowstorms."

"Holy Mother, if this is the way the real world works, then I've never been in it, lass. Ireland or Alaska, the doors are always open."

"Los Angeles or New York, the doors are always locked," Sass responded and he smiled at her. Not a big smile, not a wide one, but certainly not one that hid the pain she had seen so horribly etched on his face as they sat in front of a dying fire. She smiled back, her heart suddenly at peace. She had thought it was the loss of his book that made her feel so sad; now Sass knew it was the loss of his presence. Shay Collier brought the magic of con-

She was close to him and, without thinking, she reached for his hands. He drew back so imperceptibly she wasn't even sure he'd moved. All Sass understood was the fear, the instantaneous pain, he felt at her closeness. Her hands fell to her side. She understood so much now. Shay Collier's manhood had been destroyed, his trust crushed. Those who supposedly loved him had betrayed him in ways that were almost unimaginable. Sass sighed, wandering away to give her attention to a butter-yellow hibiscus that blossomed in the California winter. It would give him time to compose himself if she looked away from his pain.

"I've never been abused the way you were, Shay. I've never experienced the treachery you had to deal with. But then again I've never . . ." She paused, knowing she was about to speak the truth, and it was one she had never faced until this moment. "I've never loved like you have, either. I'm not sure I'll ever feel the things you've felt. But make no mistake, I have emotions that run deep. I like to think I'm a sensitive person and an ethical one. I would never want to gain— financially, creatively, or personally— knowing that *The Woman At the End of the Lane* is based on your life and your hurt. That makes it different, Shay."

Knowing she had to say the next face-to-face, Sass turned, her skirt catching a breath of sea air and lifting above her ankles. Shay's eyes flickered toward the shine of her stockinged leg, the wine-glass still cradled between his two fingers swayed, but she saw none of this. Her beautiful face was turned toward him, her eyes on him and her red-gold hair, caught in careless ringlets by a cloisonne clip, fluttered about her head. That hair gleamed in the night, caressed by the hidden lighting nestled in the lush landscaping. Sass's body, long and languid, demanded his attention and he gave it freely. It would have been hers whether she asked for it or not. Hadn't he thought of nothing else but her since he left her at the hotel in Petersburg? He'd been so sure he'd never see her again.

Yet Shay had seen her. In his dreams, in the drift of the snow, in the clarity of the sky and the solitude of his home. She was everywhere and, at first, he was angry because she left so much of herself behind. Then he was angry at himself for being weak, unable to banish the memory of Sass's face and form the way he had banished Moira's. Then one morning, the anger turned to apathy and he was fooled again.

The moment Shay Collier thought he had finally washed himself clean of the recollection of Sass Brandt, he knew he had failed. Shay's passiveness was nothing more than a moment for his memory to rest before the next wave of sentiment came washing over his heart and soul. He found himself longing for her once more: a moment to hear her voice, to see her lying half naked in front of his fire, another to breathe in the scent of her freshly washed hair. He wanted to wake and find her standing beside him as he had that morning, standing in the light of the embers, dressed in his old robe, looking like a saint come down from heaven. And those moments drove him to this one.

Now Sass was looking at him, more beautiful than the first time he had laid eyes on her and he never wanted her to be out of his sight again.

Looking closer, though, Shay Collier saw that Sass
Brandt was not going to speak sweet words to him.
Her brow was furrowed, her hands were clasped in
front of her. She considered him intensely and the
seriousness of her thoughts was evident in the dark-
ening of her eyes.

"What is it you want Shay?" she asked quietly.

"Begging your pardon, lass?"

Sass moved a defiant step forward.

"What is it you want? Or maybe it's something
you need. Only one of those two things could have
brought you here. If it's money, then I can have
Lisabet write you a check, if it's . . ."

Suddenly Sass was no longer in control. Shay's
hand shot out, curling easily about her upper arm,
squeezing through her beautiful sweater as he
pulled her toward him until, her faced raised to
his in surprise and anticipation, Sass thought Shay
Collier might kill her— or kiss her. Yet he did
neither.

He was so close she could see the fine threads
of gray just at his temple, in the thick black beard
that covered his jaw, in his mustache that lay over
his inviting lips. She imagined it was square, that
jaw of his, but not harsh. No perfectly chiseled jaw
could host lips that came together, even in anger,
to evoke times past. Times of men who spoke in
words that became poetry, and kissed, not to con-
quer, but to bring pleasure and make memories
and capture a heart forever.

All these things, Sass thought, in brief fleeting
seconds that were so overwhelming she was
amazed she could think at all. She knew the force
of each of his fingers as they pressed into her arm.

She breathed in the smell of him, part the wilds of Alaska, more the lingering scent of heather and heath from his island home. Sass looked into his eyes, but saw the sweep of ebony lashes, the tiny scar just below his left eye, above his cheek, the wave of his hair over a brow lined by sorrow. Sass felt her body in a way she'd never experienced it before. Shay called her to account, his very stance insisting that she attend to him and his sudden anger. Astonished, she could only do as he wished, waiting for him to tell her what it was that had caused this sudden siege.

"You ask me what it is I want, woman? You assume 'tis something from you that I have to take? Money. Money, Sass! I cannot believe that, after the time we spent together, after the things I told you, that you can insult me with your talk of money. God in heaven, I've come to you for more than that. I've come to give *and* receive, and I thought that was why you had come to me in the first place. But I was wrong. All your talk . . ." He released her, disgusted. "Ah, don't look at me, Sass. I was wrong. I thought you wanted to do the same. Give and take. A business between us, woman. Nothing more, but a business of the heart and soul."

Sass thought she might sink to the ground without his hand to hold her up. It was as if a life-giving connection had been broken and, if she were anyone other than Sass Brandt, she might have swooned as Shay threw up his hands. He walked a pace, then turned again as if he couldn't remember which path it had been that brought him to this moonlit place with Sass Brandt.

"Lord in heaven," he bellowed, "show me the way out of this labyrinth, for I've made a mistake in coming here."

"Wait a minute! Don't get on your damn high horse." Sass was alive, spurred by his anger, charged by his confusion and most definitely intrigued by his indignation. "You don't have any reason to be angry. Look at this situation. What am I supposed to think? At least when I came to you I was up front. I told you what I wanted, what I was willing to give in return. You broke my heart that night when you told me about that book. You tore me in two and made me feel ashamed for having pushed the matter so far that you were forced to relive that pain. God, Shay, I felt awful. I felt exactly like what you believed I was— a money-grubbing, pushy broad from Hollywood.

"So here I am, roaming around feeling terrible that I'd made you feel even worse and you show up on my doorstep to tell me you've changed your mind. What am I supposed to think? That you changed your mind because you'd had a change of heart and you should just hand over the rights? You're not that good, Shay Collier. Nobody is that selfless unless they're ready for sainthood."

Breathing hard, Sass's chest heaved with the effort of confrontation. Her sweater had slipped off her shoulder, baring it to the cool air. Her hands were fisted at her side, clenched against the surprising rage Shay Collier had ignited. He was striding down one of the bricked paths and Sass was out after him.

"Don't you dare pull that high-and-mighty nonsense with me, Shay Collier. First you act like I'm the scum of the earth for wanting to make that movie, now you're shoving the rights in my face and you expect me to believe there isn't some big payoff for you somewhere. If it isn't money, then you tell me what the price tag is because I'm damned sure it's going to be a big one." Sass stopped, tired of chasing him. Hands on her hips she called after him. "Do it like a professional. Do it like a man. But don't you dare walk away from me because I suggested it might be that you needed something from me. Goddamn it, Shay, turn around and look at me."

Shay stopped cold, then turned on his heel and headed back to her. Tall though she was, he towered over her, his eyes blazing.

"I did want something from you. I thought you could give it to me, but you can't. You can't because you're a self-centered movie star who doesn't know the first thing about people. Sure didn't I think we understood each other the night you were with me. I thought you figured the whole damn thing out, and that when I came here you would fathom not only what I had to offer, but what I must have in return."

"What's to understand? You're going to sell me the rights. What you don't understand is that I don't want to do it anymore. I'm not going to make money or anything else off a story like that. That's what you don't get, Shay Collier. There's an ethic here, a morality that has to be acknowledged. Opportunity isn't based on personal pain. I thought you of all people would respect that. I was only offering money, or whatever else you need, because I assumed you wouldn't have made the offer if you weren't desperate."

"You're right about that, woman!" Shay hollered.

"Good!" Sass snapped back. "We agree on one thing."

"That we do!" he bellowed.

"Then what?" Sass threw up her hands, flabbergasted that their conversation had come to this dead end. The man was out of his mind, stubborn as a mule, wanting her to guess what motivated him. But Sass wouldn't play. It was a game she couldn't win. "What do you want?"

Shay's eyes blazed, his lips parted, his right hand rose, clenched as it hit his chest. There was a moment of silence. His fingers relaxed and his open hand now lay against his shirt.

"I want my heart back, Sass. I thought you could give it to me. I thought you understood that."

"Hah! You want . . ." Sass's voice screeched, ready to attack again when she realized she was shouting into the wind, saying things that had no bearing on reality. Pulling in a deep breath Sass counted to ten. She hung her head, relaxed her shoulders, pushed her sweater into place. She tipped her head and looked at him, ashamed and curious.

"You want your heart back? What kind of thing is that to say? That's the kind of dialogue you find in a script."

"Or a novel or a movie," he said softly. "But, Sass, this is my soul talkin' to you, and you must listen. 'Tis the reason I'm here, lass. The things you said that night in my cabin made me believe in you. You said you *saw* the book, understood the woman and knew the men. You said you could make sense of a story like that without tricks or any such thing. Sure you promised to make a beautiful film and I want you to do just that. Show me the visions you see so that I can look back and understand what happened to my wife, my father . . . my life. I want you to show me with your film so that I can live again. Don't you understand, woman? Lord above, say you understand."

Shay Collier's plea ended in a whisper, his hands raised to her as if begging. Sass reached out without thinking, and took both in hers and they drew together until they were so close only a sliver of darkness kept them apart. She closed her eyes, feeling the roughness of his skin, the tenderness of his touch. Sass shook her head, and raised her face to the cool night air. Even here, so far from the house, she could hear the odd pulse of party conversation, the sudden laughter erupting from one guest then another. She had forgotten them all and she'd forgotten how she and Shay had talked that night. How could she have been so stupid?

"Yes, I think so," she answered, not at all sure that she understood the enormity of what he was asking. She qualified herself knowing she could be nothing less than honest. "I don't know, Shay. I can try."

Sass shook her head and felt him move into her. They were so close now, a whisper away from each other. Shay's voice lowered, her eyes fluttered closed, then opened. They were liquid gold, moist from shame. How could she have thought him a man to sell out so easily after all they'd been through?

"You do understand, Sass. 'Tis only that this is more than you bargained for. Isn't that what scares you?"

"Yes. I don't want to think of it. I saw only a beautiful story, I envisioned only the scenes and the elements of the movie. I don't want the responsibility for your life or your heart or any of that nonsense."

"By the Virgin, 'tisn't nonsense. No voodoo here. I'm an uncomplicated man to whom worldly predicaments are a mystery. I used to write about such things, but I never believed they happened. Now I cannot write, I cannot see far enough to put one foot in front of the other to bring myself back to the world. Please, Sass, help me find the way back."

"That's all you want?"

"All?" He laughed gently and the spell was broken. He stepped back, still holding on to her, spreading their arms wide as if to dance. "My goodness, I'm askin' a lot, don't you think?" He chuckled again and shook his head, looking tired until he raised his eyes to her. Then she saw that there was determination, if not the flicker of life, in them. "No, that's not all. Do you think me crazy? Surely I expect payment."

"Ah-ha! Not quite so altruistic as all that." Sass laughed, too, and their voices joined together to make night music. His faded first, the notes sliding through the garden, hers joining it until they laughed no more. Sass was ready to hear Shay Collier's demands.

"I must write the script," he said.

Sass dropped her hands. "Impossible, Shay. It's never done. We have professionals who can . . ."

"Remember the words that were honestly spoken in the house at the end of the lane? The way we all looked? The tears? The horror in Moira's eyes? I think not. Only I'm left to remember. 'Tis my soul that needs purging. I write the script or the movie isn't made. This will be my release, my purification. I ask only that. Let me work on this because I've almost forgotten how to work. Let me create this because, when Moira died, I felt all creativity drain from me. Let me show my father for what he was, then rewrite the script without bitterness. I know I can do this. More than that, Sass, I must do this or my life will go on as you saw it on the mountain. You will go on never knowing what could have been. Please, Sass. Please."

Through the shadowed dark they considered each other, each opening their hearts, each understanding without another word being spoken that they were talking about more than a script and a movie here. More than just Shay's peace of mind. They were talking about . . .

"There you are!"

Curt hailed them from the bend in the path. Startled, Sass felt her heart pound. Not from fear, because she knew it was Curt who had come upon them, but because she felt oddly ashamed, as if he had stumbled upon something intimate, something so personal it couldn't even be shared with him. Throwing a pleading look toward Shay, Sass went to Curt, her skirt billowing behind her, her heels clicking on the brick. She held out her hands as if touching Curt could erase the memory and regret she felt at sharing so much of herself with Shay that she'd never shared with the man who lay beside her every night.

"Sweetheart, I'm sorry. Have I been gone that long?"

Curt's arm enfolded Sass, protectively, purposefully, as he continued to look at the tall, black-bearded man. They moved toward Shay as a couple, Curt holding Sass close.

"Only long enough for half the party to leave without saying goodbye to the guest of honor," Curt answered, a little laugh punctuating his reprimand. He felt stiff beneath the hands Sass placed on his waist. Before she could offer her apologies, his free hand was out, offered to Shay. "Curt Evans."

"Shay Collier."

Their hands met. They shook and stepped back, considering each other. Sass kept her eyes on Shay, fearful of looking closely at Curt. What if she found him not quite so handsome, not quite so loving as she remembered.

"I know. Lisabet told me you were here. Sass forget her mittens at your place?"

Shay tipped his head, his brow knit. "Sure I don't think she did. I came with nothing that belonged to her."

"Forget it. Joke." Curt waved him off, then grinned at Sass, giving her an extra squeeze. "So, you about ready to come back in? The place is beginning to thin out, you should probably be on hand to say your goodbyes. This was a party to cheer you up, after all, I'd love it if you could show people it worked."

"Better than I ever expected," Sass answered, unable to keep her eyes from darting back to Shay Collier. "I have wonderful news to share. Shay's kindly offered to sell me the rights to *The Woman At the End of the Lane*. I'm going to make my movie, Curt."

Curt's grin faltered. To his credit his lips remained up, frozen for an instant as he looked from Sass to Shay and back again. There was something in the way she dropped the news that bothered him, something that immediately cut through his gut. Then he realized what it was. Sass had said she was going to make *her* movie.

"Hey," he said with gusto, "haven't you forgotten something? I've been for this since day one. Aren't we going to make our movie, Sass?"

"Of course *we* are," she answered, pulling away from him, her hand still holding his. There was a little tsk in her tone, a reproach for being so juvenile. "All of us are going to make this movie. Shay has agreed to write the script."

"Is that so?"

" 'Tis so, sir. I'm looking forward to working with the both of you."

"It should be interesting." Curt turned Sass back toward the house. "Time to get back, honey. I'm sure Mr. Collier won't mind if we leave him on his own a bit."

"Don't be silly. Shay, come back to the house and have something to drink," Sass said over her shoulder, dancing along beside Curt as he headed back, her hand in his. "We'll seal our bargain with a toast."

Shay raised his hand, waving her on and watching her disappear down the path. Certainly he'd go back to the house. Just not yet. Now he wanted to see her walk away from him. He wanted to think about Sass Brandt and try to figure out what it was he found so compelling about her. To sell her his story was to sell her his soul. Yet somehow he felt it was in the right hands.

Sitting down on the little stone bench he picked up the glass of wine she had left there and put it to his lips. On the rim he tasted her lipstick, before the exquisite wine. He drank until there was only one sip left. It was then Shay Collier raised the glass and toasted the woman who lived, not at the end of the lane, but in the house as big as a castle.

"Our bargain's been sealed, Sass. There's no turning back now."

"Interesting guy," Curt noted as they skipped up the steps to the patio and walked toward the living room.

"How would you know?" Sass teased, perturbed and trying not to show it. "All you did was stand there giving him the macho once-over. You didn't even try to be civil. If I didn't know better I'd say you were jealous, Curt Evans."

"Don't be ridiculous." Curt gave her hand a final squeeze and kept his eyes studiously fixed on the party-goers inside the house. "If I thought your taste ran to mountain men, I'd be out of here in a flash. I'd never be able to live up."

"Curt, I don't believe something that simple could make you cut and run. You'd never be able to leave all this . . ."

Sass never finished her joshing, her words cut short as Curt whirled her into his arms. His lips were on hers, hot, insistent and familiar before she could utter another sound. Instinctively Sass's arms went around his neck, her long fingers burying themselves in his thick hair as her body bowed into his. They stood in a pool of light, illuminated for all to see. Sass Brandt and Curt Evans: a couple, a commitment. No one who saw this display of affection could doubt that these two people belonged together. Theirs was the perfect union. Two beautiful people, astounding careers behind and ahead of them, money, life to live. Neither could ask for more. Yet when they parted, Curt still nestling Sass in the crook of his arms, there was at least one person who watched and wondered if perhaps Sass's eyes didn't sparkle a little less brightly and Curt's hold wasn't a tad too possessively tight.

"They make a fine couple."

Lisabet jumped and moved away. The voice that whispered over her shoulder was neither familiar nor pleasing. Covering her discomfort Lisabet moved away from the window and faced a guest she didn't know, her guard immediately up.

The woman was interesting, not Sass's type of friend at all, and certainly not a starlet looking for a break. Perhaps she was a friend of Curt's. He seemed to prefer a more exotic group of acquaintances. Yet there was an intelligence in this woman's eyes, a hardness that made Lisabet almost certain this was no friend of Curt's. A woman like this would eat him for breakfast.

Though not tall, she gave the impression of strength. Her hair was short and blacker than even Shay Collier's, her heritage Asian, carried by some beauty who passed along exquisitely almond shaped eyes and golden skin. Yet part of that coupling that produced her was obviously not of the Eastern persuasion and the mixture made her a citizen of the world by looks alone.

She was dressed in jade green from head to toe, her skirt terribly short, her legs fabulously attractive. She wore only one piece of jewelry, a diamond and jade pin the size of a golf ball. Exquisite and more expensive than Lisabet could imagine. Lisabet disliked everything about her. So much, in fact, that she had no desire to find the answers to any of her questions.

"They've been together a long while," Lisabet answered perfunctorily.

"Charming."

With that, and a sly last look at Sass and Curt, the woman was gone, floating away on those lovely legs of hers, touching a man here, sliding her eyes toward a woman there, missing nothing, somehow made more powerful and intriguing by the sparseness of her gestures. Oddly Lisabet thought she saw people move away from this woman, almost bow out of her presence as though they were afraid of offending her, but hoped not to be noticed by her, either.

"Interesting, isn't she?"

Richard moved easily into the recently abandoned space by Lisabet's shoulder. This time Lisabet wasn't startled. She knew Richard. She understood Richard. Richard could, if need be, be a friend.

"Who is she? A friend of Curt's?"

"No. I don't think that lady has any friends."

"Then what's she doing here?"

"I don't know; but I'd hate to be the poor slob who got roped into bringing her. That woman is bad news, and if somebody's thinking to score off her they have another think coming."

"She can't be that bad. What does she do? Own half of Hollywood?"

"That, Lisabet, is closer to the mark than you think. That is the money woman, Sloane Marshall. You want financing for a movie and can't get it anywhere else, you go see Sloane. You've got gambling debts, you see Sloane. You need to pay off one too many ex-wives. See Sloane."

"Really? A banker."

"A ballbuster."

"Funny, I've never heard of her."

"Thank your lucky stars if this is the only time you ever do. Sloane's contacts aren't the healthiest. Lot of money, no finesse, and the strangest ways to collect on debts. Yes, indeed, we should all thank our lucky stars that Sass is Sass. If she wasn't we all might belong to someone like Sloane. Hook, line, and sinker."

With those final words Richard went off. It was getting late and he didn't have much energy left. Sass and Curt floated into the living room and began to make all the right noises. The party was over. Lisabet knew she should begin seeing to the cleanup and the servants. Instead, she waited, hoping to catch a glimpse of Shay Collier. She could feel him out there in the dark, waiting for something. Waiting for Sass.

Lisabet let her eyes roam over the dwindling crowd. Sass and Curt, their arms wrapped around each other's waists were saying goodbye, smiling as if this were any other party, on any other night. Stupid people, Lisabet thought. Even Sass didn't know what had happened tonight. Even she wasn't aware that Shay Collier would change everything.

Sooner or later, some part of Sass Brandt's world was going to be turned upside down.

Eight

Curt Evans was a very, very lucky guy. From birth—the last of six children—his fortune had been predestined. Parents who were older, more affluent, shocked and proud of their late-in-life fruitfulness, showered their surprise child with the best they could give. Good middle-class things. Material things that weren't outrageous in scope, but certainly were the envy of many children with whom Curt played.

High school came and the glow grew brighter. Mom and Dad aged in the stands while their darling dribbled in the gym, was mobbed by blond and willing cheerleaders who found his good looks irresistible and his Camaro the right place to express their window-fogging appreciation of his charms.

College was next. Curt went all the way to California and UCLA, leaving Missouri behind. Mom and Dad waved him a happy goodbye. Though they loved Curt to death, they were heading down that last road and, in their late sixties, were tired of the girls and the phone calls and Curt's unbounding, always engaging, sometimes thoughtless, energy.

But life wasn't quite the same for Curt at UCLA. People, a thousand different kinds, called it their home away from home. Everybody had their own agenda and few were willing to give Curt the devotion he had come to expect. These people actually wanted an education, they really wanted to learn something. Luckily, Curt was a resourceful young man. He sniffed out a pocket of youthful, beautiful people who thought like him and lived like him, all of them doing just enough to get the grades to remain in that little slice of collegiate heaven. Happily ensconced in that protective little bubble, Curt's life was looking good again.

In his junior year Curt finally began to wonder about the rest of his life. A few of his friends had dropped out of school. One or two married, making responsible adult noises. They sent shivers down Curt's spine when they advised that he start doing the same. Not that he didn't see himself in a position of responsibility someday. He did and it would be grand. Just now, though, the picture was a little fuzzy, the end result a tad hard to visualize.

Then it happened. One particularly beautiful Saturday in the spring of his junior year, Curt waved his friends away, sending them off to the Venice Beach bike paths to strut their stuff while he stayed on campus to consider his future. He was sitting under a tree, on one of the more secluded hills, outside one of the more stately buildings on campus, as he thought about his future and his singular lack of ambition. He was wondering how he could possibly build a career on his good looks, when along came a crew of people toting a camera.

This wasn't just any camera. This was *the* camera and the lens showed Curt his future. That camera pointed his way, ready to shoot a man-on-the-street commercial for a sneaker company. Lo and behold, those sneakers happened to be on his very feet. By the time they found Curt, the crew was tired. Not many people wore those particular sneakers and they'd been searching for a final subject since early that morning. Wrapping up with such a devastatingly handsome and personable subject made them ecstatic. They invited him along to a celebratory lunch. There he filled out paperwork and was told he would be sent a check each time his commercial appeared on TV. Easy bucks. The film crew picked up the lunch tab and the lady account executive picked up Curt. He was in seventh heaven.

To this very day he chuckled every time he thought about that encounter. How he raved when he received his first check. But when he saw himself on the tube— well, UCLA was minus one out-of-town tuition.

Things picked up immediately. A commercial here, a small movie part there. By the time he was twenty-one Curt Evans was considered a star. Surprisingly, Curt wasn't a bad actor. More surprisingly, Curt found something he was willing to work for. He was damned proud of his labor and getting better at it with every movie, every appearance, every opportunity to test his acting ability.

Now, though, Curt was beginning to think he'd met his Waterloo. There was no way he could act his way through the anger and frustration and, yes, jealousy he felt every time he saw Shay Collier's dark head put together with Sass Brandt's red-gold one.

"Can you believe that?"

"What, Mr. Evans?" The question was punctuated with an extremely painful, but satisfying, assault on his biceps.

"Jesus, Marcia, who are you ticked at this morning? Are you trying to kill me?" Curt muttered. He sounded like Cary Grant with his chin scrunched into the massage table that way. It was a damned uncomfortable way to talk while the masseuse worked. Marcia wasn't the most fair of face, but that failing could be forgiven considering the rest of her.

Tiny white shorts covered a tight rear end, a cropped white T-shirt skimmed the fullest, plumpest breasts and only the most pristine tennies and slouch socks adorned her small feet. Her legs were long and she was gorgeously tanned, her flesh incredibly silky. She'd either be dead from skin cancer by the time she was thirty or wrinkled like a prune. For now, though, it was an absolute delight to be mistreated by her and satisfying to vent to someone who was so innately in tune with human nature. That and her incredible discretion made her inordinately attractive.

"Sorry, Curt, but you're tighter than a spring. If you don't get it worked out it's going to start showing on your face and if it . . ."

"Shows on your face, it's going to show on the camera, then I'll ruin a day's shooting," Curt finished for her.

"Well, it's true," Marcia pouted, hating to be made fun of.

"I know. I know. I just despise it when you're right. But look. Look out there." Curt lifted a hand just enough to make an impatient gesture toward the window. Marcia did as she was told and threw her rhythm off by a millisecond. Knowing he had her attention, Curt followed suit, his eyes narrowed, his anger growing by the minute.

"Yep." Marcia's head was down again, once more fully intent on working Curt's shoulder muscles to a pulp.

"Yep? That's all you have to say?" he complained.

She glanced out the window again just to be sure she'd figured it all out.

"He's a good-looking guy, Curt. What do you want me to say?"

"I want you to say that you think this is just a little weird. Sass moved him into the guest house, for God's sake," Curt sputtered.

"She told me it's because they're working on some major project." A punch, a knead, and that shoulder was done. She was onto the next.

"Bull." Curt reared up. Marcia flattened him with an expert hand on the crown of his head. "Bullshit," he muttered, chin back on the table, "they're working on a literary thing. An art house movie. Hell, it should have subtitles it's going to be so obscure. Not that it doesn't have some merit, but I'm talking about the execution. This guy is a novelist. He's not a scriptwriter."

Curt backtracked quickly. He was, after all, playing the male lead. It would be a nice change from all the shoot-'em-ups he'd been doing lately. If this thing actually did work he'd prove his range much broader and deeper than the business gave him credit for. Much as he trusted Marcia, you never did really know who you were talking to so he grumbled some more, but gave it a different spin. "I mean, it's a good story, a solid story. What I'm saying is that Sass is spending too much time on it. She should be out doing some publicity on *Crossfire*. Hell, if that guy can't write the stupid script on his own, why is he on Sass's payroll? It's a waste of money, if you ask me. Either let Collier get on with it or let Sass write it, but does it really take two?"

"Only to tango." Marcia slapped his shoulders, then his butt. "Roll over, Curt."

"That's not funny, Marcia." Reluctantly Curt did as he was told as the blonde above him rearranged the small towel so it covered his most private and, as she had seen, interesting part.

"If I didn't know, I'd say you thought there was more going on there than just writing a script," Marcia commented, using her magic fingers just below his collarbone.

"Don't be ridiculous. I just don't like her inviting a stranger to live with us. We don't know that much about the guy. Sure, he was a literary genius. Nobel-prize material. But he didn't follow up, did he? He just ran off and hid in Alaska when things got rough. Jesus, Alaska! Now tell me that just isn't the kind of thing somebody who has a loose screw or two would do!"

Curt maneuvered on the massage table, unable to get comfortable. He sighed. He closed his eyes, not liking the image he saw dancing behind his lids. They looked like fucking good and evil out there, Collier's dark head and Sass with her long gold hair.

"I don't know, I think it's kind of romantic. I want to run away sometimes, but I'm too chicken. I think it's sort of neat."

"You would."

"Hey, what do you want?" Marcia worked without cracking a smile. She wasn't there to enjoy herself after all, but opinions were part of the package. "I just don't see anything wrong with Sass working on something that really interests her. I've never heard her talk this way about anything before. She talks about everything, not just the schedule. It's the characters this and the costuming that. I think the movie sounds great. I can't wait to see it."

"It's a woman's thing. It'll never fly big. It'll do good with the three-hanky crowd, but it just isn't worth the kind of effort Sass is putting into him . . ."

Marcia stopped kneading. Curt stopped speaking. Silence hung heavy and full in the room waiting for one of them to say something that would ease over Curt's slip. Ticked, Curt whipped off his towel and hopped off the table.

"I've had it for today, Marcia. Thanks. I've got stuff to do. Want me to send Sass up after I'm dressed?"

"Sure. If she's free."

Marcia was out the door without a second glance at Curt's body. It wasn't hers to enjoy so no sense losing a whole lot of sleep over lusting after it. Marcia was a very sensible girl that way.

The minute the door closed Curt went to the window and laid an arm along the sill. Leaning on it, he watched Shay Collier moving away, leaving Sass sitting on the long, low wall that stretched down the walking path. Though her eyes were hidden behind huge sunglasses, Curt knew she saw nothing but the man pacing back and forth in front of her. Shay Collier's hands rose, came together, gestured toward the ocean and reached to the sky. Curt snorted in disgust. He could just hear that voice, with that accent, talking all that literary junk. Yeah, Collier had Sass eating out of the palm of his hand. Curt was getting damn tired of the only conversation being about Shay Collier, the only reading material in the house his latest script draft, Sass's unwillingness to party because she wanted to be around in case he— *he*— wanted to bounce around an idea. Most definitely, Curt was sick of this. Something had to change. He wanted Sass back, damn it. He missed her and he loved her and things were going majorly awry. Collier was making his life hard.

That was something Curt Evans just couldn't abide.

"It's beautiful. Yes, it's perfect."

Sass swung her legs and clapped her hand, excited by what she'd heard. Pushing her glasses up her nose she grinned and, surprisingly, Shay grinned back. It was the first time she'd seen him completely free of his sadness. How she would have liked to think that it was a result of their friendship, her belief in his talent. If she was help-ing to heal him, then she had actually done some-thing worthwhile and real, something necessary.

Fortunately, Sass was not so vain. It was the work that had done this to Shay, and she was only the doctor who had prescribed the medicine. No mat-ter that the subject was hurtful to him, Shay had done what only the most exquisite artist could do. He had stepped away from his personal reality and drew on the depths of his soul, the corners of his psyche, to take this bitter pill. Now he held out his work proudly, reciting the speech that Liam, his character in the book, spoke to Moira's coun-terpart, Eileen. His voice was low and smooth as he described the characters lying in bed, not touch-ing but reaching out to each other with their eyes, their whispered words. In her mind Sass saw ex-actly how she'd play the part, exactly how Curt would react. It would be marvelous and she was happy to tell him so.

"You really think so, Sass?" Shay's eyes were wide with excitement, not really expecting a re-sponse. "Sure, I thought maybe I drew Liam's dia-logue out a wee bit. I was up last night until all hours working on that so it was just right. I may change a little more, shave it a wee bit, you see? Right here."

In three strides he was by her side, standing next to the wall, leaning toward her as he read the script over her shoulder. Sass grinned. How mar-velous it was to see a man like this at work. How wonderful to feel the energy leap off him, spilling over her until she thought she couldn't wait an-other moment for the shoot to begin.

"No," Sass said and shook her head. "I don't think you should touch it. Look, that speech is only two minutes out of ninety. I'm afraid if you cut, it will seem too abrupt. I want the audience to feel the love these two have for each other and sex isn't the way to go. You've given me exactly what I want. There's respect here, there's a sensuousness that I don't think you could improve on with words. You might destroy it— or at the very least take away some of the tremendous impact— by making it a more physical scene. Don't you think?" Sass held the script, looking at it still, reading between the lines to see if she had missed something. Realizing that Shay hadn't answered her, Sass abandoned her reading and looked up. "Don't you think, Shay?"

It was a moment before he spoke and when he did, the words were gentle, almost a whisper. "Yes. I do."

Sass froze, unable to respond to such a simple statement that could mean so many things. This man of words was so confusing. At the oddest moments, he almost forgot to speak. When finally words did pass his lips they could be strangely promising.

Their eyes locked, Sass shivered. The breeze had kicked up and the smell of the sea wafted toward them, surrounding them like a blanket tying them together. Shay's eyes closed, his dark lashes kissing his cheeks as he raised his face to catch the coolness. He sighed, deep within, breaking their visual connection. But Sass's heart held tight to the moment.

" 'Tis been a long time since I've smelled the

ocean, Sass. Too long." He looked at her once again, eyes open, face forward so they spoke as equals. "I miss my home. I miss my island."

"Is it helping, Shay? Working this through the way you are?" Now it was Sass's turn to look out to sea. She didn't want to look too deeply into those eyes of his again.

"I think it is." He considered the question once more, then spoke more definitively. " 'Tis helping, and I have you to thank for that. Certainly there's no miraculous healing for me, is there? Only a better treatment than I'd managed on my own. Don't you know, the scar will always be there."

Shay reached for her and, for a moment, Sass thought he was going to pull her up into his arms. Instead, he touched her curls and plucked a petal of the palest yellow from them. He held it up for her to see, then released it on the wind, watching the little velvety bit of flower tumble away. He considered it as one would a child skipping on ahead: with a wistfulness, a gentleness, a smile on his lips as if he wished it would come back to him again.

Moved, Sass touched his face, feeling the silkiness of his close-cropped beard, wondering how she could have resisted it for so many months. It wasn't for her pleasure she made this gesture, but to assure him of her concern and friendship. These were the things she had to give Shay Collier and nothing more. Yet touching him felt right, and that they could not have. So she answered him quietly, bringing him back so gently to life that it made her heart fill to bursting.

"You're right. The scar will always be there, but

it's no longer a red and angry welt, Shay. Yours will be a thin pale line once this is finished. When it's done, you'll understand Moira better. I can see that already. Your written words evoke sympathy for her confusion instead of hatred for her betrayal. I promise I'll make it even better than you have. I swear to you, Shay Collier, that scar will be forgotten before long. When we're shooting, when we're in Ireland . . ."

Shay's hand shot up, grasping her wrist. His face clouded, his eyes darkened just as she had seen it do that morning she appeared uninvited on his doorstep. His lips were open to speak, his fingers tightening so Sass thought she might have to cry out to make him stop. But there was no time. They were not alone.

"Sass! Collier!"

Shay stepped away, loosening his grip and finally releasing her when he heard Curt's voice.

"What?" Sass whispered, confused and concerned by this strange mood. "What is it?" But he couldn't answer, if indeed he had one. He only brought one hand to his face and laid it across his eyes for a second.

"There you are." Curt was upon them.

Shay dropped his hand and turned toward the other man. He stepped farther away from Sass in the process, leaving her question unanswered. His face still carried the sign of his discontent. But what was it? Anger? Frustration? Pain? Knowing this was not something she could question in front of Curt, Sass hopped down from the wall upon which she sat and smiled. She moved into his arms with grace and confidence. A beautiful performance. Allowing Shay his privacy, Sass knew she wouldn't soon forget this moment because it was the first time she had hurt him.

"We've been working on the script. It's coming along so nicely, Curt. I know you'll adore your part," Sass said brightly, knowing Curt heard the forced sparkle in her voice.

"I already do," he said, sweeping an arm around her and kissing her grandly. When he let her go he called, "Collier, are you happy with the script?"

"That I am." Shay shook back his dark hair, that puzzling vague expression on his face once again. "I don't see that there will be any problem finishing in the next month. But, sure, it won't be finished at all if I don't spend more time at the computer than here in the garden."

"I was about to suggest the same thing myself."

"Curt," Sass objected, knowing full well he meant to be rude.

"No, Sass, he's certainly right." Shay chuckled a bit and gathered up his things. "I'm off. I'll call the house when I have something more. For now, I'll wish you good day."

And he was gone, Sass moving only when she was sure Shay was well out of hearing distance. She shook off Curt's arms, unable to hide her irritation.

"Curt, that wasn't very nice."

"What? The man isn't a guest in our home, Sass. He's on the payroll, and I think you should get what you're paying for."

"How dare you!" Sass snapped. She couldn't even look at him so she tugged at the huge sweater she wore, adjusting it over her shoulders, talking all the while. "How dare you suggest that I am unable to determine my own affairs! May I remind you that it's *my* money paying Shay Collier's salary and *my* eyes that will read every word he types and *my* voice that will speak them. I don't need you to tell me what to do when it comes to making a movie. In fact, I think I'm doing a damned fine job! For some reason everyone wants to poke their noses in and tell me that I'm not doing things right. I've heard it from Richard about how much money I'm spending, I've heard from Lisabet about how much time I'm spending, and now I'm hearing from you. Well, I've heard enough. Now, is there something more pleasant you'd like to talk to me about or shall we just go our separate ways until you can come up with a topic other than Shay Collier, the movie, or my bank account?"

Finishing with a flourish, she lifted her chin and glared at him. Curt, to his credit, took it like a man. There weren't many who could look into Sass's eyes when she was angry and hold their gaze.

"Jesus, Sass, give me a break. I didn't mean anything by it. I'm just kind of tired of you spending every waking minute with him." Curt jerked his thumb in the general direction of the guest house.

"That is your imagination. If I spent every waking minute with Shay, then I wouldn't have signed the last secondary actor to contract today. I wouldn't have the costuming well in hand. I wouldn't have signed off on the last of the locations. I have managed to contract for a director and a crew. I've made every decision I should make and been every place an executive producer should be. I'm not sitting around waiting to learn my lines, Curt. This is different from anything I've ever done, and I resent you trying to reduce something this important to a silly flirtation."

She was on a roll now, all the frustration and the exhaustion of the last months coming to a head on this gorgeous day.

"This is business, nothing more, nothing less. If I choose to have Shay Collier housed on my property until this script is complete and shooting begins, so be it. You can complain when I start spending the night in the guest house. But until then, don't pull this nonsense, Curt. Now, if you'll excuse me, some of us have work to do."

She stormed past him, incredulous that Curt who understood her need for this project, could be so petty; incensed that Curt, who knew he was loved, should regress to such paranoia. But Sass got no farther than Curt allowed. He twirled and jogged a step or two, then moved in front of her and backstepped to Sass's rhythm, smiling his apology.

"Sass, I'm sorry. Come on, honey. I miss you. You've been so immersed in this thing I hardly get to see you anymore. How can you blame me for acting like an idiot?"

"Don't give me that." Sass's cheeks flushed scarlet as she bulldozed ahead. "You've been just as busy as I have. Off to Arizona to finish up that reshoot on the *Jackson* film, but I don't go chasing after you and telling you you're spending too much time with the bevy of beauties they have on that set."

"But, Sass . . ." Curt protested.

Sass wasn't listening. She dodged him and headed round but he caught her, laughing now because she looked so delicious when she was angry.

"Sass . . . come on."

She stopped long enough to shake off his tentative grasp. He touched her gently and that slowed her down so at least they could walk together. Sass crossed her arms and pouted; Curt dipped his head and grinned up at her.

"Thanks. I appreciate the second chance. The point is that I'm on a set and this is our home. You don't even make a decision anymore without consulting him. I just feel him always there, hovering about, waiting to ask how high when you say jump."

"Curt, be sensible. He's not hovering about . . ." Sass scoffed.

"He is," Curt insisted. "I can feel his mind working. Every time he has another thought about that script he's on our doorstep. Every time I turn around to look for you, you're in conference with him. Every time I pick up the private line, you're talking to him."

"So what!" Sass wailed. "It's not like we've ever had the place to ourselves. There are servants. Winifred and Lisabet. What about Lisabet? I see her all the time and she lives in the house with us."

Curt stopped and kicked at the walk. "That's different."

Sass stopped, too, turning around to face him, dispirited and wishing he wouldn't waste so much time pouting and angling for time she didn't have to give. "How different? How could it be different?"

"Lisabet's . . . well, Lisabet's Lisabet."

"And that makes it okay with you?" Sass's bad mood was back. She had been ready to give Curt the benefit of the doubt if he had a reasonable objection to Shay's presence, but this was ridiculous. "Let's put it another way. Lisabet is quiet, she's a woman, she keeps out of your way and she doesn't demand my time. Right?" Sass offered a wry grin. Curt hung his head and she bent to catch his eye. "Right?"

Curt came to attention, smiling that devastating smile that thrilled women every time his face hit the silver screen. Sass wasn't immune; her heart melted when he turned it her way.

"Right. I'm a macho jerk. I'm making up stories just to flex my muscles. If I had a club I'd knock you over the head and drag you into the bedroom. There," he said, taking her by the shoulders, "happy? I admitted I'm an idiot. A jealous, manipulative idiot. I hate to share. I always have, and I doubt I'll ever change."

"Whew!" Sass laughed. "I'd say that just about covers everything."

"You could have danced around a bit. Maybe given my ego a break."

Sass's hands touched his waist. "We've never been anything but truthful with each other. Why change now?"

Curt slipped his arm around her shoulders and she snuggled into the crook of his arm. The sun was shining, the air was crisp and she was living the.perfect life. Sass shivered.

"Cold?" Curt murmured and tightened his hold.

Sass shook her head. No, she wasn't cold, but someone had walked across her grave. Suddenly she was anxious, fearful with her first inkling that perfection could never last. Why she should question her good fortune now, of all times, was beyond her. But foreboding sat on the horizon of her lovely life and she hadn't even seen it arrive, much less creep close.

Banishing this apprehension with an instinctive movement, she wound both arms around Curt's waist in one of those embraces that made it difficult to walk, but marvelous to try. She laid her cheek against his chest, reveling in the feel of his cashmere sweater. Curt relaxed and buried his lips in hair that smelled like gardenias and felt like ropes of silk.

"Ah, honey, I'm sorry. I'm so sorry. You know, he's the first guy I've ever seen you with that makes me jealous. I can't explain it, except that I don't trust him."

"What's not to trust?" Sass asked dreamily. "Shay Collier's giving more to me than I am to him, Curt. He asks only for what's owed him: payment for the rights and his salary as the writer. I had to almost force him into the guest house."

"I know. I think that's what makes me so uncomfortable. Everyone has a plan, Sass. You know that. Everybody except that guy, if you believe him. When you can hide it that well it must mean what he wants is pretty spectacular."

Sass raised her head and looked into Curt's eyes. She knew him as well as she knew herself, and this baseness wasn't like him.

"Can't you just accept that he's doing what he wants to do?"

"No." Curt chuckled, but there was no mirth in the sound.

"No?" Sass pulled away without letting go of him. "No? That's it? So simple after such complex ravings?"

"I suppose. I'm sorry. I simply don't feel comfortable with him. I might actually like him, but I can't get past this feeling that he's taking something away from me— or he's going to. Sometime soon."

"Sometime when hell freezes over, Curt." Sass held tight and teased him with her beautiful, barely parted lips. "That's the only time Shay Collier will take something from you. Come on. What could he possibly take? What could he possibly want?"

There was a heartbeat between them. A December cloud passed overhead shadowing the gardens and plunging them into a place that was cold for an instant, but the memory of that chill lasted inordinately long. It was the calm before the storm and when it hit, it hit hard.

"You, Sass. He might want you."

She should have laughed that off. Sass should have squeezed him and tickled him and kissed his face until their fun turned to passion right there on the brick path under the winter cloud. But Sass did none of these things. She simply held on to Curt. Her smile lost a spark or two of its dazzle, some of its trifling quality, her eyes a bit of glow. They still stood close, but she no longer touched him. Sass spoke seriously, quietly and, Curt thought, a little sadly when she finally overcame her surprise.

"He wouldn't want me. I don't think you understand how deeply Shay Collier has been hurt, how damaged he is. If he ever loves again it will be a very special woman who can bring him back to life because she has the time to do it. My life is too complicated. I'm not the kind of woman he would want."

"You've made him work again."

Sass shook her head and her light hair glistened so brightly Curt thought he'd never seen anything so beautiful.

"I offered him the chance to work, to manage his pain, that's all. But that's something to help him. Not someone to help him."

"Okay, Sass. Okay." Curt sighed. He sounded tired as if he'd been working hard for a long time and still didn't see an end to his task. He wanted to convince her she was wrong. He wanted to hold her and explain the inexplicable. Curt knew what he knew. Men couldn't stand in the same room together with a woman and not understand someone else's intent. Even if they were fooling themselves, Curt wasn't going to take a chance that one day, one of them would wake up and really look at the other.

Sliding his arm from around her shoulders, he took her hands and kissed her fingers. Suddenly Curt knew that sometimes love was not a pleasant thing. It was easy to say how much he loved Sass in the morning just before they came together, kissing and caressing and doing what they did best. It was easy to touch her, to hold her hand, smile at her across the room and receive the same. That was the easy part of love. Now the hard part was upon him and there was nowhere to go but forward. He had to find out exactly how much Sass loved him and it scared Curt Evans half to death. He held her hands tighter, her gaze more enthralled. He couldn't ask her how much she loved him so instead he said, "Sass, marry me."

"What?"

"Marry me. Please. I love you so much. I don't think I realized how much until Shay Collier came into our lives. I love you, I want to prove it, I want to make sure people know you love me. I don't want anyone second-guessing us anymore. I want a commitment. I want to make one to you, and I'm asking you to make one to me. We've talked about it. Let's do it. Now."

"Curt," Sass breathed, "I can't believe this."

Fear was as cold as an icicle plunged through his heart. She was going to say no, and he was powerless to do anything about it. God help him, he would lose his mind if she said no. Quite suddenly, Curt knew she meant the world to him.

"Sass . . ." he began, but his voice quavered, then caught in his throat. No act this, only the honest emotion of a man terrified of losing what was precious. Curt had never experienced disappointment, and he steeled himself to weather this first, horrific blow.

"Curt," Sass whispered back, her hands sliding over his face as though she could memorize it through her touch. That gesture gave him courage. He looked into her eyes only to find hope. Tears pooled in those eyes, and Curt dared to believe they were tears of happiness. "I do love you, Curt."

"Then marry me. Please, be my wife. Be anything else you want to be in the world, with anyone else in the world, but let me know it's me you love, me you'll wake up to every morning for the rest of your life. I'll never make you sorry, Sass. I promise to adore you, to love you. Let's have beautiful children together. . . ."

"Children!"

Now she did laugh, but she caught it back as a tear slipped from the corner of her eye. She wiped it away with a small sniffle. The cloud had moved on, leaving Curt and Sass bathed in the glorious December sunlight. All around them the flowers and bushes swayed in the breeze and somewhere far away a gull cried as if urging her to answer. Curt joined in, convincing her with all the words he knew.

"Why not? Can you think of two better people? Our children will be gorgeous. They'll be intelligent. They'll be talented . . ."

"They'll be loved," Sass cut in and with those words stopped Curt in his tracks.

His mouth was still open, ready to continue with his litany of wonders she could expect if only she said yes. The next word was almost out of his mouths before he fully understood what Sass had said.

"You mean they will be loved when we have them?" he asked quietly. "Or, if we have them they will be loved? Or if we ever had them they would have been loved?"

Sass chuckled, lowering her lashes, teasing him.

This, she was sure, was happiness. "I mean that when we have them, after a respectable time of marriage, when we're sure that this is going to work and . . ." She waggled a finger, looking at him once again. ". . . when this film is finished, I would be honored to be Mrs. Curt Evans. Honored and delighted and thrilled. I think it will be the most fantastic Hollywood wedding anyone has ever seen because we actually love each other. That I know. That I understand. It's been the one constant of my life for three years." Sass moved forward, melting into Curt's arms. "I adore you, Curt. You've never demanded anything of me, never expected me to give more than you give back. How could I say no?"

"God," Curt breathed. "My God, Sass." He pulled her closer, held her tighter. Hardly able to believe his luck. He had no words to express his boundless joy, his limitless relief. So Curt did what he always did when words eluded him. In one fell swoop Sass was in his arms, lifted off the ground and laughing at their promise. She laughed with sheer delight and saw herself in white. She saw the garden in bloom. Sass saw Curt waiting for her by a bower, his hand outstretched.

Curt, as he twirled her, kissed her, held her, and yelped with sheer joy, saw only one thing in his mind's eye— the empty guest house. Shay Collier would be gone, out of their lives, leaving Sass and Curt alone again and forever.

Nine

"You didn't come in for dinner."

"I'm not one for celebrating, Sass."

Shay lifted his hands on the arms of the pool chair, turning his head just far enough to politely acknowledge her, but leaving Sass to wonder if he wouldn't have preferred to be alone. She felt far too marvelous not to try to include him in this festive occasion, though. So she left Shay no choice. She joined him. A beautiful balmy night was no time to be sitting staring morosely into the pool. He had kept his own counsel too long. Sass motioned him down with one hand, holding up the bottle of champagne with the other.

"Not even if the celebration is a small one, just between friends?"

"That might be another matter," he said and smiled.

When on earth had he begun to make a habit of that? She'd hardly seen him since early December. Keeping to himself, she imagined he was working hard. Still, it was difficult not to be asked for an opinion, to be part of the birth of the next scene or see the excitement in his eyes when he felt he was on the right track with the script.

At first Sass had been worried by his silence. She was concerned Shay might be drawing away from the world again. The last thing she wanted was for him to feel pain as he made her dream a reality. But then Sass would see him walking on the beach, sitting at the window in the guest house, his head bent over his work, and realize he was only doing what came naturally. Still, his self-imposed exile wasn't all good. She felt at odds and ends without him, especially with Curt gone during the holidays. Feeling better now, she sat herself down next to him.

"Oh, I've forgotten glasses. There are some in the guest house. Would you mind?"

Shay hesitated, not at all sure if he was ready to sit this way with Sass. He had been so conscientious about staying out of her way. Curt's message had been more than clear. It hadn't been all that hard. These had been good weeks, hard-working weeks and he'd accomplished so much alone— and, yes, lonely. He'd even managed not to wonder what she was up to, up in that big house of hers, with that man of hers. Still, it was over now. What harm could there be? He pushed out of his chair only to be back a moment later, giving her the glasses, taking the bottle for himself.

"Sure, lass, you're not strong enough to do this," he murmured and, before she could protest, the cork popped with a sharp sound. The champagne spilled out over his hands, a shimmering waterfall of sparkling wine. He held it up, triumphant, his eyes dancing with delight. Sass almost sighed. What a waste these last years had been for a man like this. He loved life so dearly and had removed himself from living for so long. Instead, she kept quiet and simply smiled as she held up her glass. He filled it and said, "There you are. Champagne for your New Year's Eve celebration. Sure, shouldn't you be dressed in one of your gowns and off to the ball with your man?"

Shay dutifully filled his own glass, abandoning the bottle and sitting in the chair once more. Sass rearranged herself, sipping before she answered. The champagne was delicious, the company as marvelous as she remembered.

"Not tonight. He still hasn't come back from Arizona. But you wouldn't know that because you've been keeping to yourself for the last six weeks."

"That I have," Shay answered, looking intently at his glass.

"Shay!" Sass objected. "That was an opening. You're supposed to tell me what's been going on. I've been on pins and needles wondering how the work's going. I've committed half my liquid assets to this movie. I'm paying out on a daily basis, and I'm waiting for the one thing I need to begin work. You don't even come up to the house anymore! How much more do you think I can take?"

"Do I detect a bit of a whine, Miss Brandt?" Shay cocked his eyebrow, sliding his amused eyes her way. "There's no man dancing attendance, and we're a bit lonesome, are we?" he teased.

"Don't be silly. I'm thoroughly modern," Sass sniffed, lifting her glass as if to toast her independence. "I don't need a man to make me stop whining. I need a script. An honest-to-goodness sheaf of paper that has every word, every scene, every nuance I'll need to shoot *The Woman At the End of the Lane.* That's what I need, for sure, Shay Collier." Sass's Irish lilt was near perfect as she leaned forward, looking up at the black-haired man next to her. "I've put my money and my reputation on the line. So far there isn't anything I have to show for the effort."

"Ah," Shay breathed, "that is a bit of a misery, isn't it?"

Shay raised his glass, intent on drinking the champagne just so. It was so hard to look at her. The odd light, the late hour, the shadows playing across her face made Sass look so young. Her face was contoured by nature so that it wasn't quite as defined as it was during the day. Her skin was shaded so it wasn't the light gold from hours in the sun, but of a paleness so pure she looked as if she might break.

Seeing her as she was now reminded Shay of a child at Christmas, hoping against hope that her da had managed to find the money for that special present, knowing in her heart she would die without it. He chuckled softly and, to keep himself from touching her, put his glass down carefully.

Leaning over, Shay hid a grin. His broad-shouldered body tilted only a bit as he retrieved a package beside his chair. Shay held it in both his hands while he considered the pretty wrapping. Not as good as some of the wrappings he'd seen this Christmas. The shops in this place were something to behold. All gilt and gold, with things inside so expensive anyone of them could feed his small village for a week. He'd not found the perfect gift to thank Sass for what she had done for him. Pretty, senseless things she could buy for herself a dozen at a time. So he settled for a most beautiful paper to wrap his gift in, the one and only thing she wanted. How hard it had been for his hands to make the bow just so. But done it he had— gift and wrapping— and now it was time to see if it would please her.

"Sass Brandt, far be it from me to spoil such a fine holiday for you. I didn't have this for Christmas so we'll say our Happy New Year's with a gift."

Sass received it reverently knowing exactly what it was he had given her.

"Thank you," she whispered. "Can I open it?"

The spell was broken. For a moment Shay thought it had been him alone that brought such a look to her eyes, but that would be too much to ask. Too much to hope for.

"Of course, Sass. Open it and read it and I'll sit here with you in the dark until your eyes go bad."

With that Shay sank into his comfortable, poolside chair. If he had a hat he would have cocked it over his eyes. Instead, he closed them, his champagne flute dangling from two fingers.

For a moment Sass watched, her eyes playing over him, from the top of his beautiful hair to the tip of his worn boots. Shay Collier was an incredible sight. Sass shook her head and pulled at the bow. Watching Shay too closely, on a night such as this, might make her forget that Lisabet was in the house and Curt was far away.

She might even forget that it was Curt's ring she wore on her finger.

Tearing her eyes away, Sass unwrapped the gift

that, to her, was more precious than any jewel. One hundred and twenty pages of talk and movement that only someone like she could fully appreciate. And as she read, in the dim light by the pool, the pictures played in her mind, the words reverberated in her head. Sass longed to say them, she longed to become Eileen and for Curt to become Liam. She wanted to make real to the world the moments Shay had lived through in a private torment. She wanted this, not to hurt him, but because it was a story of human failing and, ultimately, human triumph.

When she was done, when the last page was turned, Sass laid her hand on Shay's arm. His eyes opened slowly, but the only movement he made was to turn his head, tip his lips in a bittersweet smile. Neither spoke, neither moved until Shay reached out with one hand. With a slow and tender movement that took Sass's breath away, he wiped the tear that had fallen from her eye with his fingertip. When he drew that finger kindly down her cheek and tipped her chin, Sass's heart was overwhelmed by a torrent of emotion. She was crushed by a cruel and immediate need for more of him. She hung her head, ashamed of such feelings, knowing they were experienced because the scene was set and the players so perfect for their parts. Desperate to believe it was nothing more than that, Sass forced herself to speak.

"It's wonderful. Not a word will change, I promise you. You won't be sorry, Shay."

His hand fell away, hovering as if he might reach for her again, before laying it on the arm of his chair and turning his head back so that he looked at the stars in the sky instead of those in her eyes.

"I've never been sorry, Sass, not from the day you came to me. I can't tell you what you've come to mean . . ."

"Shhh. Don't let's talk of anything we might regret. It's the night, and we're alone and the story has us in its grip. Please let's not say anything more."

"Sure, 'tisn't that the right thing. 'Tis the story. 'Tis the past that's making this present so odd a thing for us."

"I know. I appreciate what you've done for me, too. I think we were meant to find each other, don't you?"

Shay closed his eyes, wishing he could banish the sight of Sass Brandt from his mind. But he could no more do that than wish himself blind.

"Shay?" Sass sat up straighter, brushing back her hair, a quizzical expression on her face. She saw him change. Those eyes hooded and darkened and she knew all was not right. Perhaps he was suddenly feeling the loss of his work only to find he was mourning it. But then he spoke and the sound of his voice was heard as if from afar.

"I see that you've had another fine thing for Christmas, Sass."

"I have?"

He nodded toward her hand. She pulled it away from her hair and looked at the ring on her finger as if surprised to find it there. Her ring. The one Curt had made sure was under the tree even if he couldn't be the one to put it there. Lisabet had wrapped it. Lisabet had helped him pick it out. A huge square ruby surrounded by diamond baguettes. A hard-to-miss addition to Sass's usually naked hands; a gift impossible to misinterpret.

"Oh, yes. It's beautiful, isn't it?"

Shay sat up straighter, on his best behavior now, the electricity between them switched off as surely as if someone had cut the current.

" 'Tis a most beautiful ring." He nodded and it was obvious he was trying to think of something else to say.

"Yes," Sass answered, laughing self-consciously. "Curt did go a bit overboard. I suppose you missed all the excitement, buried out here as you were. Curt's asked me to marry him."

There. She said it. Strangely, Sass expected something; she just wasn't quite sure what. Perhaps some pithy dispatch that would finally give voice to the disapproval she'd felt from him all these months that he lived with them. Perhaps she expected, somewhere deep in her heart, an objection that was more personal, something that would draw on all the things that were special between the two of them. But what he said, and the way he said it, were not at all what Sass thought she would hear from Shay Collier.

"Congratulations, Sass. It's wonderful news. When is the wedding?"

Sass swallowed hard, startled that she should feel just a bit hurt by such cool good wishes. She almost laughed, realizing her reaction was nothing more than a bruised ego. Hadn't she believed somewhere in the back of her mind that Shay Collier must have fallen in love with her the way everyone did?

"I don't know, actually. After we finish the film, I suppose."

"Curt's a lucky man. I wish you the best of luck. You'll make a beautiful bride. I should like to see you walkin' down the aisle."

"You will. The way Curt's been talking he's going to have the preacher at the wrap party. He'll probably have you add the vows onto the last lines."

Sass joked only to find the words hurt her in some indefinable place. She didn't want to laugh. She wanted him to talk to her. Sass needed him to . . .

"I'm afraid he'll have to be doing his own writing, Sass."

"I'm teasing, Shay. Honestly," she insisted. "Is there a sense of humor lurking behind that black beard of yours, or are you determined to be a brooding Irishman the rest of your life?"

"Neither, Sass. I'm just here. Just taking the one wee step I can take after all these years. Do you want to have a clown at your feet?"

Sass shook her head, serious again. "No, of course not. I want a friend by my side. I know I haven't told you— you don't make it easy to tell— but you've given me much more than this script. You've slowed me down, made me look at things in life I've never had the opportunity to consider before. I used to think myself lucky that I'd never experienced half the emotions I play in my characters. Now I'm beginning to wonder if that wasn't a failing instead."

Sass inched closer to him, instinctively hugging his script.

"You've shown me happiness is a marvelous thing, but without pain or sorrow or introspection

a person can never be truly happy. I understand
now that everyone must experience the worst to
truly appreciate the best in life.''

"But you wouldn't want the pain, Sass. Sure,
doesn't it add little to the happiness in the long
run?''

"No, of course I would never want the pain
you've experienced. But I'd like to know that I'd
be strong enough to handle it if it ever came into
my life. You've made me look at myself with clear
eyes and see my strengths as well as my failings. I
appreciate that, Shay.''

Sass looked about, trying to gain inspiration
from the beauty around her. Where were the
words that would make him understand how much
she needed him? When she spoke it was with gentleness, almost with introspection.

"Funny that we should have met as we did.
Strange to have almost died on your doorstep only
to find a dear friend when I came back to life. I
can't tell you how your generosity has influenced
me. I doubt I'll ever know why you changed your
mind and sold me the rights to your father's book.
But I'm so grateful you did. I can only hope you've
gained something, too. I'd hate to think that all
you have now is money.''

"Not to worry about that, Sass." Shay swept the
champagne bottle from beneath his chair. He re-
filled his own flute, though he had hardly drunk
half, then held out the bottle toward Sass. She offered her glass. Neither of them had done justice
to the first round. Now the sparkling wine bubbled
up and Shay became animated, his speech hearty,
his gestures expansive. It was unlike him, but Sass

would not shame him by calling to task his performance. Something important was happening here and Sass wasn't quite sure what the next plot point would be. Shay was writing the script, all she could do was keep her eyes open and let him set the pace.

"I've gotten exactly what I bargained for, Sass, my girl. Someday I might sit myself down and realize I've been given more than that . . ." He cocked his head, thinking. Muttering to himself she heard, "Much more than what I had expected. . . ." Sass strained to listen, thinking he was going to tell her the complete truth. But the actor came back and he was convivial once more. The perfect picture of an Irishman toasting the bride, an intention that was not his. "Yes, I think I've got what I came for, though I must admit I almost turned back. Now I'm glad I didn't."

"So is Kelly Karter," Sass said wryly, wondering when her friend would ever give up hope. "She's still asking when you might give her a call."

"Holy Mother of God, I don't think that would be a match made in heaven." He laughed. "Don't you think both of us have more to consider than whether or not I should take to courting?"

"I suppose you're right. What are you going to do, though, between now and filming? We won't start shooting for another four or five weeks."

"And, my dear Sass, I don't anticipate hearing you say the first words, or watching you make the first gesture." Shay downed his champagne in one swift movement. He held the crystal toward the moon, but it only reflected the lights in the pool.

"Shay! You can't mean that!" Sass dropped the script, appalled at what she heard.

"Oh, by the Virgin." Shay laughed a bit too heartily as he retrieved the fallen script and gave it back to her without ever once looking her in the eye. "You make me feel a special man, indeed, Sass, my darlin'. But you'll have enough folk to admire you as you make this movie. You don't need me."

"But I do need you," she insisted and even to her ears her insistence sounded frantic. "I need you to be watchful for me so that I don't get too far afield with this. I want to do this story justice, Shay, and I can't unless you're there to make sure that I manage properly."

"But I've made sure already, don't you see?" Shay slid back onto his chair, leaning over the arm so that he and Sass were closer. He breathed deeply hoping that the scent of her perfume would come to inspire him as he lied. "Every word in that script is proper. Don't change it, and you'll be doin' fine. But, lass, I cannot watch while you do this, don't you see?"

"Oh, Shay." Her eyes opened and they were the palest shade of gold, like a sunrise. "I'm so sorry. That was stupid of me. I'm sorry. Of course you wouldn't want to watch us film this story. But please, please don't leave. There's so much you can do."

"Sass." He put his hand over hers and there was no question of his sincerity. "There's nothing I can do. You must believe that. I'm not a person to make films. I'm a writer again, thanks to you. That will be what I will do. But you can't expect me to sit here and wait in your guest house. The perennial visitor? What would Curt say after you were married? Unless, perhaps, he'd want me around to watch the wee ones when they start coming? Sure, wouldn't I make a fine nursemaid?"

"I don't mean that you're a convenience and you know it." Now her hand covered his. Sitting by the pool, in silence that was bought by wealth, their hands entwined. Both tried to ignore the contact, both failed and neither dared look to see how lovely it was, his flesh close to hers. "Of course you can stay as long as you wish, but I assume you'll want to find your own place . . ." Sass paused, her eyes flicked away for an instant. ". . . you'll want to establish your own life. I'm not so selfish to think you wouldn't want that."

Shay sat back, his hand sliding from hers easily and, for a moment, he wished she would pull him back. It was neither meant to be nor proper.

"I will establish a life, but I'm not sure California is the place for me."

"Ireland?"

Shay shook his head, "Not now. Someday."

"Not Alaska again."

"Why not?" Shay said quickly. "Have you ever seen a more serene place, a better place for me to weave my tales?"

"Have you ever seen a place more perfectly suited to hiding out? How will you resist, Shay, when the call is strong and the memories come flooding back, and there's no one for you to talk to? Do you think I'll lie down in the snow for you again, and freeze myself until I'm almost dead, just so you have something to do with your time?"

Despite himself, Shay laughed and Sass felt her

entire body give way to relief. How she worried about him, this handsome, troubled man. He seemed better, but Sass knew he wasn't quite healed. Now he was going to walk away, disappear, and Sass just knew she couldn't let him. He didn't have the strength of soul yet. He needed her. Didn't he?

" 'Tis kind of you, Sass, to worry about me, but don't. Sure it's a waste of those fine thoughts of yours. I've been on my own a long time. I've traveled and I might again. But for now I'll go back. I've my home, don't you remember? I've missed my chair and my fire. I've missed being alone in the woods and walking in air that has nothing in it but the goodness God gave it. I've missed that, Sass."

"You need a friend, Shay," Sass answered helplessly, knowing the decision was made. Powerful though she was, she wasn't strong enough to change his mind.

"And I've got one, Sass. Do you think I'd ever forget that? Do you think I'd ever forget anything about this time we've had together?"

Sass hung her head, defeated by his righteousness. There was nothing here for him. She was spoken for, as she always had been, by one person or another.

"I never thought I was selfish before, Shay. Now I find that I was lying to myself. Here I am trying to make you stay when it's only the best thing for me, not you."

"That's not a bad thing, Sass. If I was off to make this movie, wouldn't I want someone beside me who believed as much as I did in it?"

Wish You Were Here?

You can be, every month, with Zebra
Historical Romance Novels.

AND TO GET YOU STARTED, ALLOW US TO SEND YOU

4 Historical Romances Free

A $19.96 VALUE!

With absolutely no obligation to buy anything.

YOU ARE CORDIALLY INVITED TO GET SWEPT AWAY INTO NEW WORLDS OF PASSION AND ADVENTURE.

AND IT WON'T COST YOU A PENNY!

Receive 4 Zebra Historical Romances, Absolutely _Free_!
(A $19.96 value)

Now you can have your pick of handsome, noble adventurers with romance in their hearts and you on their minds. Zebra publishes Historical Romances That Burn With The Fire Of History by the world's finest romance authors.

This very special FREE offer entitles you to 4 Zebra novels at absolutely no cost, with no obligation to buy anything, ever. It's an offer designed to excite your most vivid dreams and desires...and save you almost $20!

And that's not all you get...

Your Home Subscription Saves You Money Every Month.

After you've enjoyed your initial FREE package of 4 books, you'll begin to receive monthly shipments of new Zebra titles. These novels are delivered direct to your home as soon as they are published...sometimes even before the bookstores get them! Each monthly shipment of 4 books will be yours to examine for 10 days. Then if you decide to keep the books, you'll pay the preferred subscriber's price of just $4.00 per title. That's $16 for all 4 books...a savings of almost $4 off the publisher's price...and there's no additional charge for the convenience of home delivery!

There Is No Minimum Purchase. And Your Continued Satisfaction Is Guaranteed.

We're so sure that you'll appreciate the money-saving convenience of home delivery that we guarantee your complete satisfaction. You may return any shipment...for any reason...within 10 days and pay nothing that month. And if you want us to stop sending books, just say the word. There is no minimum number of books you must buy.

It's a no-lose proposition, so send for your 4 FREE books today!

YOU'RE GOING TO LOVE GETTING

4 FREE BOOKS

These books worth almost $20, are yours without cost or obligation
when you fill out and mail this certificate.
(If the certificate is missing below, write to: Zebra Home Subscription Service, Inc.,
120 Brighton Road, P.O. Box 5214, Clifton, New Jersey 07015-5214

Complete and mail this card to receive 4 Free books!

Yes! Please send me 4 Zebra Historical Romances without cost or obligation. I understand that each month thereafter I will be able to preview 4 new Zebra Historical Romances FREE for 10 days. Then, if I should decide to keep them, I will pay the money-saving preferred publisher's price of just $4.00 each...a total of $16. That's almost $4 less than the publisher's price, and there is no additional charge for shipping and handling. I may return any shipment within 10 days and owe nothing, and I may cancel this subscription at any time. The 4 FREE books will be mine to keep in any case.

Name _____

Address _____ Apt. _____

City _____ State _____ Zip _____

Telephone ( ) _____

Signature _____ LF0595
(If under 18, parent or guardian must sign.)

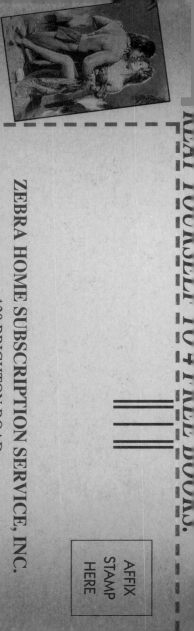

"Yes, I suppose," she murmured, knowing there was more to her desire to keep him close than an actor's superstition. Sass refused to think too deeply about that and grinned at him. "How does it feel, being a talisman?"

Shay followed her lead, returning her smile in kind, adding a very gentlemanly, if not modest, bow. "Very fine, thank you, lass." And then he was serious again. "But the time is over, and you'll go on to do things I have no understanding of. Imagine me tagging along on this huge undertaking? I could get your coffee, nothin' more. I'd be useless, so I have to go. I've been useless too long in my life. I've finished my work. I can't stay and watch you . . ."

Shay didn't finish his sentence, leaving them both to wonder if it was simply the making of a movie he couldn't watch, or her, once she wore Curt's wedding ring. Some place in her heart, the heart that seldom reveled in such vanities, Sass wanted him to admit it was her he couldn't bear to see: not in the arms of another man, not standing in the sunlight, not poring over the pages of a script with him. To look at him, though, Sass knew these feelings had no basis in fact. For Shay Collier considered her as he always had: openly, respectfully, perhaps affectionately. It was hard to tell what was there in his black eyes. For the first time in a long while, Sass Brandt gave up, and gave in, graciously. Her head rose up and her eyes looked forward and Sass was as confident as the star she was.

"Then I should close my lips, and not utter another word that will make you feel guilty for doing what you want to do. I'm forever in your debt, Shay. I wish you nothing but the best. I only hope you won't disappear. You won't disappear, will you?"

"I'll never be far, Sass. Never in my mind or in my heart."

"Then I can't ask for anything more, can I?"

"You could ask, but I've only so much to give," Shay answered and she thought she saw pain in his eyes. Not the scar of old but signs of a new fresh wound.

"Haven't we all, Shay?"

It was time to leave. She stood up and clutched the script, knowing that it was part of Shay Collier's life she held in her arms. He stood with her, looking up at the sky.

"I think it's late, Sass." He looked back at her. "The new year's begun. It will be a special one for me. I hope it will be for you, too, lass."

"It will, Shay. I have no doubt."

"Then I wish you the best in the days of this new year, and all the years to come."

With that Shay Collier turned and leaned toward her, coming close until their lips met in a kiss so gentle Sass was not sure they had touched. But her eyes had closed and when they opened again Shay Collier's face was still close to hers, his breath warm on her cheek, his lashes lush and dark against his own. For that instant, Sass wanted them to remain there forever, caught in this tender moment of time. When he moved away, when she lowered her eyes, that instant of intimacy was gone.

"You're still up?"

Sass barely acknowledged Lisabet as she came up behind her. She knew exactly what the blond woman looked like. No New Year's Eve surprises here. She would be dressed in a robe of chenille, a gown of flannel. Her hair would be pulled back, her face scrubbed clean. Deep in the pockets of her robe, Lisabet would have stuffed her hands, one clutching a tissue. And, without looking, Sass knew the other woman's eyes were trained on her, hungry for her companionship. Lisabet's expression would be tight, far from relaxed for fear she might miss an opportunity to do Sass's bidding.

All this had never bothered Sass before. Neither had Curt dancing attendance. But suddenly their attention felt cloying, not affectionate, and Shay's announcement was not like parting but abandonment. With him friendship had never been demanding; instead it had brought space to breathe. Now Sass felt herself suffocated once more.

"I just didn't feel like going to bed. I suppose I'm so used to being out on New Year's Eve. My psyche is disturbed by all this quiet." Sass laughed sadly, and Lisabet knew she was lonely.

"You should have gone out, Lisabet," Sass said as she walked away from the great bank of windows that overlooked her estate.

"No, I wouldn't want to leave you alone." Lisabet was hurt, her voice tight, but Sass didn't seem to notice.

"Sometimes alone is nice, Lisabet." Sass looked at Lisabet as she spoke and was immediately sorry. She might as well have driven a lance through the other woman's heart. Damn Lisabet for her neediness, especially tonight. Ashamed of her selfishness, Sass made up, with a smile and a retraction. "But most of the time alone is the pits." She laid her hand on the other woman's arm, letting it trail over the chenille robe as she passed. "Come on, I'll fix us some cocoa. Then we can both snuggle down for the night. The script is done. We'll be up to our eyeballs in work soon, so we might as well enjoy this while we can."

"You're right, of course," Lisabet said. "We should enjoy the quiet. Each other's company. We don't seem to do that much anymore."

Lisabet spoke distractedly and Sass, halfway across the room, hardly heard her. Instead of following, Lisabet took a moment for herself. She moved to the windows and stood close to the wall of glass, her hands still stuffed deep into her pockets. In the indirect light Lisabet looked lifeless, a statue long forgotten or ignored. Her face was shadowed, dark over one side, under her eyes, in the hollow of her cheeks. She looked hard and cold and frightening. But there was no one to see her, no one but Shay Collier still sitting by the pool with the bottle of champagne in his hand and he didn't look up. He was alone with his thoughts and Lisabet knew those thoughts were of Sass.

She turned her back on the scene, hating Shay Collier's presence almost as much as she now hated Curt's. Both of those men had taken a part of Sass away and it galled her. It was she who gave Sass what she needed most— loyalty and love— yet Lisabet was most often discarded as if she were a person of inconvenience instead of worth. She hoped things would change. One day everyone would understand how important Lisabet was in Sass Brandt's life. One day.

He knew the moment she left the window. He had felt her watching, felt the questions in her heart, despite the fact that glass and concrete separated them. Shay knew Sass understood this thing between them as much as he. How could he describe it, this electricity, this bond that went so far beyond the creative effort they had shared, this bond of heart and soul?

Sass had not acknowledged it, he knew, and that was as it should be. Wasn't her heart pure, her love given to one man alone? She hadn't even allowed herself to look into the depths of her heart. If she had, Sass would have found him waiting to give her what even Curt never could. For how could Curt understand what a woman like Sass needed? He thought one-dimensionally; reality was what he could see and touch. Curt Evans had no idea that the soul was something of greater value than the face, the body, the sense of the person to whom you professed love.

Yet Curt Evans's ring graced Sass's finger, he shared her bed and Shay Collier would never do anything to disturb her life. Hadn't his been disturbed for lesser reasons than love? Hadn't a man come and taken the woman he adored from his bed and from his heart and hadn't it almost destroyed him? He would never do that to Sass, nor even to Curt, a man he didn't much care for. Should his life go on a hundred years, never would

he bring shame or hurt or anything but goodness
to Sass Brandt's life.

Ten

"What does the village wizard say?"

Sass laughed and lay back against the door. It blew open a bit and she pressed harder, turning away from Curt long enough to make sure the latch was set.

"That wind is incredible! Can you believe this weather? Talk about a romantic setting, all this wind and rain and fog! I've never been in such a fabulous place. I keep expecting to hear Heathcliff moaning for Kathy. Or was that Scotland? I can never remember. But I don't know why I'm surprised. Shay told me the weather is like this every day this time of year, kind of wild and unpredictable. I don't think I really believed it until now."

Door finally secured, Sass pushed back the hood on her yellow slicker, freeing her hair, shaking out the prismlike drops of rain that had managed to find their way through her huge raincoat. She tossed the coat at the door, then headed for the fire, stopping long enough to give Curt a passing kiss before dropping to her knees by the hearth.

"So, what do they say, those guys at the pub?" Curt didn't move. He stared into the fire as he'd been staring into the fire all morning long.

Sass shot him a quick look and knew nothing had changed in the few hours she'd been gone. Even in this weather, the lay of the land was marvelous. Curt would feel so much better if he just got out a bit and walked, exercised, did something other than wish he were elsewhere. Seeing his face still clouded with discontent Sass turned back to the fire, reached out her hands and leaned toward the warmth.

"Oh, that's so much better," she said. "Mr. O'Toole says that it's rain through today. Lighter tomorrow with the wind still up. It's perfect. Absolutely perfect. I think this was exactly how Shay envisioned that final scene when he wrote it. We couldn't ask for anything better."

Curt bent forward. The cottage was so small they had no choice but to trip over each other when they happened to stand up at the same time.

"How about asking for dinner at Spago's? Our own bed? Our own house? Warmth. Sunshine. How about asking for an end to this interminable shoot so that we can go home. God!" Disgusted, Curt pushed himself away from Sass and flopped back in the worn chair, his fist pounding once on the arms for emphasis.

"How on earth, Sass, do you manage to stay so upbeat when we've been in this village for six weeks filming, waiting for weather breaks. Filming again. Waiting again. Even when it's not raining, it's not sunny. Fog, overcast, every depressing weather condition imaginable. It's boring. Sass, tell me you're going to listen to the village idiots and film this last sequence tomorrow, no matter what. We could get out of here by the end of the week."

Sass rubbed her hands, glad Curt couldn't see how tired she was of all his complaining. Knowing it wasn't really his fault, she brightened and hoped her mood was catching.

"You've been on worse locations than this," Sass said, laughing.

She put her arms behind her and hung her head back, her long hair brushing the hearth rug. She grinned, but Curt was too dour and self-absorbed to see that she'd never looked more beautiful. This wild land and quaint village suited her far more than the architecture of her life in Hollywood. Sensing his mood, Sass dropped the tease and sighed, wishing Curt could feel half of what she did about this place and this movie. Sitting straight again, she told him what he wanted to know.

"Yes, we're shooting tomorrow no matter what. Shay told me that the day he and Moira had this confrontation there was a light rain and it was overcast. I was just hoping the wind would die down a bit. We'll do the rest at the studio. But this . . ." Sass wrapped her arms around her knees and breathed in, loving the smell of the fire, of old wood, of small places. "This is heaven, Curt, and I wish you could see it that way." She swung her head toward her lover, her eyes and voice softening as she pleaded. "If you would only stop thinking about home, you would appreciate Ireland so much more. It's everything . . ."

"Everything Shay said it would be," Curt snapped. Sass jumped, the smile melting from her face. "Isn't that what you were going to say?"

Sass turned her head away. He might as well have slapped her, because the angry edge in his voice hurt just as much. Never, in all the time they had been together, had Curt shown so much displeasure. His easygoing manner had been replaced with irrational irritation and, for Sass, this trip had been one unhappy surprise after another. He was either mad or peeved, put upon or vexed. It was almost as if a different person had stepped off the plane at the airport. Swiveling, putting her back to the fire, Sass crossed her legs and gave Curt her full attention. It was time to work this out.

"Maybe we should talk about it."

Sass trailed a finger down his leg, but Curt remained aloof and cold. His macho exterior was dented and he was determined to milk this miserable mood.

Sass felt herself blooming in this solitude, among these simple people who laughed at their Hollywood shenanigans as the crew dragged cables and cranes and wardrobe all about the cliffs and lanes. Sass realized she was smiling and immediately wiped the grin off her face, replacing it with an expression of concern she honestly didn't feel. But she was going to put that spark back into Curt if it killed her. She couldn't have the male lead giving less than a hundred percent once the cameras started rolling, not to mention that she found his attitude a tad tiring on a personal level. It was only a day or two more, after all.

"Curt?" she urged. "Let's talk."

"What's there to talk about? That's what you were going to say, wasn't it?" Curt demanded.

"Sure, I admit it," Sass said, choosing her words carefully. "I was thinking that Ireland is exactly what Shay Collier said it would be. Don't you think that's an appropriate remark? I mean, this is Shay's home. This is where his story took place. While he was working on this script we talked about so many things: characterization, costuming, location. It's natural he and I would have discussed Ireland in detail. What kind of producer would I have been if I'd simply taken his script and sent him packing without finding out all I could about his experience?"

"You'd never have done that."

"You're right," Sass answered. "I'm too professional. I'm too interested in the story. I'm too . . ."

"Too head over heels, Sass?"

"Oh, Curt," she said wearily through her melancholy smile. "Are we going to go through this again?"

"Are you going to deny it? Again?" He crossed his arms and buried his chin in the high neck of his sweater. "You know you had a thing for him. All that mountain man, Irish broken heart stuff. You always fall for a line like that."

Sass's heart sank with those last words. Curt was looking for a fight and this new side of him worried her. Is this how things would be when the going got rough— imagined or real? If she'd done anything to deserve this treatment Sass would have taken it. But she hadn't, and that made this situation so dismal. Hadn't she been at Curt's side almost since the day they met, loving him, listening to him, encouraging his career and helping when she could? There was absolutely no reason for him to attack her this way and that hurt more than she could say.

"True," Sass admitted, unable to keep herself

from calling his bluff. Her shoulders slumped, she lowered her gaze. It was time for Curt to hear the truth.

"You're right. I can't help throwing myself at men's feet. The more rugged they are, the more I want them. I'm shameless. A terrible woman who thinks nothing of dishonoring love and commitment. They're just concepts to be discarded when I no longer have any use for them. When a man with great shoulders comes along I forget all my responsibilities. How you can still want me?"

Sass moved forward, draping her arms over his knees, raising her beautiful eyes to his face, her expression one of utter remorse. "How you can still desire me is a mystery. You're a good man, Curt. Too good for the likes of me." She managed an Irish lilt now and a finger tickled his ribs. This all sounded so ridiculous she couldn't even stay angry with him for his silliness. "Sure, I don't deserve you, such a fine gentleman as yourself."

"Cut it out, Sass." Curt squirmed out of the way, batting at her finger.

But Sass was relentless, getting into the spirit of things. It was a full-fledged tickling he was in for and, despite his best efforts, a chuckle or two proved her efforts worthwhile. She was up on her knees, both hands moving about his body. But Curt's mood changed suddenly and strangely. He caught Sass's hands in his, squeezing them together at the wrist until they hurt.

"Curt!" Sass laughed her objection, sure he would release her when he realized she was in pain. But one look at him and Sass saw this was no laughing matter.

This was more than cabin fever or missing Hollywood. Here was no pose of jealousy, but the real thing. Curt's grasp was hard and tight and Sass had never been touched that way by anyone, not even Shay Collier who had wanted to strangle her the moment they met. Now the man who hurt her was the man who professed to love her.

They remained frozen: she kneeling like a wayward slave, he kingly on his throne of a worn chair in a castle crowned with thatch. The moment of their reckoning stretched into an eternity where neither could find the truth of what they felt. But the moment became too long and too telling for Sass's liking. Her hands had curled into fists, not to fight against him, but in an instinctive move of fright.

"Don't tease me, Sass, and don't lie to me," Curt said quietly. "I felt something between the two of you the minute that guy showed up at the house. The electricity was there." He shook his head sadly. "I'm not crazy. It's still there, that feeling. The minute we set foot in this village Collier was here again, standing right beside us. No, he was right between us!"

Curt lowered her hands, his grip weakening until her wrists lay gently in his palms. He leaned close to her. Their foreheads were touching and Sass could feel his deep, deep turmoil. "I just don't feel like we've been ourselves since this whole thing started, Sass. Now, more than ever, I feel cut off from you. Over and over again I saw you in the garden with him, talking, smiling, always so excited by everything he said."

"We were working, honey. Just working. You

know how much I loved the book. I was excited because this was the project I dreamed of." Sass soothed him with her low, whispery voice.

Curt was adamant now and shook his head against the truth. He didn't want to hear it, and refused to believe anything but his own interpretation.

"I saw you looking for him, Sass. At night. You'd sit on the sofa and look out, waiting until you saw him, no matter what the hour."

"Curt," Sass breathed, her hands cupping his face, fingers spreading to touch his lips before giving him one small kiss of reassurance. "I was watching the ocean, the night. I've done that since I moved into the house. You know that. Tell me you know that."

Curt sighed and lifted back his head, but he didn't look at her. Instead, he stared into the fire. Sass's hands dropped so that they now held Curt's.

"It was different, the way you used to look out at the night. Your eyes weren't the same, and they weren't on the horizon. Maybe you didn't even know they were sweeping the grounds. Sometimes you didn't even know I was watching. Sometimes you jumped when I came into the room. You used to smile and hold out your hand and invite me to sit with you.

"I know what you were thinking about, and I know what you're still thinking about. His name comes up every time you open your mouth. Shay this and Shay that. I'm sick of hearing his name, Sass. Something about that guy got under your skin and you can't shake it. It's like you came to Ireland and really did become Collier's wife. I've never seen you perform the way you have on this project, and I finally realized why I can't admire what you're doing." He slid his gaze back to her and the unhappiness deep in his eyes was almost too much to bear. "I can't admire your performance because it's no act, is it, Sass? You're living your fantasy. You look at me, but it's Collier you see standing in front of you. You're saying words that aren't lines anymore but real arguments of a woman trying to get her man back." Curt threw up his hands in frustration. "What's worse is you want it that way. You'd rather he was the one here. Sometimes I wonder if you don't wish he was the one in bed with you at night."

"Curt . . ."

Sass could say no more than that one word. She fell back on her heels, pained to the very center of her being. His name sounded more like a thread of wind blowing in through the ill-fitting windows. It was meant to be consoling, the tightening of her grip intended as a gesture of solace and reassurance. But even she knew both fell short of the mark. The sound wasn't emphatic nor spontaneous, the touch was a bit too hesitant. And, as she realized this, Sass berated herself.

Curt was right in some respects. He seemed to think the memory, even the reality, of Shay Collier was Sass's obsession. To Curt, Shay was a danger. Curt couldn't be more wrong. The excitement she felt being with Shay, or thinking about him, was only a reaction to that which was foreign and fascinating.

Shay had none of the affectations of the men who surrounded her. His good looks weren't con-

structed by plastic surgeons or kept sound by a myr-
iad of trained personnel. He wasn't a man whose
talent was questionable, built by publicists and
press. Shay Collier wasn't a man impressed or
swayed by her wealth, her looks, or her influence.
And more than anything else, Shay Collier had always done exactly as he pleased. He had never had
his life planned and packaged and that was what
Sass envied and admired.

It was these things that made Shay unusual and
curious and, yes, attractive. Not just to Sass, but to
everyone who met him. Everyone except Curt, of
course. Sass let her hand slip away and pushed
herself off the floor. Going to the window, parting
the worn curtains, she looked out on the village
and the hills beyond.

Ireland was so green. A beautiful place. A forth-
right place. And, yes, if she were to be honest,
there was something in her heart for Shay Collier.
And, yes, she would call that something love. But
it was love of his creativity and concern for his
pain. It was not the kind of love she had for Curt,
Sass was sure of it.

Knowing this, confession would not be good.
Curt would never understand that love could have
a host of shadings. What Sass felt for Shay Collier
was such a complex emotion that even she didn't
fully fathom it. He had saved her life. He had
shared his hurt and pain with her. He had listened
to her. How grateful she had been for that! Shay
Collier had given her the gift of self-determination
when he turned over the rights to his father's
book. And, yes, when she stood next to him and
breathed in his scent, looked into those black eyes,

caught the deep blue-blackness of his hair in the light of the moon, Sass felt a stirring inside her. She had wanted to touch him and feel his arms wrapped around her lovingly, not in the panic of near death. And, when he had kissed her, just that once, she thought there was nothing sweeter in the world than the feel of his lips on hers.

But it was to Curt's bed she returned, to the life that was hers. She could do no less. Behind her was a history that made her Sass Brandt, a star. An encounter with a damaged man, a man in need of the kind of a special, selfless love was simply that— an encounter. Sass would treasure their adventure forever, and Sass knew she would make this movie as much for him as for herself. But thinking of him, dwelling on what they had in the short time they were together, was an unhealthy thing. She was stronger than that.

In time, Shay Collier would fade from memory. She might think of him someday when she had children and they wanted to strike out on their own. It would be a marvelous memory that had nothing to do with her real life. Sass would banish Shay Collier to a small, but lovely space in her heart. She would do that now for Curt's sake. For hers, too.

Looking back, Sass saw that Curt hadn't moved. He still stared into the fire and the light of it shadowed him so beautifully she was reminded of a painting; an old master whose hues and tints of the oils were used boldly to create the illusion of great delicacy.

"I love you, you know," Sass said.

Though unintentional, the declaration sounded scripted and flat. But the wind was blowing, the fire blazing, and the brooding man looked so overly dramatic she had been afraid to add her full voice to the mix: Going back to Curt, she sat beside him on the floor and draped one arm along his arm, the other over his knees as she laid her head against his strong leg.

"I love you." She spoke in a cadence that took on a life of its own, knowing she must make him believe. His hand lay tentatively on her hair, then stroked downward. Relieved, Sass realized he understood and tightened her hold.

"I do, darling, love you so much," she said again and this time she worried that perhaps she was trying to convince herself.

But Curt wound his fingers into the hair Shay Collier had found almost irresistible. He pulled her head away. Gently, he maneuvered until her face was tipped up toward his and he could see her lips moving, saying her words of love.

Sass's eyes were closed, her lips tinged with the same peach-color in her cheeks. The flames brightened the right side of her face, the blaze reflected in her porcelain skin. Her dark lashes lay against her cheeks and her lips moved and moved, saying the same words, whispering the same words one after the other.

There was nothing left to do but kiss her. Once begun he couldn't stop. Kisses and kisses, over and over again. Lips upon lips, then cheeks and eyes, Curt's body slipping off the chair and taking hers to the ground with him. He pulled her tightly to him, his hand never loosening in her hair. They rolled close to the hearth and felt the heat of the flames fanning the fervor of their desire.

Soon Sass was lost in the feel of Curt's body against hers. Even the ringing of the phone could not stop them until they were satisfied. Nothing could stop them as they tore at each other's clothing, laid their bodies together. Nothing could stop them except one thing and that was Sass Brandt's mind.

There the remembrance of the tall man who had left her so many months ago with part, but not all, of him, lay silently waiting to be called up. But Shay would never be back. He wasn't part of this life of hers. So Sass buried her face in the warm, inviting place near the base of Curt's throat. It was there she could feel the pulse of the life within him, there she found her purpose and desire exploded within her.

Memories of Shay, thoughts of a man so inappropriate to her life, were banished in a darkness that was as black as Shay Collier's eyes.

Lisabet smoothed the skirt and checked the buttons on the blouse Sass would wear in the morning. Such plain clothes. Clothes that transformed Sass into someone Lisabet hardly knew. Everything appeared to be taken care of. Wardrobe, as usual, was right on top of things but Lisabet preferred to check for herself. She would hate for Sass to wait or be inconvenienced because someone didn't take their job seriously enough. Bending, Lisabet looked at the low-heeled pumps that had been carefully pinched and scrunched until they looked as if they'd been walked in a lifetime. Finally, the scarf that would wind about Sass's neck was rearranged and passed scrutiny.

Yes, it all looked quite nice. Even Curt's things. Lisabet gave his costume a pat for good measure though she had little interest in the way he looked. He was just Curt, dressed in a costume, saying lines. It was Sass who changed, saying words that made her become the woman at the end of the lane. It was almost frightening when the cameras rolled. Sass became, not a star, but a simple woman who talked about love and commitment and failing as if she knew about it all. There weren't many who understood those things and none who understood as well as she, Lisabet, did. The last thing she wanted was for Sass to feel the pain of failure.

With a final flick of her eyes she gave the wardrobe trailer a once-over, slipped into her coat and hat, then out of the door. The rain still fell, soft and cleansing, on the little village high above the sea, but the wind had died to nothing more than a whispering breeze. It was almost five yet the sky was dark. Lights had come on in the houses, the pub, the church. If she listened closely Lisabet could hear singing coming from the little place of worship. Choir practice. Wednesday night. They'd been here long enough to know every ritual of every family in the village.

Quickly she headed toward the cottage she shared with two other women. Her roommates weren't objectionable, both quiet for the most part, but Lisabet would have preferred staying with Sass. If Curt hadn't been cast in the lead, that's exactly where she would have been, taking care of Sass's every need.

Thankfully they would wrap tomorrow if all went well. A day or two to clean up, pack, and say their goodbyes though it was only Sass who seemed to worry about the latter. At least Curt and Lisabet still had control of their senses. The crew was acting like this was fairyland and good Irish folk sprites of happiness. Lisabet would be damn happy when they were finally back home again.

With a flip of her wrist, the collar of her coat was turned up. Funny, but the wind was whipping again. Lisabet hurried on to her cottage. Soon it would be time for supper. Soon it would be time to go home.

Richard put down the phone and leaned back in his leather chair. It was there, bouncing in the chair, gazing out at the smog layer that had settled over downtown Los Angeles, that his secretary found him ten minutes later.

"Knock, knock?"

She was pretty. A redhead. Didn't see many of those in Southern California. There was so many blond-haired beauties around that a fairly attractive young woman like Shirley seemed quite special simply because she was natural and different. Richard smiled, but Shirley had been with him long enough to know it wasn't one of those self-satisfied, excellent-day kind of smiles. He waved her in.

"Come in," Richard said, righting himself.

"Anything I can help with?" Shirley scooted toward him. Her heels were sensible, her legs anything but. Richard admired them for a split second, but it wasn't a day for fun and games. Not that he ever indulged himself anyway. Business always came before pleasure.

"I don't think so. Is Doug here yet?"

Shirley raised her brows and dealt some files onto his desk. "I didn't know you were expecting him. He's not on the calendar."

"I called him, asked him to come over to discuss these spreadsheets."

Shirley glanced over the sheaf of papers Richard pushed her way. It was only a gesture. She didn't understand half of the paperwork that went through this office. She typed, she took dictation, she even got him coffee. Shirley was an old-fashioned kind of girl, and Richard treated her fairly. But both of them knew she didn't have the ambition to aspire to anything mightier than secretary. That was good. Richard didn't need anyone second-guessing his decisions. What he did need was some explanations. If what he saw on those spreadsheets was correct.

He snapped to attention, suddenly all action. The last thing Richard wanted was for Shirley to see him shudder with fear.

"What have you got?"

"Just a few letters for your signature. I've got two new scripts for you to look at and see if you want them sent to Sass and I need to know if you want me to renew your subscription to *Car and Driver.*"

Shirley grinned and Richard appreciated it.

"Finally, a decision I can make with my eyes closed. Yes. Sign me up for two years."

"Feeling magnanimous today," she said, laughing. "Oh, and that woman called again. Sloane Marshall?"

"Anybody home?"

Doug Whittaker called but was already in the office, briefcase in hand looking every inch the representative of an accounting firm, before he could be invited in. Slicked-back hair, Armani suit, suspenders, polished shoes, nails and clipped tie.

"Doug, good to see you." Richard stood up. They shook hands with the desk between them. They'd worked together on Sass's behalf for years and had never become friends. Richard had stopped worrying about this lack of closeness long since. Richard nodded to Shirley who was already closing the door behind her. "Thanks, Shirl."

They both heard a murmur and understood she'd said something appropriate. They sat. Richard pushed the printouts toward Doug.

"Want to explain this to me?"

Doug shrugged, "This could have been done over the phone."

"I needed to have you here. Just needed to see your face when you explained to me what this is all about." Richard clasped his hands on the desk in front of him to keep from wiping his forehead, which he was sure gleamed with perspiration. Doug didn't seem at all perturbed.

"I thought Sass would have told you. In fact, I was under the impression Sass had done this with your knowledge." Richard shook his head and now Doug was feeling a bit uncomfortable. The thought that Sass Brandt had acted independently to make such an enormous decision made him feel unsettled, too. Still, it was her money.

Doug sighed and unbuttoned his double-breasted jacket. "Okay. This is a current overview of Sass's estate. As you can see she's liquidated all her bearer bonds and sold off her interest in Jade Productions. That netted her about sixteen million. She can't touch the money she's put in trust, but she's pretty much run rampant through the rest of her investments. She's drawing on an account that I've been feeding with money for the last six months. She picked up another ten million from investors and is ten mil in the hole to the banks. Basically, Sass is down to about a third of her assets from one year ago. She's depleted much of her estate in order to fund this movie. So, what's your question?"

Doug sat back and looked frankly at his counterpart. He knew that Sass didn't have a legal relationship with Richard— not one that made it necessary for him to sign off on her financial dealings— still, this was a surprise. Sass's independence could mean a lot of things, not the least of which was that Richard might be out of the picture. She was a big girl now, maybe she was getting ready to make a switch in management. If that was the case he'd be first in line. More than likely it was nothing more than Sass being overwhelmed. The whole industry knew she had gone just a bit crazy. Sass's folly, that's what they called it and nobody could convince her it wasn't worth the millions she was spending. Not that Hollywood didn't have faith in her.

Anybody would have bankrolled a movie for Sass Brandt the actress. But Sass Brandt the producer? That was a questionable gamble. Despite rumors to the contrary, Hollywood wasn't willing to throw its money after just anything.

"Richard?"

"Huh?" Richard looked up, startled to realize he had drifted off.

"Questions?"

"Why didn't you call? Why didn't you tell me about this?"

Doug offered him a skeptical look instead of a explanation so Richard recanted. "Okay. Sorry. You had no obligation to tell me. Sass is my client, and I should have been on top of things. I've blown it big time. I should have . . ."

Richard was up and moving around his plush office. He looked less dapper than usual. The hair he tousled with one hand was sporting more gray than it had six months ago. His workout had been neglected and his suit was a bit rumpled. Possibly his financial house wasn't in good order, either. Sass's frivolity might affect Richard more dearly than Doug had at first imagined. There had been some talk that Richard had been seen with Sloane Marshall. No one was seen with Sloane Marshall unless they owed the lady.

"Is there anything we can recoup?"

Doug shook his head. "I don't know that there's anything I should, or could, do at this point without Sass's permission. If she didn't see fit to fill you in on the specifics, I don't think I can. It's her money, Richard. I think she can do what she pleases with it."

"But she shouldn't be throwing it away. Sass has

been acting irrationally ever since she got her teeth into this project. She needs guidance. She isn't able to function on this level by herself."

"Then I suggest you guide her, Richard. I gave her my input when she had me liquidate the bonds. The distribution of funds has been such that she's as protected as we could make her in a tax situation. There's going to be a big bite April fifteen, but we've done what we could. Other than that, what can I say? She earned the money, I guess she can blow it any way she wants. Now, do you want me to go over this line by line or can I leave?"

After Doug was gone, Shirley was back on the firing line.

"Want me to try to get Sass on the phone again?" she asked, knowing the look on Richard's face. She'd seen it only once before when Sass was hospitalized with pneumonia. Though Richard loved Sass like a daughter, bottom line was, she was a client— his only client— and she was as precious as Fort Knox.

"No." Richard shook his head, then went back to his desk. He gathered up the papers and held them in his hand, considering them. "No," he said again. He looked at Shirley, a decision made. "I want you to book me on the next flight to Ireland. A direct on Aer Lingus, if possible. No matter what, I want to arrive tomorrow morning. I've got to talk to Sass in person and it won't wait. She's gone too far. Everything we've worked for is on the line. Get me on a flight, Shirley. Get me on one now."

The snow was long gone but still the weather was cold. Shay had warmed the cabin with an expertly kindled fire. The long-drawn curtains were thrown back so the light streamed in, changing the face of the place he had lived so long. The pipes still froze, the wood still had to be carted in and lamps lit, but it was a better place than he had left it. The reason for all this was Sass.

First, and most laughable, living in her mansion by the sea had shown him exactly how much he loved his cabin. Beautiful though Sass's home was, it was not a place for him. He would be forever grateful to her for showing him that riches were not what he desired most in the world.

But Sass had also shown him the folly of his reclusive ways. Though he didn't like everyone he met these days— in town, on the road, those he had talked to at Sass's home— at least he had found his voice once more. Hiding was existing, not living, and hiding from memories was the most futile task of all. So he began to work again and it was a painful liberation. Yet no more the layabout Shay Collier, thanks to Sass.

Last, and certainly most important, Shay knew his house was different because she had been in it. Now and again he would have a vision, see her sitting by his fire, wearing his robe, lying upon his couch and realize that her presence would always be there to warm this place in which he lived.

So he sat looking out the window, considering the forest and the northern sun beyond, knowing he should be working. But today his mind was wandering. This was the week, if things had gone right, that Sass would finish shooting their— her—

movie. Funny how proprietorial he still felt, as if he had some stake in what she was doing.

Absentmindedly, he fingered the postcard Sass had sent him from Ireland. A silly thing, this picture of the cottages tourists loved and citizens hated for the lack of heat and the horrible plumbing. He didn't even know why he kept it except that every once in a while he thought he could smell Sass's scent clinging to it. Sometimes he assumed there was a flourish in her signature, an embellishment done to bring a smile to his face at her put-on pride.

When he realized what he was doing, Shay Collier rose from his desk and put the postcard back into the little cubbyhole where he kept the small items that were dear to him in this life. He went to the kitchen, pulling his well-worn sweater tight about his middle, running a hand through his long, wavy hair.

Though it was the middle of the day, he fixed himself some coffee with a dollop of whiskey in for good measure. Then Shay Collier set himself down in front of the fire, stretching his legs in front of him while he sipped from the steaming cup. Lazily he let his mind wander, hoping all had gone well for Sass. And, as he stared into the blaze, felt the warmth climbing from the soles of his feet to the middle of his heart, he realized that the color of the flames reminded him somehow of Sass. Perhaps her hair, perhaps her smile, perhaps only the suggestion of brilliance the fire brought to mind made him think of Sass.

Laying back his head Shay closed his eyes. In that darkness he saw her face that last night, the first day, every moment he'd known her; Shay, his heart newly born, his mind working once more, let himself be comforted by the thought of her. He was happy that she had her dream, happy that it was almost over and she would soon see the fruits of her labor. Perhaps he would go see the movie. Perhaps he could bear to live through that story again if only to see Sass Brandt's face once more.

Eleven

"Sass, come on, the light is looking good."

"Coming, Charlie."

Sass leaned into the mirror and flicked a tissue over her cheeks. Darling though she was, Meriam insisted on making her up as if this were opening night. She was supposed to be an Irish housewife, and housewives, especially when they are about to face their wronged husband, do not take time to do their face. Satisfied, Sass hopped down from the high chair, crumpled the paper bib at her neck, and tossed it away. Lisabet was on her in an instant.

"Here, let me."

Sass almost turned away. Lisabet didn't have enough to do and Sass knew, the second day in Ireland, that she should have been left behind to take care of the house. But, since she was here, Sass let her fuss. She raised her chin. Lisabet straightened the little lace collar, the simple strand of pearls that was the only adornment to Sass's costume. Finally she spent a moment on Sass's cardigan and stepped back.

"How do I look?" Sass asked, though the last thing she needed was Lisabet's input. She could feel how she looked. Perfect for the part. She was Moira.

"Fine," Lisabet answered.

"That's it?"

Lisabet's eyes clouded with confusion, unsure how to answer. She hadn't a clue that Sass was joking. "You look marvelous. But I still think you shouldn't be so dowdy. You've covered up your figure completely."

"And this isn't a beauty contest." Sass turned once more to the mirror. "Shay was very specific about the kinds of clothes his wife wore. That's what makes the betrayal all the more poignant. She wasn't a sexual creature in the sense that she flaunted her beauty, seducing the old man. That's the whole point: we are all vulnerable."

Satisfied, Sass grinned at Lisabet instead of the mirror and put her hand on the other woman's arm. "I don't know what I'm going to do with you and Curt. Honestly, you both have faces as long as anything I've ever seen. I thought you at least had some feel for this project."

"I do," Lisabet assured her, immediately responding to the praise, her face brightening until it almost looked beautiful. "Oh, Sass, I know this movie is the right thing for you now that you've done it. I just would like to see more life in it, that's all, something to show off your spark."

"This is better," Sass said brightly. "This shows off my heart, and that's what I've wanted to do for so long now. I was tired of choosing scripts because they showed off what was physically pleasing about me. Be happy, Lisabet. Look past the physical the way I hope the audiences will."

With that, Sass was out of the trailer, breathing deep of the gloriously pristine day. She greeted the crew as she saw them. Soon Lisabet could hear only the sound of her voice, not the words she used to call out her happiness. She moved to the doorway. There was a spring in Sass's step that had never been there as long as Lisabet had known her. With a sigh, Lisabet stepped down from the trailer, happy that the rain had stopped at least. She was tired of it and as anxious for the warmth of the sun as Curt.

"Feeling left out, Lisabet?"

"Richard!" Lisabet's head snapped up, her eyes narrowed. She didn't like surprises and this certainly was one. "What are you doing here?"

"Thought I'd pop in and see how things were going."

"And I'm Saint Patrick," Lisabet drawled, crossing her arms as Richard fell in step with her. He was dressed for L.A. in a suit and tie, shoes that had been beautiful until they hit the soggy soil of Ireland. He carried a briefcase, holding it tight as if it were precious.

"What a misery finding you," he complained.

"I wouldn't think it should be hard. Everyone on this side of the island knows we've been filming out here."

"I suppose I should have said it was a bitch getting here. The roads aren't exactly well kept."

"Beats sitting on the freeway though, don't you think?" Lisabet kept her eyes on Sass while she spoke. If Richard was here that meant trouble and Lisabet wanted to hear it first. That way she could figure out a way to soften whatever blow he was about to deliver. "What are you doing here, Richard?"

"Business."

"I figured that," Lisabet said. "What kind? Things are going well. There's nothing you could possibly do to wrap this up any quicker, and we're due back in L.A. in a few days. Somebody die while we were gone?"

"Almost. Sass has used up a good deal of her money shooting this thing."

"Just a good deal?"

"More than that," Richard said. "I'm worried."

"It's her money, Richard."

"It's our jobs, Lisabet," he reminded her, "and Sass's career. She's young, but not young enough to put back everything if this project fails. I don't think she understands that."

Richard stopped and Lisabet with him. They had come to the edge of the crowd that watched the goings-on. Old men dressed in black held their bicycles upright, young boys stood in knots chattering like magpies. Behind them the village silently stood guard over the antics. Ahead the land dropped off into the sea at the bottom of the cliffs. Richard had to admit this was a grand sight and a moving one. The film would be visually marvelous, he was sure. What he didn't know was if it would make any money. Before he could speculate Sass saw him and came running across the grass.

"Richard! My God, Richard! What are you doing here?"

Holding out his arms, Richard hugged her tight as she flung herself toward him. If Richard hadn't heard her voice he would have had to look twice at this woman to know it was Sass, so he held her away to get a better look. She was beautiful, shining with a loveliness he had never seen before. She glimmered, she shone, the light reflected from her only to come back and dance around that fabulous hair of hers.

"Sass, you look great," Richard said, feeling small. Somehow the worry about money seemed minor compared to the happiness the spending of it had brought. How could he possibly be so base as to think all the money in the world wasn't worth this? Thankfully, he came to his senses. Sloane Marshall held a personal note from him and was anxious for repayment. There was no time for sentimentality. "Sass. Listen. We've got to talk. Are you almost done?"

"We haven't even started." She laughed, pulling him along through the crowd, greeting some of the watchers by name as she went. "Give me a clue though. What horrid thing brings you here? Why didn't you call? Why . . ."

"Sass!"

Before she could finish her sentence, the director bellowed.

"I've got to run, Richard. Norman is a bear. But I think we're going to do it on the first take so it won't be long. We're in the home stretch, Richard, and it's looking great!"

With a kiss on Richard's cheek, Sass ran back to Curt and the cameras leaving Richard enthralled with her, the place, and this project. Lisabet had watched this too long to be overly interested.

"How long has she been like this?" Richard asked without looking at Lisabet.

"Since we got here. I think she's possessed."

"I hope it shows on film. She might actually have a hit on her hands if it does, and by God she needs it."

"Then she'll get it. She's Sass Brandt."

"Sass, come on. Cut the chatter."

Norman Childress, director and taskmaster, was in no mood to dillydally. The light was right and he was going to get this all important shot no matter what the star wanted to do. She could goof off when they wrapped.

"Sorry, Norm. Really. I'm sorry." Sass hid her smile behind her fingers. It was beginning, that wonderful giddiness that gripped her just before she knew she was about to step into a momentous scene. Desperately she tried to control her nervous giggles.

"Thank you," he answered. "Now, you're here. This is your mark." He drew a line in the patch of dirt. "Don't move from this mark until Curt let's you have it. When he slaps you, then you fall back and to the left. Once you're down on the ground, we'll cut. I'll shoot the expression after the actual slap."

"Okay. Got it."

Sass calmed down quickly, professionalism overcoming the mischievousness. Norm had Curt in hand now and was moving him back, exactly two steps away from Sass who gazed out over the fabulous sea. The view was fantastic, a coastline of cliffs that rivaled any natural wonder in the U.S. It was a gorgeous place.

"Sass!"

"Sorry, Norm." Sass adjusted her stance. She had to stop daydreaming.

"You're driving me nuts, Sass. Keep your mind on things."

Sass nodded, properly chastised. She forced herself to watch Curt and listen to Norm's instructions.

"Okay. Curt, you're arguing with her. You're hurt, you've just found out she's slept with your father. You've loved this woman all your life. I want to see the pain beneath the anger, and I don't want you screaming at her. I want your voice modulated as if you're keeping it all under control. But that pain is there, straining every word you manage to get out. Sass," Norm's hand was on her arm for emphasis, "tears. Streaming tears, but no frantic feeling in your voice, either. You know each other too intimately. You understand the depth of this man's feelings." Sass nodded. "Then, Curt, I want to see the welling of all that pain just before you slap her. Only I don't think I want a slap. I want you to backhand her. Pull that hand over your shoulder like this."

Norm showed them what he wanted, taking Curt's place to demonstrate. In slow motion he brought his hand over his shoulder and down at an angle toward Sass's face. She responded, equally slow, to get the feel of the cadence. Her head snapped back, her hands went to her face, she feigned a fall but remained upright so she didn't ruin her clothes until the camera was rolling. She smiled. It would be perfect with the sound effects and the proper camera angle.

"You try." Norm stepped away and Curt stood his mark. Once again they played the scene. Two then three times. "Think you're ready?"

The actors nodded. Norm stepped away and behind the camera. He checked the angle and the focus. He talked to the cameraman, giving last-minute directions. Curt looked down at the ground, building up his pain and anger. Sass stared out to sea, mesmerized by the color and the smell and the sound of the waves crashing below. She brought tears to her eyes, thinking of the saddest thing she could. It was Shay she thought of. Shay and his pain and the moment he and his wife stood like this on the cliffs trying to find a way to ease the anguish they both felt.

The tears came, blurring her vision. She barely heard Norm call for action. It was as if the crew had disappeared, as if this was reality and not just the retelling of it. She turned her head toward Curt and saw Shay. She listened to the words Curt said and heard Shay's voice. The accusations she heard, and the grief she felt, were her own.

So lost was she in the moment, Sass hardly knew if the words she spoke back were scripted. There were tears trailing down her cheeks, falling onto the plain blouse the likes of which Shay's wife would have worn. She felt her hands tremble and her knees become weak as if it were her sin that caused such heartache. In those moments, she, Sass Brandt, became the woman who lived at the end of the lane; she took upon herself the sins of that woman. Sass Brandt spoke and hurt and felt and moved as if here and now was the truth of it.

And, as she lost herself in the words, and threw

herself into the role, Sass Brandt moved as she wasn't supposed to move. Sass's feet left their mark by only an inch, for only a split second. But it was a split second too soon. Curt Evans had put everything he had into his role and his raised hand came down swift and hard, not missing her by an inch as a stage strike should, but catching her off guard. The blow landed square on the cheek sending her, not backward as it should, but forward to the right. Forward where the earth crumbled beneath her feet and no one was fast enough, or courageous enough, to reach out and try to catch Sass before she plunged off the cliff to the hard wet sand a hundred feet below.

"I thought she was dead."

Curt paced, though there was precious little room to do so. He hated Ireland for its small spaces, especially in a place like this. Here, where a person felt like they were about ready to jump out of their skin, there was a need to run or at least manage a long stride. "Where are those doctors? God, I can't believe this happened. Not in a place like this. We should be back at Cedar's where Sass could get the best care possible . . ."

"She is getting the best care possible, Mr. Evans."

Curt swung about. The doctor stood in the doorway looking tired, his surgical greens rumpled and stained. Curt blinked, not wanting to imagine what those stains might be. He moved back, still standing but aligning himself with Lisabet and Richard who sat on a low couch beneath a high window. The doctor joined them, falling into a chair that had seen better days. He lit a cigarette and ran a hand over his head, baring a balding pate as he wiped the green paper hat off with that gesture. Curt made no move to apologize for his statement, nor did anyone else speak. They allowed the doctor to rest a moment; he would say what he had to say in his own good time. It didn't take long. He snuffed out his cigarette, wasting most of it, then looked at the anxious group.

"Ms. Brandt is in very bad shape. We've done what we can, but so much of her was broken. Crushed actually." The doctor's voice shook a bit at the last. He had himself in hand a second later. "The wet sand was like concrete. It took the rescuers so long to get to her, then transport her properly that damage was done just by the passage of time. Ms. Brandt lost quite a lot of blood from the cuts and contusions she suffered as she fell." The small man shook his head and took a long, slow breath, his hands clasping and unclasping as if that might ease the stiffness in his fingers from the long hours of surgery. "Sure, Irish cliffs are as treacherous as our hills are gentle, and your work was taking place on a particularly unsafe point. Now I can't imagine that you'd chosen a place like that, or that someone hadn't warned you there might be some danger. So near the edge . . ."

He sighed with the thought of what might have been, but the lament triggered Curt's anger. He stepped forward, his body taut as if he might leap on this little man who had so recently held Sass's life in his hands.

"Goddamn you, do you think we wanted this to happen? Any of us?" Curt's head swung left and right, but Richard looked away and Lisabet let her lashes cover her eyes. "Do you think I did this on purpose? I swear, you think I don't have a brain in my head. It wasn't anyone's fault. It wasn't my fault. I swear, she moved just at the wrong time. She just stepped a little this way." Curt minced a step as if that would convince them all that he was blameless. Then he held out his hands to anyone who would listen to his plea. "It was an accident."

Lisabet was up reaching for Curt's taut body, touching the fists balled at his side. The tone of his voice frightened her. He was crazed with guilt and grief as they all were, but he felt the blame more painfully. He was the one who had inadvertently sent her spinning to the beach below and nothing could change that. Lisabet grasped his arm. He shook her off. He didn't seem to notice her at all, caged as he was in his anger, locked in a death stare with the doctor. Curt assumed he was accused— by all of them.

Lisabet swept in front of him in one deft movement. She took both his arms, holding on tight and shook him gently. Curt still wouldn't look at her. She tried again. Richard began to rise, but Lisabet stopped him with a look. His assistance wasn't needed.

"Curt," she said, so softly only he could hear. "Curt, no one is blaming you for anything. Do you hear me? We all saw it. It was a tragic, horrible accident. Do you understand? Curt?"

Surprising even herself, Lisabet reached up and laid her hand around the back of his neck. She felt him shudder, then he shivered and finally his frantic eyes were on hers. For the first time in their relationship Lisabet felt a bond with Curt Evans. Poor man. The horror he was reliving must be devastating.

Gently, Lisabet pulled him forward, urging him to her until she was able to wrap her arms around him. When finally she held him, Curt melted, giving in to his anguish, needing the comfort and companionship this woman had to offer. When he realized she wouldn't let go, when he realized it was all right not to be Curt Evans, the movie star, he collapsed into Lisabet's arms, wrapping his own around her as he sobbed.

"I didn't mean it, Lisabet. Honestly, I don't know what happened. How could this have happened? My Sass. How could it be?"

Hushing him like a child, Lisabet lowered him to the couch, Richard moving, reaching up to touch him, wishing he had the guts to simply break down and cry, too. He felt it, the sense of loss that surrounded Sass. It had been that way since the moment they hovered around her in the helicopter on their way to Dublin. They had left the crew, the townsfolk, they had left the equipment and the scripts and rushed with her, the only sounds uttered prayers for her life.

Now Richard imagined they should have perhaps prayed for her death. This doctor was giving them news that was far worse than that which they had all imagined. The doctor began to talk again when he thought they were ready to hear what he had to say.

"Miraculously, Miss Brandt has suffered no major head injuries. She has a concussion, there were many stitches. Her right arm was cut rather severely. It appears she can't move it and we're not sure why. No nerve damage is evident and the muscles are intact. The paralysis might simply be a function of shock, of her inability to respond to our directions because of medication. Until she's conscious we won't truly know what is wrong with that arm." The doctor shifted, moving his weight forward, looking each in the eye in turn. They were down to it now. "Her pelvis is broken, ribs, too." Lisabet moaned but remained rigid. "Unfortunately her legs took the full force of the fall. Her left was shattered, her right isn't in much better shape, but I doubt it should need additional surgery."

"What do you mean, shattered?" Richard asked, realizing the implications could be far-reaching for him as well as Sass.

"I mean that it will be amazing if her leg can be saved," came the steady answer.

The doctor made a routine prognosis. With it, all sound in the room ceased. The three people on the couch stopped breathing. The echo of Curt's muttering and sobbing hung in the air, vying with the reverberation of the doctor's pronouncement. It was the doctor's words everyone remembered. They crashed about in Richard's head, screamed in Lisabet's, and shrieked in Curt's. A less than perfect Sass. Sass no longer whole. Sass no longer beautiful. Sass no longer bankable.

" 'Tis sorry, I am," the doctor whispered. He had given this kind of news a hundred times. It was no worse, nor any better, because the woman

in question was a movie star. The news hurt and
shocked the same, rich or poor.

Lisabet nodded. Curt fell back onto the sofa and
Richard just sat, unable to move, his face as pale
as a new moon. Finally he lowered his head and
buried his face in his hands.

"Can we see her?" Lisabet asked, recovering her
sense before the other two. There were things to
be done, after all, and she wanted to see the situation for herself before any decisions were made.

The doctor drew a weary hand over his tired
eyes. "It won't do you much good. She'll be se-
dated for quite a bit."

"I understand." Lisabet rose and was almost out
the door when she turned back. "Curt?"

He looked up, his eyes unfocused, face drawn
and not quite so handsome any longer.

"What?" he asked, his voice hollow and his
query only a rote response to the calling of his
name.

"The doctor said we could see Sass."

"Oh."

He looked at Richard as though the older man
would give him permission to stay where he was.
But Richard didn't bother to look back. For the
first time in his life, Curt Evans was on his own.
Nobody was going to tell him what to do, give him
what he wanted or make sure he was comfortable.
This was a life lesson Curt had imagined he would
never have to learn. Ugliness had been skirted all
of his years, though he confidently thought he'd
left it behind. Now something monstrous had run
right around him and was waiting up ahead. To
his credit, his moment of indecision lasted no

longer than the blink of an eye. He pushed himself off the couch and ran his hands through his hair.

"I'm coming."

He joined Lisabet and, arm in arm, they followed the doctor who walked ahead of them. He led them to a room that seemed larger than the others and stood back. Lisabet went in first; Curt hovered at the door needing to feel comfortable with the scene before he stepped in and faced his lover. When he did, he took it all in with a practiced eye. The white room, bare and painfully clean. There was no television, no radio, no phone. The walls were empty except for a rough-hewn crucifix above the bed and even that was not much to see. Obviously this was not a state-of-the art situation. But the bed was high and narrow and the bedclothes pristine. A window, open to the air, graced the opposite wall. Now and again the gauzy white curtains that hung over it fluttered, rising on the breeze like the wings of an angel in flight.

And finally, there was Sass— Sass whom he could barely recognize. Her head was wrapped in bandages, her long hair, he imagined, was gone, cut to allow the doctors to do what they had to do. An IV ran into her right arm, dripping gently into a needle inserted under her pallid flesh.

Curt looked away, his hand covering his muscled stomach. For a moment he wasn't sure if he could do this. The paleness of her flesh was unnerving. There was no contour to her cheeks, no delicacy to those hands that had so often held and caressed him. Her slimness was shocking, her body so inordinately delicate Curt feared the breeze might pick her up and whisk her away, scattering Sass Brandt to the winds of Ireland before she was ash.

And her face. Her beautiful face! Both eyes were blue and purple and black, one side swollen grossly so that half of her was unrecognizable. That Curt could accept. Yes, he could understand that she was bruised and beaten, but when he looked further, his eyes traveling down to the legs that so worried the doctor, he had to turn away. Both were in casts. Her left was contorted and raised to a most horrid position. Huge pins stuck out from the plaster at the oddest of angles. The right was equally formidable, dressed in plaster but there were no pins, no unearthly twist of flesh and bone.

Curt's stomach heaved and his head felt light. He swayed, reaching for the jamb to hold him steady only to find a warm soft hand at the ready. Curt opened his eyes and found himself staring at the kind of woman central casting adored. She was so very small, slight and kindly looking. From head to toe she was swathed in black, her wrinkled little face framed by some kind of starched white fabric, a veil covered her from crown to heel. The lady had the ear of God, certainly. She'd pledged her youth and her love to him in another millennium, Curt was sure, and his symbol hung heavily on her breast.

"She needs you, sir," the nun said, her brogue adding a touch of wisdom to her sincerity.

"Yes, Sister," Curt answered, wishing she would let go of his hand. But God was with her, and she was determined to pass along His comfort to Curt Evans.

"She may never be the same, you know. To be sure, you'll have to care for her, watch her, help her face the life she must live now."

That was enough. Curt pulled his hand away from her two small dry ones. She patted Curt on the shoulder and walked away, the soft click of rosary beads sounding her leaving.

"Jesus," Curt muttered, sweat popping out on his forehead, a chill grabbing hold of his body until it quivered almost uncontrollably.

He knew what had frightened him, he understood why he felt so bad, but there was no way in hell he was going to admit it to that woman. He loved Sass, and to think for a minute that he couldn't love her scarred, was to betray her. What kind of bastard was he to even allow that thought in his head? Frantically he wiped his brow, tugged at the collar of his shirt, realizing for the first time how unkempt he was.

He hadn't thought to change, hadn't even considered what had happened to him as he desperately scrambled down the cliff toward Sass, screaming her name, cutting his hands as he was turned back time and time again by the lay of the land. That, he assured himself, proved he loved her. He had tried to save her at great personal risk. The other—that horrible thought that he might not be able to love her now—had been an aberration.

Drawing on the only reserves he had, Curt willed himself to become a hero. In his mind he saw himself saving Sass and this, going to her bedside, was the first scene. After that he would nurse her, make sure that life returned to normal and

Sass remained the star she was. He would make her beautiful again. His fortunes would rise with hers; his story would be equally as moving. They would meet the world together, paragons of virtue and courage in the face of tragedy. That's how it would be. He was ready for this moment, because the ones he saw in their future were still filled with notoriety, riches, and beauty.

Shaking back his hair, looking once more at the scratches on the palms of his hand and the dirt embedded in his nails, Curt became the champion he could never be in reality. He went to the bed where Lisabet already sat holding Sass's hand. Lisabet looked as if there wouldn't be a tomorrow.

Curt smiled. He was the only one who knew. There would be a tomorrow. Of that he was sure. He didn't allow himself to wonder if he would be there to share it with Sass Brandt. He was here now. That was all that mattered.

"Don't, Lisabet. Don't do that. I don't want to do those damn exercises. They hurt."

"Sass, if you don't you're never going to get any better. Your legs need to have movement on a regular basis or you'll lose all the ground you gained after the last surgery. You should be so grateful that you even have both your legs, but now you're acting like a spoiled child. You've got to get back on your feet."

"It doesn't matter if I'm on my feet or not," Sass complained. "Even if I could walk, I doubt I could storm into anyone's office and get a straight answer about anything. I don't know what's happening with the production. Richard is always out of town these days, Curt's either telling me to hush or he's acting like Florence Nightingale or he's gone on location. I'm sick of doctors and sick of therapists and I'm sick of Curt disappearing the minute I ask him for something a little more intimate than a bouquet of flowers or my pillows fluffed. And you! You act as if everything would be set to rights if I could just get up and take a stroll!"

Lisabet swallowed all the words she wanted to say. Instead, she simply said, "Sass, you're going to upset yourself."

"I'm already upset, Lisabet," Sass wailed, her fingers plucking frantically at the long linen skirt she wore to cover her injuries. "I feel useless and unhappy and out of control. Why can't anyone understand that? Why can't someone just sit down with me and give me a rundown on the *The Woman At the End of the Lane?*"

"Have you ever thought that we do understand what you're going through, and we're all trying to help you in every way we can? Nothing matters about the movie except that it's on hold. Nothing can happen until you get yourself on your feet again and shoot those last scenes."

How easily those words spilled out of Lisabet's lips. She didn't even blink as she spun her tale. Those scenes would never be shot, everyone knew that. They had all moved on with their lives. Curt was working, Richard floundering about for new clients. Curt was enjoying a boon while Richard found the going rough. He was too old now and had been exclusive too long. The hot properties he hoped to represent were already happily ensconced with other managers. Only Lisabet remained with Sass and was content to do so. The small lie wouldn't hurt and that carrot might be enough to get her up and moving with a cane. Sass would soon enough figure out what was what. Lisabet smiled, and if Sass had paid attention she would have noticed the shadow of patronization.

"Don't be ridiculous," Sass complained. Her voice strained as she tried to twirl the great wheels on her chair so that she could at least look at Lisabet as she flitted about the room. Giving up, she steadied herself and pled her case. "There are five scenes left to do. We could do all of them without me standing. That's not a problem. My voice isn't affected."

"What about your hair? The entire thing was shot with you in a long bob. What are you going to do about that?" Lisabet countered and Sass thought there was a note of triumph in her voice.

Sass clamped her mouth shut and turned her face away to look out of the bank of windows. That one hurt. She almost reached up to touch the fine silky hair that had grown so slowly in the last six months. How she missed her long hair. It would take forever for it to grow back the way it was. Even with all the fabulous talent in Hollywood, there wasn't a hairdresser in town who could do anything to make her look gorgeous until she had enough hair to do something with. Looking in the mirror was always such a shock. Her doelike eyes peered out of her head above pinched cheeks and under the fringe of bangs that looked so little like the full waves they had cut off.

"We could work with wigs," she muttered, knowing she was grasping at straws.

"Not on the close-ups, Sass," Lisabet answered before coming 'round the wheelchair that had become Sass's lifeline. Bending her knees, Lisabet balanced on the balls of her feet and imprisoned her charge as she put her hands on the arms of the chair. "Listen to me, Sass. You can't act now. That's all there is to it. You don't look like yourself. You're an invalid. You've been very ill and it shows. I don't mean to hurt your feelings, but I have to be blunt. You know this yourself. I've seen you look away from the mirror. I've helped you in the shower and know that you haven't even taken the time to really look at your injuries or understand them."

"Would you, Lisabet?" Sass shot back. "Would you want to look in the mirror and not recognize the person you see? Would you want to wake up in the morning and stretch your legs only to find that one won't go as far as the other? Would you want to try to hold a cup only to find that you need both hands?"

"No," Lisabet answered. "I wouldn't want a moment of the pain you've suffered, but I would take it from you if I could. I would take every scratch and bruise as my own if it would help so that you could get back to that precious movie of yours." Lisabet's hand let loose of the cold metal and hovered near Sass's cheek, but fell back in place when she saw Sass stiffen. Lisabet pushed herself up and away, ashamed she had so embarrassed herself.

"But, Sass, I wouldn't want to do what you're doing now, either. I wouldn't fool myself that a bit of makeup and a wig could make me what I was. You may never be like you were. You have to consider that. You have to make plans for a future that doesn't include acting."

"Don't be absurd. The doctors I have are the best. They tell me I'm going to be just fine."

"Did they say you'd be perfect again?"

Lisabet towered above the woman who, at one time, had seemed larger than life. Funny how good that felt, to look down on her. Not that it gave Lisabet a sense of power, only a sense that she was needed. Though it was hard to acknowledge, Lisabet knew, that in the cold light of day, this accident had been the best thing that ever happened to her. There wasn't a place Sass could go, a task she could perform without some help and Lisabet was always there to give it. Curt's devotion had been surprising initially, but it soon became evident he would only lavish his care in the most romantic, and staged, ways. When it came to the necessities— dressing Sass, bathing Sass, fixing her food, holding the phone when her arms tired— Curt had more often than not slipped away.

Yes, this felt good to Lisabet and now Sass was tiring of it all. She wanted to work again. Though Lisabet nagged at Sass to do her exercises, to follow her therapy, secretly she was glad that Sass seemed unable, or unwilling, to find the drive to do so. Lisabet sighed, disappointed in herself. Sometimes her thoughts were awful. But those times came less often as Sass came to rely upon her more and more.

"Did they tell you they would make you as good as new, Sass?" Lisabet asked again.

"No, no one has told me that," she said. With that admission went another bit of her energy, another bit of hope and Lisabet rejoiced at its passing. There would be plenty of time for Sass to tackle something new.

"Then you should tell them," Lisabet insisted for show. "You should show them what Sass Brandt can do. Do it for me, for yourself, but don't do it for that movie. That's not going to happen right now. It's just not, Sass."

Lisabet smiled, positive she'd given her speech with just the right inflection of concern and resignation.

Sass swung her head toward Lisabet, her eyes hooded and suddenly mysterious. For a long while she looked at Lisabet, considering what had been said, weighing her options. She had never been so tired in her life. The exhaustion dogged her from morning to night, the pain woke with her and slept with her— more often than Curt did these days. She didn't want to work on her body, she simply wanted it back. She didn't want to look at her legs or find out that she'd never be able to raise her arm higher than her shoulder. If she was working, then she wouldn't think about these things, then her body might heal on its own. But of course she knew that was silly; a hopeless wish. She was just so damn scared and there was no one she trusted to tell.

Curt was seldom home anymore. Lisabet seemed content to stand guardian angel. And Richard! He had managed to all but disappear. She'd hated all of it, but not until this moment did she realize what she detested most about all of this misery: if Lisabet was right, then Sass's promise to Shay would be broken. All the talk of dreams, the vision they had shared, would never become reality. Not that he would ever know. Shay hadn't called. He hadn't even bothered to send a note or inquire from Lisabet about her progress. Shay Collier had forgotten her just as sure as the rest of the world had.

"Lisabet," Sass finally said, "I want you to call Richard now. I want to meet with him at four. Don't take no for an answer. Then I want you to come back here. Bring me a sandwich and some ice cream, a piece of cake. Anything with calories. I've got to put a few pounds on. You're right. We're going to exercise. That movie will be finished. If I don't look right now, I will in two months or four or six more. There will be a day when I'll look right and sound right. I might even walk right. But that movie will be finished if I have to kill myself doing it."

"Sass, you know this isn't what I meant when I said you should exercise," Lisabet objected.

"I don't care what you meant," Sass answered, smiling for the first time in a very long while. "I need a challenge. I need to get my act together. I might even take it on the road." She laughed, thinking how wonderful it would be to find Shay and hand him a finished reel even if he had been a heel and kept his distance during this awful time. "Now get a move on. I haven't got all day. I've wasted too much time as it is."

Lisabet opened her mouth only to shut it again. There was no arguing now. This was the old Sass, and Lisabet didn't like the resurrection. It was too soon. If Sass did what she said, if she managed a miracle just to finish that movie, then everything would be as it was before. That was something Lisabet couldn't abide. Sass shooed her away. Off Lisabet went, wanting to be alone to think. Ignoring the kitchen, she went directly to the phone. Lunch could wait.

"Richard? Lisabet. Sass wants to see you today at four." Lisabet listened to all the objections, to the lame excuses. She knew exactly what was going on. Richard was a coward and didn't want to tell Sass what Lisabet already knew. There wasn't much money left. Hadn't Lisabet already seen the effects of Sass's idiocy with this movie? The therapists and doctors and healing paraphernalia were costing a fortune Sass didn't have anymore. The gardens weren't as pristine as they were before, the chauffeur was no longer available, the grocery no longer delivered their exotic wares.

When Richard was done with his excuse, when he had exhausted every reason, Lisabet said again, "Four o'clock. I expect we'll see you?"

To that, Richard answered with a very weary and resigned yes.

Twelve

Lisabet slipped into the darkened bedroom. Sass still looked out the window seeming not to notice that the day had departed and night was upon them. Her huge eyes looked through that window, toward the wall topped with barbed wire, to the sea that lay calmly beyond. She didn't acknowledge Lisabet: not when she came into the room, not when she straightened the covers that lay across Sass's lap, not when Lisabet murmured words of comfort and encouragement. The silence scared Lisabet half to death. Sass had never been like this. Even after the accident and the surgeries, she had managed to speak. Even then she moved to let Lisabet know that all was not lost. But this silence, these hours of banishment, Lisabet couldn't stand. It was as if Sass had gone away, forgetting to take her battered body with her, expecting Lisabet to pack it up and send it along when she could.

"Sass?" Lisabet couldn't help trying once more. "You should eat something."

Silence.

"Maybe you should sleep instead of sitting up in bed. Let me help you lay down. You'll be more comfortable."

Silence with a twist. There was an almost imperceptible stiffening when Lisabet came close with arms out to cradle Sass and ease her on to her back. Lisabet panicked.

"I'm sorry," she said, flustered, dying to help and to hold and to make Sass's worries simply disappear. If only she could wipe away the last few months she would, she would have died rather than have Sass go through the last few hours.

There seemed nothing to do. She looked around the room that was so familiar and at once so foreign. In the old days she had hated watching Sass go into this room every night with Curt. Now she would rejoice if Sass leapt from her bed and locked her out of the room forever; she would be delighted if Sass threw herself into nights of wild abandon with Curt, or any man for that matter. If only Sass would say something to let Lisabet know that she was not forgotten, not shut out completely.

Taking a deep breath Lisabet was about to try to communicate with Sass again when she realized they were not alone. In the doorway stood a man, a shadow that filled the doorway. Lisabet gasped and stepped to the side, ready to protect Sass with her life. But it was only Curt moving into the moonlit room. He walked slowly and sadly as if he, too, had taken the melancholy in this house as his own.

"Sass?" He spoke quietly, ignoring Lisabet. "Sass? We need to talk."

"Not now, Curt."

Lisabet had come around the bed, reaching out, touching Curt and pulling him back toward the door. He shook her off.

"Cut it out, Lisabet. I've got to talk to Sass."

"Now's not the time. Richard was here. She's not feeling well."

"I'm sorry," he said, keeping his eyes on the still figure in her bed. "Sass, I need to talk to you. It's okay to talk to you, isn't it?"

Slowly Sass swiveled her head until she faced the two people at the foot of her bed. She looked at them blankly and didn't speak. Curt Evans needed no other consent. He didn't smile; what he had to say was nothing to smile about.

"Get out of here, Lisabet." Curt didn't look her way, his gaze was riveted on Sass.

Lisabet tried to touch him again, but he moved out of range, rounding the bed to sit beside Sass in the dark. Angrily, she watched the two of them. It was almost as if nothing had changed. In the moonlight Sass looked beautiful even with the short crop of hair.

Banished, knowing there was nothing to be done now, Lisabet turned on her heel and left them alone. She closed the door behind her. When she heard the click of the lock, Lisabet lay her cheek against it, wishing she could help. But wishes did no good. Slowly, sadly, she pushed herself away from the door, but found it impossible to leave. Quietly she went across the hall and settled herself in the guest room. There she watched Sass's door, listened for the sounds of love or distress, listened for anything that would give her a clue as to what it was Curt Evans was saying to the suddenly silent, suddenly beaten Sass Brandt.

* * *

"It's good to see you. I guess I didn't realize how long it's been since I've been home."

Curt waited for some sign that she was ready to listen, but Sass remained mute, unable or unwilling to give him her full attention. That was just as well. He wasn't sure he could look directly into her eyes when he told her what he had to say. Courage waning, Curt moved toward the bedside table, his hand on the lamp when Sass said, "Don't."

Her voice was lifeless. She didn't move. Curt did as she asked and backed away without turning on the light. It was a relief in a way. He'd rather do this in the dark.

"Okay, no problem." Curt stuffed his hands into the pocket of his trousers. The dark and Sass's demeanor were eerie. Suddenly he felt the need to open the door or the window, to get a breath of fresh air into this room. It looked less like a boudoir and more like a hospital every day. But he knew she wouldn't want him to do any of those things so the only thing left was to talk. "Okay, Sass. There's no other way to do this."

He rounded the bed and sat near her, but not close enough to hold her, touch her. Sass looked at him without curiosity; it seemed she looked right through him. Her gaze, once focused on that faraway horizon, still saw the ends of the earth and not the man sitting so close.

"What I have to say is going to hurt you, Sass. Hell, it hurts me and I know it's a cowardly thing to do. But I think it would be worse if we didn't clear the air." Curt moved on the bed, smoothed the covers, took a good long hard look at the ruby ring on her finger. He did everything he could think of that would keep him from looking at her. "What I mean is, this is difficult. I'm afraid to say the words, but I'm afraid not to because I think I'm going crazy with the way things are, Sass." Sass blinked, but she didn't speak. Gathering his courage, Curt took a deep breath and said, "I'm leaving, Sass. I've made arrangements to move into a place of my own. I think it will be better. You'll have the house to yourself to recuperate. I'm hardly here anyway, I've been so busy lately. I . . ."

What else could he say? He expected to feel better and he only felt worse. Why wouldn't she cry or something? That would at least prove she'd heard him. It would, at least, be some punishment for what he knew was a spineless retreat. Just when he should be attacking with all his might, trying to save the woman he loved from a worthless future, he was running.

"Sass, say something. I know I'm a heel. This is about the worst thing I could do to you, babe. I've really tried to do what's right in this situation. Nobody could fault me for not trying, could they, Sass?"

Curt stood up. He paced in front of the window. Her eyes followed him. Those huge eyes, so big and sad and looking so blankly out of her gaunt face. He looked away, angered that she hadn't the courtesy to meet him halfway, to help him through this awful moment.

"Sass, I can't help it. I have a life, too. I need to be able to work and go out and not worry if you need something. I've gone to therapy with you, but the therapy isn't working. I keep trying to hope and you know I love you, but I guess I don't love you the way I should. Sass . . ." Curt stopped. The least he could do was to be completely honest. "I thought I loved you the forever kind of way, but I was wrong. I can't think of you as being Sass when you can't walk and you don't look like you used to.

"I didn't know that what I felt for you was tied up in the way you look, but how couldn't it be? I mean, the way you look is what you are, Sass. That's why you were in the movies." He heard himself use the past tense and cringe. Quickly he defended himself. "Even you'd have to admit to that. Even you have to admit that you can't feel the same way about yourself." Two strides and he was beside her, kneeling by the bed, his hands clasping hers even though he didn't want to touch. He feared she would cling to him and beg him to stay. She did neither.

"Sass, say something. Tell me I'm a shit. Scream at me. I know that this isn't the kind of thing that's supposed to happen in a great love story. But I'd do you no good if I stayed away and resented you, or couldn't touch you or love you the way you should be loved."

He was running out of words now. The more he talked the more horrible this whole thing sounded. Maybe he was the lowest of the low, but Curt couldn't help the locked-in, useless, frantic feelings he had. That was reality and the best script in the world couldn't make this sound good.

"Sass, come on, talk to me. Say you under-stand. Let me go with your blessing, and then you can get on with your life. I won't be an extra burden. Sass."

Curt waited, aware that Sass's eyes hadn't moved, her hand hadn't responded to his touch. She stared at a spot he had once occupied but paid no attention to him now. Curt shot up, embarrassed and tired of begging. She wasn't going to get to him with this act of hers. He wasn't going to belittle himself anymore.

"Please, Sass, do me the courtesy of looking at me. It's taken me weeks to get up the courage to do this. I know everybody's going to hate my guts for a while, but I've got to do what's good for me, too. I'll take my licks, just don't play this game with me. Say something now, or I'm out of here, and that's not the way I want it to be."

Sass blinked. Her hands jerked. A tremor ran along her jaw. She looked at him as if she'd been rudely awakened from a deep, restless sleep.

"I've no money left to do my movie, Curt. There isn't anything left."

Curt froze. This wasn't what he expected and the surprise threw him off guard. When Sass laughed, a dry and guttural sound, a shudder gripped him with such force he almost lost his footing.

"Richard told me the banks are calling in their loans. The investors are taking their losses, and won't give me another cent. The insurance has already begun to pay off. It's like I'm dead, not injured. I've run through more than two-thirds of my own money producing the movie. I haven't any more money to give."

Sass sighed. For the first time she looked at

Curt, truly looked at him. Her eyes sparkled in the moonlight, luminous and frightened and disillusioned.

"Oh, my God." Curt leaned back against the wall, his mouth open as he stared at her. "Sass, that can't be. You own half of Malibu, you've got . . ."

"Nothing I can touch," Sass finished for him, her voice weak with resignation. "Real estate that can be sold for pennies on the dollar, tax-free funds that can't be liquidated. I can't even run the household the way it used to be. Winifred's already gone. Richard even suggested I sell this place if I can. But the market is bad."

Sass's eyelashes fluttered. It seemed hard for her to keep her mind on the conversation. With a great effort she tried to smile.

"So you see, Curt, you're not the only one who wants to leave. You're just one of many, my love. Just one of many. So go away and leave me alone. I'm tired. So very, very tired."

Sass lay her head back on the pillows Lisabet had so carefully piled behind her. She sunk into the down, adoring the richness of the Egyptian cotton covers. All her life she had luxuriated in the fine things she owned. Sass couldn't even remember when she and her mother lived without the trappings of wealth. Since childhood, people had flocked to her, wanting her to perform, to be their friend, to help them gain something she already had. All her life she could pick and choose who would be graced with her companionship, her love, and her interest. Now backs were turning, people were fleeing, even the man she loved was bowing out of her life.

Amazingly, it didn't matter. Later it might, but these last few hours had been spent in limbo, time filled with complete and utter nothingness. Her body had been hurt so badly, her mind wounded by lack of faith, her heart was pierced by the arrows of deceitful mutterings of artificial people. There was nothing to do but stay in her bed and lick her wounds and Sass wasn't even sure if there was even the strength for that.

"Sass, I'm so sorry."

Curt's words came to her, he didn't. He stood silhouetted against the window and Sass didn't even have to open her eyes to know how he looked. He looked perfectly handsome, tall and heroic. But poor Curt wasn't a champion. He was all thumbs when it came to tragedy. He couldn't run through it or rise above it or meet it head-on. Sass couldn't blame him. She doubted she had the stuff heroines were made of, either.

"I know you're sorry, Curt," she said, but her voice was the whisper of a woman exhausted beyond human endurance. Sass had no experience to draw on to see her through this darkness; she could only hope somewhere, deep in her soul, there was a reserve of strength that would rescue her. Such a puzzle. One too complex for her to figure out now.

"Is there anything I can do, Sass?"

She wanted to laugh, to ask for suggestions. What on earth could she say? Stay, Curt? Love me, Curt? Act like the man who promised to cherish me in sickness and in health? At least there was that to be thankful for. They hadn't married.

"No, Curt," she said, her lips curling into a

smile of sorts. "There's nothing you can do that I can't do for myself. The question is, do I want to do it any more than you?"

"Of course you do," Curt said quickly and without conviction. Instead there was alarm in his encouragement. If she failed to believe she had the wherewithal to survive and triumph, then Sass Brandt might call in her marker. He owed her a lot: money, the years he lived in this house, parts she got him with a word in the right ear. She could bind him to her with a snap of her fingers. Thankfully, Sass proved herself a better woman than he was a man.

"Yes, I suppose I'll want to try again. After a while. But it will take a long, long time. I can't expect you to stay with me. I would never have expected that."

Sass turned her head; there was a small smile on those beautiful lips of hers. Curt watched, seeing in this one moment all the beauty she had possessed before the accident. His body betrayed him and for one instant he thought to slip into the bed beside her. He would touch her, hold her, and make her whole again. But the magic wasn't there any longer and he wasn't God. Nor was this a movie where the script called for a miraculous recovery, for legs to heal and hair to grow and arms to be strong to hold back. This was life at its most tragic. He could hardly wait to be gone. That was shameful, but he had to go and Sass knew it.

"There's no need to stay, Curt," Sass whispered. "I'm going to sleep now. I have to sleep. Tell Lisabet you're going. She'll take care of everything."

Curt thought something more should be said,

but the moon had disappeared behind a cloud and the room was too dark to see if Sass might be waiting to hear more. Fighting down his self-loathing, Curt raised his head high and squared his shoulders. He had told the truth. That, at least, was something to be proud of. Holding that thought, he walked the breadth of the huge bedroom, opened the door, and took one last look at the woman with whom he'd shared this house.

The beautiful ring that sealed their promise of everlasting love still sparkled on her finger, but it no longer looked quite as impressive as it had months ago. He wondered how long she would wear it, if Sass would look at it and hope he would return. He prayed she wouldn't. Because Curt Evans would never be back.

Quietly he closed the door behind him and, in the dark, Sass Brandt slipped off Curt's ring. She held it in her leadened hand and, as that hand fell over the side of the bed, as the sleep of despair embraced her, Sass let the ring fall to the floor.

Thirteen

It was a stunning day. The sun was shining, the breeze was barely there, and the temperature had hit a perfect seventy-five degrees. This was one of those I-feel-alive-and-worthwhile-and-successful days. Everyone, young or old, rich or not, was infused with the sense that anything was possible. And it was on this day, feeling this kind of soulful power, that Shay Collier drove his rental truck up the long and winding road leading to the impressive gates that closed Sass Brandt off from the world.

Months ago, returning from a hunting trip, Shay heard of Sass's misfortune. The accident, the movie closure, the fact that her dream had been just this close to reality when it was shattered into a million cosmic shards, was news that broke his heart. He had thought to call, to go to her immediately. But, torturous as it was, he held back. Sass had Curt. She had Richard and Lisabet. There was money to buy the best medical care, friends to ease her pain and, from what he had learned, Sass's injuries, while serious, weren't life threatening.

So Shay restrained himself. He lost himself in

his work only to find that every word he penned reminded him of Sass, of her smile, of her heart, of her vision. By the saints, he was worried and, until he knew the truth, nothing he wrote would be worth a snap.

So he called— and called— reaching a machine more often than not. When he managed to rouse Lisabet, he was given one of a hundred excuses why Sass couldn't come to the phone. Lisabet was polite. She was considerate. She often told Shay that Sass sent her best. But the more he persisted, the more adamant Lisabet became: Sass couldn't come to the phone.

Finally the calls left Shay troubled. There was something in Lisabet's voice, some anger that flew across the line connecting them, that left him sick with worry.

So Shay Collier put down his pen and his fanciful, fictional thoughts. He couldn't write about what might be, if he wasn't sure what was. He began to call. He called the production assistant who had first told him of Sass's misfortune. He called Curt's publicist and was told the gentleman in question was out of state shooting. Finally he called Kelly Karter, the columnist who had kindly escorted him into Sass's house the night he gave her his father's book. It was she who told him all he needed to know.

Curt was gone. Sass hadn't been seen. Work on *The Woman At the End of the Lane* had stopped. The movie was a dead issue. All was quiet where Sass Brandt was concerned— too quiet for Shay's liking.

Now here he was, standing on the shoulder of a road that had been built specifically for Sass, looking at the white palace she called home. He felt the sun warming him, the breeze tickling him. He wished Sass was here talking to him. Soon she would be if he had his way.

Leaving the truck and pocketing the keys, Shay sauntered toward the gates, his heart and mind reaching out to touch the life inside this silent place. They had done it before, he and Sass, and if she were well, if she could, she would reach right back out to him. But there was nothing. Not a sound, not a vibration, not a soul-melting moment from which he could draw hope.

His brow furrowed, his mouth turned down. Shay Collier shook back his hair and raised his hand to his neatly trimmed beard. Suddenly he was aware of his body: the strength of it, the height and width of it. It was disconcerting that the aloneness he felt made him so aware of himself, as if he were the last man standing on this great green earth.

Taking a deep breath, looping one thumb over the belt strung through his well-worn jeans, he reached up with the other and pushed the buzzer on the security box. Squinting up against the sun, he shaded his eyes and took note of the camera pointed his way. It wasn't operating, the little red light was dead and the lens was dusty. He buzzed again and once more. The final time he left his finger on the button and took a closer look at the rust on the gate, the overgrown weeds on the drive. Now he wanted in and nothing was going to stop him.

* * *

"Look, Sass, all your magazines have come. I've just gone through the mail and every single one came today. Curt's mentioned in the *Hollywood Reporter*, too. I thought you might like to see that."

Lisabet twirled into the chair next to Sass's, plopping herself down. She was so happy, felt so free now that it was just the two of them, alone in this marvelous house. The solitude was downright invigorating. Perfection would be if Sass were as happy with the arrangement as she was, but that would come in time. Until then, Lisabet would keep on her happy face.

"Sass, I've brought you some mail, too. Not as many letters as a few months ago, but that's understandable. People tend not to write as often as they should. Look, though, here's a lovely get-well card from a little girl in Indiana. She drew the picture herself. And here's another from that man who wants to marry you. He never gives up, does he?"

Lisabet clucked and fussed and arranged the mail in meticulous stacks Sass probably wouldn't touch. Not that this worried Lisabet. She would read to Sass tonight after she got her ready for bed. She would push the chair into the house, the chair Sass hadn't risen from since Curt left and Richard had delivered his horrible news. She would bathe Sass and massage her legs and dress her in a sensible flannel gown. Then she would read to her and another day would be done.

Sass had nothing better to do, after all. She couldn't make a movie if she couldn't walk. One day, perhaps Sass might write or direct, but first she had to come to grips with the fact that the glory days were over. With one more abrupt thump on the mail pile, Lisabet stood up again and touched Sass's hair.

"Well, I suppose you don't need anything. Do you want me to comb your hair? It's growing out rather nicely. A bit curlier than it was, but that's all right. I think it makes you look very sweet." Sass shook her hair, unaware she was trying to shake off the hand that touched her with such familiarity. "All right then. I'll go in now, and get us some lunch. It's such a lovely day, we can eat out here, then it will be time for your nap. That will be nice, won't it? A salad? Maybe a sandwich? I'll see what we have."

Lisabet fairly danced up the steps and across the large veranda, through the huge glass doors that at one time had been opened to interesting, creative people. She didn't miss the noise at all and was almost sure Sass didn't either— not that Sass ever said anything one way or the other.

Inside, the house was cool and dark even though the sun shined through the floor-to-ceiling windows. Lisabet moved like she owned the place, straightening this, fluffing that until she was in the kitchen with Marie who was the only staff left. But Marie didn't notice Lisabet come in, she was busy on the security phone, reaching for the button that would unlatch the gate and allow a visitor entrance.

"Marie!" At Lisabet's screech the young woman almost dropped the phone. "What are you doing? We're not expecting any visitors."

Marie lay her hands over her heart and breathed deep, afraid that Ms. Lisabet would let her go like all the rest.

"He's a friend of Miss Sass's. He's come to see her. I thought she might like a visitor."

"Who is it?" Lisabet demanded, coming close, her hand held out for the phone.

"Mr. Shay, Miss Lisabet. He was so nice when he lived here. He worked so hard on Miss Sass's movie. I think he would be good for her, don't you?"

Marie watched Lisabet narrowly, and the taller woman was well aware of the scrutiny. If she could just run this place on her own she'd let Marie go so Sass could have the privacy she needed. But one servant was a necessity. No sense running her off unless it was absolutely necessary. Lisabet smiled, realizing her worry was all for naught. This was a situation easily taken care. No need for a scene.

"I think I should talk to Mr. Collier before you let him in, Marie. Why don't you tell him that I'll be down in a moment."

Marie was about to suggest they be polite and let the man at least come past the gate, but Lisabet was already gone, out the door, without another word. With a shrug, Marie delivered the message, then went back to scrubbing the stove. This was none of her affair. Still, she felt sorry for Miss Sass. Sitting all day. Waiting. Waiting to die it seemed.

Lisabet had completely forgotten Marie by the time she closed the front door behind her. She hurried past the wide entry and down the drive that led to the front gate. Damn the man. She thought she'd taken care of him ages ago. Stupid for him to come here. He wasn't needed. It was appalling that she had to deal with him face-to-face. Had he no sensitivity?

As fast as her feet went, Lisabet's mind whirred faster until, by the time she saw Shay Collier lounging against the grillwork of the gates, she was furious. She stopped, just to look at him, trying to control herself. How damnably smug he seemed, laying casually about that way, as if this were nothing more than a social call. He had no idea what she— and Sass, of course— had been through the last months. Now he was here, pretty as you please, thinking he could just waltz in and make himself welcome all over again. Well, Mr. Collier had another think coming. Things had changed since Sass had taken him in.

Squaring her shoulders, pulling her cardigan tight around her angular frame, Lisabet calmed herself. Anger would only pique his interest and fan his insistence. She walked slowly toward him, keeping her eyes forward as he stood back, waiting for her to come.

"Mr. Collier?" Lisabet managed a smile. It faltered when Shay turned those inky eyes on her. How much more this man saw than Curt Evans ever did. She'd best be on her guard.

Lisabet slowed her step, stopping a yard or two from him. He had wrapped his fingers through the wrought iron as if he were Samson and could tear down the pillars of the temple with hardly a thought. Lisabet's smile faltered. "I'm surprised to see you here. Is there something I can do for you?"

"I should say there might be, Lisabet. You can open up this portal. I've come to see Sass, now that she's not feeling up to going out of the house much these days."

Lisabet shivered. The man's voice, so low, so soft, the smoothness of it made musical by the Irish lilt, was the worst thing about him. Lisabet would never let that voice whisper to Sass if she could help it. He would bring nothing but disappointment like all men did.

"Why on earth would you think that?" Lisabet asked.

Shay tilted his chin toward the great white house. "I've heard she stays in there all the time now. 'T'were the lovely people I met while I worked with Sass that told me. Sure, don't they say Sass hasn't seen anyone since right after her accident. I even heard the accident was quite a horror, Lisabet. So bad that perhaps Sass is sicker than anyone knows. But then no one seems to know the truth."

Lisabet moved her head, a deferential little gesture indicating she wasn't to blame for the nonsense he'd been told.

"I'm afraid none of these people have been around to make that judgment," Lisabet answered. There was a rudeness in her tone and a coldness creeping over her. This man wanted to share, and Lisabet wasn't about to let him into the sandbox. "Hollywood is a chatty place. People talk before they actually know what they're talking about. Friendships here are quite different, I'm sure, than on that quaint little island you come from. We're not a village that rallies around the flag in an hour of need."

"Perhaps you've taken the flag down, miss, so that no one knows where they can rally?" Shay countered lazily.

Lisabet had never been his favorite, but he had

never felt what he was feeling now. There was a wariness here and this, he was sure, was a dangerous woman, not a giving heart. She was not a risk-taker, either. Lisabet would follow the safe road to the point of self-destruction if she had to, and that made Shay a prudent man.

"I assure you, I'm doing everything I can to help Sass."

"Then let me in to see her, Lisabet," Shay countered, moving along the fence to keep abreast of the woman who squirmed opposite him. "A friendly face is just what Sass needs, and, sure, don't you need a break, too, after all your good service? 'Tis my understanding Curt no longer lives in this place. And, from the looks of things, 'twould seem that not many of the servants have been about, either. By heaven, I would imagine I'd be a welcome sight."

"I'm sure you would be if Sass was up to seeing you." Lisabet rubbed her arms as if she was cold, her eyes darted this way and that, lighting anywhere but in line with Shay's. "But, Mr. Collier, you must understand, Sass's recovery is a very delicate thing. To upset her now . . ."

"You think I'd be upsetting to her, then?" Shay's voice was stronger now, the edge more finely honed.

"No, not you in particular." Lisabet backtracked. This man was so quick. "I think anything out of the ordinary would be upsetting."

"By the Virgin, I would think everything is out of the ordinary for Sass now. Last I saw her she was Queen of the May. By the saints, it would seem no one's dancin' now, Miss Lisabet. Perhaps she's waiting for a friend to fill up her dance card."

"I'm her friend, Mr. Collier. I've been her friend and helpmate for a very long while. I know what's best for her. I will continue to follow my heart and my judgment in regard to Sass's condition. Now, if you'd be kind enough to give me a number where you can be reached, perhaps, when she's feeling stronger, I can call you. You could talk on the phone."

"Seems I've tried that," he reminded her, his gaze darker than ever. Lisabet's hands clutched tightly, all her energy going into controlling of her fear and anger.

"Then I'm sorry, I'll have to be quite frank with you. You're not needed here, Mr. Collier. You are the one who is responsible for what happened to Sass." Shay turned away, loosening his grip as he scoffed at Lisabet's suggestions. His cavalierness infuriated Lisabet and her voice rose, tight and cold and shrill. "Oh, yes, you are. Don't try to deny it. You and your pain and your anguish. That story. That book made Sass a crazy person. She didn't sleep, she hardly ate wanting it so badly for her own. I was happy when you turned her away. It was the best thing that ever happened to her. Then there you were, just as you are now, coming out of nowhere, giving her things she shouldn't have."

"She wanted that book to become more than she was, Lisabet. It was her heart she was taking care of. That's why she chased it down, and took it for her own," Shay answered without a second thought.

"You gave it to her without considering what it might do to her."

"Woman, you're daft! I was nowhere near that accident," Shay cried, amazed at this woman's persistence.

"But you gave her the rights. You made it possible for her to be standing on that cliff. You are as responsible for her injuries as if you pushed her yourself."

Lisabet seethed, instinctively moving closer, her hand upon the gate to steady herself in her outrage. There was nothing more to say. For the first time in her life, Lisabet wanted to strike out. But she missed her chance. Shay threw himself against the black iron, his large hand covering hers, holding it there so that she had no choice but to face him, breathe in the scent of a man who made no pretense of his manhood. He smelled like the high forests he came from, and the green island that had been his home. He smelled like power and purpose and Lisabet wanted him far away from her, this house and Sass whom she adored. But Shay's grip was hard and it ground her thin fingers into the cold, hard iron. His lips came close and she turned her head away. There was no escape. She had to listen. She was his prisoner.

"Open this gate, Lisabet. Open it now because I'm thinking that Sass has nothing to say about who she sees. I'm thinking you're a witch who cast a spell over her weak soul. Sure, I am not responsible for whatever has happened to that dear woman. You are. You're the one who is playin' games, Miss Lisabet, and I'd like to make the sides a bit more even, if you catch my drift."

As he spoke, Shay's grip tightened. Had it been anyone else Lisabet would have cried out. But this was Shay Collier, and she knew he was a threat the moment she had laid eyes on him in Alaska. To show weakness would be to lose this battle, and she'd come too far to surrender. Purposefully Lisabet stared into his eyes, barely moving her lips as she spoke.

"Let go of my hand, Mr. Collier. Leave this property. That is your only choice. You are not welcome here and the movie is finished. If you do not leave this place now, I shall call the police and have you arrested. It is as simple as that. This is Sass Brandt's home and you are nothing but a trespasser."

They had said their piece and now stood linked to each other in their anger and frustration. Two tall people standing in the sunlight, their faces close together. They could have been lovers, kept apart by a jealous father; they could have been friends intimately sharing their secret. In truth, though, they were enemies and there was no misunderstanding that.

Suddenly Shay's grip went slack though he still held Lisabet's hand to the metal. She narrowed her eyes, holding his glare until finally he backed off. Still, she held on to the great barrier that kept him away from the woman he had come to see. When Lisabet managed words, her voice shook, but it was a small embarrassment. She had won.

"Goodbye, Mr. Collier. I think, perhaps, it would be better if you left now."

"Sure, don't I think you're right, Miss Lisabet." Shay answered with a calm so unnerving Lisabet felt the lie of it in her heart of hearts. Perhaps he wasn't finished with her. Perhaps . . .

Abruptly he turned, the heel of his boots crunching into the gravel of the drive. God, she'd done it! He was leaving. Lisabet's eyelids fluttered shut, her free hand clutched her middle. How that man frightened her. When she opened her eyes again it was to see Shay Collier getting into the cab of the hired truck. She listened as the engine ignited, she watched the cloud of dust kick up as he turned tightly in the drive and sped off. He was gone. Gone.

With a deep breath Lisabet calmed herself, taking one more moment to thoroughly compose herself before walking slowly up to the house. There, at the door, Marie met her, an expectant smile on her pretty little face. But when Lisabet walked in and closed the door, allowing no one else entry, Marie knew better than to open it again to see if Mr. Collier had been left on the doorstep. Quietly she went back to her dusting.

Poor Miss Sass, she thought. But then she'd had that thought before. No need to waste her time thinking it again.

Poor Miss Sass.

Shay parked the truck a mile down the road. He could hardly see Sass's place, only the glint of glass off the extension he knew to be the second-floor wing. How often had he seen her sitting, watching the night. Shaking his head he left the truck, knowing that was enough to guide him.

Rolling up the sleeves on his all too warm flannel shirt, Shay started off. There was a spriteliness to his step that belied his size or his concern, but was testament to his confidence. He would find Sass just as she had found him so long ago. He would go sneaking and barging and banging at her barriers until she paid him some mind. Then he would take a look at Lisabet's face and she would see who was the more cunning of the two of them. Stupid woman, to think he would leave so easily when there was obviously so much awry.

"Holy Virgin, thank you for small favors," Shay muttered, coming upon a low wall that surrounded the mansion skirting Sass's property on the left. He was over it easily, a hand down on the brick, long legs flying over to land on the soft untended earth beyond. Looking about he saw the journey would be an easy one. This bit of land was not one that was monitored by cameras or dogs ready to take half his leg off for trespassing. It was only the buffer between the two great estates that neither of the rich folks could claim.

Breaking into a jog Shay ran the length of the property. To his right the wall was high. Sass's wall. The enclosure used to keep out people who might hurt her was now used to bar her friends. Shay kept his eyes forward toward the sea so that he couldn't see the barbed-wire high atop this structure. Fifteen minutes later he had managed the beach and was skirting the wall that faced the ocean, searching for any possible entry onto Sass's property. There was none to be found. The gate was too high to jump and heavily padlocked. Only a key from inside could open it for him and he doubted Lisabet would do the honors. On he walked until he came to a place where the ocean had kindly rearranged the lay of the land.

The tide had left a wonderful dune laid up against the white stucco. It was high enough to stand atop and, with one small leap, Shay could reach the cap of the structure. With a wee bit of muscle he'd be able to hang on. But then what? That damn barbed wire was stilled laced around the top.

"Well, Shay, my boy, nothin' to do about that now, is there?"

Muttering to himself he closed his eyes, drawing on all his inner strength, he prayed that there would be a way to get through that wicked wire with little more than a scratch. When he felt his courage waning, Shay Collier gave a cry and leapt forward. Up he went but his prayers weren't answered. The barbed wire caught him at the shoulder, ripping away the shirt and tearing at his skin as he threw himself over the wide top of the wall. He dared not look for fear he would give up if he actually saw the blood that trickled between flesh and cloth.

"Argh!"

Shay bit his lip against the pain. Damned barb wire hurt more than he would have thought. Instinctively he raised his hands clasping at anything to keep his balance, but it was another twist of sharpened metal that caught his palm. He cried out in earnest now, but kept his position, waiting for the pain to subside.

Blinking, fighting the tears that welled in his eyes, Shay tried to focus. He could just barely make out the inches where he might actually grasp without cutting himself further. Gingerly he lifted his hand, blood coming from the puncture. Carefully he lay it on an expanse of wire between two barbs. With that he swung his leg up, thanking his lucky stars for his heavy boots and jeans. For a moment he half lay atop the wide wall and listened. No alarm, no dogs to announce his arrival. Lisabet hadn't exactly made this a prison and that was good. Painful, but good.

Breathing hard, Shay scooted along the wall, moving his hands cautiously from one safe place to the next as he searched for a weakness in the wire. It was damnably well made, this stockade, and he looked like Christ crucified by the time he found that flaw.

Cursing and muttering, Shay pushed down on the wire. It gave enough to let him ease over with only a few more scratches here and there. Finally, with one great bound, Shay threw himself over the edge. Landing in a crouch on the other side he rolled forward and lay prone. He felt his injuries before trying to push the pain out of his mind. Knowing the enemy intimately was half the battle.

Finally ready, Shay sat up and looked about, fully expecting to see Lisabet rushing at him with a broom to drive him back. When all remained silent, when the only movement was a gentle breeze through the trees, Shay got up and dusted himself off. Trying to stave off the flow of blood from the wounds on his chest and arms, he ignored everything else.

Breathing deeply, Shay truly looked at the ground around him. It was good to be back. This was such a beautiful place that Sass had built. But, sure, weren't her visions always those of beauty? Yet, though his eyes saw splendor, his heart knew the radiance was gone from here; though his mind was open, he couldn't sense Sass.

Curious and concerned, Shay moved carefully, unsure whether there were security measures he hadn't been aware of when he lived here, so close to the woman who captured his imagination. He went through the dense gardens at the periphery of the estate. Beyond lay a vast expanse of grass wound about with more beds filled with trees and bushes. He pushed aside the fronds of a huge fern and peered toward the house. Half of it was obscured by the lush landscaping, but he could see there was no one about, not even a gardener. From the looks of the place, the gardener hadn't been about for a good long while. The grass was longer than he had ever seen it and brown in spots. The bed in which he stood was littered with overripe fruit and leaves and branches that had fallen, never to be picked up.

Shay stepped out from his hiding place. Though the sun lighted him, on this side of the wall there seemed to be little warmth. Cautiously he made his way toward the house, watching his step, keeping an eye on the windows as each came into view. He saw the great flight of glass on the second floor where Sass sat with her legs tucked under, watching the night, thinking her thoughts. How often had he watched her, letting his eyes feast on that beautiful woman? Too often. It was those moments that had opened his heart and his mind and his soul to the possibility that passion might once again be part of his life. Perhaps he could feel again. No! That was wrong. By the time he had packed his bag and left this place he *had* felt again, and it was pain that fell upon Shay Collier as he departed.

He was almost 'round the last of the large flower beds and still there was no Lisabet; no servant here or there to stop him. The closer he moved toward the house, the more poignant was the sense of despair. Squinting up toward the roof of the house, to the third floor where Sass's bedroom was, Shay saw that paint was starting to peel from the gutters, a roof tile was broken and hadn't been replaced. Underscoring the sadness of this sorrowful place, Shay saw that the curtains over Sass's bedroom window were drawn tight against the glistening sun.

It was that window that held Shay in thrall as he stepped from the grass and gardens onto the brick that paved the way to the pool and the house beyond. So intent was he, Shay was almost upon her before he realized it. And when he did, Shay Collier's heart froze. Never, in his wildest dreams or his amazing imagination, did he envision this. Not this, Mother in heaven.

"Sass?"

He whispered her name, never thinking that there might be an answer. This was a specter, a shade, a spirit. Here was a lost soul who had somehow wandered out of purgatory and settled itself by Sass's pool. A tremor clutched at Shay's throat, a ghostly fist caught him in the gut. My God! The cry was there waiting to be released, the tears had pooled and needed only his permission to fall.

He had felt a pain like this before in his life: inflicted by his father, his wife, himself. He understood anguish so well, but this! This was more than his heart could bear. Hardly aware that he was moving on, stumbling once, then again and not caring who might be watching behind the glass, Shay went forward.

"Sass, my girl," he said gently. He called again and again more to convince himself it was her rather than to prompt a response. She didn't move, her eyes didn't flick toward him. If she would only look his way, he might be able to quell the terror that had gripped his heart.

He murmured sweet nonsense, coming close, standing in front of the woman who sat so still in the wheelchair. He hardly knew her. The glorious hair was gone, shorn off and grown back with not a care for style or comeliness. The face that had one time turned up to his so expectantly was drawn and wan, the peaches and cream that had colored her lovely skin had drained away, leaving her flesh waxen looking. And those eyes that wouldn't look his way, those eyes that had one time shined on him, warming him, bringing him back to life with their belief in his talent, they were dead behind the long lashes. Her skeletal hands lay on a lap covered with an afghan the color of the sky, a hue so startling it only underscored the fragility and infirmity of the woman it warmed.

It was toward this silent creature Shay went, moving as if a wrong step or a sudden noise might cause her to shatter into a million pieces at his feet. As he drew near, Shay reached out and he saw his hand was shaking.

With a Herculean effort Shay took those last steps. Coming alongside Sass, he lay his hand atop her head, drawing it down, petting the softness until his hand lay where her hair curled in odd little ringlets at the nape of her bare neck. Slowly he bent his knees, balancing on the balls of his feet. His other hand hovered over hers as if he wasn't sure if the weight of it might break those long delicate fingers. Finally they came to rest, laying his hand over hers, carefully pressing his warm flesh into her cold skin.

"Ah, my Sass. My girl," he said once again as he lay his head upon his own hand in her lap. For a long while he lay there, holding himself still so as not to disturb her. Yet when a sob rose in him, when a tear slipped from his eye, Sass found the strength to come back from the limbo to which she had banished herself.

"Shay?" she whispered. "Is it really you?"

Fourteen

"Oh, My God in heavens, Sass. Sass!"

Shay's head snapped up, his hands cupping her face as he let the tears fall in earnest. But his joy was short-lived. Sass had fallen back into her silence, drifted away from him once more. Frantically he tried to call her back.

"Sass, listen to me!" he cried, his hands moving her head until she had no choice but to look at him. "Don't you do this. Not now. You've saved me from myself, don't you even think to lose yourself to your sorrow. Sass, you talk to me." Shay's hand slipped to her shoulder, his fingers pressing into her, finding nothing but skin and bones to hold onto. Though he hadn't meant it, Shay shook her, terrified that she might float away from him like a leaf upon the pond. "Talk to me now, Sass. By Saint Patrick and those blasted snakes, you can do that."

Sass blinked. She shook her head and one of her hands drifted up to his, clutching it as best she could. Desperately she tried to focus.

"Shay? Shay?"

" 'Tis me. Yes, 'tis me." Shay gulped a great sob. There was no time to waste on his own sorrow. Frantically he swiped at his tears with the back of one strong hand, then held her again, more gently this time. He forced a smile into his words. It was coaxing she needed, and he was there to give it.

"I've come to see how you are. Sure, didn't I just happen upon you at the right time, lass?" Shay tried to slip his hands from her shoulders, but Sass was coming 'round now. She wouldn't let him go. Her frail fingers held on as if for dear life. "Shhh, love. Hush. By the saints, I'm not going to leave you. 'Tis only to sit with you that I want. Just to sit next to you. Sass, let go now so I can sit like a proper gentleman calling on a lady."

Gently he eased his hand out of her grasp. With the utmost care he lay hers back in her lap, arranging it just so, unable to look at that face of hers, so stricken and fearful. When she was settled, he took a chair and pulled it close to her, lowering his voice until it was no more than a murmur, a verbal caress.

"I just want to see what's going on with you, Sass. Let me look at you. What's happened to you? I don't remember your hair being so short." Shay tried to laugh, but he could no more make light of this than he could dance a jig at a funeral.

"I fell," Sass answered, her voice hesitant as if her illness had been that of the soul and not the body.

"But sure, Sass, when I heard, they said you were doing fine."

Sass let her head list to one side, perhaps trying to turn it away. The conversation was already beginning to tire her. She was slipping away and

Shay hadn't the foggiest idea of what to do. He took a steadying breath, knowing everything was up to him. Sass would be no help, poor thing. Whatever had caused her to be like this would not easily be pushed away or explained away.

With great care Shay reached for the blanket on Sass's knee. Her face still turned from him, Sass jerked, her hands instinctively tightening, pressing down to keep him from what he wanted.

"Now, now, Sass, 'tisn't anything to worry about. It's a lovely day. The sun is bright . . ." Slowly he moved the blanket with one hand, holding her hands with his other. ". . . you won't catch your death, I promise. I'm here with you. I'll be watching out for you."

The blanket was off and Shay saw that she was dressed in a long robe, her feet encased in slippers. Easing himself from his chair, he crouched beside her.

"Ah, you're dressed warmly for such a lovely day, Sass. Wouldn't you like me to help you off with these slippers?" Off they came. "And only for a moment, Sass, let me see where you're hurt, my darlin' . . ."

"No, Shay. No," Sass whimpered.

"Yes, love, yes. I've got to see what it is that's going on here, or there's no helping you, don't you see? And what good is it to be a friend, Sass, if one cannot be of service," Shay soothed, his fingers touching the hem of her gown. Slowly grasping the fabric he rolled it up as he spoke, baring those legs that had been so beautiful not so long ago. "I only want to know what it is you've done to yourself, woman. Sure haven't you been the witchy one, causing everybody to be crazy with worry."

He saw the first of the scars on her ankle, still red as a new wound, where once surgery was done. Thankfully they were healing nicely. The sight of it gave him hope until he pulled her gown a bit higher and saw that the leg was half shriveled, another, wider and deeper injury starting midcalf and running the length of her leg. There the skin was indented and Shay questioned whether the surgeries were finished. No doctor in his right mind would leave a star of Sass's caliber so damaged. But then he saw it. The leg itself was not quite right. At her thigh, so sadly without tone or shape from long hours in this chair, Sass's bone was askew, not quite in line as was her right. He wondered if she could stand, if she could walk, if there was nerve damage, if . . .

"What are you doing here!"

Lisabet was on him so fast Shay was knocked backward as she wedged herself between he and Sass. Angrily she yanked Sass's long robe down around her ankles and grabbed at the slippers Shay had left beside the chair. In her fury, Lisabet dropped a slipper, retrieved it and pushed them both back on Sass's feet. The woman in the chair cried out, but did nothing to stop the assault. It was Shay, on his feet, who was ready to fight.

"By God, don't you hurt her!" he cried. Grabbing Lisabet he twirled her around to face him. Her expression was one of utter hatred, all color had drained from her face and her hazel eyes sparked with enmity.

"Don't touch me! Get away from me!" she screamed.

"Don't you touch *her!*" Shay snapped back. "You're the one that should be gettin' away. 'Tis you that's done this to her, I'd swear."

"It's me that's kept her alive while everyone else deserted her. You and Curt and Richard. Where have you all been this while? She needed someone and you couldn't be bothered."

"I didn't know about this. You never called to tell me. I had to hear it from some good soul who traveled to Ireland with her. I was an afterthought, but thank God that person acted or sure I'd never have seen this horror."

"Yes, this is horrible. But Sass and I are managing just fine." Lisabet reached for the afghan and clutched it to her breast. Warily she moved around Sass's chair, keeping her eye on Shay while she tucked it about Sass's legs. "We don't need you. Just go away. Get away from us. We're managing fine."

"Managing is all you've done here, isn't it? Perhaps you've forgotten that living is what you're supposed to be about. Sass is no princess to be held by you in this fortress. You've sent everyone away save for yourself and you're killing her."

"I sent no one away. I had to let them go. Every last servant. Sass hasn't the money to pay for them. The others, they just drifted away. See how they cared for her? No one comes. No one." Lisabet saw that this was not what the great suffering Irishman expected to hear. For a split second he was speechless and she moved in for the kill.

With great determination, Lisabet grabbed the

wheelchair and twisted it so that Sass faced the house with Lisabet guarding her from behind. She shook back her hair, triumphant as she looked at Shay.

"It isn't so easy to condemn me now, is it, Mr. Collier? Sass hasn't the money for anything except the doctors and the therapists and the mortgage on this fine castle of hers. She's broke. She can't sell off her long-term investments or cash them in. I stay because I care for her, and I've managed things because I love her. Now get out of here before I press charges."

Lisabet was quick. Her heels were clacking across the brick, Sass collapsed to one side of the chair. She'd almost made it to the first walkway when Shay caught up with them.

"Leave her be, Lisabet. Don't take her now. She doesn't want to go. Sass! Tell her!" In three great loping strides he was upon them, scooting around in front of the chair, his arms out to stop them, Shay's face a play of fear and hope. Still Lisabet came at him, using Sass as a weapon. "Sass, darlin' woman, don't let her take you in there. If you do you'll never come out. Never."

Grabbing the arms of the chair he pushed it back, holding it steady as Lisabet tried to move it around him. He ignored her, talking only to Sass, pleading with her to come back to him just long enough to let him know she wanted to fight; long enough to let him know that she understood what this woman was doing to her.

"Sass, say one word. Blink or nod or touch your nose." He laughed and there was an hysterical edge to it as if his time on this earth were running out and only she could give him more. "Sass, one word. Sure, that's all we need from you. Just say my name, and I swear I'll throw this baggage over the wall and be done with her."

He had run out of words, nothing left to say that might convince her of his devotion. Certainly she must know he wouldn't run the way the others had, nor would he bury her as Lisabet had done. In this pause that lengthened into an endless moment, Lisabet remained still, Shay looked into Sass's forlorn face and they all waited for the dead to come back to life. And then she spoke. Small and difficult though it was, Sass Brandt smiled and gave him just what he wanted.

"Not over the wall. Just ask her to go inside."

With that Shay grasped Sass's small and waiflike face in his big strong hands and kissed her, his lips laying gently upon hers to bring her no pain, only a promise that now the world would begin for her again.

"Do you want something more to drink?" Shay held up the water glass that Marie had brought but Sass shook her head. "Tired?"

This time she nodded. "My legs hurt."

"Of course they do. But that will go away. You just need some exercise. You say you could walk after the accident?"

"Yes, for a bit. But Lisabet thought it would be better if I sat in the chair. Just for a while."

"And how long has this while been, Sass?" Shay made a show of replacing the water goblet on the tray behind him. He didn't want Sass to see any more anger. If it killed him, he would try to work with that horror who called herself Sass's friend. But every time he thought of her keeping Sass on this estate, cut off from everyone and everything that was familiar, he wanted to . . .

"I don't know. A few weeks. A few months. Shay, I'm so tired. I can't think. I haven't had company in so long." Sass's voice trailed off. Her hand came to her neck to play with the curls of new hair she found there. She licked her lips. He saw so much in her small gestures, understood more than she knew. Gently he touched that anxious hand and said, "You're a fine-looking woman, Sass, only a bit drawn. You're not to worry about how you look. That will come. Mother in heaven, everything will come back."

Sass shook her head and under her lowered eyes Shay saw a great tear squeeze out to hang on the tips of her silky lashes before sliding down her cheek. This he wiped away without a word, letting the silence be filled by the beautiful sounds of nature. In the distance he could hear the sea, to the right, a bird harbingering the end of the day. Leaves rustled and the air tasted of salt. He willed Sass to feel all these things, hear them because it would be the small signs of life that would give her back a bit of hers. Just like the moment when he felt her shallow breath, and her skin began to warm under his on that day in the snow. It was that tiniest evidence that life still existed that made Shay Collier start living again.

"I don't think so, Shay. I think it's over, the life I had."

"Now don't you go sayin' that. How could a star the likes of you come crashing down to earth without leavin' a crater the size of Ireland itself?" Shay chucked her chin ever so gently, yet still she didn't look at him. "I didn't hear a thing on the news, lass, about a nova destroying itself in the grand space above all of us ordinary people. So it must be that you're simply winking out for a bit, don't you think?"

"I'm tired, Shay."

Sass lay her head back. The one smile she'd managed had been too long ago. An hour or two since Lisabet left them angrily and unwillingly. Since then the conversation had been scattered. A bit about Curt, but nothing about the misery he had caused. Shay's fury was enough for both of them. Should be ever see the man— but that was best left to rest in his gut. Now there were more important matters to deal with. The movie. Sass's financial situation. Richard, who seldom called anymore. Shay knew there wasn't much to say— no offers of roles, the press should not see her as she was— but still Richard could have found some way to keep her dream alive.

"Do you want to go rest, then we'll talk some more over dinner?"

Sass shook her head.

"What is it you want, then?' Should I see you in the morning, Sass? Take you down by the ocean to get a bit of the breeze? You just say it, and I'll be making it happen."

Her head tipped to one side, Sass looked at him with doleful eyes. The tears were long done, but they had taken their toll, wearying her until it seemed difficult to even move her lips to speak. But speak she did.

"I want nothing to happen, Shay. I want you to go away now." With a great and shuddering sigh, Sass forced more words out of lips that hadn't spoken so many in a very long time. "I have nothing for you anymore. No dreams. No movie. Nothing, Shay. I'm not what I was, and you can't make me that way again. Please, Shay Collier, go away. Leave me be."

Her speech complete, her message delivered, Sass looked at him and waited. There would be a parting now, of that she was sure. Exhausted beyond endurance she waited for him to rise from his chair. When he did her lips tipped up. A goodbye gesture that couldn't blossom into a smile. Yet instead of coming to her, offering a final touch, a kiss brushed atop her head, Shay Collier simply towered over her, standing so straight and fine in the dying sunlight, illuminated red by the ball of fire sinking into the sea behind him.

"No, Sass. 'Twon't be that easy. Not like a goddamn movie where I walk out leavin' the theater in tears over your tragedy. No, my darlin', it won't happen that way."

"Shay . . ."

"Don't even try it. Sick you may be. Hurt and tired and estranged from everything you ever knew. That I understand. I know how those things can kill the spirit. But yours isn't dead, and I didn't half kill myself getting to you to have you give me any of your actress bunk." Shay forced a huge grin and stroked his beard, a wise man talking to one who had underestimated him. "Ah, you think I didn't know, but I do. This is a show." A wave of pain creased her face, her expression so anguished that Shay thought he, too, would be wounded by it. But he couldn't stop now. He would use whatever he could— truth or lies— to make her come back to the world and to him. Her hands were on the wheels of her chair. She was trying to run and that was good. A spark of spirit left. He moved in toward her, her little hands so ineffectual on those big, big wheels.

"Did you see what happened to me getting to you? Did you see, woman?" Shay ripped open his shirt as he hunkered down beside her, showing her the scratches and gouges left by the barbed wire. "I don't think your front bell was working so I had to come in the back way. But 'tisn't much, Sass, not when it's a friend in need. I've come to you, and the least you can do is meet me halfway."

Sass's head was shaking hard now, back and forth, denying that she could or would or even wanted to start living again.

"I won't be the same. I couldn't be the same."

"So who is it in this world that says you must be?"

"Just that, Shay," Sass answered back, her voice gaining strength as he egged her on.

"Just what, explain this nonsense to me. Explain that your hair was shorn off and now you stand accused of what? Of being hurt and not perfect so that the cinema will throw you out on your ear if you dare to come to it and say I'm ready to work again?"

"That, yes." She gasped as if for air. "And more. More."

"More what, woman?"

"Myself. I can't find myself. Not in this body. Not the way I look. It is who I am."

"Ah, Sass, that was never true. Never."

Shay stood looking at her, his heart breaking in two. How beautiful she still looked to him now. Nothing to do with the length of her hair or the scars on her legs. In her was the beauty of the heart, and that would be destroyed if she stayed as she was much longer.

"It is, Shay." Sass's voice was so small, the sudden quickening of it fading into weariness as she resigned herself to her fate. "Curt left me. Richard hardly comes anymore. It's all gone. All the people who I cared about aren't here anymore. All the people I loved have gone away from me. Everyone. Gone. I'm not who I was. I can never be again. Not the woman people loved."

Sass's head fell forward, resting on her chest. From where he stood Shay saw the gentle shake of her shoulders, the fragility of her demeanor. He knew that tears were falling from her eyes, and it wasn't a lament for the lost beauty she was feeling. Shay knew it was the loneliness, the sadness that love could so easily slip away until there was no one left for her, who had given so much.

Shay gave way. He could no more look at her in such torment and not feel it, than he could walk on water. His body was seized by an anguish so deep he could do nothing but give in to it. Sinking to his knees, Shay Collier crossed his arms over his chest, as if that might ease the torture Sass had dealt him. He fell back, sitting on the heels of his boots, his head turned up toward a sky that had no right to be so stunning. He heard the birds and the whisper of the breeze. Beyond them, all around them, was the distant rush of water against sand. And finally he heard the faint, helpless weeping of Sass Brandt. All this came together, crafted to build for him a monument to ruin. He felt weak in the shadow of such despair, but finally Shay found his voice, frail though it was. He couldn't leave her like this to simply fade away, die under the watchful eye of Lisabet who would grasp at Sass's very soul.

"Sass," he called, but she didn't move. Those shoulders still shook, the tears still fell. Shay moved, walking on his knees to her, slowly as he held out his hands, then his arms, calling all the while. "Sass, you can't leave now. Don't give up, my girl. Sass?"

He could say nothing more. A sob ripped from his own throat, and Shay Collier stopped his movement. His arms fell to his sides, his head bowed in defeat. Had he ever felt pain like this? Not Moira's, certainly, for it was pain of her own doing. But this? This was God's handiwork and it made Shay want to curse the spirit who had done this to Sass Brandt. Agonized, he raised his head again, his body paralyzed by the futility of it all. How could he think that he had the strength to make this better? How could anyone make this better? But his lips moved. He said his piece as best he could, and now prayed for a miracle.

"Sass, don't I love you? Haven't I come to you? Aren't I here for you now? Sass . . ." He could say no more. The tears coursed down his fine, high cheeks only to nestle in his beard. His eyes narrowed against his anguish and hers. She had no strength left to even raise her head. "I love you, Sass. You've given me my life. 'Tis nothing to me if you take yours from me now."

That was the end. He knelt in the fading sunlight, at Sass Brandt's feet, little left to do but watch her fade from his sight as the tears fell fast from his eyes. And just when he thought they would spend the rest of their lives as they were, just when it seemed they would drown in their own veil of sorrow, Shay saw the most marvelous of sights. Though he wept and tears clouded his vision, Shay knew Sass's arm was raised. She reached toward him not to implore, but to meet him halfway. There was the will and the desire, to come back to this land of the living.

Fifteen

"By all the saints, Sass, that's it! Keep it up now or surely I'll have something to say to you about your performance."

"Don't be ridiculous. I could whop you with one hand tied behind my back."

Sass didn't hear Shay's laughter as she put her face in the water and kicked as hard as her legs would allow. How good it felt to move again, breathe again. Her lips and eyes closed, she felt the whirl of bubbles, the tickle of the water as she laughed underwater. One last, best effort kick and she pulled her head out of the water, gasping for air as she laughed and laughed.

Shay was on her in an instant, his strong hands spanning her waist as he pulled her upright, flipped her around and held her against the water.

"Excellent job, my sweet. You're doing just fine."

Sass lay back, listening to Shay's voice filter through the water. Her eyes were closed and she could feel the hot summer sun baking away the moisture beading on her lashes. Her arms floated, crosslike from her sides and she shook her head slowly, loving the feel of her hair now

that it reached her shoulders. For a moment, in
that self-imposed blindness, Sass flashed on her
legs, still ugly and scarred and her smile faded.
But the image was put aside, there was more to
think about than the cosmetics of her healing.
Shay's lips were on hers as he slowly moved in the
shallow end of the pool, twirling her, letting her
lay in his arms, so trusting of his care that her
body was given over to him completely. He moved
his lips only to bring them down upon hers once
again. Another and another followed. Kisses that
had nothing to do with sex, but everything to do
with desire. But Shay was wise in his courtship.
He held Sass, kissed her and moved with the caution and tenderness of a man come upon a beautiful fairy in the forest.

Finally finished, her lips kissed dry, he raised
her up and Sass's arms came 'round his neck. She
would never tire of touching him, though never
had she breathed this secret to him. They had
been so busy, the two of them, to think of what
might be. Too busy, thank God.

"Now, are you feeling better having this little
workout?" Shay asked, obviously content to stand
in the pristine water of the pool he had cleaned
himself, happy to hold her close while her legs
moved slowly, pushing against the water to
strengthen every muscle.

"I'm done in. You're a taskmaster, and I'm going to fire you any day now," she teased.

"By God, wouldn't that be a hard thing to do?"

Sass shook her head. Her face gorgeous with her
hair wet and pulled tightly back from it. How naturally beautiful she was, he thought.

"Not difficult at all. I'll snap my fingers, and you're out of here. I'll get someone to throw you out, just as soon as I have servants back to do my bidding."

"Again I say, impossible," Shay said and pirouetted, creating a whirlpool around them. "You don't pay me. You don't own me. You can't be rid of me even if you wanted."

With that Sass's eyes opened and instinctively Shay stood his ground, tightening his hold on her. A small smile played about her lips as she looked at his face. Carved out of stone he would like people to think, but touchable and wonderful and easy to smile she knew.

"Do you promise, Shay?"

"What?"

"Promise I can't be rid of you?"

"Ah, lass, sure I'd be like that bad penny. Throw me away, and I'd turn up again"— he kissed her— "and again." He kissed her once more. "And again."

"Shay." Sass breathed, wanting to say so much more. Her arms tightened about his neck, she pushed her body into his. Close was not close enough.

"Sass!"

Her eyes flew open but she clung to him. Lisabet. Her timing was incredibly poor as usual. Sass turned her head.

"Yes? What is it?"

"Lunch." Lisabet's eyes flitted toward Shay, then back to Sass. "I've brought you both lunch," she reluctantly added.

Shay held Sass away, both trying desperately to

control their giggles. Poor Lisabet. How she hated the life Shay had breathed back into Sass. Or perhaps it was Shay she hated. But Sass forgave her, understanding how desperately the woman needed to be needed. Perhaps she would have felt differently if Shay had told her how Lisabet kept him from her. But his counsel was his own, and he hoped he would never regret that decision.

With a final twirl, he scooped Sass up and waded toward the side. There he put her onto the warm concrete. Lisabet brought her a towel and draped it over her shoulders. Shay was beside her, pushing up on his strong arms and setting himself in place, water pouring from him. Quite the king of the deep he looked as he shook back his black hair and grabbed a towel for himself.

"You're looking so wonderful, Sass. I wouldn't have thought it a few months ago. You've done amazing things for yourself."

With a final twist of the towel he draped it around his neck and looked at her.

"We've done amazing things. I think I'd be dead now if it wasn't for you."

"I can't even imagine such a thing," Shay answered quietly, his brow clouding. Sass almost apologized, sure he was thinking about a long-ago love who had taken her own life. Little did she know that it was the thought of never seeing her again that caused the dark cloud to descend upon him. "Thank the Virgin I don't have to imagine. You're here, and I think you might just be better than before. Let me take a look at you?"

He leaned back, thoroughly surveying her from

head to toe. Playfully, Sass pulled the towel behind her shoulders, posing for him.

"Yes, you're looking mighty well, Ms. Brandt. A few pounds have done you a world of good." He reached out and tapped her arms. "Very strong. Very good. And those legs, lass. Look at those legs." Shay reached for them but Sass pulled away, her head dipping and her arms instinctively lowering to protect that which she abhorred. But Shay was too quick for her. He caught her hands and lifted them to his lips. "Not to worry, Sass. Let's just take a look. Sure, it's not like I haven't seen those legs before, 'tis it?"

Sass shook her head. "No. I just don't want you to look too closely."

"Sass, think back to what those legs looked like in the beginning. I saw them then and I thought you'd never have the strength to make them work again. Now, come, my darlin', let me see."

Reluctantly Sass lay back, her hand supporting her weight as Shay gently lifted first one, then the other leg from the water.

"Sass, you should be proud of what you've accomplished. Look now. Look and see how lovely they are."

"Ugly." Sass frowned.

"Scarred, yes. Ugly no," Shay reminded her. " 'Tis your badge of courage, these scars. Soon even they'll fade. Didn't the doctor tell you you've had the last of those operations. There's nothing more he can do, so we'll do the rest. Now, let me see how they work since they're all muscled and tan and lovely again.

Shay was up before Sass could beg him to carry

her just this once. Mischievously he winked at Lisabet, still getting glares in return. He retrieved Sass's cane and brought it to her.

"Up you go now!" Shay's strong hands wrapped around her, just under her arms. His voice was heartier than his touch. As he encouraged her, Shay watched her legs flail, then begin to work. He lifted her gently until she was on her feet, standing on her own, but happy to have him beside her to lean on. He was the balance in her life now.

"Now, woman, have you ever done anything so magnificent in your life?"

Shay stepped back, his hand to his chin as if inspecting a rather fine piece of merchandise.

"Shay, stop!" Sass laughed and leaned on to the cane. It was a beautiful thing, very old with a silver knob atop. A present from Shay in those early days. He had told her she'd look like a queen walking with it. Under his scrutiny, she felt like one. "You're being silly, and I'm hungry. Now, can you please help me to the table?"

"I think not. Perhaps today it's time for you to help yourself to the table." With that he turned his back on her and walked toward the shaded area where Lisabet had laid lunch.

"How can you do that to her?" Lisabet complained as he passed.

"Shay! Come on," Sass called. "Help me."

"Leave her be, Lisabet. I mean it," Shay whispered. But Lisabet ignored him and started off. It was only a strong, quick hand on her arm that stayed her. Shay's brows rose, commanding her to stay where she was. He looked over his shoulder to see Sass struggling but moving forward as she called.

"Shay, come on. I'm tired enough as it is . . ."

His grip relaxed as he saw that Lisabet had given up.

"Lisabet, if you don't let her be, she will be hurt more in the long run," he said quietly.

"I know that. I know," Lisabet answered curtly. "It's just I wanted to be the one to help. It was supposed to be me."

She turned on her heel, heading back to the house before Shay could convince her that it was up to both of them to see Sass through this. He hung his head. Pity Lisabet couldn't share. Her cooperation would have finally made this a completely happy home.

"Shay!"

Quickly he turned, catching Sass just before she lost her balance. Instead of panic, though, she laughed, clutching him as she righted herself.

"Look at me. Look how far I came!" she cried gleefully.

Shay looked and looked and looked. He couldn't keep his eyes off her. Without a thought he pulled her to him and the silver-tipped cane clattered to the brick and concrete. Never had he felt so much for one person. Not all the hatred for his father, nor all the love and remorse and disappointment he had felt for Moira, could match the pure and unadulterated adoration he had for the woman in his arms.

"God, I love you. I love you more than life itself." He kissed her forehead and Sass's temples, unwilling to kiss closed those eyes that looked at him with such wonderment. "I love you, and I want you with me always. Say that you're mine. That should another man more handsome, more powerful, more wealthy come into your life you'll send him on his way. Sass, my love, you are a wonder. I'm proud of you and grateful to you."

Though his passion was overwhelming, Sass, who had looked death in the eye, could only answer him with the gentlest of smiles. Life was so fleeting. Whatever her forever was, it belonged to Shay Collier. Winding her fingers through the thick waves of hair drying at his temples, touching the lovely tip of his mustache where it met beard before running her thumbs over his full, sweet lips, all Sass could do was smile and murmur and finally say, "It's I who am grateful. Twice now you've saved my life. Twice you've come to my rescue. What more powerful man could there be in my life, Shay Collier?"

"Sure, I don't know, Sass," Shay answered softly, "but there are days I fear . . ."

"Shhh." Four fingers were on his lips now. She would hear no more. This was love as she'd never known it. Anything, anyone, in her life before this moment was simply a trial. "Don't ever be afraid. It will never be a man who comes between us. Perhaps my own stupidity, my weakness when I feel I can't go on, but never another man."

"Then I'll be there with a hand for you, Sass Brandt. I'll always be there."

"See that you are, Shay," she teased. Then more quietly, "Please see that you are."

One last kiss. He took her affection and gave his own. Careful, he was, so that this woman would know he felt more than passion. That would have to wait, but not much longer. The healing they both had to do was coming to an end. The last of his pain was being put in its place. Soon he would exorcise it completely.

"I've a surprise for you."

"What?" she murmured, wishing she never had to leave the safety of his arms; knowing she must if she were to give him the kind of love he needed from her.

"Come on. Lunch first. I'll show you while we eat."

"That's just a sneaky way of making me eat," Sass said as he retrieved her cane. Dutifully she maneuvered herself toward the table and even managed the chair on her own. Palms raised, she gave Shay a victorious smile.

"Nicely done, Sass," he raved. Snapping her napkin he leaned over her shoulder and lay it across her lap. Sass smelled the chlorine, the sun, and the salt air in his hair. It was a heady combination: his closeness, his scent, the heat from his near-naked body. But Shay was in a high, fine mood. He chuckled, pushing her chair gently closer to the table. "Ah, chicken again. Doesn't Lisabet think a good piece of red meat might be in order now and again?"

Sass giggled, "I'm never sure these days if she's watching the budget or my figure."

"We'll leave the budget to her, I'll be the only one watching your figure," Shay said and kissed the top of her head.

Sass picked up her fork, letting it hover over her salad. But she sat alone. Shay had disappeared.

"Shay?" she called, and was about to look over

her shoulder when he reappeared, putting an envelope beside her plate. Leaning close, laying his cheek against her hair, he rested his hands on the arms of her chair.

"Your surprise, my darlin'," he whispered into her hair. A kiss. His lips lingered there for an instant. " 'Tis time you went back to work, love. Time we both made our dreams come true."

The sun was going down and Shay stood outside Sass's room. He knew the evening would be long and Sass would tire in the face of it. He understood that Sass's head was probably filled with thoughts of business and not of him. Yet, there he was, his hand on the knob, his heart urging him on while his head sounded retreat. Twisting the knob, he knocked lightly on the door.

Sass hadn't responded to his rapping, yet Shay knew he had done the right thing the moment he slipped into her room. Though papers were strewn around her on the huge bed, she was ignoring the lists and charts. Her eyes had been on the door as if she'd been waiting for him, as if her heart had reached out and willed him there. Gently Shay closed the door and stood facing her. Their eyes locked. He offered neither a flicker of a smile nor allowed his eyes to light with hope, for fear he would bind her to him out of gratitude, or she would offer herself because of a perceived debt.

It took no more time than the twinkling flight of the fairies Shay was so fond of spying for Sass to lay aside her work and open her arms. In that moment she banished his wariness. She held her arms straight and sure toward the man she had loved since the moment she laid eyes on him. They'd been rendered helpless by their old worlds and built a new one in which they were strong and unafraid. No longer did dead or departed lovers stand between them. Only the length of the room kept them apart. Shay closed that space slowly, savoring the perfect composition of the picture as he went.

Freshly bathed, Sass was swathed in terry as white as snow. Her hair lay in ringlets about her cheeks, glistening in the light from the bedside lamp. It dried in wisps so fine it might have been a halo about her head. Her skin was tinged with shades of pink and peach with cream running underneath. The bath must have been deliciously warm to heighten her color so. Another step and Shay was vaguely aware of the satin-covered bolster of the bed, the inviting fluff of the coverlet. He felt, rather than took note of, the ever lengthening shadows that reached across half the huge room. The other half remained gloriously bathed in the last golden rays of the sun.

Rounding the bed, unable to take his eyes off Sass, Shay stopped for a split second. He raised his head to breathe in the sweet smell of soap and flesh tinged with the ever so slight scent of pine. Without a word he sat beside her. The bed gave a bit but there was no creak, no sound that his weight was unwelcome. It was Sass who touched first, reaching out for him instinctively before changing her mind. The last thing she wanted was to waste a single moment. She wanted to savor them, explore Shay, watch him until the time she was blinded by her desire.

Gently Sass touched his cheek, soft just above that silky beard of his. She smiled hearing Shay's instantaneous intake of breath. How he would love her to think him stony in the face of this gentle affection! The Shay of old. But Sass knew better. She touched his lips, the full bottom one that had opened slightly, the equally satiny upper. Both closed and kissed the tips of her fingers. She let them lay there, her own eyes closing now against the amazing sensations such a caress brought.

How wrong she'd been all these years. Acting her movie love scenes with rote responses. Loving Curt without the depth of feeling he deserved. Never had Sass imagined that loving and touching could be like this. Somewhere, deep inside her, there opened a most amazing and new space waiting to be filled up by whatever Shay had to give. She would take it all no matter how little or how much. She would cherish his affection, care for it, and happily wait until he had more to give.

"I truly love you, you know," Sass whispered and grinned that grin of utter happiness Shay had only seen again in the last few weeks.

"God, woman," he whispered back, unsure if his voice would hold in the face of what was to come. "I hope you do. I couldn't be so close to you any longer if you didn't."

Those were all the words he had and the only ones Sass wanted. There was nothing left to say, only things needing to be done. One mind, one body, one heart, they reached for each other at the same time. Sass laughed softly. Her hands dropped, her eyes lowered. Someday this would be so natural to them. Tonight she wanted to be led, she wanted to experience only joy and forget all the pain of the last, long months. Selfishly she let Shay take command, which he did with tenderness and awe.

His hands were skilled. They pushed the robe just off her shoulders and no further. They ran over the slope of her delicate shoulders, lightly over her flesh until she shivered with anticipation. When he lowered his head, laying his lips along the line of her throat, Sass's head fell back, her hands touched his hair. Holding his head lightly she wound her fingers through the thickness of his hair and pressed him closer, all her senses alive with the very idea of him, the reality of him.

Sass felt him tug at her belt. She moved. It came untied easily in his hands. For the first time in a long while Sass didn't give a moment's thought to the pain in, or the scars on, her legs. Her own hands released his head, ruffling his hair once more. She tipped his face up, looked hard and lovingly at him for a moment, then unbuttoned his shirt: one, two, three, four until his chest was laid bare and she kissed the expanse of it. Burying her face in the dark curling hair she found there, Sass moved her lips from nipple to nipple, reveling in the shudders and quivers that threatened to overwhelm Shay.

She laughed and he did, too, before falling silent once again. There was no one to hear, yet they felt like children about to embark on a forbidden, fanciful adventure.

"Oh . . . God . . . Sass, you're so beautiful."

He looked with wonder at her body. So lovely in the fading light. Lightly he ran his fingers the length of it pushing her gently back until she lay on the bed. Without another word Shay joined her: she naked, he almost so. His hands were everywhere, his lips following close behind. Sass laughed now, then shut her lips long enough to kiss whatever bareness she could unearth as she struggled with the last of his clothes.

"Shay," she murmured as he rolled over, taking her with him until she lay atop him and spread her arms wide over his, stopping their craziness for only a moment.

"Sass," Shay moaned with a chuckle. "Have you no sympathy for a man in my condition? 'Tisn't time for talking."

"I have a feeling your condition will last as long as you like." She chuckled. "Now shhhhh, my love. Just for a moment, don't speak." With that, arms spread so that they made a beautiful and entirely human cross on the big bed, Sass lowered her head to his chest and lay her ear against his heart. "There. I can hear it. Strong beats. So alive. We're so alive, Shay. This is the reason we had to meet. We had to heal each other."

Shay slid his arms from beneath hers and wrapped them around her, running his hands down to the small of her back and up again.

"Enough talk. We're healed. We're healthy, lass, and there's more to life now than worrying what was. There's the future and there's lovin'. I mean to do quite a lot of lovin' starting today."

With that he rolled her over once more and captured her mouth with his. This kiss was unlike the others. It was masterful and long and deep and Sass returned it to him in kind, her body opening to receive him without a second thought or another word. Finally, when he entered her, when they became one and their past and future were abandoned for the ever more electrifying present, Sass learned what it meant to love completely. Shay would be hers now and forever. Everything she would do from this point forward would be for him. With a small cry, a shudder, a tightening of her arms around his neck, she wordlessly promised that their destinies, their dreams, would never part ways. They belonged to each other now and nothing and no one would ever change that.

The outdoor lights bathed Sass Brandt's compound in a marvelous white glow. It was all so beautiful. She finally felt beautiful. Sass, standing at the huge bank of windows overlooking the grounds, could almost believe that her life hadn't changed at all. It was as if the house was just waiting for guests to come through the door, greetings and kisses all around. Lisabet would be riding roughshod on the caterers, laughter would filter out of the house, past the patio and toward the sea as naturally as waves roll to shore. Everyone would have something interesting to say. Sass would listen, pulled this way and that, laughing, running here and there, sitting to sip a drink with an old friend, stopping to wind her arms around Curt and give him a kiss.

Sass stiffened, clutching the silver head of her cane tighter. Funny she should think of him now when she was so happy. But the moment of hurt passed quickly, contentment and common sense lying in its wake. Soft light couldn't make her life the way it used to be and she wouldn't want to live it again anyway. So much of that life had been a mere facade; white lies told because no one knew what the truth was. Certainly she didn't. And if she didn't, how could she have expected Curt and Lisabet to recognize how shallow their emotional bonds were. No, she wouldn't go back. Even the pain and suffering she experienced with her accident had been a blessing in disguise. It had brought her time to sort through her life, to come to terms with the realization that lip service was a way of life in Hollywood and true caring was the exception not the rule. Her pain had brought her Shay. That was worth falling a thousand times from a hundred higher cliffs. Oh, how well worth the pain that was!

A private smile curling her lips, Sass thought of going back upstairs for just a moment. She had been reluctant to leave their bed at all after this beautiful first time of loving. But Shay insisted. She had worn him out, he said, and dutifully Sass had laughed. She knew full well it was she he worried about. As if such delightful exercise could ever be detrimental to her health. Yes, perhaps she would just go right back upstairs and . . .

"Are you all right?"

Sass looked over her shoulder just as Lizabet finished arranging the crudités on a silver platter on a low table in front of the couch. Startled, Sass's free hand fluttered to her neck as if to cover the blush that flared just above her heart. She almost laughed at her own embarrassment. It wasn't as if Lisabet didn't know about the marvelous things that could happen between a man and a woman. Still, this was Sass's own private time, she wasn't ready to share it with anyone just yet. She and Shay. What happened between them would stay between them, their magical moments, for as long as possible.

"Better than ever, Lisabet," Sass said brightly, moving her cane first then her legs. She was still a bit awkward, but even Lisabet couldn't deny the amazing progress she had made in the last few months. Sass stopped just before she reached the sofa. "Do I look all right?"

"Fine," Lisabet said. Stepping back she surveyed the table, not Sass.

"You didn't even bother to look, Lisabet," Sass said softly, hurt that the other woman should disregard her.

Lisabet let her eyes roam over Sass, "You look wonderful. Never better, actually. Now, did you want me to be here when Richard comes?"

"Of course! Lisabet, after all we've been through do you think that I wouldn't want you here for this meeting?"

"I just thought that Mr. Collier would be sitting in, so there was probably no need for me to be here," Lisabet sniffed.

"Don't be ridiculous," Sass said, moving to the sofa. She was getting tired. Her left leg was not as strong as it looked despite all the exercise. "Lisabet, sit down. I can't stand long and you make me nervous towering over me."

"I've got so many things to do, I better . . ."

"If you want to keep your job, you're going to sit right down here and talk to me," Sass insisted, grinning, hoping to lighten the mood.

Lisabet slid onto one of the overstuffed chairs, as far away from Sass as she could get. She didn't want to be close and smell her perfume or see that her clothes no longer hung on her, or her eyes didn't beseech her for help. Her legs, hidden by the wide-legged pants she wore, were the only evidence that all was not right with Sass Brandt. Her hair skimmed her shoulders, curlier than it had been, more beautiful than it had been, and long enough to be styled as it had been in Ireland. Her skin was glorious, kissed gently by the sun, never enough to harm her, just enough to set her aglow. And those eyes. They were the most dramatically different. No longer haunted, all Lisabet saw in them was purpose and confidence and it was Shay Collier she had to thank for that. Even when Curt was here Sass never looked so assured, she had always been just a bit empty.

"Lisabet?" Sass was leaning forward, her hand out as if she might touch the other woman. But they were too far away from each other so Sass's gesture was only that of the suggestion of intimacy. "Lisabet, what is wrong with you lately? We hardly ever talk anymore. Not the way we used to."

"It's been a hard year, Sass."

"You're telling me?"

"I'm telling you," Lisabet answered coldly, "that it's been hard on everyone. Including me. For months I was the one who did everything around here. I got you up and dressed. I fixed you breakfast, lunch, and dinner. I chauffeured you to the doctor, stayed at the hospital twenty-four hours a day when you had your surgeries. And where was everyone else. Where?"

"Lisabet, come on," Sass soothed, honestly shocked by Lisabet's outburst. "I'm sorry. I never said thank you. I never told you how much I appreciated everything you did for me when everyone turned their back on me. I apologize. Forgive me?"

"This isn't about forgiveness, Sass. It's about appreciation."

"I do appreciate you. But you have to understand. I wasn't myself for a very long time."

"I know that better than anyone."

"I know you do. I've never disputed that." Sass threw up her hands, hardly knowing what else to say. "So can't we start again? I think it's time we get back to the way things used to be. We used to smile at each other, sit and have a cup of tea."

"There's no time for that now, is there?" Lisabet shot back.

"Of course there is. Lisabet, what on earth is the matter? You should be thrilled. We're going to work again."

"*You're* going to work again. And you certainly don't need me when you have him."

"Shay? Shay isn't an employee. He couldn't possibly replace you. Is that what this is all about? Are you afraid I'm going to send you away?"

"No, of course not. You couldn't send me any farther than I already am. Ever since he moved back in here I've been persona non grata."

"Lisabet, don't be ridiculous."

"I'm not. He doesn't like me. He doesn't want

me here, and I don't know that I can take much more of this." Lisabet shot out of her chair. Her hands were shaking and she clasped them together; her knees felt weak and she paced to keep them from knocking together. There was a knot in her throat and she took a few deep breaths as she spoke so that her complaints were a staccato jumble. "I don't feel like I belong . . . Never able to help you with anything he can't do better . . . I just feel so useless. . . ."

"Lisabet, don't be silly." Sass struggled to get up, almost forgetting how difficult it was for her. She was halfway up when the tip of the cane slipped on the hardwood floor and she crumpled to a heap, catching herself on the coffee table, falling with a yelp of surprise. Lisabet was on her in a second, her arms gently lifting Sass back to the sofa, brushing her off, pushing back her hair until Sass caught her hands.

"Lisabet, I'm fine. I'm fine," she said softly until finally Lisabet relaxed, her muscles softening until Sass was able to pull her toward the couch.

"You don't need me anymore," came the soft and despairing admission. "I see it. I love you, Sass, and it's not enough for you. I never got the chance to show you how much. But now, I'm truly not needed."

"Lisabet, stop. That's nonsense. I love you, too. I've never had a better friend, a more loyal employee."

"No." Lisabet's head snapped up. Suddenly she seemed strong and angry and Sass was taken aback. Though she still held Lisabet's hands, their contact was taut and wary. "That's not what I am.

I'm not an employee. I haven't been for years now. I thought you understood that. You included me in everything, I was the first one you told good news to. I was the one who took care of every single thing you needed. There was more to us than just friendship. We have a bond of love, Sass. Don't you understand that? Why can't you understand that?''

Suddenly Sass realized that she was no longer holding Lisabet's hands. Instead, Lisabet had hold of hers, was leaning into her as if she could force Sass to understand. Her expression was distraught, her tone frenzied and Sass couldn't find the words to begin to soothe her. And that was when Lisabet understood. Looking into Sass's confused eyes, seeing her mouth open in an expression of amazement, Lisabet realized that Sass had never felt what she did.

"Oh, no," Lisabet groaned. "You don't know. You don't know how I love you. Sass, I never had anyone else. No family. No sister. No one to love and then there was you. You took me in, gave me a job even though I wasn't beautiful or witty or any of the things that you are. I thought I had some worth. Don't I have some importance? Don't I?"

Nothing was said. In the glow of the indirect lighting, Sass Brandt listened to the words reverberating in her head. Never, in her wildest imagination, would she have foreseen this. Her heart moved in her breast, heavy with sorrow and regret. Lisabet had given her life to Sass for love, the kind Sass could never return.

"Oh, Lisabet. I didn't know. I just didn't . . ."

"It's all right." Lisabet pulled away, digging in her skirt pocket for a tissue.

"No, it's not. I'm sorry. I'm sorry I didn't understand all this before. I've taken advantage of you and I apologize. If you want to leave, I'll understand."

"I don't want to," Lisabet said. "I just want you to look at me again and really see me. I want you to be my friend."

Sass reached out. "I'll always be that. But I can't be anything more. You must understand. I've been given a second chance to live my life. I want to live it to the fullest this time. I can give you my love as a friend but I can't give more than that, Lisabet. I know you understand. We aren't sisters. We are friends, just as you want. If somewhere in your heart you need more than that, I'm sorry. I'm so sorry I'm not all you want me to be."

"But you are, Sass." Lisabet bent and gathered Sass's hands in her own. This was the moment when everything had to be said. "You are everything to me. I never had anyone to care for me. When I was desperate for a job you took me in. I know I wasn't the smartest or the most beautiful, but you saw something in me and I . . ."

"There you both are!"

Lisabet's declaration was cut short. Shay had found them. Her head bowed. Instinctively she pulled Sass's hands closer, only for Sass to ease them back and away. When Lisabet looked again, Sass's eyes were on her, honest and clear and the message they sent was not the one Lisabet wanted to see.

"We've been waiting for you." Sass spoke to

Shay, keeping her gaze level with Lisabet's until the other woman leaned away, her face closing, her body compacting until there was not a thread of sentiment between them. Lisabet stood. Sass watched with a breaking heart. Poor Lisabet. She'd been too guarded here, too susceptible to the facade. She thought nothing would ever change and now it had.

"I don't think I need you now, Lisabet," Sass said softly, doing her best to give Lisabet a dignified way out.

"You will, Sass," she said. She left without so much as a glance toward Shay. Looking over his shoulder, he watched her before joining Sass.

"I think I interrupted something important."

Sass sighed, "You have no idea."

"Bad?"

"Sad. I had no idea, until this accident, that Lisabet was so obsessed when it came to me?"

Shay looked at Sass as he always had, with frankness and forthrightness. He always told her the truth, but this time, the words that came out of his mouth were half that.

"I think we've all been a bit surprised by Lisabet's dedication to you. It's a wonderful thing, to inspire that kind of friendship, lass. 'Tis a sad thing not to understand there are limits to everything. I think Lisabet is a sorrowful lady. But if she had to choose who to give all of her love to, then it is a fine person she chose in you."

Her eyes pooling with tears, Sass touched Shay's cheek. No pretense in Shay Collier. He was everything Sass ever imagined in a man and more. Was it any wonder she found herself loving him more desperately each day?

"Thank you. That was so kind," she whispered, leaning close and kissing his lips.

Suddenly Shay's arms were around her, pulling her close, her cane falling to the floor between them.

"Ah, Sass," he whispered when their lips parted and his cheek was next to hers. "I'm not so kind. I think that I need to have you in my bed, beside me, loving me and that's all I think about. These words come out of my mouth and I say what needs to be said, yet I can't think of anything but you. Touch me once more, touch me like that again, with all the grace and gentleness that is in you and I'll forget you were ever hurt, I'll forget what we're about tonight."

"Shay," she breathed, feeling the heat rising from him, infecting her until she was almost lost in the passion of his speech.

"I mean it, Sass. Say the word. Say it now and I'll have you upstairs before you know it. God, I love you. I don't care about Lisabet." He held her away, roughly, but the face he showed her was smiling, laughing. "Am I a fool, or what, lass? I don't know what's come over me. Sure I've been as reserved as any man can be with you while you worked your way back from limbo. I don't know what's come over me tonight."

"Whatever it is," Sass said, cupping his face, smiling up at him with all the love and life she had in her, "I fully approve."

"Are you joking with me, Sass?" Shay asked, grinning when she shook her head. "You mean . . ."

The doorbell rang, and Shay's words hung on the tail of that chime, riding it away until both of them broke down in laughter. What joy there was in loving. What fun. Sass wondered how she could have survived all her life without it.

"Did I come at a bad time?"

Still laughing, Sass looked up to see Richard. How he had aged. He stared at them with a quizzical look on his face as if happiness was the last thing he expected to find here. With a most affectionate smile, Sass sat up, retrieved her cane and stood, waving away Shay's helping hand.

"Richard, you never come at a bad time. I'm so happy to see you."

"Me, too, Sass," he said, coming forward, leaning toward her to kiss her cheek. They stood together for a moment, both aware that Richard was more like a prodigal son than the wise father figure Sass had once thought. Both also understood that there was nothing to do but go on. There would be no recriminations from Sass and no apologies from Richard. Business, in this town, was business. Sass turned around, gesturing to the couch.

"Sit. Next to Shay." Richard did as he was told, nodding to the black-bearded man, grateful he saw no accusations in Shay's eyes, either. "Would you like a drink, Richard?"

"No thanks, Sass. I've actually got a dinner engagement after this. One drink and I'd be asleep."

"New client?" she asked, joining them.

"Maybe. You're still my one and only."

There was a bit of gloom to this admission, and Sass suddenly realized how much some people had depended on her. If only she'd managed to pull herself together sooner. Well, that couldn't be helped, but now, soon, though, things would be right.

"I'm glad to hear it, Richard." Sass put her hand briefly over his. He smiled cheerlessly.

"You're looking great, Sass. I never would have thought it." He looked over his shoulder. "We have you to thank for that, Shay."

" 'Twasn't a hard thing to give this one some bucking up." Shay grinned but looked past Richard toward the object of his affection.

"Richard," Sass said, tugging at his sleeve, "that's not all we have to thank Shay for. I want you to look at this." Sass handed over the sheaf of paper Shay had given her earlier that day. "Look, we can finish *The Woman At the End of the Lane*. He's figured out how we can rewrite that last scene. We wouldn't have to go back to Ireland to finish up. It would save a ton of money."

"You were even contemplating that?" Richard asked, shocked the movie was still under consideration, not to mention reshooting that last scene.

Sass shivered, "No, I honestly don't think I could stand on a cliff again. In fact, I know I couldn't."

"Thank God." Richard sighed and snapped the papers. From the breast pocket of his jacket he pulled his glasses out and slipped them on.

"But the way Shay's written it we can take it all the way up to the two people on the cliff— we've got that on film— then fade out to a scene with Curt on his own, sitting in his home after the funeral. We can shoot the dream sequence in the studio. It will work so well. After that," Sass pointed toward the third page and Richard dutifully turned it, "we've got maybe three months of editing. It's going to take someone really fine to do that and there's distribution, of course. Also, we've allowed for a substantial advertising and promotional budget. We're going to need it. They could use the accident for drama to draw attention to the movie."

Sass was grinning from ear to ear, peeking past Richard to Shay, who managed a wink. Man that he was, he kept his enthusiasm to himself. Richard sat between them, bent over as if studying the work intently.

"I can't believe he found time to do all this and play nursemaid at the same time, but Richard, I think it's feasible. Really, I do. I want you to liquidate whatever you can. Come up with the cash it will take to finish it. I can't believe I'm going back to work, but this is it! We're finally going to do it."

In her enthusiasm Sass failed to notice Richard's sigh or Lisabet slip into the corner of the huge room, her face dour as she watched the proceedings. She didn't see Shay's expression change to one of caution. It took her more than a minute to realize she was the only one smiling; everyone else was taking their cue from Richard and he was just about to call for action.

With great care he slipped his glasses off and lay the proposal on the coffee table. A click echoed in the room as he folded his glasses and put them away. His heavy sigh was added to the mix and, when he sat back, the huge sofa seemed to swallow him.

"Sass, it just can't be done."

"What are you talking about?" she scoffed good-naturedly. "Of course it can be done."

"I'm telling you it can't be done. I can't get the money. You're tapped out. If you liquidate anything else you'll be taking losses as high as fifty percent. Then you'd have to worry about capital gains in April. I don't think you could fund this kind of effort even if you managed to unload this place." He wearily ran a hand through his hair. "Sass, I can help manage your money and if you want to get back to work we can find guests spots that can accommodate you, but . . ."

"Richard, what are you talking about?" Sass laughed. "I don't need to be accommodated. I need to finish my movie. Shay's shown how it can be done creatively, now all I need is the money. If you're worried about liquidating, then let's get a loan."

"Sass, don't."

Richard stood up, his hands buried deep in his pockets as he paced. The silence grew to immense proportions. Once he stopped just to look at Lisabet. Did Sass see a nod of agreement? Of sympathy?

"Richard, look at me."

He looked sad and old when he did as she asked. "Sass, nobody will bankroll you. They don't think you can draw anymore, they worry that your injuries might keep you from finishing anything you start. You know how this business is. Rumors, innuendo. Half the town has you on your death bed."

"Then let's show them I'm not," Sass insisted

without hesitation. "Sell everything, Richard. Do it now."

"And if I can't?"

"Than get me six million dollars. I don't care how you do it, but I'm going to finish this movie if I have to crawl around this town with a tin cup. Now, are you going to go begging or am I?"

Sixteen

Richard hated Sloane Marshall's home, if that's what it could be called. It sat high on a hill, fashioned of stucco, glass, wood, and metal forged into exaggerated wings that pointed east and west. The place was about as inviting as a fortress, as hard looking and cold feeling as the mistress it housed. The interior was no more engaging. The furniture was sparse and what there was of it was spare in design. The backs of chairs were rigid and elongated, the paintings, angry splashes of color on overbearing, unframed canvases. The one and only table, in what Richard assumed was the living room, was nothing more than a sweep of glass atop a glass pedestal. Perhaps Sloane hoped that no one would notice it, no one would ask for a drink to put atop it, no one would consider it an invitation to try and make oneself comfortable in this tortuous shrine to spare, and supposedly artistic design.

With no small detail of architecture or ornament to distract him in this cavernous room, Richard paced. He put his hands in his pocket and moved his feet. But the sound of his heels on the bleached wood floor, the echo of every sigh as it drifted up to the impossibly high ceiling, unnerved him. He had no idea what he was doing here. He should leave, he knew that. Turning on his heel, already planning how he would admit defeat to Sass, Richard pulled up short and every single syllable of every single apologetic word flew out of his mind. He was not alone.

Sloane could have been one of her carefully chosen objets d'art so still did she stand. Impossibly slim and exotic as a bronzed Erte she watched him, one arm outstretched, her long fingers barely touching the white wall, the other arm draped across her waist. She was dressed in white from head to toe: wide pants, a tunic that reached to her knees and cut a deep V from her throat to her waist. Beneath that, a shimmering tight shirt of some sort pushed her small breasts up into beautifully, delicate mounds above the scooped neck. On her throat was a slash of gold, a collar that twisted and turned as if, with life, it might strangle her. And above it all, regally held, was a head and face so stunningly proportioned that it was almost startling to look at. Sloane's hair was short, just this side of shaved, so that the blackness of it, the gleam of it wouldn't distract and the viewer could admire her huge, dark, almond-shaped eyes, the small, straight nose, a mouth too full and ripe for someone as exacting as she.

"Richard, what a surprise. I thought our business was finished."

"It is, Sloane. I have your signature on a note to prove it."

"Then this is a social call. How endearing."

Sloane moved, but somehow Richard couldn't

find a word in his vocabulary to describe how she floated toward him. Perhaps she slithered, perhaps she levitated, witch that she was. He didn't hear the click of her heels on the floor yet he saw that she wore stiletto-heeled slides; he didn't hear the swish of her clothing, yet he knew her garment was silk and should have at least sighed in her wake. And he hated the look on her face. It was one of complete and utter amusement; a vicious cat with a cornered mouse. Sloane could smell need a mile away and her only pleasure in life was meeting those needs— and setting the almost unbearable terms of repayment.

Richard shuddered as she passed. How could it be that a woman as beautiful as she, a woman who smelled of spice and the Orient, should make him feel as if the grim reaper had crossed his path? He turned on his heel, followed her lead and sat on a black-lacquered couch covered with intricately embroidered pillows, the only color in this joyless room. Sloane reclined on a matching couch that faced him over the expanse of a glass table. Lazily she lay her head against her upturned palm and drew her legs up, tucking her feet under the pillows. Had China an emperor, certainly Sloane would have been the favored concubine.

"I . . ." Richard began but found the words difficult to say. His palms were sweating, his body heat alternating between hot and cold. This was so wrong. But, damn it, so necessary. For Sass. He shook his head, knowing that he was lying to himself. All this was for him. Sass needed to finish this movie. If she didn't, both of them would be completely ruined. Sloane was their only hope.

"Richard, I do believe we're tongue-tied. I had no idea I had that effect on you."

Sloane laughed, drawing her long, buffed nails over her chest, lingering on the rise of her breast, caressing herself casually, as if without thought, as if she had no idea how provocative this was.

"Sloane, listen, I need a favor. But I need good terms. It's a long shot so I can't afford to commit to your usual rates. I need money, Sloane, and it's for a sure thing. Honest it is. You'll get every cent back."

"How much do you need, Richard?"

"A lot."

"I assume you've been to the banks?"

Richard nodded. He held his hands clasped tightly between his knees, doing his best to hold her languid gaze. There was no reason to lie to her. She had her sources and would know who he had talked to. He saw Sloane's eyes harden, her smile flatten. She was getting ready to deal.

"Another real estate investment, Richard? I thought you'd learned your lesson last time."

"No, nothing like that."

"Good." Sloane sat up, swinging her legs over the edge of the couch, reaching to the side table. In her fingers was a long cigarette. She lit it gracefully. The scent was that of incense, always exotic. Nothing normal here for Richard to hang on to and understand.

"My employers weren't happy, Richard, with our last deal. Even they knew that real estate in California was a lost cause. They only advanced you the loan because they knew how solid your position was with Sass. I knew payback wasn't a problem. But if you're getting risky again, I'm afraid we can't do business. Sass is out of the picture, so to speak," Sloane paused a moment, chuckling at her pun, "and from what I hear you haven't been awfully successful in signing up someone new to replace her."

"I don't need anyone to replace her," Richard said, hoping Sloane wouldn't see the uncertainty in his eyes. "She's working again."

"So the little lady has staying power. What's she doing? A TV movie of the week?"

"She's going to finish *The Woman At the End of the Lane.*"

There, he said it and he was getting the kind of response he had anticipated. Sloane would never be so gauche as to verbalize her surprise. Instead, a delicate arched brow was raised, a last drag taken on the cigarette before it was carefully put out in a huge crystal ashtray.

"That's interesting. She must be doing quite well. I thought she wasn't even walking."

"She's walking and talking, Sloane. No one is going to believe the change in her."

"Are we talking miracle here?"

Richard raised a shoulder, warming now in his excitement. She hadn't thrown him out and she knew damn well what he wanted.

"Close to a miracle. Shay Collier. He came back. It's your knight in shining armor story. She's given a hundred and ten percent to him and it's paid off. She looks better than ever. They're inseparable, and together they're going to make this movie a piece of film history."

"Richard," Sloane said, laughing, "you weren't that excited about that movie in the first place.

Everyone knew it, so don't try to sell me a piece of goods."

"I'm not. But things have changed. Think of the publicity value of Sass's accident. People will come to see the film just to see the before and after Sass. Everybody knows where the filming stopped, the scene where the accident happened. If nothing else they'll come out of curiosity."

"And you flatter yourself. Sass has been out of commission for over a year. It's still a literary piece. It will be shown in art houses, maybe get some play on the East and West coasts, but that's it. It will never make it into the Midwest and the South."

"It will if the PR and advertising are right."

"Since when has anyone been able to coordinate the kind of magic for an art house film?"

"Since Sass Brandt's name is on the marquee," Richard said evenly and found he believed it even in the deepest recesses of his heart.

Sloane was silent, sitting straight in her almost colorless clothes in her almost colorless house. She was thinking, doing her magic, reaching into his mind with hers to weigh the probabilities of success. Her eyes narrowed, those long lashes of hers shadowing the most telling part of those black orbs.

"How much do you want, Richard? How much for Sass to finish this movie?"

"Six million."

She didn't laugh. She didn't smile. Sloane didn't even do him the courtesy of repeating the amount as if she had any interest. Instead she stood up.

"I'll make a call."

She was gone, leaving him alone in the room, disappearing into the bowels of this house to an office, a bedroom, a chamber of horrors he had never seen. What kind of person made a killing preying off other people's needs and weaknesses and dreams? People like Sloane, obviously. And it was people like him and Sass that made it all possible. Except Sass didn't know he was here. Sass should be told. But she would draw the line if she knew Sloane was involved. And if Sass did that, not only would the movie never be finished, Richard's life would be over. Jesus! Failure in Hollywood at his age was a one-way ticket to oblivion. Much as he loved Sass, it was his future that frightened him. Sass, at least, had Shay. Richard would have nobody. No hope, no money. Nothing.

"Richard." Sloane never asked for anyone's attention. She demanded it and it scared the living daylights out of him to find she'd traversed the hardwood floor without a sound and was now towering above him. He looked up. She smiled, a wicked little grin. "I've talked to my employers. They're most interested in Sass's recovery. They congratulate her on it."

"The money?"

"They'll be happy to oblige. Six million in an escrow account until the papers are signed."

Richard could feel himself pale and wished to God he was a better man than this. "And the rate of interest, the terms?"

"I think you'll like them, Richard. My employer is a great fan of Sass's. He doesn't think much of this current project. He's read the book. But he does have an interest in the film industry." Sloane turned away, her long, ephemeral coat fluttering in an unfelt breeze as she walked toward the huge glass doors that led to an impeccably kept Japanese garden. She lay one hand upon the glass but turned to look at Richard. "My employer would like to give Sass a fighting chance. No interest on this loan. A straight payback."

Richard half rose, startled by such generosity. The words of thanks were on his lips, the expression of gratitude already bubbling up from his heart, when he saw the slow and vicious smile slither across Sloane's face.

"You didn't think that was all, did you?" Sloane laughed and the sound was incredibly girlish, a sound of pure and utter delight. "Oh, Richard. You've not kept up with the times." Sloane's expression hardened once again, the glimpse of the girl was gone and the woman who wielded power like a double-edged sword was back. "This isn't a gift, Richard. This is a proposition. My employer will stake the final six million for *The Woman At the End of the Lane.* He will hope for the best. But, if the movie is not a success, if it doesn't recoup the investment, then Sass will be under obligation to star in a movie funded and chosen by my employer."

"Your employer isn't . . ."

"Exactly the most reputable? Tell me you don't listen to gossip, Richard." Sloane moved toward him and lay her hands on the low back of the lacquered couch. "Of course you do and the stories are all true, Richard. My employer dabbles in many things: drugs, arms, art, women. You name it, he can move it. That's why my employer has money to throw away on Sass's ridiculous movie. That is why my employer is able to be magnanimous with his funds. Everyone knows this. You knew it when you borrowed for that real estate deal. It didn't bother you then, it shouldn't cause you any concern now."

"But that was for me. You're asking me to commit Sass to an unknown project, produced by, by . . ." Richard was at a loss for words.

"By a shady character? Hah! That's rich," Sloane drawled, laughing cruelly, obviously enjoying his discomfort. Suddenly Sloane was serious, tiring of the game. "This isn't the forties, Richard. People make their money in many different ways. Some make it on their own steam like Sass, some make it by siphoning off part of that steam because they don't have a talent of their own. Much like you, Richard." Sloane paused and let the insult sink in. "And some make it any way that can, like me and my employer. Nobody cares how it's made anymore, all they care about is that they've got it. And isn't that what you care about, Richard, that you've got the money you need?"

"Yes. Yes, of course," he muttered.

Now Richard was up, unable to sit any longer on that odd, uncomfortable, yet luxurious couch. He ran a hand through his hair. Unlike Sloane he made noise as he paced. His steps sounded heavy on the hard floor, his breath shot ragged into the still air and there was the metallic sound of the change jingling in his pocket where his other hand had found a refuge.

"Richard, I don't have time for this nonsense. Either you're interested or you're not. If you're

not, then I've other things to do." Sloane rounded
the couch, letting her hand trail along the smooth
lacquer before settling herself down again. She
looked bored and that alone was enough to make
Richard nervous. "I thought you were a risk-taker,
Richard. More than that, I assumed you had Sass
in the palm of your hand. Seems you're getting soft
in your old age, and you can't even control a
woman who can barely walk. I think that's sad,
Richard."

"I never controlled Sass."

"She used to listen to you."

"That was before Shay Collier came into the picture," Richard said, turning to look at Sloane.
"She listens to him now. He's the one who's got
her ear."

"Then let him get her the money she needs."
Sloane lifted the hem of her garment and picked
at it as if one of the exquisite stitches displeased
her. She tossed it away and looked at him with
those big, black eyes of hers, an expression of apathy settling over her lovely features.

"He can't. Nobody can. You're the only one
who'll give us that kind of money," Richard con-
fessed.

"I know. And I'm willing to do you this favor.
In fact, I would suggest that the terms are truly
incredible. Accept, and you may never have to pay
the dividend. Come on, Richard," she teased,
"you're about ready for a run of good luck. You
believe in Sass. She believes in her movie. If it's a
success, you pay back the principal and Sass is
none the wiser about the little deal you made. If
you lose, and the movie's a flop, then you find a

way to make her see that this next project is in her best interest. It's as simple as that."

Sloane was becoming impatient with Richard's hedging, it bothered her immensely that he should care so much about Sass Brandt.

"Come on. She's not that good, Richard. Nobody is as saintly as Sass Brandt wants us all to believe. She'll see the light when the time comes. Look at it this way, she wants money and you're getting it for her. Did she ask any questions? Did she insist on knowing where it was you were going to find a hunk of change like this? I doubt it. Sass Brandt knows what's what. She's got her pretty little hand out. Put the money in it. One way or the other she'll thank you for it. Who knows, my employer's film might be just the thing to put her back on top if this little artsy one fails. She'll thank you, Richard. Take my word for it."

Richard stared at Sloane. He saw her lips move, those beautiful, beautiful lips. They formed sounds and words and, unfortunately, made sense. She was right. This was a no-lose situation. If *The Woman At the End of the Lane* failed, Sass would need exposure if she still wanted to act. If *The Woman At the End of the Lane* was a success, she need never know about the deal he cut with Sloane. He was the manager, she the star. So all he had to do was manage this situation.

Now it was his turn. Sloane had stopped talking and her lips were curled into a hard, mean little smile as she waited for his answer. In one blinding flash Richard felt a momentary panic. He should run and not look back. But the moment was gone as quickly as it had come and, to his surprise, he heard his own voice, so calm and assured, ringing strong through the house.

"When can you have the paperwork done?"

"A few hours, Richard. Just a few hours and the money is yours."

Richard nodded. He didn't feel any different now that he'd sold his soul, and promised Sass's along with it.

Seventeen

"Ouch! Marcia, that hurts."

"Of course it hurts," Marcia said, her voice sharper than her touch. It hurt as much to massage Sass's legs as it did for those twisted muscles to be touched. Thankfully Sass was lying flat on her face and couldn't see that. Marcia's own was screwed into an expression of sadness and concern. Everyone on the crew knew that Sass hated to be treated as if she were any different than she had been a year ago. Of course there had been the initial whispers. "Poor Sass." "Did, you see her limp?" "Did you see the scars?" "Awful!" "Poor Sass!" But that didn't last long. Sass didn't want sympathy, and her excitement was catching. She was working again, gloriously healthy looking except for her legs, energized and thrilled to be back with them all to finish her movie.

And who could blame her? Shay Collier was by her side, treating her like a queen. If he worried, no one ever knew. He had eyes only for her. Those black eyes watched her movements, watched her lips as she spoke her lines, watched her in silent contemplation as she moved into her character. That man was the envy of every guy on the set, and the desire of every woman. Yet he never gave one of them a second glance. A polite hello, a softly told story, a compliment with that marvelously rich brogue of his were always at the ready, but it was to Sass he went and with Sass he stayed. The man was in love, and was no less the star of the show because of it.

"There." Marcia gave Sass's good leg a playful slap and backed off. Sass swung herself up, her face aglow.

"Oh, I feel so much better. I shouldn't have eaten that huge sandwich for lunch. I'll be lucky if I can get my skirt buttoned."

Tucking the towel tight around her breasts she eased herself off the table in a ritual Marcia was getting used to. First her right leg, then gingerly her left leg would come to the floor. Sass would adjust her weight until it was just so and walk with barely a sign of a limp— most days. But today wasn't one of them.

"I wouldn't worry so much about your skirt if I were you, Sass. What's the use of getting dressed if you can't stand up and show it off?"

"Don't be silly," Sass scoffed, releasing the table to prove that she could very well stand on her own. Marcia in her cute little shorts snapped a towel and leaned back against the wall, one brow raised, challenging Sass. "I'm doing just dandy."

"And I'm the Queen of Sheba. It doesn't take a rocket scientist to figure out that leg's been bothering you royally."

"Then work your magic better," Sass said, laughing.

"I'm not a doctor, and I can't make it better. I can only ease the muscle strain. I think you should tell Shay you need to cut down on the shoot schedule."

"Absolutely not!" Sass moved across the floor of her trailer and grabbed her panties. She slipped them on, standing first on her left leg as if that would prove her pain was only a figment of Marcia's imagination. Sass pulled them up and let the towel slip away. Even Marcia had to admit that, as a package, it was hard to believe Sass felt anything but marvelous. She was as gorgeous as the first day Marcia had been called to service. She sighed and rolled her eyes. Sass didn't miss a trick. "Stop it. You're acting ridiculous. Look at me!" Sass snapped on a bra of peach silk and held out her arms. "Do I look like I need a doctor?"

"No. But the reason you're a star is because you're a damn good actress. I think you ought to at least clue Shay in on the fact that leg is fatigued and needs some rest."

"This leg needs to get to work, that's all."

Sass twirled away and started to dress. The costume felt good. With each button, each zip, with the cardigan over her shoulders Sass felt herself becoming her character. There were only two more scenes to shoot. Two more and they were finished. She and Shay could run away for a few days until editing got underway. Then she'd be off her feet, looking at every frame, watching for any discrepancies. That was when she'd worry about this leg of hers and the exhaustion.

"Okay. Okay." Marcia leaned down and snapped up the towel Sass had discarded. "You won't hear another word about this from me."

"Good," Sass said sweetly. Love could cure a whole lot of things. Maybe it could cure that damn leg, too.

"I only had your best interests at heart. . . ."

"I know. I know." Sass scooted in front of the mirror to check her hair. "Oh, this darn makeup. Do me a favor, send Lisabet in to help me get this sweater right. And see if you can dig up that makeup guy. I can never remember his name."

"Pierre," Marcia drawled.

"Yeah, Pierre. I sure wish we'd been able to afford to get Artists Inc. back again." Sass sighed. "Oh well, it's only a few more scenes and we've got the camera crew, and Norman directing out of the goodness of his heart."

"And this movie has the star who will carry it through," Marcia reminded her and Sass grinned into the mirror.

"Thanks, I needed that."

Marcia shrugged. "Only the truth, Sass." She put her hand on the knob of the trailer door. "I'll send Lisabet and Pierre in. Just try to stay off that leg till it's time to shoot, okay?"

"Okay. I'll do my best."

With that Marcia was out the door and Lisabet in. Ten minutes later Sass was ready to go, stepping out onto a set where people smiled and laughed and pitched in where they had to in order to make this movie work. For a moment Sass watched and thought that this was an even more vital effort than the first had been when money was plentiful. Now, with less money, it seemed that everyone was simply giving their best.

"You look lovely, lass."

Shay's arms were around her, her back to him and she lay against him adoring the feel of his lips in her hair.

"Bet you say that to all the girls." Sass laughed gently.

"Only those 'twill listen, my girl."

Sass slipped about, her arms now winding about his waist, her face tilted up so that he could see the marvelous sparkle deep inside her eyes where the gold melted to the color of mink.

"I'm all ears," she murmured and he kissed her as he knew he must. Neither could be so close without a kiss or a caress, and neither would have it any other way.

"I'm afraid if we have this particular discussion we'll forget what we're about, and this fine costume will suffer for it."

"If that's a promise, I'll call a break. We'll start again, maybe after dinner?"

"Now don't be putting ideas into either of our heads. Are you ready?"

"More than ever. Did you check on the cliff scene?"

Sass slipped her arm around Shay's waist as they strolled toward the set.

"I did and I don't think we'll need to be having Curt back to shoot again. The editing looks good. But then again, mine's an untrained eye. You'll have a look for yourself after this."

"Absolutely. But I trust you. I'd rather not have to rework that scene. In fact, I'm not even sure Curt would be available."

"I understand. But I wonder sometimes, Sass, perhaps you don't want to face Curt. Could it be that maybe you've not done with him in your heart?"

Sass stopped short, pulling back on the tall man next to her, "Shay, how can you even think that?"

"I don't think it," Shay answered, then smiled gently. "At least not often."

"Then don't think it ever. Curt is long gone, from my home and from my heart and . . ."

Sass's words trailed off just as her eyes tracked toward the door of the sound stage. Shay looked over his shoulder, his hold tightening on Sass.

"She's here again," Sass muttered. "Damn. I wish that woman would just go away."

"Sure there's nothing wrong with her being here, is there, Sass? She's doing no harm."

"Shay, wherever Sloane Marshall is there's harm. Believe me, I've heard the stories. Mark Coogan was ruined by that woman. He couldn't repay a loan and she took everything he had. Mark even told me that her so-called business associates paid his wife a call while he was gone one day. She's trouble, Shay, and I don't want her on the set. Oh my God!"

"What?" Shay peered closer, but the Asian woman had moved into the shadows and it took him a minute to focus as she sauntered into the light again. It was then he saw what so infuriated Sass. Richard Maden strolled with Sloane familiarly on his arm.

"I can't believe it. They look like old friends. My God, Richard should have more sense than that."

"Richard has a great deal of sense, Sass. Perhaps he doesn't want to offend the lady. She's taken an interest in your film. If she knows such powerful people, maybe it's a good thing."

"Nothing about Sloane is a good thing. It's like she's The Shadow. She just kind of appears and no one knows why. Well, this is my set and I don't want her here. I don't like her watching me while I work."

Sass slipped from the protection of his arm and was headed for the duo before Shay could stop her. Not that he had any intention of doing so. Sass knew what she was about and, if the truth be known, Shay was glad to see her so feisty.

"Richard?"

Sass stood well away from the two. Richard's shoulders stiffened but when he turned, it was a smile he showed Sass, an open arm he offered to her. She didn't move into it. Instead, she kept her eyes on Sloane, that beautiful and exotic woman who Sass knew only by horrid reputation.

"I'm sorry, but perhaps you didn't know. This is a closed set. I'm afraid your friend is going to have to leave before we start shooting," Sass said just as Shay came up beside her. Surprised when no apologies were forthcoming, when there was no flurry of goodbyes, Sass raised a brow. The silent question was directed at Sloane. In response, she moved closer to Richard, smiling with incredible audacity.

"Sass," Richard said, "this lady is here as my guest."

"Really?" Still Sass's gaze didn't waver. Instead, she stuck out her hand. "Sass Brandt."

"Sloane Marshall."

"I know who you are," Sass said, not meaning

to be rude but sounding it nonetheless. "I'm sorry, but I will have to ask you to leave. Only those I have personally cleared are allowed here during the shooting."

Sloane looked at Sass a minute longer, ignoring the actress's hand. It was obvious she wasn't going to move, nor was she going to do Sass the courtesy of answering her. Instead, those almond eyes of hers glittered with delight at her own impudence and slid their way to Shay.

"And who might this be?"

Sass stepped forward, moving in front of Shay as if to shield him. But Shay could hold his own.

"Shay Collier. Invited and working on this film."

"Good for you," she said.

"Yes it is, and I'm afraid he has things to do in order to ready the next scene. Richard?" Sass looked at Richard, noting his pallor, the sheen of sweat across his forehead. "Would you mind asking Lisabet to make sure that lunch is ready on time for the crew today? There seemed to be a problem yesterday."

"She's taken care of it, Sass."

"Please," Sass said quickly, authoritatively, "check again. I'd hate for anyone to have to wait after the morning we have scheduled."

"Go, Richard," Sloane goaded. "Ms. Brandt obviously wants to slap my poor little hands in private. Go on, see to lunch. I'm sure you can do that very well."

"Sass, I think I should stay."

But Sass was no longer paying attention to him, so Richard backed off and Shay went with him.

The men gone, the two women stood alone. Sass moved first and Sloane fell into step, walking more gracefully in her high heels and tight skirt than Sass did in her flat shoes and dirndl. It was a failing noted by Sass only. Sloane kept her eyes straight ahead as they moved slowly toward the doors and Sloane's eviction.

"You've been on this set quite a bit. I was surprised when I saw Richard with you."

"Men will always surprise you." Sloane chuckled. "I'm sure you didn't think I was his type?"

"I never underestimate men, nor would I presume to make assumptions about Richard's private life. What he does on his own time is his business. I care about him a great deal, but I've no say in his social life. What he does on my time is quite another matter, though. And, this . . ." Sass stopped, turned and surveyed the set that looked so much like the cottage in which Shay's wife had taken her own life. "This is my time. And these are my rules. You are going to have to leave. Please."

Sloane smiled. She took two deliberate steps toward the door as she pulled on lambskin gloves that were the color of persimmon.

"I'm afraid, Ms. Brandt, that you aren't quite right about that."

"About what?" Sass shook her head, confused.

"About this being your time. Actually," Sloane said with a sigh, snapping her shoulders toward Sass, cutting a beautiful figure in her Armani suit, her Hermès scarf draped over her shoulders, "this is my time. Or at least a portion of it is."

"I beg your pardon?" Sass laughed hard and

short. But Sloane didn't move, her stance ever more irritating, her arrogant expression infuriating. Sass was disgusted. "Don't be absurd. You're wasting time I don't have. Now, please, leave the set and don't come back. If you want to see Richard, do it after our work is done."

Sass turned on her heel, a pain shooting up her left leg, a frantic jolt of terror clutching at her belly. She wanted to run but couldn't; she hated the fear she felt and was powerless to banish it. But she wasn't a step away when she heard that luscious, unhurried, pompous voice following her, lassoing her and dragging her back.

"I'll do whatever it is I damn well want here, Sass. It's my set. My employers paid for it, and for you, and for every sandwich you're going to serve your crew at lunch. My employer's money will pay for editing this film and advertising it. And I'm here at my employer's specific request to see that his money is being spent properly. So don't order me away. I bought the right to be here, and I will make sure, that every cent of my employer's money is spent as it should be."

Sass's breath disappeared. Her hand found her throat and she thanked God that her back was to this woman. The room was spinning and the words Sloane spoke were whipping around the whirlpool of her mind. Fast. She had to think fast. Could it be that Richard sold her out? That Sloane Marshall was actually funding the completion of *The Woman At the End of the Lane*? Forcing the breath back into her body, squaring her shoulders, Sass clasped her shaking hands in front of her. She turned her best face to Sloane. Sass the actress was haughty and righteous, but Sass the woman was dying inside.

"Richard would never have come to you for money."

"Then you don't know Richard as well as you thought." Sloane abandoned her pose. Her languorous body melted into a sinister stance. "The deal is done, Ms. Brandt, and it's what it is. If you're little gamble pays off, you're paid back free and clear. Not a penny of interest."

"That's quite generous. From what I'd heard about the way you do business, one takes their financial life into their hands when they make a deal with you. A noninterest loan seems a bit out of character."

"Not really. This was a special situation. My employer was most happy to do you this favor. He's quite a fan of yours."

"And he's a businessman, I'm sure, who doesn't let sentiment get in the way."

"Right you are." Sloane laughed as she walked over to a high stool and rested a foot upon it. She was a gorgeous woman and one completely without appeal. It was hard to imagine anyone touching her with affection, anyone speaking to her in friendship or whispering words of love. "Though his regard for you is high, he couldn't possibly let loose of six million dollars without some assurance that he would recoup his investment."

"He'll get back every penny. This is a fine movie."

"That's for the critics to say— and the public, of course. They may turn two thumbs down on you, Sass. Then you'll be sitting on a pile of debt."

"I assume there's some provision in that eventuality?" Sass heard the tremor in her own voice and looked closely at Sloane.

"Of course. But it's of little consequence now. Why don't you go and finish your film? Do what you do so well. If the time comes when we must talk about the specifics of our arrangement, we'll do so in more comfortable surroundings."

"We'll do so now."

Sass was no longer afraid. Her anger had found a space in her heart and was pushing everything else aside. This woman's veiled threats had to be more terrorizing than any reality. It was the fear Sloane enjoyed. Sass could deal with anything, any terms Richard negotiated, but she couldn't continue with the film in this limbo filled with dread. Sloane sighed theatrically, batted her lashes coquettishly and finally acquiesced.

"All right," she clucked, falsely exasperated. "If you must know. But I certainly don't see what good it's going to do. Richard is your manager, you're the actress. He should manage, and you should act."

"I manage myself, thank you. Richard is my advisor. Now, if you please, the terms of your agreement with him?"

"The terms are so simple. If *The Woman At the End of the Lane* does well, you pay back the loan and my employer is delighted. If, on the other hand, the film appears that it will fail at the box office, and you cannot pay back the principal, we are willing to take your talent in trade. My employer has a movie he would like to produce. If *The Woman At the End of the Lane* fails, all you have to do is star in that film. A simple, straightforward barter. See?" Sloane held her palms upward. She flashed a grin. "Nothing up my sleeve."

"And nothing in your coffers if this movie fails. I wouldn't work for your employer if he were the last man on earth. I've heard enough to know that this man's fortune wasn't made by the sweat of his brow, but by the misfortunes of others. Drugs, I believe. Drugs and prostitution and God knows what else."

"Oh, Sass." Sloane hopped down from her stool and smoothed her skirt. "Please don't be so saintly. So you recovered from an accident. It wasn't a miracle. God didn't reach out his little finger and bring you miraculously back to life. You just worked at it, and now you're pushing your way back into the spotlight. You want to be a star again? You want the money? So what's the difference between you and him?"

"I don't hurt anyone. I use my talent. I work for what I have."

"So does he!" Sloane laughed. "Come on. That fall of yours didn't knock you senseless. You think the banks that extended you loans before the accident didn't make some shady deals? Of course they did. Everyone does. My employer just happens to be more up front about things. Don't be an ass. Richard accepted our deal, and you are bound."

"But he didn't tell me."

"And you didn't ask, from what I hear," Sloane countered. "You didn't want to know. You're as selfish as the rest of us, pretty lady."

"I'll take you to court."

"I'll take what's most important to you."

"Is that a threat?"

"I don't know." Sloane slid past, coming so close that Sass felt the brush of wool against her shoulder, smelled the scent of ginger and spices that followed the woman who now turned back and looked into her stricken eyes. "Not really, I suppose. As they say in the movies, it's just fact. Funny how easy it is to find out about people. The general assumption would be that status and wealth are most important to you. People would imagine you might be self-centered. But I know that's not the case. You're very unusual for someone in your position which, actually, is rather refreshing. It would be so boring to simply take *things* from you. No, you actually have priorities. You have a soul. You have . . ." Sloane looked over her shoulder. Shay was conferring with Lisabet, Richard hovered near the dressing room. Sloane's eyes were hard as flint when they turned back to Sass. "You have people you love. They truly, honestly love and admire you. Those are terrible things to lose: love, admiration, people. So much harder to part with than mere things. Don't you think?"

Sass couldn't move. She couldn't bear to look at Shay or Lisabet because Sloane was right. Those people meant more to her than anything in the world, even Lisabet with her neediness, her deceitful way of keeping Sass to herself. Even Richard after this. Suddenly she was tired. To have come so close only to find misery at the end of the road. A tear slid down her cheek, gliding, stopping, choosing a path and continuing on. Sloane reached out with that gloved hand of hers, one

finger extended and caught the tear. The persimmon leather of her glove stained to blood red.

"That's touching. So touching," she whispered.
"Hold the mood. From what I've seen of the
script, despair is the perfect emotion for this final
scene. Perhaps, if you play it right, you'll never
have to worry about my employer again. Perhaps,
if you can pull it off, you might have a hit. Then
all those people you love so much will get to go
to bed every night, safe and snug."

With that, Sloane was gone, leaving the set the
same way she came: as if she owned it.

Sass slipped out of bed, careful of her leg since
she'd been still for so long. Quietly she pulled on
her mint silk robe, belting the waist as she walked
quietly out of the room. Sass didn't look back at
the fabulous view, nor the black-haired man who
lay peaceful in her bed. It was the first time since
she met Shay Collier that he was not nestled in
her thoughts. Her mind was elsewhere, her soul
was troubled and she believed herself to be completely, utterly alone.

She had made it through the day, performing as
she had never performed before. She couldn't
bear to talk to Richard. He had been smart enough
to leave before she had to ask him to go. Lisabet
fawned, and it was all Sass could do not to brush
her away, scream that she needed time to think.
Shay, considerate of what he imagined was her exhaustion after the final and dreadful suicide scene,
had bundled her up, taking her home in loving

silence, never guessing that the very heart of her had been ripped out by Sloane and her threats.

Sass begged off dinner and she locked herself in the bathroom, immersing herself in a steaming tub. But there was no consolation in her isolation. When her eyes were closed she saw Sloane's laughing ones and envisioned herself without Shay, without Lisabet, alone in a dark world that had been made blacker by that woman. Once she left her room, ready to tell Shay everything, or confide in Lisabet if she were the first one stumbled upon. But Sass turned back when she heard the two of them speaking, civil, almost friendly in their concern. If they could put their differences aside out of love for her, how could she tell them that her love had created danger for them?

With a heavy heart Sass had gone back to her room and climbed into bed, pulling the covers high against her chin, shivering though there was no chill. Sleep was feigned when Shay slipped in beside her, kissing her, laying a protective hand upon her hip. But she could no more pretend that she was asleep than make the stars wink out.

She had turned toward him with hope, the feel of his lips still upon her cheek. She wanted those lips on hers. She wanted him to kiss away the thoughts that refused to leave her head. Wordlessly Sass raised her face to his, wound her arms around his naked waist and pulled Shay ever closer. He needed no further encouragement. A word escaped that marvelous mouth of his. Some wonderful term of endearment, a muttering of her name, before he kissed her, soft and sweet and ever more deeply.

Sass pushed the sound out of her mind. It wasn't words she wanted, but escape. They had lost themselves in each other so often, banished the world at a moment's notice, that Sass hungered for that magic now. But it wasn't to be, reality was stronger than illusion. Desperation was a wall against pleasure. Sass closed her eyes and concentrated on his every movement. Shay's hands were on her back, under her gown, pulling at it, tugging it over her head and throwing it to the ground, in one swift movement. But he was too slow, too gentle, Sass couldn't break down the wall and cross to the other side of ecstasy where oblivion waited.

Frantically Sass rolled atop Shay, laying herself over him. He laughed, misunderstanding her need. She kissed him harder and grasped his hands, pushing them against her breasts and between the two of them until he had no choice but to catch the heat of her need. He laughed with a deep, guttural night sound that signaled his joy and his desire. In the blink of an eye she was on her back, eyes closed, offering herself up to sensations his caresses, nips, and bites brought. She prayed to find the place where lust becomes passion and passion opens the door to a universe without thought or fear.

Despite her love for Shay, despite the joy their coming together brought even in such a time, Sass couldn't cross the threshold to forgetfulness. It was over, their act of love and Shay had held her. He murmured endearments, laying his head upon her shoulder until, exhausted, sleep claimed him. Sass was left alone to stare at the ceiling, fighting back her tears and terror.

Now she was alone in the dark house that had known so much joy and so much sorrow but never, ever, fear. Silently she glided down the stairs, pulling her robe closer, the shivering coming again. She hated the visions running through her head: Sloane and Shay, her accident and Curt's desertion, Lisabet's cloying devotion, Richard's betrayal and Sloane's face ever present in her head. She headed toward the kitchen but changed her mind. On the table was the folder that had been thrust into her hands as she left the set for the last time.

Sitting, Sass opened it, peering at the pages through the dim light. She turned the light up slightly. Page after page was turned, turned back and referred to again. Sass held her head in her hands hardly able to believe what she was seeing. She had been so careful, checking and rechecking expenditures. But things had happened, the stage needed more work than anticipated, shooting in studio had proven more expensive than if they had wrapped on location. Reediting to save the scene on the cliff so that Curt wouldn't have to be called back, had been excruciatingly expensive. Bottom line. Another seven hundred thousand was needed to finish and promote the project.

"A little light reading, Sass?"

She jumped, Shay was at her side. "I didn't hear you. You scared me."

"Sure, 'tisn't that the last thing I've ever wanted to do, my love."

He kissed her head and sat beside her, a com-

forting hand on her arm. She sat up straighter, shy-
ing from his touch. She didn't want to love him any
more than she already did. If she lost Shay, if something happened to him, how could she bear it?

"In a mood, are we, lass?" His hand slid away
from her.

"No." She shook her head and flicked at the
papers in front of her. "Nothing like that. Just
more bills. More money." Sass put a hand to the
side of her head, then let it fall. "I'll have to get
some money."

Shay nodded and slipped onto the chair next to
her.

"So, 'tis money that's bothering you, is it?"

Sass threw back her head, offered a weak smile,
her face turned toward him while her eyes studiously avoided his. Yet she saw everything. Shay's
eyes lowered as he studied the table, his hands
clasped in front of him on the gleaming surface.
His hair was sleep tousled, two high spots of color
stained his cheeks. He'd been sleeping deeply,
dreaming well and beautifully. Now he was sitting
beside her, judge and jury, deciding how much of
this story he believed. When he raised his head,
he also raised his hand and tipped her chin, forcing her to look at him.

"That's not all, Sass. 'Tisn't just money worrying
you. You've not been yourself, and it's a deep sadness you're carryin'." Shay's eyes bore into her as
if he could pull the truth away from her mind and
open her heart at the same time. "What is it, Sass?
It's not like you to hide things from me. We've
been to hell and back, you and I, and there's nothing you can tell me that will make me feel any the

less for you. If you've a dragon, let me slay it. If you've a heartache, let me heal it. I'll save you from whatever it is that hurts you, the way that you saved me."

Sass sighed sadly as she clutched his hand gently, kissed his fingertips, then put him away from her.

"You've already saved me. You don't owe me anything."

"You rescued yourself from those injuries. I'm talking about something deeper here, Sass. If you can, don't lie to me. For certainly, by all the saints in heaven, that may be the thing I couldn't stand."

"Oh, Shay."

Sass buried her face in her hands, her exclamation so weary that he could barely contain himself. He felt the pain coming from her as if it were the heat of a fever burning so hot it left her feeble. He wished he had the cooling hand to lay upon her brow. Instead, he lay that hand on her upright arm and let it lie. She would face him when she was ready. He was relieved, at least, that the aura of despair about her, on a day that should have been so joyous, had not been his imagination. When she looked at him again, she looked almost childlike in the early morning light. And, like a child, her wide eyes showed a helpless worry worn so openly that Shay's heart almost broke from looking at it.

"You're right," she said. "The last thing I could, or should, do to you is lie. This is about money, Shay, but it's about so much more. It's about everything. Our vision of this movie, our dreams for the future . . . it's about our lives, Shay. Our very lives."

She'd never heard anything like it, not in this house. The walls themselves trembled with the rumbling and thrusting noises that pushed up through her bedroom floor. For a long while Lisabet lay still, waiting to hear it again, trying to identify the noise. When she did, she could hardly believe her ears. Lisabet had prayed for such a ruckus in the beginning, but now she hoped she was wrong.

Slipping into her robe and slippers, she hurried down the long hall to the top of the stairs that overlooked the main room of the house. Slowing, she stopped only when she saw them. In her deepest, darkest heart, Lisabet could never have imagined a scene such as this.

"That is the most ridiculous thing I've ever heard, Sass. Don't play these games with me. Don't try my patience!"

Shay's hand swept the huge and heavy pillows from the couch, scattering them across the room. His voice boomed, shattering the brittle atmosphere in the room. His face was flushed with anger, but no more so than Sass's. She stood her ground, well back, as if she was afraid Shay might lay those powerful hands on her and fling her about. Or, perhaps, it was her own fury she feared, for she was tense, poised like a cat ready to pounce on its prey.

"Don't say that!" she screamed. "You make it sound like I'm playing some kind of game. This is no game, Shay, and you can't just ignore this. You can't make it go away. Goddamn it, listen to me. I know about this woman. I know about the people she works for. This isn't a movie and this isn't one of your novels. This is real and she threatened you."

"I don't care if she threatened half the country. There are laws, and there are police, and she will be taken care of. But you don't . . ."

Shay threw up his hands, his breath was coming hard. He tossed his head back and struck the wall with a fist, his other planted at his hip. His shirt was open, never having been buttoned, his jeans were zipped but the snap at the waist was askew and Lisabet saw the fine line of dark hair that ran down his taut belly, disappearing beneath that sheath of denim. His feet were bare and somehow that made his anger all the more poign-ant.

Now his voice was quiet, quivering with the effort to control it. Lisabet could have sworn it was tears she heard beneath the begging and the fury. "Don't, Sass. Sure, you're going to throw it all away if you do this. What good is your movie, or your recovery, or our love if we both know that you've sold your soul to people who should be visitin' together in hell? What good will we be to each other with that between us?"

Sass's shoulders sagged, but her head was up, her eyes still wary.

"But it won't be between us long. If this movie fails, then I make the one they want me to make and it's over."

Shay twirled slowly, his back against the wall, his head thrown back against it, too. The cords on his long strong neck stood out, the great sob of frustration he uttered could be seen coursing through his throat, his lips trying to stop it before it was torn from him.

"Ah, Sass. Ah." Then he doubled over, catching himself with his hands on his knees. He spoke to the carpeting, to the air, to anything but her. "Sass, it won't be over then. What's to keep them from comin' back and comin' back if they choose? What's to keep them from threatening one more time so that you'll do that one last favor?"

Sass shook her head, short bursts of denial. "It won't happen. I'll see that it won't."

" 'Tisn't that dandy, Sass. You're afraid for us now, but tomorrow or the next day you'll see that everything will be rosy. A rich thought, lass. A very rich thought. . . ."

Shay's head swung back and forth and he pushed himself upright once more, only now re-alizing that they had company. His flashing eyes narrowed as he speared Lisabet with a look. "Ah, Lisabet. Have we wakened you? Wakened you with our spit and fire down here in the queen's palace. Well, come now, join the row. Sure, doesn't it have to do with you, too?"

Shay's head swung back Sass's way and he im-paled her with his black gaze. When she didn't move, he did. He was up the stairs two at a time, his huge hand covering Lisabet's. Down he went again, taking her with him. "Now, Miss Sass, ask your friend here how much her life is worth. Six million dollars? One million? What about peace of mind? What's the dollar sign on that, my darlin' girl?"

Sass turned away, crossing her arms over her robe. "Shay, please."

"No, you please!" he roared.

"Shay, Sass, what's going on here? I could hear both of you all the way up in my room." Lisabet looked from one to the other, her face pinched into an expression of dread. "Please, someone tell me what's going on."

"Sass, do you think you should do the honors?" Shay asked sarcastically, but Sass remained silent, her back to them, her rich red-gold hair tumbling to her shoulders. "Nothing from the mistress of the house? How unusual since it's she who seems to know what's best for everyone who lives under this roof."

"Shay?" Lisabet breathed. Much as she didn't care for the relationship between Sass and this man, Lisabet could not have imagined a day when he would have spoken with such disdain, when his voice would have held such venom.

"This isn't my fault. Richard's the one," Sass said quietly.

"Oh, no, Sass. Oh no!" Shay threw himself forward, clutching at the sofa. He dug his fingers into the fabric, and would have done the same to Sass's soft skin if he had his hands on her. "Don't you dare blame this on Richard. He was doing only what you told him to do."

"I told him to get funding. I never told him to . . ."

"You told him to do what he had to! And he did it, poor man. There isn't a way in heaven to say no to you. Sure, don't I know that firsthand. Back you came, almost killing yourself, to get what you wanted when you sought me out that first time. Holy Mother of God! Did you not once think of what would have happened to me if you'd died at my door? Never once did you imagine what I might have felt if you died. The guilt would have been dreadful. I, already damaged by one woman's death, would now have two on my head."

"I didn't know about your wife then," Sass cried angrily, spinning toward him.

"Did that matter? No! What mattered was your willingness to sacrifice me, and my peace of mind, for what you wanted. The same way you were willing to sacrifice Richard's. All or nothing, Sass. Richard understood that, and because he loved you, he did what you wanted. He got you money. Did you ever once ask where it came from? Did you?"

"No." Sass seemed to shrink away, the fight going out of her. The silence left in the wake of her retreat was eerie. Crossing her arms, running her hands over them she stepped toward the window, unable to look at Shay. "I never asked," she said quietly.

Lisabet skirted around the couch where Shay still stood, his anger keeping his body tensed at angles that looked hard and unwelcoming. Her hands shook as she reached Sass. She wanted to touch the honey-haired woman but found she couldn't. Too many things were happening here in this room between these people who had loved and respected each other beyond all bounds. Lisabet was afraid a touch might shatter Sass or the protective aura that was so delicately draped around her.

"Sass, what is it? What's wrong here?"

"I'll say what it is, Lisabet," Shay answered her. "I'll say because you won't get another word out of Sass. She's hiding behind her very deep and abiding love for us. She's using us, Lisabet, and I want no part of it. Richard, it seems, secured the funding to finish the movie from a woman named Sloane Marshall." Shay moved slowly around the couch, looking at Sass while he told his story. "Sloane is not a very nice woman, 'tis she? Her investors have agreed not to charge Sass exorbitant interest on her loan if *The Woman At the End of the Lane* is a success."

Lisabet shook her head, looking from one to the other, "But that's wonderful."

"Ah-ha!" Shay bellowed, "That's the rub!" A sly and ugly smile came across Shay's face. Still, Sass didn't look his way. Only the muscle that defined the beautiful line of her jaw trembled under his scrutiny. Instinctively Lisabet moved closer to Sass. This time she did reach out, laying her hands lightly on the other woman's shoulders. It was Lisabet who met Shay's angry eyes, Lisabet who held his gaze.

"Lisabet," Shay said quietly, "there is another part to this deal of Richard's. If the movie fails, Sass must make a film for Sloane's employer. A man of terrible reputation. A man who traffics in drugs and other distasteful things. A man who thinks nothing of taking a life. This is who Sass will be indentured to. This is the man whose shadow Sass will live under the rest of her life if she does this thing."

"Tell the rest, Shay. Go ahead, tell the rest. Let's

see what Lisabet thinks about why I won't give the money back," Sass challenged.

"Oh, this is the rich part, yes. The final codicil. If Sass does not fulfill her bargain, 'twould seem these fine folks, these business people of such high repute, will do you and I and Richard bodily harm until Sass does exactly as they say. Now," he went on sarcastically, "what has Sass decided to do? Give the money back, and let the movie lie until she can fund it herself? No, our grand lady here has decided to go ahead with this deal. She has such faith in her movie that she is willing to throw us to the wolves, Lisabet. You and I are now the collateral with which Sass deals."

"Stop it, Shay! I've heard enough. You make it sound so simple. I already owe these people six million dollars. It's spent. It's done. The film is almost finished. Do you honestly think they'll let me walk away now? I can just hear it. 'Oh, Sloane, sorry about that, but could you hang out until I manage to get another role that will pay me six or seven mil. I promise I'll give you everything I owe you then.' " Sass laughed ruefully. "Sure, she's really going to wait around for that! Her goons would be after all of us like that." Sass snapped her fingers and shook Lisabet free.

"Then we go to the police, Sass, darlin'!" Shay cried in despair.

"And they get us when the police lose interest. Shay, there's no other way to do this. I have to finish the movie. I have to take this chance. It's not just for me. It's for all of us. This is the only way that we can make Sloane go away. What's done is done, Shay. That's all there is to it. I'll finish

The Woman At the End of the Lane. I'll make it a success. I'll make everything all right.''

"No, Sass. You're wrong. You're throwing us all away, you're risking everything. Not only our lives, but your own reputation. Think, Sass. Think with your head and not your heart. Good lord, woman. I know how long you've wanted this to happen for you and it breaks my heart that all your hope and all your suffering and hard work has come to this. But, Sass, who will want you to act for them when they know who you've sold yourself to? It's not just this movie, it's the rest of your career, the rest of your life. For God's sake, Sass, think about the ramifications of what you're about to do.''

"I have, Shay. I have,'' Sass insisted. "Lisabet, tell him that I can do this. He doesn't have the faith. I can pull this off. The movie will be finished and Sloane will get her money and we'll all be fine. But that's the only way. I have to finish this movie. I have to take the risk.''

Sass's arms reached out toward Shay, hovering at a halfway mark as she watched and waited for him to meet her there. But when he stood he simply looked at her, his face a play of emotions: anger and confusion, disappointment and longing and over it all a blanket of tortured love. Finally he moved, but it wasn't toward her. His back to Sass and Lisabet, his voice already sounding so far away, he spoke.

"I can't take the risk, Sass. I can't watch you destroy yourself. Perhaps I'm not a strong man. I thought I was at one time, but now I see how weak I am. I cannot watch another woman I love destroy herself. I cannot stay here and hope and wait.''

Shay's head hung. He shook it sadly, his black curls glinting in the light of the sunrise. "I've got to go Sass. I love you beyond my life, so I want you to know 'tisn't me I'm afraid for, my darlin'. 'Tisn't me at all."

Without a backward look he was gone, up the stairs, disappearing into the still dark hall. The two women watched, they waited and listened but heard nothing. When Lisabet thought the silence between them might become unbearable, Sass laughed, a short and painful little sound.

"He doesn't mean it." She tried to keep the trembling from her voice, but failed. "He doesn't, Lisabet. Where would he go? Back to that cabin of his? I don't think so, do you? Do you?"

Sass spun toward her companion, a desperate smile on her beautiful lips. There in the early morning light Lisabet thought she'd never seen Sass look more beautiful. But Sass had lost something, a touch of her talent. Though her lips were pulled back, though her eyes were shining, even Lisabet could tell this act was less than convincing. There was terror behind the sparkling eyes and cowardice behind the smile. But Lisabet loved Sass and Lisabet would never criticize any of her performances.

"No, Sass," Lisabet said quietly. "I don't understand how anyone could ever leave you."

Eighteen

Hollywood lost something the day premieres gave way to private screenings, theaters turned into multiplexes, and two thumbs up replaced an all-night party at the Derby while the beautiful people waited for the early-edition reviews. But now, just for this one night, Hollywood was everything it had been in the golden days and Sass Brandt was the lonely star waiting for her cue to step into the spotlight.

From her Oggioni silk teddy to the antique Lalique pin carelessly pinned to the breast of her Fendi chemise, Sass Brandt looked every inch the star.

What she felt was another matter entirely.

Sass was tired even though the last few days had been spent in quiet reflection of what had been and what was to come; lonely despite the fact that Lisabet sat next to her in the limousine. Sass sighed, and leaned her high clear brow against the glass, closing her eyes for only a moment. How she wished . . . How she wished . . .

Nothing. There was nothing to wish for any longer. Even if the film was a fabulous success, Shay hadn't come back. He wasn't there to give her strength, to wait with her, to love her and believe in her. How hard it was even to believe in herself now. How could she have expected that from Shay when she had failed the task so miserably?

"Curt's arriving."

Sass opened her eyes, reluctant to be drawn back into the present. She glanced over her shoulder in time to see Lisabet nod toward the entrance of the theater. Sass's eyes followed suit, looking out the rain-cloud-colored window and hating the tint. Limousine windows were the ultimate conceit. They kept people from looking in, as though her face was too precious for them to see. She almost laughed at the thought. Tonight the darkened windows were blinds, hiding the coward she had become. Now the solitude of the car symbolized less her hubris, than her fear and aloneness.

Richard had stolen away, terrified, trying to sit the fence until he figured out which side would come out on top. Curt, well Curt was the most honest of all. He had places to go and things to do, and he had left Sass long before this problem with Sloane. Shay's leaving had been the worst and hurt the most even though there was righteousness in his decision. Sass couldn't help but wonder, though, if there was honor in it. If you love, shouldn't you love unconditionally? No, that wasn't right, either. Lisabet loved unconditionally, she remained by Sass's side, and Sass was still lonely.

"There."

Lisabet's voice, her raised hand, reminded Sass she couldn't afford the leisure of her own company.

"I see him," Sass murmured, as she caught sight of Curt passing his car keys to a red-jacketed underling. He was in perfect celebrity form.

Rounding the back of his Ferrari Curt hesitated the way actors do, pirouetting and waving to the crowd as he brushed aside the attendant and opened the passenger door. Though Sass couldn't see, she could well imagine what was happening now. Long, slim legs were easing out of the car, a beaded gown draping around them, letting the spectators glimpse just enough of a perfectly formed thigh to know what they were missing. Then . . .

Sass sat up straighter. Old habits died hard. At the last moment, just before Curt's date was seen in all her glory, Sass realized she was as anxious to know who had accompanied Curt to the premiere as everyone else. She smiled when a head of long, blond hair followed broad shoulders and, indeed, a daring, baring beaded gown was seen on a spectacular body. Stargazers behind the barricades grinned, heads turned, catcalls were hooted. The blonde kissed Curt deeply and the crowd went wild.

"Curt's taste in women has changed," Sass noted wryly. "He used to like them a bit shorter, with more red in their hair."

"He was never worthy of you," Lisabet murmured, the disdain in her voice evident. Sass smiled sadly and sighed. Touching the hem of her chemise she made conversation that was still surprisingly painful.

"Curt was a good man, Lisabet. I was happy with him." The reprimand was gentle, but even to

Sass it sounded hollow. What did she know of loving when she and Curt were together? They had
mutual admiration. She and Shay had had love.
And that was water under the bridge. There was
nowhere to go but forward. Sass checked her watch.
Lisabet did the same and spoke first. It was her
job, after all, to keep Sass's life in order.

"It's time."

"I see that," Sass answered wistfully, sad that her
life, her dream, her vision had come to this tacky
showdown. Sass pressed a button and spoke to the
driver. "Kim, we're ready now."

On command, the sleek, gray car moved forward, stopping only when they reached the theater entrance. Kim, a sultry redhead dressed in
impeccable livery, opened the door and stood
back. Lisabet stepped out first looking wonderful
in her new dress. Sass had insisted upon the gift,
more for her own sake than for Lisabet's. Tonight
Sass only wanted to see perfect, beautiful people.
That would be her talisman. Impeccable clothes,
flawless grooming, exact timing would all somehow influence the outcome of the premiere for
the better. Lisabet smoothed the back of her
mushroom-colored Herrera as though she could
lengthen the skirt. Stubbornly it ended in a startling hem far above her knees.

For that instant, between the time Lisabet slid
her legs out of the car and the time she stood up,
Sass Brandt was alone and the world outside came
tumbling in at her, assaulting her senses and pin-
ning her to the leather seat.

Klieg lights ravished the surprisingly clear, amazingly black night. Car horns sounded angrily, pro-

testing the closing of a full lane on Sunset Boulevard. And the people gathered to watch made an all too familiar, all too inviting noise of their own. It was that collective voice swelling and diminishing with a life of its own that, in happier days, had washed over Sass like a welcoming wave of cool water. Now she closed her eyes and breathed it in but the healing of the adoration was not to be had. Still, she would remember the sound for the rest of her life in case tomorrow these beautiful, fickle people didn't want to know, much less love, her.

Sass bent her head, then threw it back quickly. Tears stung her eyes. How had it come to this? Her lips trembling, Sass sought to gain control again. She thought of nothing but the woman she had been so long ago, and the one she was expected to be that night.

She was Sass Brandt.

Superstar.

Her name drew millions of dollars and people to the theaters.

She was talented and beautiful and healed.

Tonight would end the way she wanted.

The world was hers.

She was Sass Brandt.

She opened her eyes, took the chauffeur's hand and let herself be drawn slowly and regally into the night. This was the beginning of the end.

A young man was the first to call her name. Others took up the chant. Sass raised her head higher, her coppery hair swinging down her back. Every inch of her body responded to their outcry: her beautiful breasts and tiny waist, the swell of her exquisite hips, even the still painful scars that

ran down her legs under her opaque stockings.
The shouts surrounded her, cloaking her in adulation and, for that time, Sass was safe. She was
loved. But the safety was false and the love too collective to be comforting. Yet Sass continued to
smile. No one was close enough to see she was in
pain.

Out of nowhere Curt came and stood beside
her, the blonde firmly attached to him, snuggled
securely under his left arm. His right was around
Sass's waist and she could smell his marvelous
cologne as he bent to kiss her cheek. Instinctively,
desperately, Sass turned her head just at the right
moment and his lips met hers. She pressed her
body against his. Smaller than the blonde, Sass
became a part of him once again until both his
arms surrounded her, the blonde momentarily
abandoned. Around them the crowd cheered the
one-time favored couple. Their breakup had
made the front page of every tabloid, saddening
their fans who thought it a mistake. Sass now
knew it wasn't. She released her hold on Curt
and leaned back to look at him, her smile one
of affection, not love.

"Maybe I should have held on a little longer,
Sass," Curt said, grinning at her. His incredible
face was beginning to show signs of aging. This
had been hard on him, too. She had been selfish
not to realize that.

"I don't think so, Curt." Sass laughed gently.
"After tonight you'll be big even if the movie is a
flop. You've got lots of things to do and challenges
to meet. I've already done them and met them.
You don't need me."

"You might be right. Still, I should have . . ." He gave her an opening to interrupt and Sass took it to save him face. She still cared that much.

"Should have doesn't count. What you do does. We've accomplished a lot—together and apart. I think apart is probably better."

"You might be right." With a quick kiss on Sass's brow, Curt reined in the blonde, and became part of a couple again. Sass still held him lightly, but she knew she stood alone. A microphone was shoved between them and they parted, their smiles still glittering, their manner warm and inviting. All of it had been second nature for a long time.

"Sass! Curt! You both look wonderful. You must be so excited tonight." Kelly Karter wielded her microphone like a deadly weapon.

"We're thrilled, Kelly," Curt said as his date giggled ridiculously.

"Sass." Kelly turned a sympathetic eye toward the star and Sass reached for her hand. Kelly squeezed it, but the show went on. "I know this is a really big night for you. Are you feeling triumphant?"

"This is a really special night for me, Kelly. Making *The Woman At the End of the Lane* has been a personal challenge from the beginning. I only hope all of you find the story as exceptional and compelling as I do. I'm so grateful that I was allowed to bring this story to the screen. I can't tell you how appreciative I am." The last was said like a prayer and Sass, realizing how much she meant it, hoped that somehow Shay was hearing her.

"Like a dream come true," Kelly whispered, her

microphone held aside so she could offer her friend her encouragement.

"Yes, like a dream. A vision become reality," Sass whispered, but she was no longer paying attention. Curt was forgotten, Kelly Karter had disappeared, Lisabet, standing a respectful distance away, didn't exist any longer. There were other, more important people, she had to impress with her confidence.

Sass walked up the red carpet to the theater entrance. She went slowly, approaching them warily. Richard was turned out in an impeccably tailored tux, his gray hair slicked back from his patrician forehead. His usually sharp eyes pleaded with Sass to remember what they were about and not make trouble. There was fear in those eyes and that was strangely satisfying to Sass.

Beside him Sloane stood impossibly erect, her tight, athletic body encased in a stark, remarkable gown of iridescent green. The dress seemed to move of its own accord as though it, rather than the woman, was the thing alive. But life was only an illusion. The dress was laced with peacock feathers that rippled as people moved passed her. She was a vision of the next century, glistening and glowing, her gown undulating, readying its mistress for intergalactic travel. Unfortunately Sloane remained sadly grounded to this time. Her almond eyes betrayed nothing as they locked on Sass. Her wide, full mouth, tipped at the edges in a caricature of a smile. Her lipstick was blood red, her skin made up to Kabuki whiteness, her raven hair was nothing but a cap of color on her beautifully formed head. Heavy jade earrings brushed her bare shoulders. Pain shot up Sass's legs, a reminder of the beginning. It tightened her muscles until she thought she might stumble. Thankfully she didn't.

"Sloane."

"Sass." Sloane's sleek head dipped ever so slightly, just enough to let Sass know that no respect was intended. "You look quite smashing this evening. I always said one should dress as appropriately for their triumphs as their failures. Don't you agree, Richard?"

Sloane really had no interest in his opinion. Richard had never been anything but her conduit, and his expression of timidity was not surprising. Everyone eventually displayed a nervous habit in Sloane's presence, but she had long since lost interest in the manifestations of fear. Eyeing Sass though, she was intrigued. Sass stood perfectly still. Not a twitch or a quiver betrayed her. Sloane wasn't at all sure she approved of that.

"Sass, I'm sorry," Richard said, taking a step forward. She waved away his apology. Or, perhaps it was meant as an excuse for his behavior. Either way it didn't matter. He meant nothing to her any longer. He wasn't a person. He was an owned thing and the one who controlled him was Sloane.

"I'm dressed for success, Sloane. I won't be the one feeling wretched when this night is over."

Sloane laughed that strange, girlish laugh of hers. "I've read the book, darling, and you're kidding yourself. Olivier might have been able to turn a piece of Irish angst into a commercial success, but not you."

"We'll see, won't we?" Sass answered, her bravado as false as the jewels she now wore. She could remember when both had been real.

"Any minute now, Miss Brandt," Sloane said, her voice low and deep. Sass reached out and Lisabet was there, instantly taking her arm. Sloane raised a thin arched brow noticing Lisabet for the first time. "You're alone tonight?"

"On the contrary. I am here sharing this night with my dear friend and confidante. Who better for a night like this?"

"A man? Like the one who interested you dearly not so long ago?"

Sass's heart lurched. How dare this woman even think of Shay, much less speak of him. Sass turned cold.

"He's not here. I don't know where he is."

Sloane grinned and Sass saw she had small, white teeth, beautifully formed. Sloane leaned close and whispered, "Not to worry. I do."

Sass reeled, her body trembled in direct response to the quaking of her heart. The wound was too raw. It wasn't possible that Sloane would still hurt him now that he had left Sass's life, was it? Lisabet held her tight, aware that no one must see Sass weak. Lisabet would die before she allowed that.

"We better be getting in, Sass. They're waiting for you."

"Yes. Of course." Sass nodded, but her agreement was fragile. Quickly, Lisabet led her away seating her in the darkened theater moments later. There Sass remained silent, her eyes raised to the screen. She waited. She prayed. The film began.

Ninety seconds before the credits rolled Sass

rushed from the theater leaving Lisabet behind.
Her lips trembled and tears spilled from her wide,
bright eyes. Ignoring the pain in her legs and the
pounding of her heart, Sass ran across the carpeted
lobby and pushed through the huge doors, pulling
the cool night air into her lungs as desperately as
a drowning woman suddenly rescued from a raging
sea. She needed air and she needed to understand
what had happened in that theater, before she
could face anyone.

Collapsing, Sass closed her eyes as she pressed
her body against the cold concrete of the building
and clasped her arms around her body. In moments people would pour through the doors and
the truth would come with them. Opening her eyes
Sass stared past the lights of the theater, past the
now abandoned barricades that had held back the
adoring crowds. She focused on the dark as she
tried to settle her thoughts.

Yet, as she stared, the night, not her thoughts,
took on shape and substance, solidifying into a
form familiar and unexpected. It was only a motion in the darkness at first, a quivering of the
blackness before it became a shadow and, finally,
the contour of a man. He came slowly, confidently
toward her without a hint of hesitation. He came
with determination, without regret or question.

He came for her.

"Shay."

Sass's voice shook with disbelief. She called his
name, but the sound was as delicate as a wish
dreamed before waking. She wasn't sure she'd spoken at all. He came silently until he was close
enough to touch her. Wordlessly he took her. Ex-

pressive hands wrapped around her shoulders before pulling Sass close, enveloping her in arms she
knew so well and had missed so much. It was then,
before they could speak, before truths could be
told, that the doors of the theater opened and
Sloane stood silhouetted in the back-light of the
theater. Her black eyes glittered, her dress undu-
lated as she came toward them, closer and closer
until she was almost part of them. Her lips curled
upward, her beautiful, delicate face tilted toward
them until Sass wondered if Sloane might lay her
head against theirs. Lovers all, waiting for the kiss
of death or the breath of life. Instead, she stayed
quite still, her lashes lowered, her breathing so
quiet she might not have breathed at all.

"So he came back for you, Sass," she whispered.
Her lashes raised. Those horribly cold and beautiful eyes were on Sass's golden ones. "He came
back just in time it would seem. Good for you. No
one should be alone when they meet their destiny."

" 'Tis a pity, then, there's no one to stand beside
you," Shay answered, quietly.

"There are times I feel that, too," Sloane said
and backed away as the theater attendants threw
open the doors in anticipation of the movement
of the crowd inside. But no one came through the
doors, no one moved from their seats. Instead, the
sound of cheers and applause rushed through
those doors washing over Shay and Sass as they
watched Sloane melt into the blackness, banished
from them like a bad dream.

"Sass . . ." Shay began but her fingertips found
his lips. What words could there be that would add

to her joy? He was here, with her. That was all she ever wanted.

"Shhh, darling. Just listen. Listen."

Gently, he lay his cheek against her hair and closed his eyes, listening as she asked him to do. The sound he heard was one of success, one of appreciation for Sass's craft and it lifted his heart to heaven to hear it.

"It's for both of us, you know." Sass pulled back a bit so she could look into his loving eyes. "You and me and our courage. You came back without knowing how things would turn out."

"Sure, that's not courage, my love. That's daftness. Love has done that to me. By the saints, I couldn't live without you. Not in Ireland, nor Alaska, nor the moon."

"Then don't try. Stay with me, my love. The past is a dream. We'll start again."

"And the future?" Shay asked, pushing a silken thread of hair away from her eyes.

"The future is a vision that I see so clearly. Happiness is in the future. Nothing but happiness. The movie is a success, the ghosts are put to rest. It's over. . . ."

"That's where you're wrong, lass. For us it's just begun."

With that Shay Collier lowered his head and kissed Sass Brandt. He kissed her long and well while the applause drifted through the doors and lay upon them like a blessing.

Epilogue

"Sass!" Shay bellowed. "Woman, where in the blue blazes are you!" He slapped the bed and thought of calling once more but time was running out. Action was needed. Leaping from the bed half-naked, Shay rushed out of the bedroom only to run smack into Sass climbing slowly, laboriously, up the stairs.

"You'll wake the dead, Shay Collier. Hush. If I don't see it, I don't see it. The news will still be the same." She grinned at him but it didn't make a dent in his pique.

"You can't tell me that you aren't just about bursting to know whether or not your movie is going to win the Academy Award for best film," he insisted, peeved that she was so calm.

"Yes, I am bursting," she said laughing, "but I think it has more to do with the half a chocolate cake I just ate than . . ."

"Enough of this nonsense. Time's wasting," Shay wailed, sweeping her into his arms, almost losing his balance as he did so. Amazing what a bit of weight could do.

"Shay, you'll break your back." Sass giggled, but wound her arms around his neck nonetheless and nuzzled her face into the crook of his neck happily.

"I'd break every bone in my body to get you back in front of that television. I know I was the one who insisted we not go to the ceremony, but that didn't mean I was willing to ignore the entire thing! I don't want you coming back to me in six months, blamin' me for missing this night of nights."

In a flash Shay had her back through the door. He lay her gently on the bed, arranged the pillows behind her and slid one under her legs. Those poor legs. He could barely see the scars now, but they were so swollen. Swooping down, Shay kissed each knee, then pulled a coverlet over her. In the blink of an eye he was beside her, his arm wrapped around her shoulders.

"Are we ready?" Sass teased, tickling him playfully. "Maybe we need to turn up the heat or open the windows or . . ."

"Hush. You're talking nonsense," Shay complained. He brushed her fingers away, then clasped them in his own, raised them to his lips and kissed them to end her jesting. "Now, it's coming. Listen to that. Sure, the jokes are terrible this year."

"Most definitely," Sass murmured and cuddled into him. She could care less about the host's jokes or who was wearing what to the prestigious awards. But Shay was intent upon watching to the end so Sass trained her eyes on the television.

There they were. All the people who thought her crazy when she first started to make this film, all those who abandoned her during her time of need, those who cheered her on when it looked as though *The Woman At the End of the Lane* was going to be a movie with legs were sitting at the music center wondering if Sass Brandt's magic had held. There were also friends in the crowd that filled the Dorothy Chandler Pavilion on this Oscar night and she couldn't forget that, but Sass had no desire to be with friends this night or show off her good fortune to her enemies. Shay was by her side, the movie was made and she, as an artist, was vindicated. What more could she want?

The Oscar, naturally.

With a giggle, she cuddled closer to Shay. Why fight it? She was just as excited as he.

"Okay, you win. I'm dying to find out who the winner is."

"Then hush, woman. The man's got the envelope." Shay grabbed the remote and hit the volume button before laying his cheek on Sass's hair, holding her ever more tightly and whispering a prayer just loud enough for Sass to hear.

"God, you're a wonderful man," Sass breathed and closed her eyes.

"Save the praise, darlin'. The time has come." Sass settled down, her eyes on the set once again. He had already said "the winner is" and now the tuxedoed host was ripping open the envelope. Shay threw his other arm around her and buried his face in her hair. "Ah, Sass! I can't watch!"

"Shay Collier. All that nonsense, and now you're going to be a coward. Open your eyes." Playfully she pulled at him, trying to turn him around. But her antics were cut short. The announcement was being made.

". . . is *The Woman At the End of the Lane!*"

The crowd of gorgeous people on the television went wild and the cameras panned to capture every-

one's reaction. People stood, they clapped and
cheered as Lisabet half ran up the aisle to collect
Sass's award. Beside her, Sass felt Shay slump. She
chuckled and pushed his head up so that she could
see him.

"Well," she said quietly. "We did it."

"Mother of God, I feel as if I've been holding
my breath for the last two years. Pinch me, Sass.
Pinch me and make me know it's true. You've
done it, haven't you?"

"Don't be ridiculous, Shay," she whispered
warmly. *"We* did it. The both of us. And I have no
intention of pinching you." Carefully Sass sat up.
It was difficult these days, but she managed. With
a great effort she reached over him and took the
remote. A second later the television was off and
the phone downstairs was ringing. It would ring
all night long probably, but Sass could ignore it.
She'd bet she could make Shay ignore it, too!

"Come here, Shay Collier," she murmured and
gathered him into her arms, "let's celebrate."

"Sass," he warned, looking not at all sure about
this, but she shook her head.

"I'm not going to be put off," she insisted.

"But your legs . . ."

"Nothing to worry about. A bit swollen. It's only
natural."

"And . . . this?" Reverently Shay reached out
and touched her stomach. It was big and round
and the most beautiful sight he had ever seen.

"This?" Sass raised one beautifully shaped brow
and tried not to laugh. "It's our baby, darling. The
newest little Collier. It's not a this or a that. Our
baby is in there sleeping, not a kick or a punch in

the longest time." Sass lowered her voice conspiratorially, a twinkle in her eye as she ran a long nail down his bare chest. "I promise, if we're careful, very careful, I bet we won't even wake little Shay up while we celebrate."

"But I don't want to hurt you . . ."

"As if you ever could," Sass breathed, her hands running over his shoulders as he inched himself down beside her. Predictably his hands were beginning a trek of their own.

"Sass . . ."

"Shhh . . ." she soothed.

"Perhaps you're right," he muttered, his beard brushing her cheek a moment before his lips traveled past toward the hollow near her ear. Gently his hands cupped her breasts, made even more beautiful by her pregnancy. Sass's hands covered his. She felt the hard metal of the ring that now adorned his finger. Not even a golden Oscar could mean more to her than that simple band. "There, nothing to worry about, my darling?"

"Nothing, Sass. Nothing in the whole wide world will ever worry me again."

"I'm so glad to hear that, Mr. Collier," Sass said as her lips lay against his cheek.

"Not any happier than I, Mrs. Collier. No one could be happier than I."

With that, his lips covered hers, his body pressing tight against the woman he adored and the new life they had made. There was nothing left to say. Only loving to be done, a child to be born and dreams— always dreams— to be dreamed.

didn't expect it, but Sass Brandt and Stan Corn became enchanted in my eyes. I live, I person— everything here can become. Together they

Dear Reader:

I didn't expect it, but Sass Brandt and Shay Collier became enchanted in my eyes. They personified everything love can become. Together they were magic, apart they were desperate, and when adversity threatened, the stronger protected the weaker. To me that is the ultimate test of love.

I hope you enjoyed following their lives as much as I enjoyed helping their story unfold on the pages of *Dreams*.

May all your loves and dreams be as special and enduring as theirs. Thank you for letting me be a part of your reading. I would love to hear from you soon. Your words are always valued and appreciated. I'm currently working on my next contemporary, *Seasons*, which Zebra Books will be publishing in May 1996.

Best regards,

Rebecca Forster
P.O. Box 1081
Palos Verdes Estates, CA 90274

CATCH A RISING STAR!

ROBIN ST. THOMAS

FORTUNE'S SISTERS (2616, $3.95)
It was Pia's destiny to be a Hollywood star. She had complete self-confidence, breathtaking beauty, and the help of her domineering mother. But her younger sister Jeanne began to steal the spotlight meant for Pia, diverting attention away from the ruthlessly ambitious star. When her mother Mathilde started to return the advances of dashing director Wes Guest, Pia's jealousy surfaced. Her passion for Guest and desire to be the brightest star in Hollywood pitted Pia against her own family—sister against sister, mother against daughter. Pia was determined to be the only survivor in the arenas of love and fame. But neither Mathilde nor Jeanne would surrender without a fight. . . .

LOVER'S MASQUERADE (2886, $4.50)
New Orleans. A city of secrets, shrouded in mystery and magic. A city where dreams become obsessions and memories once again become reality. A city where even one trip, like a stop on Claudia Gage's book promotion tour, can lead to a perilous fall. For New Orleans is also the home of Armand Dantine, who knows the secrets that Claudia would conceal and the past she cannot remember. And he will stop at nothing to make her love him, and will not let her go again . . .

SENSATION (3228, $4.95)
They'd dreamed of stardom, and their dreams came true. Now they had fame and the power that comes with it. In Hollywood, in New York, and around the world, the names of Aurora Styles, Rachel Allenby, and Pia Decameron commanded immediate attention—and lust and envy as well. They were stars, idols on pedestals. And there was always someone waiting in the wings to bring them crashing down . . .

YOU WON'T WANT TO READ
JUST ONE — KATHERINE STONE

ROOMMATES (3355-9, $4.95)
No one could have prepared Carrie for the monumental changes she would face when she met her new circle of friends at Stanford University. Once their lives intertwined and became woven into the tapestry of the times, they would never be the same.

TWINS (3492-X, $4.95)
Brook and Melanie Chandler were so different, it was hard to believe they were sisters. One was a dark, serious, ambitious New York attorney; the other, a golden, glamourous, sophisticated supermodel. But they were more than sisters — they were twins and more alike than even they knew . . .

THE CARLTON CLUB (3614-0, $4.95)
It was the place to see and be seen, the only place to be. And for those who frequented the playground of the very rich, it was a way of life. Mark, Kathleen, Leslie and Janet — they worked together, played together, and loved together, all behind exclusive gates of the *Carlton Club*.

Taylor—made Romance From Zebra Books

WHISPERED KISSES (3830, $4.99/5.99)
Beautiful Texas heiress Laura Leigh Webster never imagined that her biggest worry on her African safari would be the handsome Jace Elliot, her tour guide. Laura's guardian, Lord Chadwick Hamilton, warns her of Jace's dangerous past; she simply cannot resist the lure of his strong arms and the passion of his *Whispered Kisses*.

KISS OF THE NIGHT WIND (3831, $4.99/$5.99)
Carrie Sue Strover thought she was leaving trouble behind her when she deserted her brother's outlaw gang to live her life as schoolmarm Carolyn Starns. On her journey, her stagecoach was attacked and she was rescued by handsome T.J. Rogue. T.J. plots to have Carrie lead him to her brother's cohorts who murdered his family. T.J., however, soon succumbs to the beautiful runaway's charms and loving caresses.

FORTUNE'S FLAMES (3825, $4.99/$5.99)
Impatient to begin her journey back home to New Orleans, beautiful Maren James was furious when Captain Hawk delayed the voyage by searching for stowaways. Impatience gave way to uncontrollable desire once the handsome captain searched *her* cabin. He was looking for illegal passengers; what he found was wild passion with a woman he knew was unlike all those he had known before!

PASSIONS WILD AND FREE (3828, $4.99/$5.99)
After seeing her family and home destroyed by the cruel and hateful Epson gang, Randee Hollis swore revenge. She knew she found the perfect man to help her—gunslinger Marsh Logan. Not only strong and brave, Marsh had the ebony hair and light blue eyes to make Randee forget her hate and seek the love and passion that only he could give her.

Available wherever paperbacks are sold, or order direct from the Publisher. Send cover price plus 50¢ per copy for mailing and handling to Penguin USA, P.O. Box 999, c/o Dept. 17109, Bergenfield, NJ 07621. Residents of New York and Tennessee must include sales tax. DO NOT SEND CASH.